W9-BVU-818

The
LAST
WOMAN
STANDING

Center Point
Large Print

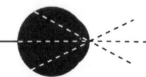

**This Large Print Book carries the
Seal of Approval of N.A.V.H.**

The
LAST
WOMAN
STANDING

THELMA ADAMS

CENTER POINT LARGE PRINT
THORNDIKE, MAINE

This Center Point Large Print edition
is published in the year 2017 by arrangement with
Amazon Publishing, www.apub.com.

Originally published in the United States
by Amazon Publishing, 2016.

This is a work of fiction.
Names, characters, organizations, places,
events, and incidents are either products of the
author's imagination or are used fictitiously.

The text of this Large Print edition is unabridged.
In other aspects, this book may vary
from the original edition.
Printed in the United States of America
on permanent paper.
Set in 16-point Times New Roman type.

ISBN: 978-1-68324-294-9

Library of Congress Cataloging-in-Publication Data

Names: Adams, Thelma, author.
Title: The last woman standing / Thelma Adams.
Description: Center Point Large Print edition. | Thorndike, Maine :
Center Point Large Print, 2017.
Identifiers: LCCN 2016056316 | ISBN 9781683242949
   (hardcover : alk. paper)
Subjects: LCSH: Earp, Josephine Sarah Marcus—Fiction. | Earp, Wyatt,
1848–1929—Fiction. | Frontier and pioneer life—Arizona—
Tombstone—Fiction. | Tombstone (Ariz.)—Fiction. | Large type books. |
GSAFD: Western stories. | Biographical fiction.
Classification: LCC PS3601.D3975 L37 2017 | DDC 813/.6—dc23
LC record available at https://lccn.loc.gov/2016056316

To my three Ranalds,
and my only Elizabeth

CHAPTER 1
FEBRUARY 1937

Tombstone kicked my ass and I kicked back. No one expected that of a little Jewish girl from a no-name family. I wasn't invited to the dance near the O.K. Corral with my husband, Wyatt, and his brothers Earp, or those irascible Clantons, or my ex, Sheriff Johnny-come-lately Behan. I was just a woman—a footnote—expected to tuck my skirts under my tail and inspire male bravery when I wasn't baking corn bread or childbearing. That was never my idea of the wild frontier life for which I'd run away from a good home. I had big dreams and big brown eyes and lashes like whips. I wanted to straddle my man like a pony and ride into the sunset.

Pardon me for spreading my legs so soon. You hardly know me. But you will.

You may not like me—I'm not the first beautiful girl to be conceited, and my mouth tends to shoot off faster than my brain kicks in. But, you'll have to admit, I got a long way from folding kreplach in my mother's kitchen and brushing egg white on the braided challah at my father's bakery for a lass lacking much talent for singing or dancing or debauchery. And since this all happened in a time

7

before archives, in a territory with a longer past entrusted to the songs of the Apaches, sometimes I think that a lie is as good as the truth if it's prettily wrapped.

I've finally come back to where it all began for Wyatt and me. Not by steamer and train and stagecoach, but by automobile in one straight shot, no Apaches. Not in furs but in wool flannel. It's my 1937 one-last-look tour with friends who are hoping the trip will inspire some memories that I haven't already shared, and maybe make me a buck. Wyatt and I were a boom-or-bust couple who never saved a dime. He's become a cottage industry of myth and legend and outright bullshit. I have the real stories locked away, gleaned not so much from pillow talk as being nosy whenever I had a chance to watch or listen. And I didn't bunk just with Wyatt—I first took my turn with Johnny Behan: sheriff, politician, and friend to cowboys and ranchers and the anti-Earp gaggle. Johnny hated me for switching partners in the middle of the dance, even if I caught him riding another woman in our bed with his own son, Albert, by my side as witness. Men are funny that way. They put a brand on your ass and expect you to behave while they're out lassoing another man's wife. I don't know how he missed that irony, but as smart as a man is (and Johnny was, book-learned and all, with a head for figures), if he's a womanizer, there's never any shortage of lies he tells himself and those who love him.

I've always been a good talker and a better listener. I'm curious about people and things. Not so much politics, but how folks jockey for power and goodies when there's so much joy on this earth to go around. What I learned from Tombstone is that God is in the landscape: in the big sky and the hovering moon, in the scent of mesquite and wood smoke. He's embedded in the chests of rare men like Wyatt, and in the communion between a man and a woman that leaps like flying embers from the physical to the spiritual until they become one flesh, two hearts.

Now I'm listening to the wind banging loose boards, standing alone in the corner window on the second floor of the Tourist Hotel directly across from the old Oriental Saloon where Wyatt had the gambling concession. I've told my friends I'm napping, but I'm really hiding out. I could never sleep at a moment like this: too many emotions. I just wanted to feel them as deeply as I could without all the chatter and explaining. Tombstone hasn't fared much better than I in the fifty years since we last rolled in the sheets together. The wind has its way with the ghost town, howling just for hell, bowling down Allen Street, churning dust and candy wrappers and memories too tough to die. We've crossed into the twentieth century, and I'm a relic, faded and forgotten. I don't quite know how to wrap my heart around that yet, and I'm lonesome as always since Wyatt died in our Los Angeles bungalow eight years ago.

We had a long run as Mr. and Mrs. Earp—I swear there's a marriage certificate somewhere—but I'm not eager for my final curtain call. I could say God isn't ready for me, either, but I'm not prepared for him. I was raised Jewish, but he never spoke to me in a synagogue with all that Hebrew mumbling of men. I never entered a church—not once, my whole life, not even for Wyatt's funeral at the Congregational Church in Los Angeles. I skipped that formation, spurning the gawkers and celebrity seekers and Hollywood pallbearers. I couldn't face screen cowboy Tom Mix's tears without Wyatt beside me. Afterward, I carted his ashes up north. I buried them beside my parents in the Little Hills of Eternity, the Jewish cemetery in Colma, California. The graveyard's lush stillness offered no peace; beside Wyatt, my empty plot beckoned. I have as yet declined.

Wyatt and I met in Tombstone in 1880 when he was thirty-two and had already made a name for himself in Wichita and Dodge City. He was dead handsome: six feet tall with broad shoulders (I like a man with shoulders), carrying 180 pounds of muscle and grit. He had thick blond hair brushed back from a broad forehead and piercing blue eyes. He called them his truth-seekers, and if you were lying, they made you uneasy. Wyatt was so much better-looking than that dullard Hollywood actor Bert Lindley who played him in that Wild Bill Hickok picture—God forbid he upstage Wild Bill. He was a sum-of-his-parts guy. His deep voice and manly presence tied the package together. A staunch Lincoln Republican, when that still mattered.

Wyatt was fearless like no one else I've ever met. I'm hardly alone in this opinion, but you'd be turning up corpses to find someone else who knew him and his bravery as well as I did. He might have been a man of few words, but every word counted. My first impression of him when I hopped off the stagecoach was that he was striking, but somber as an undertaker with his black coat and high collar. I got around that eventually and unbuttoned him. He unbuttoned me, too.

When I arrived in October 1880, I was in Arizona to be with Johnny Behan, who couldn't have been more different from Wyatt, although they were both handsome in their own ways. I can pick 'em. Johnny was three years older than Wyatt. Where Wyatt was tall, Johnny was short—not much taller than I am, though he tended to wear higher heels on his handcrafted boots. But he was dapper—a snappy dresser—and a born politician who could talk a hen out of her feathers. Likable as all hell, he had a round, pleasant face, merry black eyes, and even, white teeth in a mouth born to smile—and that was a rarity, given frontier dentistry. Johnny had a story for every occasion, which made him good company. And he was quite the kisser. If my knees weren't so arthritic, I might swoon at the thought, but then I'd stand right up because his tongue had a tendency to wander. Unlike Wyatt, who was kin to the lone wolf despite running with a pack, Johnny despised being alone.

So, when I arrived in Tombstone—just down Allen Street in front of the Wells Fargo office—covered with dust, sucking a hard cherry candy to get rid of the taste of grit and keep my tongue from sticking to the roof of my mouth, I was coming to Johnny. Wyatt had Mattie Blaylock warming his bed. I switched partners that year, but it was a bloody dance. And while you can credit the fatal gunfight near the O.K. Corral to lawlessness or booze or the conflict between cowboys and businessmen, Republicans and Democrats, or just plain male cussedness, if you don't factor in Johnny's jealousy of Wyatt, you'd be missing the spark.

When I came to Tombstone, I was afraid and excited to experience the legendary town that, according to reputation, "had a man for breakfast every morning." I left disgusted because I knew some of those men, and they were too good to be toast. The broad window where I'm standing overlooks the intersection where Wyatt's older brother Virgil got shot and crippled by the coward Ike Clanton, staggering into the lobby of the Oriental Hotel across the street to be half patched up. Virgil was a good man, even if his wife, Allie, was a shriveled little bitch. She never liked me, but she had her reasons, starting with me stepping off the stage into Johnny's arms with a big "Look at Me" sign tacked to my bosom, and I had some pair. The arrogance of me: parading through Tombstone, without a sellable skill except my own skin, without a clan to back me up, batting my eyelashes and tossing my curls. It was the arrogance of young beauty: assuming that the whole world will tilt toward you and yield its secrets. If Allie could see me now, old and squat and querulous, she'd laugh her wheezy cackle knowing that I'd got what was coming to me.

Truth is: Allie and I would get along better now, comparing our scars and scratches, our years with stubborn Earp men. Wyatt's not the only one gone. Virgil is, too, and Morgan, James, Warren, and their half brother, Newton. We women endure like grudges. I'm left to bear witness to the grave-yard of the lively town I once knew: boarded-up buildings and rotted wood and tacky neon signs that read CAFÉ and DRUGS. Not that it was ever entirely classy, but it was real.

A tourist bus bounces up in a swirl of exhaust, and the brake groans, clogged with dirt. It disgorges passengers holding their lower backs, wobbly-kneed with cameras strapped to their chests, their heads swiveling to absorb the view. If any of them looked up, they would see me, a plump, old Jewish lady with more wrinkles than curves, white hair piled up in a vanilla ice-cream cone, and no chin to speak of. No one looks at old ladies like me. We're the invisible women.

Let's face it: aging is a bitch for everybody. It's a dumb joke that's replayed every day when you awaken from dreams where you're running around in your prime, chasing after men long dead with an ache in your pants, only to find yourself as you really are: creaky and misshapen, breasts touching belly, and alone in the spare bedroom under the roof of distant relations. But for a beautiful woman like I was—and don't just take my word for it; even our enemies said I was the most beautiful woman to ever step off a stage in Tombstone—it's even harder. Sometime in your teens men just start turning toward you, waking up to you (and women begin to prickle, although you hardly take the time to understand why)—the rabbi, his son, the wealthier widowers eyed hungrily by the mothers of the congregation for their daughters. You discover your power in the world and you itch to exercise it, to leave your mother's shadow and find your rightful glorious place in the new world beyond the *shtetl* by the sea, San Francisco, where the German Jews lorded over us Prussian immigrants. And all that time when you should have been gaining character—reading books, learning languages, growing wiser, and mastering hardships—you've been busy tossing your curls from one shoulder to the next and rushing headlong into a future that you assume will catch you.

I wasn't dumb. I was just distracted by the sway of my own breasts. Beauty brings trust in the universe, and then, in that cruel joke, over time it rescinds your power. Your brow furrows, your vanity chisels your features, and the frontier wind batters your skin. That demon strand of gray weaves itself into the brown. Your chest grows and grows in a race with your thighs. One day you're walking alone down a street and no heads turn, no eyes seek you out, and you're not a pillar of society or a great thinker or the mother of a brood of scholars, but a little woman in shabby shoes long out of fashion, writing letters to the editors and trying to exert some control over a life that's disappeared.

Those tourists down on the street tumbling from the bus like circus clowns wouldn't suspect that I know all the stories they want to hear, not just the cut-and-dried tales of men shooting men at the corner of this-and-that, which the tour guide will drone at them. Oh, no. I know the juice and I drank it. Where those tourists see wormy wood, I see fresh paint. They buy souvenirs—bendy aluminum

US Marshal badges and cap-gun six-shooters and Indian warbonnets—but I saw the real thing.

Across the street and a block west from my window, I spy where Vogan's Saloon and Bowling Alley once stood on Allen between Fourth and Fifth Streets. I had a front-row seat that January for the standoff that occurred right there between Wyatt and a lynch mob aiming to hang gambler Johnny-Behind-the-Deuce after he shot and killed a mining engineer in Charleston. I shouldn't have been there, and I shouldn't have been holed up in a cathouse for safety with Johnny's son, Albert, but that day turned me: I'd never seen a man so absolutely cool in conflict like Wyatt. Admittedly, my father was a baker, so my experience was limited, but still, terrified and tucked up on a balcony on my belly, I watched Wyatt single out one leader in the stampeding crowd. He looked him in the eye and talked amiably and softly in words I could hardly hear over the roar of the mob, his shotgun open on the crook of his elbow, until the mob backed off and there was no more bloodshed.

I lied to myself that day, thinking I was still Johnny's girl. I'd been in love with love, not Johnny. That day Wyatt became the only law-and-order man in town for me. He stirred me in a way that made me hold my knees tighter together. He knew right from wrong in a biblical sense, and he wasn't going to compromise.

The same couldn't be said for John Harris Behan, although his reputation as a coward has been exaggerated. What a character. I haven't thought about him in a long time, and my anger and jealousy have all but dissipated. He was a people person, a compromiser, a consummate politician who could spin a story to charm your knickers off. That last was probably what he did best. Which is a nice way of saying he was a horndog. I'd only just arrived in Tombstone when my fiancé, who'd lured me from my San Francisco home with a diamond ring and no set wedding date, took me out to dinner at the Grand Hotel right across from Vogan's to celebrate. He dazzled me. I was nineteen and swoony, and I'd never seen anything like it: crystal chandeliers and cushy carpets and gold-veined mirrors. We were surrounded by silver millionaires and bachelor bankers in ties and tails. There was no shortage of men in that town. I'd never ordered from a menu or drunk Champagne, and Johnny had me in his watch pocket until he doubled up his bet and tried to take me upstairs for dessert in front of all the grandees. I wasn't ready to give it away, even for a fancy meal, but it was really just stalling, and we both knew it.

The Grand Hotel was just a month old then. It's not so grand now. Just like him. Dead like the rest of them. I'm impatient with the tourists with their little paper maps and their thirst for an afternoon's adventure only a bus ride away from ordinary life. Everybody who entered Tombstone then was taking a risk, I think, sifting through the memories of a time when Turkish carpets lined the Oriental Saloon across the street, and liquor-fueled cowboys stomped through the doors in muddy boots emblazoned with playing cards and stars, wearing gaudy, scarlet bib-front shirts. They had that bandy-legged walk that didn't just come from riding horses but showed how heavy their manhood was. Those folks on the bus wouldn't expect me to think like that, but I knew every step those men took was a dare: my balls are bigger than yours, my pistol shoots straighter, my horse faster, and my loving stronger. I'm old but I'm not dead yet.

I can almost hear the whole cacophony of Tombstone during that boom time. The mines and the mill ran night and day, with the whistle blowing the shift changes, and rock clacking on rock. Loaded wagons pulled by eight-horse teams pounded the streets, and the miners traveled in a herd heading to work on the hill with lunch buckets and scrubbed faces, passing the previous shift returning with rounded shoulders and cheeks powdered gray. I can see my old friend Kitty with a basket on her arm in a sweet feathered hat, flouncing to market and courting wolf whistles, and Nelly Cashman standing outside her restaurant in her big, bloody apron, having a smoke.

And I can see Johnny's nine-year-old son, Albert, walking his beloved pony, Geronimo, back to Dexter Livery Stable, which Johnny co-owned with John Dunbar. They shared Mrs. Dunbar, too, as it turned out, much to Dunbar's chagrin and my own disgust.

And there's Wyatt, standing on the corner, armed with his integrity, his boots hip-width apart, his thumb anchored in his dark vest, licking a corner of his mustache. He was patient. He could outwait a turtle. He looks up at me from the past with those steady sky-blue eyes of his. He always saw me clearer than I saw myself.

That was the main difference between Wyatt and Johnny, although there were many. Wyatt saw me for who I was beneath the creamy complexion and the big brown eyes. He knew I had a heart as big as my chest. He had the ability to read men and women, and from the very first he knew I could be his partner in adventure and his haven in a hotel room. That's a big thing for a pretty woman—to know she's loved for who she actually is behind the veil of beauty, her flaws and foibles and cussedness. Johnny loved me like a china doll, like a possession. And once he got me in the sack, that was it. I could bake his biscuits and watch his son and wash his socks tucked away in some tiny house on a side street. He liked the chase. Too bad for him: the best was yet to come. There were days when Wyatt and I stayed together right across the street at the Cosmopolitan and didn't leave our big carved-wood Renaissance Revival bed until dusk fell and he had to strap on his guns and return to work. Those days could be bottled and sold as jam. We made love in that room right there across the street, and no one knows what happened there but us—and he isn't talking. He was never one to kiss and tell.

Snatches of Fred Astaire singing "The Way You Look Tonight" float out of the café when the wind breaks, and they make me miss dancing with my man. I wasn't much of a professional dancer (despite my short-lived career in Pauline Markham's Pinafore on Wheels), but I loved to dance, and so did Wyatt. He would have liked that song. He was so good-looking, tall and solid, sober but with eyes that smiled at me. We could spend months with just each other as company, talking or not talking; it didn't matter. Neither of us was easy to live with: he had his sorrows and his moods, and I could climb up on my high horse faster than Annie Oakley. We had our booms and our busts over nearly fifty years together, and I never could have the children we wanted. But that was later, so much later, in California and Alaska. This was just Tombstone, when he was young and I was younger. This was the town where I lost my virginity and found my sex.

CHAPTER 2
OCTOBER 1880

I left San Francisco for the second time on a Friday night at dusk. The foghorns bayed in the distance, but the white mist hadn't yet swallowed our humble stoop. My mother's disapproval shrouded the dining room as densely as the coming fog, and my father's shoulders rounded in defeat. He'd turned inward at the dinner table, hardly raising his eyes from his soup. What joy Papa might have shared with a different wife, someone with simpler tastes who cherished him as he deserved to be cherished—but that would have been the end of me. I am cut from their two cloths stitched together, both fun-loving and determined to make my way up in the world. But my departure at nineteen was the definition of a *shonda*: a shameful act witnessed by a gentile.

That Christian witness was Mrs. Catherine Jones, lately of Tombstone, dispatched by my fiancé, Johnny Behan, to gather me for the first leg of our journey to the Arizona Territories. Despite Mrs. Jones's daily assurances from her Nob Hill hotel over the past three days that she would collect me, she had not yet appeared on our doorstep. My mother found this suspicious. (That she was leery was not unexpected: skepticism was a deeply ingrained part of her nature, along with a string of superstitions that she carried over from Prussia.) That night she still must have hoped that Mrs. Jones would never arrive, as if she were a figment of my imagination and I had written the letters with their extravagant curlicues on fine hotel stationery myself. I was mischievous, but not that crafty.

Although my mother's anxiety was contagious, I remained optimistic: my packed carpetbag sat atop my trunk in the dark foyer under the coat hooks. The mood around the battered table laden with common porcelain and bent utensils didn't stop my feet from tapping an anticipatory jig underneath. I kept my hands imprisoned between my thighs so my mother wouldn't notice their restless wandering. I wanted out, out, out, yet I was concerned about leaving my father, sister, and brother behind in this house of impossibly high standards, the land of never-good-enough.

The five of us—my father, Henry ("Heschie" to his friends); my sister, Henrietta ("Hennie" or my "Hen"), three years my junior; and Nathan, my mother's favorite and now a man of twenty-two—were having what seemed like our last Shabbat dinner together. The air was thick with Ma's unspoken criticism. Every prayer, even the *HaMotzi* over the bread Papa had made with his own hands, felt like a curse.

Ma wore the dark-brown taffeta she usually reserved for funerals and fasts, stiff at the elbows and tight at the waist, but I was so distracted by my leave-taking that I didn't consider her wardrobe choice. Counting back, she must have been fifty-two: tall and thin and dignified, her baleful, pale face with the pointy chin surprisingly unwrinkled, and long, aristocratic fingers with almond-shaped nail beds, reddened from plucking chickens and scrubbing laundry. A ghostly white swath emerged from her widow's peak, a rebuke to the luxuriant dark hair that she'd twisted and plaited and piled into a bun at the crown of her head. She was imposing rather than attractive, with blue eyes that only Hennie had inherited. Nathan and I returned her gaze with our father's brown eyes.

My half sister Rebecca (four years older than Nathan) had purchased this somber luxury my mother wore with money hoarded from her housekeeping budget. Rebecca had a different father—my mother's first husband—and looked out from the face of a stranger. He had gifted her with generous ginger hair that she caught up like crimped red ribbon atop her head. Rebecca's husband, Aaron Weiner, leased the dark three-story townhouse on Perry Street; the couple lived in relative privacy on the third floor while my mother cooked and cleaned for us all.

I loved Rebecca. She was my second, more

indulgent mother, who introduced me to Gilbert and Sullivan's *H.M.S. Pinafore* and its heroine, Josephine, "the lass that loved a sailor" not of her father's choosing. It was an irony not lost on Ma. She was as sharp as she was judgmental and certainly parceled out guilt to Rebecca for indulging my "artistic" side when she was supposed to be shopping a more cultured version of myself to wealthy widowers of the congregation and members of the Weiners' German Jewish circle. I harbored no anger toward Ma. Well, maybe a little. I hadn't the guts to ask how this marrying a daughter off to an older man differed from the prostitution practiced on Tombstone's Allen Street, except that the transaction remained within the faith.

We were all related on Perry Street, but it wasn't quite like living with family. We were the poor relations, the *schnorrers*, and on a Friday night, Becca and her husband ate with his grandparents and extended family in a grander house on the hill. At the end of the night, they changed shoes to trudge home so as not to break the Sabbath. We were unwelcome at their Shabbat dinner, prepared by a cook and served by a maid. The Weiners expected their son the businessman to earn his way up to a house on the street beside theirs. Everyone must pull their weight. He'd taken a step back because he'd married Becca (even though he got lucky with my beautiful sister, considering his extreme myopia, lack of shoulders, and misshapen spine).

The formal mantel mirror above the dinner table reflected the five of us as if in a painting. To my left sat Papa; Ma was on my right. Across the table perched Nathan and Hennie. Nathan resembled my mother: tall, towering over Papa, with a pointed chin and the serious brow of a scholar crawling across his forehead like a caterpillar. Hennie was a shy girl on the plain side of pretty, with a long, freckled face and heavy eyelids above pale lashes, which gave her a sleepy look that led people to underestimate her ample intelligence. Before I left home the first time, I had sat beside Hennie facing the mirror. Now I sat quarantined by myself. We clustered in the wood-paneled front room with the bay windows overlooking an identical house across Perry Street. I watched Ma with her generous brow and incongruous pointy chin light the Shabbat candles at the foot of the table. Like a hankie dropped by God, her ecru lace scarf covered her taut bun. She was the picture of martyrdom, raising her arms in their stiff leg-of-mutton sleeves. She passed slender fingers in three graceful circles over the candles, set in heavy silver—all that remained of the treasures her family had smuggled out of Prussia. I loved my mother but wouldn't follow her down her path of righteousness and sorrow. We lived in a new world. She dwelled among old *dybbuks*.

Then Papa took his turn at the table's head. Though he was eight years younger than Ma, his hair had dwindled to a few wisps, and he shrunk into silence around her. He was a gentle man whose brush of a mustache made me imagine what a dashing bachelor he must have been when he first met my mother on Manhattan's Hester Street. They were Prussian immigrants from trampled towns near each other—Ma, a recent widow with three-year-old Rebecca, and he, already a baker capable of earning a living even in tough times. Papa didn't feel the Sabbath ritual deeply like Ma, but he knew the drill, having grown up as the only son among sisters. In the rapid, mumbling Hebrew Papa used, he blessed us children (I heard Ma's breath catch when he blessed me; I knew where I got my flair for drama). Then he muttered the *HaMotzi* over the braided challah that he made at the bakery where he worked.

Ma sniffed, and we all sat down to kreplach soup with chunky carrots floating in broth left over from last week's roast. I had already served the soup. Hennie's job was clearing the table. Nathan's was studying the Torah with Ma after dinner. I lost myself in my bowl, then looked up to catch Hennie's eyes. She looked down and away shyly. This was strange. We'd always been close, even if that meant I led her into temptation— getting her ears pierced when we knew Ma wouldn't approve, buying trinkets in Chinatown, and peeking into a basement room where men lay out on cots and women gazed at us with lazy kohl-rimmed eyes, the air smelling sickeningly sweet.

Hennie and I shared a bedroom until that year. When I returned from Arizona the first time (after I ran away with Pauline Markham's Pinafore troupe and met Johnny), Ma changed the sleeping arrangements, as if my itchy feet might be contagious. She took Hennie into her bed on the second floor, dispatched Pa to sleep with Nathan in the bigger bedroom I'd shared with Hennie, and moved me to a slit of a room at the rear. No one was happy with the arrangement, particularly Papa, but it meant we all joined Ma in her misery.

Though I ultimately learned to love the silence of the Arizona (and later, Alaska) nights sharing a campfire with Wyatt, listening for the swoop of a hawk on its prey or an owl's otherworldly hoot, I never knew when to keep quiet around my own dinner table. While the rest of my family silently slurped soup, I had to interrupt the awkward peace. I began to prattle about my upcoming journey to Arizona. Mrs. Jones and I would be riding in safety on the new train to the territories. This was met with silence. Apparently, if I was going to leave, at least I should have had the decency not to discuss it. But if there was an elephant in the room, I made it stand on its hind legs and dance in the center ring. I pressed on, like the frontierswoman I believed I was: "And there won't be any encounters with Apaches this time. Even though we'll be making the final leg of the journey by stagecoach, it's as safe as taking the Market Street cable car. It's hardly even an adventure."

"You want an adventure," threatened Mama, "I'll give you an adventure."

"Leave it, Sophie," Papa said.

"Look where leaving it got us, Henry." Ma's voice rose to a level that would have worked from the *bimah* to the last row of the congregation. She could have been a rabbi, if such a thing as a female rabbi wasn't ridiculous even in her own eyes. "Do you think you are the only person to have left home, Josephine? Does that make you special?" She stared at me with those judgmental eyes of God.

"You don't want me to go, Mama, but you don't want me here, either."

"I left home once. My father sent us ahead to America, my mother and my sisters, Esther and Maida." Mama paused. I had not even known she had two sisters. After not mentioning them for so long, she looked as though just the words were painful. *Esther. Maida.* This previously hidden side of my reserved mother frightened me.

Mama pushed aside her soup. "We traveled from our village to Hamburg, and then sailed to Liverpool, and from there to New York City. The trip across the Atlantic took eleven weeks. As soon as the ship set sail, my mother began retching over the side. Maybe it was for lack of food, or seasickness, or maybe my father got her pregnant again, a going-away present. Who knows? I never saw the man again to ask. Between spells of nausea, Mama cut some treasure out of her hem—my dowry, or Maida's— then traded it to a mate for supplies so that she could make us a meal. The gentile returned a day later with a gruel made for cats. My older sister, Maida, prepared a soup from it. Mama ate a bit and then gagged. Esther was only seven. She was such a good girl that she swallowed the first bite without quarrel when Mama told her to. But then she couldn't force the foul stew back up. We gave her emetics. Nothing worked. She passed that night without a single word."

Hennie burst into tears. Nathan flushed. Papa, apparently familiar with the tale, shook his head at me and sighed, bracing for the *tsuris* my words had unleashed. I could not believe that Mama would take this moment, when I had one foot out the door and needed a positive, supportive send-off to tide me over in rough times, to reveal her past, as if to blame me for the tragedy of that voyage forty years before.

Ma continued with her eyes latched on mine alone. "Next day, when the officers discovered my sister's corpse, they immediately went to remove it. My mother wailed. She threw herself on the

29

body and begged for the chance to prepare it for a Jewish burial. But, thank the *goyim*, there was to be no burial; they tossed Esther overboard with the waste."

Ma looked straight at me as if I, who consorted with gentiles, could explain their behavior. Her face was now red, and she cried as she talked, not even pausing to wipe her nose. I'd never seen her weep, although I'd heard her sobs through the walls. It was titanic, so frightening and fueled by anger (unleashed after years of suppression) that I found it difficult to be empathetic. It made me want to put my arms over my head and hide. She told us that all her family could do to show their sadness was rip their already-torn collars. And Maida, so silent and gray during the proceedings, who blamed herself for the foul stew, slipped away the next day at dawn. "I saw my sister's eyes flicker and close, and then she was gone," Mama said. "It was the splash that I remember most distinctly after all these years, and my mother's chiding when I had refused to eat that gruel not fit for cats. Believe me, there were times, long after the boat docked, when I wished I had."

Just as Hennie leapt from her chair and rushed headlong to comfort our mother, kneeling at her side, there was an impatient knocking at the door. I pushed my chair back to run to the entrance, but my mother's stare kept me in my seat. Nathan rose instead, buttoning his vest like the banker she wanted him to be. He did not look my way.

Nathan approached the entry and cautiously opened the door but couldn't keep Hurricane Kitty from entering with the damp San Francisco air. Mrs. Catherine "Kitty" Jones, currently of Tombstone, was a plump pepper-pot with over-plucked eyebrows, bottle-red hair, and a bosom like two jostling grapefruits. She was as exotic in our somber house as a scarlet macaw in her fitted jade-green bodice and voluminous skirt, striped royal blue and antique gold. The exorbitant feather in her tiny cap caught on the door as Kitty brushed by, her arms open and cheeks flushed.

"You must be Josephine," Kitty said to Hennie, whom my mother had swept up to stand beside her when the stranger entered the dining room. My sister, her arms interlaced around mother's waist, gaped at her in something like horror. Kitty continued: "I knew Johnny liked them young, but this is excessive."

Kitty laughed loudly, alone in her mirth, as she turned to me flirtatiously, cocking a shoulder and raising her arched brows. "No, no, *no,*" she said in a high, breathless voice (I would learn that her corset pinched her diaphragm, leading to light-headedness and headaches), "*you* are Josephine. Yes. A true beauty, just as Johnny said, although those brows could be clipped by a gardener."

My family stiffened. Undeterred, I popped out

of my seat, sloshing the soup from my bowl onto the linen tablecloth Ma would have to bleach and soak. My mother flinched as I rushed to embrace the woman whom I'd never met before this day, so happy was I that she'd actually arrived.

Johnny had dispatched Kitty with a generous allowance to collect me and chaperone my return to Arizona on the new train to Tucson. While Kitty had promised to pay a call the day she arrived, she later confessed she'd been indulging in the delights of a San Francisco hotel room, rummaging through sweet shops, and fingering the luxuries of S&G Gump's, eyeing a particularly extravagant gilded mirror. Perhaps my mother had come to believe that the woman was a myth, like the engagement, and would never appear. I looked into Ma's eyes, ringed with tears and flat with rage, and swiftly glanced away so as not to be deterred.

After a brief embrace, Kitty pushed me back and handed me a blue velvet box. "Here is the ring. We must be going."

I plucked the ring from the box—a shining diamond solitaire of at least half a carat in a dull gold band—and slid it onto my left hand. A perfect fit. People say that the world stops at moments like these, but I felt like the world suddenly sped up and found true north. Johnny and I were meant to be together. Here was proof. How could this not be right?

Later, I could answer that question with the same flamboyant cynicism that Kitty taught me that day, a form of social play-acting, but not that Shabbat. This ring was a ticket out of my mother's shadow. I was again dancing away from San Francisco toward the footlights, the lass in love with a sailor—or sheriff. I went to show it to my mother, who retreated as if it were cursed. But Hennie couldn't resist. She ran up to admire the engagement band until Ma pulled her back tightly by her collar. Nathan had the sense not to come any closer.

"If we're to make the train, we have to leave," Kitty said. In mock horror she asked, "Are you taking all this?" while regarding my carpetbag, traveling case, and worn trunk. Then she exited to retrieve the coachman, leaving me alone with my stunned family. My mother still must have wondered how I could leave the house with this painted gentile. Maybe she was already planning suitable punishments. I turned and passed between the pocket doors to grab my hand-me-down cloak from the hook by the door. Then I turned for a final good-bye in the darkened hallway. Ma hugged Hennie to her like a shield made of flesh, while Nathan cleaved to her shoulder.

With a lurch, Papa rose from the table, passing the three frozen figures to embrace me. I rose on tiptoe, although he was only five inches taller than

I was. He still smelled of the sweet yeast of the bakery, even in his Sabbath suit. He hugged me around my waist with one hand, kneading my back with the strong fingers of the other. I raised my lips to his stubbly cheek, closing my eyes as he played with the curls that escaped my bun. He rested his head on my shoulder and let his chin bite into my muscle until I flinched, a game we'd played since childhood, a sign that he would not let go. We always communicated wordlessly—in touch and gesture—a code my mother observed with distaste. I was proud to be my father's daughter. He was such a good man, quiet and simply satisfied. I hated to leave him behind to clean up another mess of mine. He guided my right hand behind my back, stuffing a folded envelope inside my palm, closing my fingers around the rough paper. When he was sure I had it, he kissed my ear and retreated to my mother's side.

The coachman jostled me from behind as he lugged my trunk outside. At the sound of fabric tearing, I looked up to see my mother rip Hennie's collar on my old dress. I held Ma's eyes as she reached up to her own collar and tore the fine material of her best dress. She turned toward Nathan as I ran out the front door, my triumphant exit trumped. I rushed outside, the cold air slapping my flushed cheeks.

"Well, that was a jolly family fare-thee-well,"

said Kitty, encasing her nervousness in antic extroversion. I climbed into the coach and collapsed, stuffing my father's envelope into the carpetbag. I leaned forward and stared through the bay window to where I'd stood just a few minutes before. I viewed my empty place at the table and Nathan's back as he draped a sheet over the mantel mirror.

CHAPTER 3

I thought I would never reach Tombstone. By the time I did, I was no great beauty. I had sweat, and shivered, and sweat again through my traveling clothes. It was warm by day and cold at night. Stains circled my armpits, each new ring reaching outward like foam deposits on the seashore. I tucked my elbows, trying to keep my arms close. But attempt that for hours on end: it fails.

The journey lasted three days but felt like three years. The train only reached as far as Tucson, where we changed for the Tombstone stagecoach. The boom was on, with as many as a hundred people arriving weekly, so we queued up at 5:00 a.m. for a chilly 7:00 a.m. departure. Kitty warned me that this final stretch was the toughest. Given our sleeplessness and erratic eating—everything offered seemed to contain ham or bacon—I'd been skeptical. How tough could it be if Kitty had taken it round trip just to come and retrieve me?

But Kitty hadn't exaggerated. The dusty thirteen-hour trip was bumpy. She insisted we take the front bench that faced backward so that the leather bolster wedged against the head of the coach would support our spines. What we gained in smoothness we exchanged for nausea. The journey might have been boring except for the constant fear of robbery.

We traveled in the newest of vehicles, a flat-roofed Concord coach crafted in New Hampshire. From the box above, the driver controlled a six-horse team, his face covered with a bandana. Seated beside him with a rifle for comfort was a Wells Fargo agent (by coincidence, Morgan Earp, Wyatt's younger brother). The competition for this route was so fierce that the driver hustled the horses at a speed never intended for such a vehicle. The two-ton coach lurched, climbing steep hills, then free-falling, careening on the bends.

To maximize profit, the H. C. Walker & Company stage line packed nine passengers together in a way that forced unwanted intimacy. A childlike senorita named Marietta with a nickel-size mole above her left eye faced us from the middle bench. Sandwiched between two beefy mining engineers, she sat so near us that her knees separated ours. Despite her clean, homespun dress, her musky, days-old sweat overwhelmed us.

Experienced female travelers wore veils to

create a layer of social distance as much as to keep the dust out of their eyes, mouths, and noses. I had no veil, physical or emotional, my spirits as unprotected as my face. Every feeling announced itself right on the surface. Accustomed to a sheltered life in a close-knit family, I had not yet learned to conceal my emotions from the outside world, to tip my chin down and look away. I believed that most strangers would have my best interests at heart, right down to Kitty herself, since Johnny had sent her to chaperone me.

I may have been the wildest woman of the Marcus clan, but I carried no claim on such a title beyond my front stoop. Despite my yearning for glorious adventure, the reality of stagecoach travel wasn't half so grand. My tailbone throbbed. I lacked a plush bottom like Kitty's to soften the ride, or the comforts of the whiskey flask passed from man to man to dull the pain and induce sleep. My molars ached from the jarring hoofbeats upon the rough, new roads not yet pounded smooth. All the *schmutz* kicked up by man and mare filled my mouth and irritated my nostrils, inducing fits of sneezing.

Kitty shifted beside me, sucking her teeth as she wiggled her backside to shove me off the turf her wide hips demanded. For three days, my chaperone had chattered away. My jaw ached from wagging in answer to her questions; outlaws on the stand underwent less grilling from the prosecution. In turn, I doubted there was a story about her I didn't know, from her baby brother's cholera death and the way her mother had buried all maternal feelings like a shroud with his small body, to the china pattern Kitty would buy at Gump's in San Francisco if her husband, Harry B. Jones, Esq., finally made a killing.

The attorney had dragged Kitty to the Arizona Territories in a final effort to emerge nearer the top of the social heap, or so she said. She confessed they no longer had marital relations. Kitty was uncertain whether the inactivity was a blessing or a curse, given her husband's ineptitude in that department, too. But she still had needs, she confided, more than most women. As a virgin, I had little advice to offer. That suited my traveling companion just fine, given she had so many opinions of her own. But when pressed about Johnny, Kitty demurred, smiling impishly, which should have signaled a red flag since he was the only topic where she was discreet.

I began yet another of those virulent sneezing fits that plagued me on the journey—a run so loud I awakened the slumbering giant of a mining engineer whose mammoth feet crowded mine. "Should I have brought an umbrella?" Kitty asked. As it turns out, I was allergic to dust. While digging for my last clean handkerchief in my carpetbag, I found Papa's crumpled letter stuffed in a side pocket. I'd hid it there for safekeeping that Friday night I left Perry Street and had forgotten it in my distress. The discovery released the guilt I had shoved down to the bottom of my belly. Anxiety rose into my throat, aggravating my preexisting jitters. I was antsy to arrive and see if my Johnny was really *my* Johnny. I needed to prove my mother wrong: I wasn't a wanton wastrel, but a desirable woman who deserved a life on a bigger stage lit by more than Shabbat candles.

I knew I should wait until I had privacy, but I was no paragon of patience—not like Wyatt, whose ability to outwait his opponents and nearly all provocation gave him the edge. He could spend an hour eating a vanilla ice-cream cone. Not me. So I grasped Papa's letter, flattened the ivory envelope on my lap, then ripped it open. Out tumbled two twenty-dollar bills, which piqued the attention among men throughout the coach who I had assumed were asleep.

This was the first letter I'd ever received from my father, a man more accustomed to jotting down bakery lists than correspondence. Although he was quiet by nature, I never confused Papa's reserve with being absent in thought or deed. He made the best of a situation that had its pluses and minuses, ever appreciative that he was alive and free in America. One lesson he gleaned from the old country before his exodus: keep your head down and avoid political involvement. That caution colored his actions in domestic affairs as well.

Papa's letter had the power to restore the courage that had drained away when I watched my mother split her best collar. Just remembering that moment, and the way Hennie shunned my glance, tightened my stomach. The message read, in small, cramped writing:

My Dearest Sadie,
Sweet daughter, I hope you are reading this somewhere safe, with happy eyes. You will never be dead to me. *Shivah* is for corpses, not the living. You are a great joy to me, and that has not changed because we no longer live in the same house. That had to happen sooner or later if I did my job right as your father. Every bird must leave the nest.

Remember this, *shayna maidel*, where others see your outside charms, I know the beauty of your nature. Since the day you were born you have had a heart as big as your cheeks. You entered the world laughing and smiling (although later you could spit and scream with the best of them if you didn't get your way!). That's all right. That's who you are. Independent and freedom-loving like our adopted land.

Mama and I are people from the old

country and we see with different eyes. We made sacrifices so that you could live a new world life. Mama only holds on too tight out of fear, but I know life is a journey each pair of shoes must take on their own. Mama lives in the past. You must live in the future. You have my blessing for what it is worth. May you find love, and keep love, and have children of your own, but know that there is always and forever love in my heart for you and shelter under my roof as long as I live.

Affectionately,

Papa

I felt the gaze of strangers on my face, rough men used to seeing women cry and ignoring the spectacle. Kitty reached into my lap and snatched the bills, tucking the greenbacks into my sleeve for safekeeping. I didn't look up, letting my tears soak the paper. With the faint scent of fresh bread, I inhaled the absolute kindness of this man who loved me, not more or less than he loved his other children, or even Rebecca, but free from the bonds of expectation. He saw me not only as I really was, but also my very best self. Papa seemed to see beyond what I envisioned as the woman I could become, if only I was brave and confident enough to place one foot in front of the other—and turn around and change paths if one direction failed me. In his eyes, I had the power to break the boundaries of the *shtetls* we replicated wherever we went, the dos and don'ts to which my mother clung.

Staring at the stationery, I recalled the games we played when I was a child sitting in Papa's lap: putting my pointer finger in his mouth and withdrawing it as fast as I could, daring him to bite me (he did—and hard!); playing with his big ears; teasing the wisps of hair on his head up and up until it was a solitary plume on his scalp, adding a flirtatious femininity to someone so steadfastly male. Ma would rustle past and cluck her tongue, but we just waited quietly, inhaling with one breath until she took her endless busyness to another room. I often encircled the incorrectly set broken bone on his right forearm that popped out like a third wrist. He got it playing stickball on Hester Street. The idea of my hardworking father ever playing sports was nearly inconceivable, for he never played games anymore, except our little made-up ones. As for his broken bone, he always said that it hurt when there was fog. So many stories I hadn't asked him to tell—would I still have a chance? What were his seven sisters named? Which was his favorite? Why had he left Prussia, and where were those darlings who had spoiled him as he deserved to be spoiled now?

Perhaps I dozed off, because when I opened my

eyes, twilight had arrived. The temperature had dropped with the sun. I found myself shivering, and I wasn't alone. I looked up and into the eyes of the Mexican senorita, Marietta, who had wrapped her rough-loomed shawl twice around her neck for warmth. I looked down at my knee and saw her callused hand there, and remembered a patting sensation while crying.

I moaned to Kitty about the dust in my mouth. She wiggled her hips and retrieved a brown paper sack of bright cherry candies. Kitty offered them around, creating a circle of sweetness. Marietta smiled in thanks, a few teeth missing. Nevertheless, she was a pretty little thing, with heavy ropes of black braids caught in an opalescent abalone clip. I later learned that the stunning ornament was an engagement gift from the rancher Peter Spence. They never wed, although Marietta cleaned his house and shared his bed and brought her mother to live with them.

I heard shouting from above and outside the coach, fearing the worst: robberies were more common come nightfall. Marietta, facing front, squeezed my knee between gumdrop-sticky fingers. I looked through the curtains to see Johnny Behan galloping up out of the gloom on his bay stallion, a bouquet of yellow roses clutched to his saddle horn. The passengers shuffled so that I could sit by the window; by now everyone had been thoroughly, wearyingly informed of the man's irresistible charms. Seeing him in light of Papa's letter, my heart opened: I'd found love with a man as good as my own father. Johnny had staked a claim on my heart and pursued me recklessly despite the difference in our ages and faiths.

Outside the window, Johnny sat tall in his saddle, making his stallion dance sideways before turning to ride beside the carriage. He tipped his cream-colored Stetson and said, "Ladies," with the ease of someone who knew the value of his looks. My heart skipped a beat. Just shy of his thirty-sixth birthday, with lively, dark eyes; thick, curved brows; and a broad, intelligent forehead, Johnny sported a salesman's genial smile. He knowingly revealed two rows of even, white teeth. They were legendary in a time of few dentists, when pliers were often the dental implement of choice. His was a face a woman trusted, although I would later learn Johnny could use a heart to match. Men, on the other hand, could see right through him, and his ability to reel in good women was a source of constant amusement and side bets around the poker table.

But that fresh October evening as I entered Tombstone under a dark-blue sky stretched taut as a sheet in the wind, I was the only passenger to get such an exorbitant welcome. I was terribly in love with love. I lifted my chest, and released a hairpin to let the wind sweep my curls in a way that I knew suggested a seductiveness I hadn't the experience to support. I played the heroine of my own operetta, Josephine in *H.M.S. Pinafore*, oblivious to all the other stories on the frontier stage, the family turf wars of *Romeo and Juliet*, the malicious manipulations of *Richard III*. I had seen the Shakespeare plays with Rebecca, but when Evil arrived with a sharp knife, I was busy examining the staging and costumes, the false gems that shined like rubies on the velvet-covered chests of actresses often decades older than the characters they played.

Johnny cantered alongside the coach, beaming as if I were Queen Victoria on parade. As the driver urged the horses on even faster in a final, mad dash to our destination at the Wells Fargo office, Johnny held a one-sided conversation with me. His words flew back on the wind, so I nodded and smiled foolishly as if I understood, when all I really wanted was that first kiss once my feet touched Tombstone dirt. I wanted Johnny's lips on mine, his hands circling my waist, my lace-covered thighs pressing against his chaps. I wanted to lose myself in his scent of bay rum and horses. When I glanced over at Kitty, I noticed she, too, lit up at the sight of Johnny—in a way that did not reflect sisterly affection.

Suddenly, the stage screeched to a halt, bouncing back and forth on its leather-strap suspension. I crawled across knees and thighs (a man grimaced, but I ignored him), angling for the exit without pausing for propriety. When I stepped onto the running board, my knees failed. I felt dizzy, as if the world was racing ahead, while my insides fell behind. As I grabbed for purchase, Morgan Earp leapt off the coach box to the street below and reached a hand up to steady me as I stared into his amused blue eyes. That was how I met my first Earp.

It was some entrance for a nice Jewish girl from San Francisco.

Morgan, at twenty-nine, was the penultimate and breeziest Earp brother, a six-footer like the pack of them. His fair hair took a swirly curl off to one side with brilliantine, while his handlebar mustache protected his grin from grit and bugs on the range. Morgan gently lifted me by my waist and deposited me on Allen Street. He said with a merry laugh: "You don't weigh more than a child."

"But she kisses like a woman." Johnny stepped forward, scooped me up, spun me around, and kissed me right there in front of everyone. I smooched back without hesitation. I was hungry for his touch, despite the crowd. Back then, folks turned up to see the stage arrive, to appraise newcomers for marks and marriageable prospects. And with that kiss, Johnny trumpeted his message: *This is my woman. Hands off!* At least Johnny wanted me, even if I was no longer welcome in my mother's house.

From the beginning, kissing united Johnny and me. We weren't the first couple to have that in common. We'd met the previous year when I ran away from home with Pauline Markham's Pinafore on Wheels theatrical troupe. I made it as far as Arizona with my best friend, Dora, before the Apache scout Al Sieber dispatched us back to our anguished parents in San Francisco. I was a lousy performer—I had paralyzing stage fright and couldn't carry a tune—but I discovered my aptitude for romance. Apaches besieged our convoy, and Johnny was among Sieber's team pursuing the braves who'd hopped the reservation. Sieber's crew rescued us from an ambush, and then, while they continued their hunt, sheltered the actors at a nearby ranch and relay station. From the moment Johnny set eyes on me, there was a connection. It flattered me that out of all the beauties, most far more talented and experienced, I attracted his attention. All my theatrical ambitions evaporated with our first kiss. It was foolish of me, I know, but no more foolish than running away from my family with Dora to join Miss Markham's traveling troupe.

During those two weeks, Johnny sought Apaches by day, returning to the ranch at night. While the other hunters rushed into the building hungry for grub and the dances that followed, the well-mannered Johnny paused to wash up at the trough. Smelling sweet, he changed his shirt, waxed his whiskers, and pursued me. I wasn't hard to find.

After supper, Johnny and I would ease onto the front porch, leaving Dora and the others behind. It was on those evenings that I discovered one of my true loves—and it wasn't named Behan. I fell for the desert night, leaning against the porch railing and watching the stars fall fast with my back to the house lights and the raucous music, the stamps and whoops of dancers as the Pinafore on Wheels troupe passed the time.

Just standing there with Johnny smoking by my side, a city girl who'd just loosened her pigtails and lowered her skirts, the night called me up and gave me a sense of the universe's immensity. Maybe a coyote cried out in hunger and loneliness. A jackrabbit scampered. Tumbleweed scratched the earth's back. And I breathed in the desert air, sweet and tart and liberating.

Usually, after a bucket of stars had fallen and the men stepping onto the porch to cool off and smoke seemed too close for Johnny, he would lead me away from the lights of the ranch. Something about those desert nights opened me up from the inside out. When I took his hand, I felt an unfamiliar excitement. It was as if my life was actually happening to me, right then and right there. This was why I'd left home: to end the agonizing wait for my life to begin. I might have been a failure onstage, but I intended to be the star of my own life, not the girl with her braids tucked up under a hat (and her chest tightly wrapped), performing the sailor's hornpipe. Johnny took my hand, gently yet firmly. He knew where he was going, and I followed. I admired his broad shoulders and slim waist, his confident walk as he led me around the adobe dwelling and behind the stables. Once there, he twirled me around and gentled my back against the rough barn wood. He pressed in close against me, blocking out the sky that no longer held my attention.

It was there I had my first real kisses from a man who knew what he was doing—not a little boy playing house in a back bedroom while Ma's skirts swished nearby. At first, Johnny's urgency alarmed me. I didn't know what to do when his tongue pushed between my lips. But I was a quick study. I learned to push my body back, to let my lips play against his—and before long I was leading Johnny back to the spot behind the stables. He'd unleashed a hunger that made every part of me more alive. Miss Markham, belatedly acting the mother hen, pulled me aside and warned that I should not go outside unchaperoned, but I didn't want any company other than Johnny's. If this was danger, I wanted more.

A year had passed since those remote desert nights, a year spent cloistered with my family. The Torah boys at synagogue and the widowers Ma considered eligible did not interest me. And now,

Johnny's kiss in front of the Wells Fargo office told me what his letters could not convey: he still wanted me passionately. And, even more, I still wanted him. A year had passed for me without a single kiss, and tasting Johnny again, I didn't know how I'd survived without him.

Johnny begged my pardon and separated from me in order to help Kitty's husband load my trunks on his buckboard along with Kitty's things. I took a breath and absorbed the sights, the mix of roughness and riches, filth and fortune. Tombstone was a boomtown with three thousand residents, give or take. The hoisting works that served the silver mines dominated the view on the hilltop overlooking the town. The crunching and pounding continued night and day, like a giant chewing boulders, interrupted by the whistles that announced the shift changes.

Tombstone bristled with energy. That October the boom was still rising toward its apex. I sensed a gambler's optimism lacking in my narrow San Francisco: a day in a miner's life could make the difference between squirrel and beans over a fire, and cassoulet and Champagne at a fine restaurant. Down the road, I saw the squatters' canvas tents by campfire light set out in uneven rows, inhabited by men who found it easier to wear their clothes until it was time to buy new ones than to wash the soot and slag and sweat from the ones they wore. But the block of Allen

Street where I stood was the town's heart. Surrounding me between Fourth and Fifth Streets were the Oriental Saloon, the Grand Hotel, and the Occidental Saloon—all lit up and wearing luxurious facades that contrasted with the shanty town only tobacco-spitting distance away.

As Johnny roped his horse to Harry's wagon and Kitty nagged her stoop-shouldered husband, I felt a weight on one cheek. I sensed eyes staring at me. I don't know how that's possible, but it happened just that way, as real as the feeling of sunshine while your eyes are closed. That was the first time I saw Wyatt. He was looking straight at me. I stared right back. He was dead handsome with an athletic build on a six-foot frame, made taller by perfect posture. His hair was blond and thick like his younger brother's, with a matching mustache and unflinching eyes, the same blue as Morgan's but twice as intense.

Suddenly bashful, I glanced away and flushed. Morgan caught my eye and winked. He'd seen the Earp effect before. "Is everyone so handsome in Tombstone?" I asked him.

"Just us Earps," Morgan said, showing off a dimple.

"And my fiancé," I said with a smile. Johnny, realizing he couldn't leave me alone for a minute, approached and took my hand as if claiming lost luggage. I surrendered my arm, feeling like a naughty child caught out. But instead of leading me to safety, he led me directly over to the tall stranger in the black frock coat. His crisp white shirt seemed like a miracle in a frontier where a layer of soot covered everything. While he was as tall as Morgan, he was rangier: high-waisted and long-legged. A pair of Buntline long-handled Colt revolvers bulged at his narrow hips.

"Josie, meet Mr. Wyatt Earp." Johnny steered me forward. "If you're ever in peril, and I'm absent, the deputy sheriff is your man."

I craned my neck to see Wyatt beneath his black Stetson. He tipped his hat in greeting, nudging it backward enough to give me a look into his appraising eyes. They were deeper set and harder to read than Morgan's; he seemed as closed as Morgan was open, but that was only a first impression. When he said "Ma'am," his low, calm voice drew me in. It made me want to stand on tiptoe and listen closely over the street noise—horse-and-mule hoofs pounding, wagon wheels rattling, the sharp cries of street vendors hawking their wares, and the continual growl of the hoisting works.

With a girlish flirtatiousness, I extended my hand. "I hope I never require your assistance, Mr. Earp, but I'm pleased to meet you." The encounter resembled a play, the words part of a script, my knee dipping so slightly in a little curtsy. The current that went from Wyatt's hand to mine when he clasped it in his own was unlike anything I felt with Johnny. When I looked up, and up, and up at him as he held my hand for just a moment too long, I saw that his eyes were not guarded, but deep. They held pain and promise. The look was so intimate and searching that I felt naked right there in the middle of Allen Street, with Johnny just a step behind me crowing about my arrival, lost in the cacophony of the main thoroughfare.

I still held Wyatt's hand when Johnny grabbed my elbow and guided me down Allen Street for a tour of the town before going to dinner to celebrate my first night in Tombstone. In case my fiancé had noticed my interest in Wyatt, I whispered, "Well, he's serious as death."

"Even death laughs occasionally."

I laughed loudly but recognized the hollowness in my teasing. I considered Papa's letter, and his encouragement to find a man to love and love me back. Meeting Wyatt, I experienced a charge I'd never felt before—but I didn't trust it. I considered what I felt for Johnny love. I lacked the experience to know otherwise. I chastised myself for behaving toward a dedicated man like Johnny as if he was no longer good enough—too short, perhaps, too glib, secondhand. Fearing I was too much my mother's daughter, I tried to stuff my misgivings down in that soul cellar where I kept her disapproval and my worries that my heart wasn't nearly as good as Papa claimed. I gave Johnny's hand a squeeze. He squeezed back twice.

CHAPTER 4

As we linked arms and strolled Allen Street's boardwalk, Johnny firmly shook hands with passersby. He looked each one in the eye. In return, they smiled and nodded and replied with cordial small talk. Some men promised to meet up later that week and raise a glass at the Grand Hotel where Johnny tended bar. He seemed to know everybody—their names and, if they had children, *their* names, as well as their hometowns and their aspirations—and he'd only arrived a month before. I shared the glow of Johnny's popularity, smiling widely in return at these strangers, mostly men. They looked back at me with appreciation and welcome despite my travel-worn appearance. Although I craved a bath, Johnny had other plans—and I couldn't disappoint now that we were united. I felt as if I'd spent the last year like a troll under the stairs, hiding from the world in my mother's disapproving shadow. Now I could finally stand upright. It felt fantastic to shake out my bones, raise my head, and stare straight at the world without shame. The trip's exhaustion bubbled up into exhilaration. Here I stood, finally, on the road to becoming who I really was, ready to give all my love to Johnny and unfold in his arms.

As we passed Barron's Barber Shop with its candy-striped pole, the proprietor saluted with his shears. Johnny tipped his hat, revealing a fresh cut, a walking advertisement for the shop. Two grisly customers covered in trail dust cooled their boots on a bench outside, awaiting a shave and a haircut to return them to some semblance of civilized manhood. Johnny politely said, "Gentlemen," to the gnarly strangers as if they were Eastern bankers.

"I don't plan on tending bar forever, Josie. There's no money there. I'm running for sheriff. That's why I introduced you to Wyatt. I'm thinking of deputizing him. He's the best lawman in town, even if he is a damned Republican."

The political parties made little impression on me; if Johnny was a Democrat, so was I. However, in the coming months as tensions climbed in Tombstone, I learned that the conflicting allegiances between Johnny and Wyatt reflected the deep divide between North and South—even on the Western frontier. Only fifteen years had passed since Union General Ulysses S. Grant accepted Confederate Robert E. Lee's surrender at Appomattox. While the officers officially ended the Civil War, they failed to cauterize wounds still seeping into the conflicts between cowboys and lawmen in the Arizona Territory.

On that first day, I was oblivious to these opposing forces that would shape our future.

Instead, I savored the weight of Johnny's arm around mine. I'd never been part of a couple before. I floated beside Johnny like the heroine of a stage musical singing in a duet with the handsome tenor. When we approached a warped board on the walk, he encircled my waist to lift me over the obstacle. A shock of electricity shot through my body, reaching the crown of my head and bouncing back down my spine to, well, *that* place. Deep breath. And another.

We then encountered Mr. and Mrs. Clum, the editor of the *Tombstone Epitaph* and his pregnant wife. Their son, Woody, clutched his mother's skirts, disappearing into the blue calico when I smiled at him. Mr. Clum—five feet nine, barrel-chested, and athletic with a receding hairline—reached out his hand, then retracted his inky fingers and laughed, saying, "The stain of the truth since May 1, 1880."

"What's the latest news?" asked Johnny.

"Today we have the arrival of that famed *Pinafore* actress and fiancée of John Harris Behan," said Clum, "Miss Josephine Marcus, lately of San Francisco."

"I'm hardly famous," I said. "I was merely the cabin boy, and had stage fright at that."

"You're too modest," said Clum. "Will you help us form a *Pinafore* troupe?"

"My professional dancing days are done," I said, patting Johnny's arm. "But an amateur production wouldn't hurt, would it, Johnny? I assume you'd join in, Mr. Clum?"

"John has a beautiful baritone," said the fine-boned Mrs. Mollie Clum, her mouth curvy and eyes shrewd. Mollie's dress strained over the large bump she supported with a veined and reddened hand, her ring finger swollen beneath a square-cut sapphire on a gold band. Glancing down, Mollie said, "But we must take our curtain calls for this production before we launch another. Right, John?"

"I do fancy singing 'I am the monarch of the sea,' but you're right, Mother. First things first. Come, Woody," Clum said. The boy sidled out from his mother's skirts, revealing possum eyes, big and wary. Clum reached down and swung the lad up only to have the shy child bury his face, so that the boy's girlish curls wiggled at his father's neck.

We bid good-bye, making vague promises for future get-togethers. As we continued, Johnny hailed ranchers and cowboys by name—among them Ike Clanton and his younger brother Billy, Tom McLaury, and William "Curly Bill" Brocius. They strutted toward us on the boardwalk with the bowlegged swagger of men who spent long days in the saddle and then cut loose in town. I'd never seen anything like them in their bright-colored bibbed wool shirts and leather pants tucked into boots tooled with stars and playing cards. They resembled the rowdy chorus of sailors in *H.M.S. Pinafore*, and I couldn't keep myself from staring. The men clearly took my stares for something more, looking right back at me with eyes bright from liquor. I didn't know whether to be flattered or frightened, so I chose flattered. I felt secure with Johnny beside me. When Curly Bill winked, I even winked right back. Tom McLaury reached out for a pinch, which Johnny blocked good-naturedly as if it were a game among friends.

As the cowboys proceeded on their saloon crawl, I wrinkled my nose at the odor of horse and booze that trailed after them. Although my experience with *shickers* was limited—no one in my house drank alcohol for pleasure—I could tell there would be a demand for a sheriff with men like these running wild. As if he read my mind, Johnny said, "I've got a plan, Josie. The territorial government is creating a new county called Cochise. Tombstone will be its seat, and I have the inside track for sheriff."

"Isn't that dangerous?"

"Less perilous than prospecting in Apache territory, darling girl." The endearment warmed me. "Besides, a smart lawman knows how to shoot a gun, but he'll live longer if he knows when to holster it. A silver tongue is a better weapon than a silver bullet."

"Not if you're hunting Apaches."

"You might have a point there."

"I'll say I do. Arrows have points, too, Johnny."

"Ouch!" he said as we passed the Oriental Saloon. The square, one-story wooden building, lined with glass-paned arcade doors on two sides, squatted where Allen crossed Fifth Street. Barflies buzzed on the front walk, laughing and spitting tobacco in the general vicinity of cast-iron spittoons. Johnny said of the saloon, "You couldn't see anything finer in San Francisco," as if he himself had erected the bar and hotel and crafted the crystal chandeliers.

"Nor anything finer than me, Johnny Be-Handy," said a green-eyed redhead in a taunting Irish brogue. She sauntered through the Oriental's swinging doors, then stood before us clutching her slim hips and clucking at Johnny like a schoolteacher disappointed in her pet's misspelling. She dwarfed us both, six feet tall if she was an inch, even without the lemon-colored lace-up boots she tapped impatiently. Freckles splashed her square face, framing prominent cheekbones. A deep dimple cleaved her pointy chin. She filled out a green silk evening dress that would have suited a night at the opera. She scolded Johnny with a familiarity that chafed: "I see you've brought Albert's mother along. She's awfully young to have such a big boy."

"I don't have a son," I corrected, pulling myself up all five feet (which had never before felt so inadequate to the task). Who was this gentile giant to know my business? And anyone who examined my waist, or my smooth skin, could see I was no mother of a nine-year-old, no mother at all. I'd swung from elated to furious in seconds. I could feel that thing boiling up in me that preceded a hard stamp of my right foot, or the slamming of a door. But I was not keen to show that part of my personality before Johnny and the green goddess. The barflies had begun to laugh, though, furthering my fury. In Tombstone, everything on the street was a show, and a fight between two women always got a big audience, given the town's ratio of roosters to hens.

Johnny tipped his hat and said "Delia" in a conciliatory manner while tightening his grip on my elbow until it pinched. He backed me off the boardwalk onto Allen Street, then swiveled me around, narrowly avoiding a mule-drawn water wagon that barreled past. I flinched, and that, too, made the barflies howl with laughter.

"Hey, Albert's mum," Delia called as Johnny moved us along, "if you ever need a job dancing, tell them Delia sent you."

I tried to pull away from Johnny to fling back the response that was lurking in the bottom of my throat, but Johnny resisted. He tugged my arm and my body followed, but he couldn't keep me from hearing her sing a popular *Pinafore* song. She had a rich, relaxed soprano I envied: *"I'm called Little Buttercup, dear Little Buttercup, though I could never tell why, but still I'm called Buttercup, poor Little Buttercup, sweet Little Buttercup I."*

"Nice voice," I said sourly as we climbed the boardwalk on the opposite side of the street. Delia held a high *C* without strain, projecting across the noisy road with its speeding horses and staggering drunks. Her talent frosted me. She was probably a better dancer, too, with all that leg. "Friend of yours, Johnny?"

"Delia's no friend of mine, sweet pea."

"Then why does she know our business?" I sounded nearly as shrill as the mine whistle that announced the shift change just then, giving Johnny an excuse to exchange the topic of Delia for the more welcome subject of dinner. Johnny had reserved a prime table at the Grand Hotel, where he tended bar. We approached the brand-new two-story building conveniently located down Allen Street from the Oriental and across from the more established Cosmopolitan.

Johnny opened the hotel's frosted-glass door for me, and then followed close enough to blow warm breath on the curls at my nape. It sent a shiver down my spine. I reached back for his hand, and my palm accidentally landed somewhere high on his thigh. Awkwardly, I pulled it back. The gilded full-length mirror that dominated the foyer reflected my surprise and embarrassment. But as Johnny unwound my woolen paisley shawl, I

61

relaxed at the sight of the familiar, pearly-skinned oval face I knew so well, even if it was not as refreshed as I would have liked.

Seeing my reflection bolstered my confidence. That's who you are. That's who I am. That's why I'm here. Beneath a whisper of a widow's peak, my widely spaced eyes rimmed with dense lashes held my gaze beneath bold, dark brows, my left higher and just a little more bowed than my right. I arched that sable eyebrow with an appraising look, raising my chin to enhance the effect of high cheekbones and full lips, the lower falling open to reveal just the hint of the part between my two front teeth. Some would say that my nose was too wide, too heavy at the tip—my brother Nathan had often teased me, calling it "bulbous," picking as siblings will on one small flaw to spite the whole—but it was the strength of that feature that held the rest in balance.

"My beauty," Johnny whispered, his mouth brushing my curls. I smiled over my shoulder, raised my chin a little higher, inviting him closer, then turned back to the mirror that now captured us both. We looked into each other's eyes in the reflection, his warm and amused, framed by the lines of many past smiles radiating out. He tried to match my serious expression, sucking in his cheeks and pursing his cupid lips, but he couldn't maintain the pose. His lopsided, happy grin returned. He squinted merrily at me. I shut my eyes to save the image, as if I was a photographer composing our engagement photo: the future Mr. and Mrs. John Harris Behan, of Tombstone.

Spinning around and opening my eyes, I found myself in a setting as grand as the gilded and rouged opera houses I'd visited in San Francisco with Rebecca, only on a more intimate scale. Instead of rushing to the cheap seats, feeling like an interloper in a world of gentiles, I held my head up proudly as I had in the mirror and surveyed the scene with newly privileged eyes. I had just as much right to be in Tombstone as anybody else seeking fortune and adventure, refusing the hand-me-down destinies of all our hometowns—east and west, north and south. There wasn't a soul in the room born in Tombstone. There wasn't a plot of inherited property.

Here, in the soft light of etched-glass oil lamps, I had a chance to become who I really was. While I wasn't entirely familiar with that Josie yet, I could feel her at the edge of my fingertips. When I looked deep inside myself, I knew this excitement I felt was just the beginning. Every action I took would bring that new Josie closer to me. The first step had been making my way against the current to Tombstone, to this spot where a sparkly chandeliered dining room stretched out to my left. To my right, beyond a swinging door, the hum of the fancy bar where Johnny worked most nights could be heard. Directly before me, a wide staircase rose gracefully, leading, I presumed, to private hotel suites.

When we entered the dining room, all heads swiveled in my direction, from newly minted silver millionaires to Eastern investors and bachelor bankers. There was an intake of breath that left the cigar smoke hanging beneath the heavy crystal chandeliers. Starved for attention, I smiled and nodded at the strangers, freely making eye contact, feeling like Princess Beatrice. And many gents— for men dominated the room—smiled back warmly, but with the canny eyes of silver-ore assessors. A stiff, aged maître d' with shoe polish– black hair above a pallid face appeared before us in black tie and tails. He addressed us in a European accent that I couldn't quite place, but that I knew was neither German nor French, since I was familiar with both. Thanks to a coin Johnny slipped into his hand, the man was overly solicitous. He led us over a plush carpet, gesturing with gnarled arthritic hands to a prominent circular table for two swathed in white damask linen.

Johnny pulled out a carved walnut dining chair for me. I sat down, enchanted. He leaned close\ to whisper in my ear, asking if I was comfortable. I smiled, overwhelmed with joy. Never before had a man held a seat for me (although Nathan had pulled his share out from *under* me many times as a lark). Never had anyone treated me with the deference shown by the maître d'.

This royal treatment inflated my sense of my own importance. Johnny savored the moment. He strutted to his place across the table. Once seated, he unfurled his cloth napkin like a magician's cape and fixed me with a smile that rose from his white teeth to his dancing eyes, as if no one in the room was as merry as we were. He made me feel like I was the only person there that mattered, pulling my gaze into his own with an unwavering magnetism. As I leaned in, he put his hand on my knee beneath the fancy tablecloth. I didn't pull my leg away, but his hand felt heavy and hot, and it made me unsure of what I was supposed to do, how I was supposed to react. Was I supposed to move in closer, or retreat in a game of cat and mouse? Was this something that also happened in fancy restaurants, like having one's chair held for you, or three crystal glasses beside your china plate? I had no idea.

A sober waiter in formal dress approached with a superior look on his clean-shaven face. He handed Johnny the menu and requested permission to give me the second one, which lacked prices. Johnny nodded gravely in assent and then winked at me, which made the waiter's behavior less intimidating. Johnny's easygoing, good-time nature made my jump into the unknown world of fine dining in public thrilling. I imagined that his zest for living must be how the rest of the world dined while we at home had our backs to them. In our house, dinner was the family united around the challah by candlelight, hardly talking between prayers, under the tent of tension between husband and wife, mother and daughter.

With Johnny smiling across from me, I wasn't going to waste time worrying about my inexperience. I was going to dig in and relish the moment. So I read the hand-lettered parchment menu, deliberating between Columbia River salmon *au buerre et noir*, and *lapine domestique á la maître d'*. It wasn't kreplach, but I'd eaten enough of them to last a lifetime.

When the waiter returned, shuffling unctuously, Johnny ordered roast loin of beef. When I chose salmon, Johnny explained we weren't near the Columbia River, but in cattle country. He told the waiter: "Mademoiselle will have the beef, too, please, and Champagne." As the waiter pivoted away, Johnny added, "And keep it coming."

The waiter nodded and then headed for the bar. While we awaited his return, Johnny explained that he felt at home in the Grand. The hotel reminded him of the Harris House, owned by his grandparents back in Missouri, a state that straddled Confederate and Union in the Civil War. Located at the gateway to the Santa Fe Trail, it had served Washington Irving, Horace Greeley, and—critical to Johnny's political ambitions—the current governor of the Arizona Territory, John C. Fremont.

And then Johnny stopped discussing his roots and stared at me as if I were Helen of Troy. His eyes crinkled with his smile, looking as if he was the luckiest man in the West and didn't care what others thought. I eventually learned that opinions did matter to Johnny. Seating me across from him was part of his scheme to win friends and influence people. Johnny was playing to a crowd populated by influential men he knew briefly, or not at all. In that lavish dining room, Johnny possessed a valuable commodity: the most beautiful young woman (me!). His dominion would inspire other men to wonder what John Harris Behan had that they lacked, how they could acquire it, and how they could ally themselves with this charismatic Arizonan who had the means to attract such a prize.

Of course, I was ignorant then while Johnny reclined, smoking and embroidering stories about growing up in the Harris House on grits and fried chicken and his grandmother's famed oatmeal cookies. His father was an Irish Catholic immigrant, which didn't sit well with his mother's staunch Southern Baptists and Confederate loyalists. The Harrises had been pioneers, born and buried in Virginia for more than a century before my parents crossed the Atlantic.

Considering my mother's recent revelation about her rough overseas passage, I felt ashamed that I had no similar stories of family achievements to share. Ours had been an anxious struggle just to arrive. Ma wasn't alone among Jewish immigrants in keeping those tales private and hidden from the gentiles. While Johnny had a brick-built inn bearing his family name, bureaucrats had likely Americanized our surname at Ellis Island. I thought perhaps our name had been Marcuse. Once the Champagne arrived, I ceased dwelling upon my flawed pedigree, too dazzled to realize that all families had shameful secrets.

The waiter popped the cork and filled cut crystal goblets that sparkled like rainbows in the light. Johnny toasted "To us!" Bubbles tickled my nose as I relished my first sip. It was the antithesis of the syrupy sweet kosher wine we drank on Shabbat, swallowed and set aside before it raised anyone's spirits. After a few mouthfuls, I became lightheaded, intoxicated with the liquor as well as with Johnny, so handsome and confident and good-natured. I fell into the flattery of being his chosen woman in the nation's wildest boomtown.

Johnny entertained me with tales of his childhood pranks. Hearing that he'd once traded flour for scented dusting powder among the guests' toiletries at the Harris House, I confessed to salting the tails of pigeons in a futile effort to capture the fowl. I only caught a *potch*, a spank, from my impatient mother. We were laughing at our mischievous younger selves when the waiter served the beef. It was more tender than any meat I'd ever consumed—once I sorted out how to wield the serrated knife big enough to slay an Apache.

After the entrée, my corset chafing, I watched the waiter exchange the dishes for demitasses and a plate of oatmeal cookies "a la Harris House." Johnny doused his cigar. He reached across the table for my hands and stared into my eyes. "I love you, Josie," he said, despite being in public. His voice betrayed an emotional squeak. "You've made a big leap this week to join me. You left the security of a loving home with nothing more than this gold ring to bind you to me. Our union is riskier for you than me. But, trust me, I will protect you. My courageous Josie, jump into my arms and I will catch you."

I hadn't really considered this imbalance. And even then, in my Champagne glow, I didn't register how bold, how foolish, my actions would appear to any rational being. To me, he had made the bigger leap, choosing to love a Jewish maiden with no dowry over all the other women attracted to him, a man of real skills in the world from a fine family. I rejected what he was saying outright, although in retrospect, he was making a disclaimer as much as a declaration of affection. I *was* the one taking all the risks—alone in Tombstone, entirely dependent on his goodwill and pocketbook, with no return ticket.

CHAPTER 5

As midnight approached, Johnny rose from his chair and knelt beside me in the dining room of the Grand Hotel. I felt lightheaded and desperately in love. I was both free in the world and attached to a man who adored me. Even if I couldn't carry a tune, my life would be a song, a duet. Confidence bubbled up inside me. The words I'd never before spoken to a man besides my father flew out of my mouth: "I love you."

"I love you, too, Josephine Marcus. You're a gambler, and you've doubled down on me."

A pause followed while I awaited the marriage proposal expected from a gentleman on his knees. It didn't happen. I could have said "Marry me" right then and sent Johnny sprinting for the justice of the peace. But I followed Johnny's lead as he rose with just the slightest of creaks and eased back my chair. Together, we waltzed out of the dining room under the curious stares of strangers.

In the lobby, I approached the porter who held the glass doors ajar. Beyond, Allen Street was as lively at midnight as it was at noon. Johnny caught my elbow and aimed me toward the staircase. We climbed beside the mahogany banisters. By the fourth step, I felt like a girl being jerked awake from a dream where I was flying over the city, hand in hand with a loving friend. By the seventh, my fingers had stiffened in Johnny's grasp, his hand on my lower back less supportive than urging. I fully awoke from my dreamlike state to a figure dominating the landing above. She had a heavily powdered, pale moon face under a ruler-straight center part, her dark curls escaped and frizzed from ringlets that must have been tight as wood shavings earlier that night. Around her neck she wore five silver necklaces, some with topazes, some turquoise, and one with a large, scrolled heart-shaped locket. She stared down the remaining steps with black-flecked sapphire eyes. In Spanish-accented English, she said, "Evening, Johnny," with a soft *J*.

"Miss Timberline." Johnny nodded with a pleasant reserve, as if it was noon and he'd encountered the town librarian on the boardwalk.

"Ah, tonight I'm a Miss." The woman pulled lavender gloves over ringed fingers. "Are you working the bar later?"

"Tomorrow."

"Then I suppose I'll see you mañana. Like you, the sun goes down and I go to work." Miss Timberline descended two steps, kicking the pleat of her turquoise silk skirt ahead of her. It rustled like dry leaves. She stopped, adjusting her right glove as she peered down myopically at Johnny and me. I could smell the heavy attar of roses she wore. "So, this is the blushing bride."

On cue, I reddened from my collarbones to my scalp. I looked back toward the safety of the lobby, where I saw the eager faces of the porter and the maître d'.

"Guilty as charged," Miss Timberline said throatily. She crossed so near on the wide steps that our skirts rubbed against each other, the jewel-toned turquoise of hers making my traveling dress appear flat and worn. I watched her swish downstairs and disappear into the bar.

A door opened above. A stout old man emerged, half-hidden behind a dense white beard that floated out ahead of his chin and was of a piece with spiny sideburns. His white eyebrows extended like awnings over deep-set, canny eyes. Well into his sixties, he struggled to fasten his last vest button with rough fingers. He stopped to check his pocket watch and then descended. He nodded at Johnny conspiratorially and said with excessive ceremony, "Mr. Behan."

"Mr. Clanton." Johnny led me up past the man, who smelled of attar of roses mixed with cigar and sour sweat.

"Where are we going, Johnny?"

"Upstairs. I want to show you the fine suites with their Eastlake furnishings. You've never seen anything like them, even in San Francisco!"

"I doubt I have." My feet turned mulish and stopped one step below the landing. I steadied myself on the banister, leaning away from my fiancé. And then it clicked: the attar of roses, the upstairs rooms, the Champagne. I was instantly sober. And furious.

My mother's scolding dominated my thoughts: *That man just wants to take advantage.* That she might have been right stirred my rage. While I was a virgin, I was not entirely naive. Rebecca had been unpleasantly surprised on her wedding night. "He wanted to put *that thing* where?" It had been a shock. Always protective, Becca had refused to let me remain ignorant. Since Ma delivered dire warnings on the subject without adequate enlightenment, Rebecca initiated my lessons in human reproduction. Sitting me down, my sister distilled the facts of life. While she avoided the topic of pleasure (perhaps because she lacked empirical knowledge), Rebecca had explained intercourse with scientific specificity.

After the mechanics, Rebecca turned to more practical advice tailored to my reckless nature. Using a rough drawing, she outlined what I could and could not do before a wedding ceremony. I'd paid sufficient attention to know that going upstairs in a hotel with a man not your husband would not be conducive to keeping that line well drawn. I said to Johnny, my voice small and uncertain: "I cannot follow you any farther."

Johnny stood above me on the landing. "But you are my bride."

"Not yet, although you make me blush. I am

your fiancée, and that allows certain privileges, but not carte blanche."

"In Tombstone, we're as good as married."

"Tombstone is *not* the world."

"But it's *our* world, Josie dear." Johnny removed a room key from his vest pocket and stretched to place it in my hand.

I refused with two open palms raised to Johnny, hands that had never slapped a man but seemed to know instinctively how it was done. "I have a ring, but no license."

"On my honor, you have my undying love." Johnny, smooth and gracious, stepped down to raise me up.

"If you bought a piece of land, you'd want the security of a deed," I said. "You wouldn't build a house on a handshake."

"My love is your security, my heart your collateral," Johnny said. "Let's not discuss this here. Let's go where it's private."

"No, sir, not until we wed." Rebecca would be proud. I turned my back on Johnny and began my descent. The maître d' and the porter hovered below. When I glanced back, Johnny smiled graciously, accepting momentary defeat as he followed in my footsteps. He gently took my bare forearm from behind and kissed it softly, slowly above the wrist, moving back the fabric ruffles of my three-quarter sleeves with his lips. Enflamed, I nearly spurned Rebecca's advice. I almost took the key. My feet wanted to climb those stairs, to end the tension. But Johnny was already guiding me down, stepping ahead to lead me as if it was he who had second thoughts. The maître d' scowled after him, wringing his arthritic hands.

Kitty later told me in a moment of spite that the maître d' was among the many sporting gents in attendance who'd bet cash money on Johnny's ability to keep me upstairs and take my virginity by morning. I won. He lost.

Johnny did not appreciate my disloyalty.

CHAPTER 6
NOVEMBER 1880

A month passed before I saw Wyatt again, well after I discovered that dinner at the Grand Hotel was a rare event on Johnny's tight budget. Had I known that first night, I would have inhaled another glass of Champagne and gobbled those oatmeal cookies. One rainy afternoon, I was alone in the Joneses' cottage, humming a *klezmer* melody in a minor key and baking strudel. Using dried pears, cinnamon, and a jigger of brandy I'd snuck from Harry's decanter, I was improvising on my father's recipe with available ingredients. When the knock at the door came, I figured it was Johnny. I ran to answer it, barefoot, my sleeves rolled up above my elbows and my hair twisted atop my head. My hand, still sticky with dough, stuck to the knob when I pulled; I puckered up to smooch Johnny before realizing it wasn't him. There stood Wyatt, rain running off his big black Stetson, stamping his black boots with heels so high they pushed him up to six foot three—he was more like a tree than a man.

I craned my neck just to look Wyatt in the general vicinity of his eyes, and when he stared back, a shot of lightning ran from my eye sockets all the way down to my naked toes and back. Taken by surprise, I couldn't hide my delight at his appearance. His manly confidence was as thick and heavy as that woman Timberline's perfume. It was an aura, that's what it was. I was both intimidated and attracted. I hated being with a man more beautiful than I was, but I'd made an exception in Wyatt's case.

Since I'd seen Wyatt by the stagecoach the month before, the deputy sheriff had made the papers. He'd been helping Marshal Fred White disarm some rancher rowdies enjoying a midnight shooting party on Allen Street. Things got out of hand—as they frequently did, given the vast amounts of liquor consumed—when cowboy Curly Bill Brocius surrendered his pistol to the marshal, barrel first. The firearm discharged, and the bullet entered White's groin. After the marshal collapsed, Wyatt conked Curly Bill on the head with his pistol butt and dragged him to jail, creating an enemy for life. White lingered long enough to testify that the shooting was accidental before leaving behind a stunned populace—and a job opportunity.

Marshal White was my first "man for breakfast" in Tombstone (a spot so desperate prospector Ed Schieffelin named it after a grave marker). Kitty and I read about White's death by misadventure in the *Tombstone Daily Nugget*. Swaddled in our frontier propriety while we sipped tea from china cups, newsprint seemed like the closest Kitty and I got to any action. We may as well have been living in San Francisco for all we saw, which would have suited Kitty just fine. Me? I wanted action, the more the better.

And so, before Wyatt knocked on that stormy afternoon, I pounded strudel dough and wondered how I'd painted myself into that particular corner, an unwanted guest in another woman's kitchen. There I was in all my Tombstone glory: standing barefoot and anything but pregnant (I was still, technically, a virgin) by Kitty's stove. The Joneses had not anticipated that I would be bunking on the daybed in their two-room cottage for more than a night or two while Johnny and his son, Albert, kipped in an army tent five parcels down the road.

But four weeks and a general election later, there I was at the Joneses' house. While Republican James Garfield defeated Democrat Winfield Scott

Hancock, I was absorbed by domestic politics and my own new beginnings. I attempted to stay out of Kitty's way, but I have one of those big personalities that gets underfoot. That afternoon she'd swanned off to a cribbage-and-crab session with her circle of church ladies. Since I didn't attend Sunday worship, I was excluded from Thursday's cards and conversation, leaving me alone with my thoughts and my strudel when Wyatt appeared.

After a long, awkward pause, the deputy sheriff said, "I'm Wyatt Earp." I knew who he was—that voice, those shoulders—I was just stunned by his proximity.

"I reckon you are. I'm Josephine."

"The lass that loved the sailor."

"Aye, aye, Cap'n. You know your *Pinafore*."

Wyatt continued in songlike speech, "Sorry her lot, who loves too well, heavy the heart that hopes but vainly; sad are the sighs that own the spell . . ."

". . . uttered by eyes that speak too plainly." I recalled that electric shock he'd sent through me with a glance. I never did have a poker face; I looked down. I was barefoot, which made me feel naked. At home, Ma forbade me from walking barefoot, saying it was a sign of mourning and would cast a shadow over her and Papa's lives. I wiggled my toes. I'd never been all that conscientious to begin with.

"I'm expected. Can I come in, or should I wait here and scare the crows?"

I rocked back on my naked heels and laughed. Wyatt joined in. He had a deep, warm chuckle. Maybe Mr. Dark 'n' Stormy wasn't as serious as I had supposed. I welcomed him over the threshold, pointing out the iron wall hooks where he could hang his sopping waxed cotton coat and Stetson. After the laughter fell away, I stood there unsure what to do next without Johnny present.

"Did I interrupt something?"

"No, I'm just baking."

"Well, that's something. Find me a stool near the stove and pour me some coffee. I'll keep you company until your Johnny returns."

That was where the trouble began: in Kitty's kitchen with the cast-iron stove, newspaper plugging the holes in the walls to keep out the weather, and a lot of cozy silence. While we awaited Johnny, I poured fresh coffee for Wyatt and returned to work. Baking settled me; it brought me closer to my father, even if he was nearly a thousand miles away. I sprinkled drops of water on the dough to return it to the right texture, and then set to work. I kneaded and rolled, folding the dough in on itself with a satisfying slap until it was smooth and supple. I didn't have to look up to feel Wyatt's eyes on me.

"What's that?"

"Strudel."

"No, who's the little man?" He pointed at the dough figure I'd exiled to the table's edge.

Embarrassed, I laughed, and said, "It's for Albert, Johnny's son. To keep him company. He gets lonesome in that tent down the road without his mother."

I felt ashamed for revealing the secret sadness I'd pulled from the boy so slowly and carefully. I sprinkled flour on the table and brought the little flour gent close to finish his features and give him a soul. First, I brushed egg white over his face for shine. Then I pressed dough with a fork until it oozed through the tines to make wavy hair. I painted the bread-locks with yolk to turn them gold, and then placed currant buttons down his chest, and raisins for eyes and dimpled knees.

"Does the little man have a name?"

"Not yet. Do you have one for him?"

"I reckon that's Albert's job. I don't want to step on his toes."

I turned the little fellow in the light. "He resembles a banker for all his short pants," I said. But it was Albert I was thinking of. I'd known Johnny was a father, but it was news to me that the nine-year-old was already in Tombstone when I arrived. It was yet another detail my fiancé had neglected to share. But I'd warmed to Albert instantly. I missed Henrietta, my Hen, and Albert became more like a little brother than a son to me. I knew how to be a big sister, but I had no desire to become a mother before I was a wife.

"That's one serious little dough boy," said Wyatt, reviving the conversation.

"He could use a laugh." I looked up at Wyatt with a smile, which I immediately realized was dangerous. There it was—that spark—and I couldn't hide the way it lit up my face except by glancing down. I stretched out the dough boy's smile with cherry juice, and rouged up his cheeks.

"That's better. Is he edible?"

"You certainly play rough! Our banker won't be your man for breakfast!"

"I didn't say I would eat him, Miss Josephine, so holster your six-shooters."

"That's a relief. I wouldn't want to make a bloody mess in Kitty's kitchen. Besides, my little crusty man doesn't taste like much except salt and flour. But with all that yeast, he's an early riser!"

"Not me!"

The rectangular room that contained the kitchen, parlor, and dinner table was warm and dry, smelling of coffee, cinnamon, and fruit. It felt comforting, just the two of us as the wind hissed and scratched outside. We shared an easy silence. I stretched out over the table with the rolling pin and smeared pears on the flat surface; I scattered raisins and sprinkled cinnamon-sugar last, shaping it into a tidy, sweet package bound for the oven.

"Can you bake corn bread?" asked Wyatt after half a coffee cup of silence.

"No. Why?"

"It's my favorite." He extended his mug for more coffee.

"If there's a recipe, I can learn." I used two hands to steady the flow of coffee as I poured, pleased that we were getting along so well. "Corn bread is Johnny's favorite, too, after beaten biscuits."

I fooled myself into believing I was entertaining our guest to help Johnny achieve his local ambitions. The previous night my fiancé explained that he needed to patch fences with the former deputy sheriff, the reason as plain as black-and-white newsprint. I followed the stories in the rival papers, the *Tombstone Epitaph* and the *Tombstone Daily Nugget*, although they diverged along political lines. Johnny, a Southern Democrat, preferred the *Nugget*. The election that made Garfield president affected the Arizona Territory, commencing a pigs-at-the-trough scramble for local political spoils that had a direct impact on me.

One election in particular concerned both Johnny and Wyatt: the race for Pima County sheriff between Republican challenger Bob Paul and Democrat incumbent Charlie Shibell. At the time, Wyatt was Shibell's deputy, despite their political differences. Their working relationship ruptured with the sheriff's increasing ties to the ranchers, and accusations of election fraud.

According to the *Epitaph*, one district's votes tallied 103 for Shibell and just one for Paul, even though there were only fifty eligible voters. Cowboys Ike Clanton and John Ringo served as election officials.

Wyatt found this deceit untenable. He resigned as Shibell's deputy sheriff and joined Paul's campaign to overturn the fraudulent election results. Wyatt's loss was Johnny's gain: Shibell offered him the newly vacated position. It suited Shibell fine since Johnny had ambitions to become sheriff when the territorial government created a new county with Tombstone as its seat—a job that could pay a princely $40,000 per year. But Johnny, ever the politician, didn't want to alienate the sharpshooting Earps in the process. He'd invited Wyatt over so that they could have some privacy to negotiate.

I checked my strudel in the oven, even though I knew it was too soon. "What else do you like besides corn bread?"

"Nothing that requires cooking." Wyatt let a pause hang in the fragrant air. It hovered while I considered his intention and what it would be like to kiss that man right under his big handlebar mustache. What would that first kiss be like: rough or soft, forceful or tentative? Or would it be sloppy and awkward? And then I remembered Johnny and scolded myself for straying. Wyatt finished his thought. "Ice cream: I'm a boy in knee breeches when it comes to ice cream."

I laughed at the image, a little louder than the joke deserved. "That's Albert's favorite, too. He's die-hard tutti-frutti."

"I'm a strict vanilla man. And you?"

"I can't be pinned down: peppermint one day, chocolate the next. Albert and I are regulars at Lottie Hinkley's Ice Cream Parlor after school. These days, he needs a little extra sweetness—"

Johnny swung open the front door and stamped his wet boots on the threshold. The cold crept into the kitchen and chilled my bare toes. "What's that heavenly smell?"

Wyatt set his coffee down in the flour dust, rising to his full, imposing height. When he picked up the mug again, it had left a wet ring above the banker's head.

"Like a halo," I said.

"I've never known a banker with a halo," said Wyatt.

"What are you two doing over there?" Johnny asked, suspicious even though he set up the meeting with Wyatt—and arrived late. "Did my little gal put you to work, Wyatt?"

"No. I was just keeping her from setting the house on fire."

"It was a close call," I said. That fire had been set elsewhere.

"Well, come on over here and sit yourself down, Wyatt." Johnny pointed to the scarlet mohair armchair Kitty had shipped from San Francisco. Johnny settled on the divan opposite, reaching for the silver tray with the decanters atop the mahogany table that separated him and Wyatt. "Pour you a snort?"

"No, thank you, John. Coffee suits me fine."

I padded over and snuggled beside Johnny like a cat seeking the room's warmest spot, tucking my legs up on the sofa and my feet under my skirt. I reached over to remove the pocket watch from his vest, and he said, "Women! They always want something."

"Yes, Johnny, I want something desperately: to time the strudel."

"That's what *you* say, Josie girl." Johnny pulled me close to nestle in the crook of his arm. "Wyatt, have you heard the story about the gunfight between the Englishman and the frontier widow?"

"Can't say I have."

"When the Englishman killed her husband, the widow challenged him to draw at fifty paces. She was a crack shot, but her antagonist chose the weapons. At high noon, the Englishman handed the widow a paper parcel that matched his own. At the word *fire,* the lady opened her package, shrieked like a banshee, and dropped dead right there without a shot fired."

"What was in the package?" I asked, hooked.

"The wily Brit had gift-wrapped a live mouse. Can you beat that?"

"Can't say I can, Johnny," Wyatt said, seeming no more impressed than I with the story's punch line, and then, without missing a beat, he cut to the chase: "I hear you have something to say to me."

"You're all business, Wyatt." *Well, maybe not all business,* I thought. But I wasn't part of the discussion, so I just observed the two men. It seemed that Wyatt had turned serious the moment Johnny entered the cottage, and he maintained his poker face as Johnny launched his sales pitch: "I have a proposition that could make us both rich. You're a fine deputy sheriff, as brave and quick as any from here to Dodge City. There's not a man to contest that."

"Only you're deputy sheriff now, and I'm not," Wyatt said, shifting his big frame in the parlor chair. It was an awkward moment; Wyatt let a pause hang between them without breaking a sweat. Silences didn't seem to unnerve him the way they did Johnny.

"Tombstone isn't Dodge City," said Johnny.

"I appreciate the geography lesson." Wyatt looked over at me.

"What I mean is that, unlike Dodge, we're not a cow town that welcomes drovers at trail's end a few times a year. We're smack-dab in the middle of ranching territory. Raising cattle is as much our tax base as the silver business. We may have a Republican governor now, but the majority of Arizonans are Democrats like me. When it comes to picking a new sheriff, Governor Fremont might be looking for a Republican like you, but he has to placate his constituents."

"I'll place my bets on the governor."

"Sure thing, Wyatt, but why not spread your risk? I'm running for sheriff when Tombstone becomes the seat of this new county they're finagling. I figure you are, too. Here's my proposition: I run for sheriff, and I promise to make you my deputy."

"Well, that's an interesting twist, given that I've already been the deputy, and I'm lined up for the top job. Considering Fremont's political affiliation, I'm sitting prettier than you at the moment. I can't make sense of this marriage, since we represent opposing parties."

"Then let me clarify. The sheriff's office isn't pure politics." Johnny rushed his words, combing his goatee with his fingers. "It's more like a wedding of opposites: part of it is tax assessing and collecting, the other part's law enforcement. Hell, the job is a silver mine without the hard labor and the pickax, what with getting a cut of the tax-collecting business. The more you collect, the more you make. That's where I come in. With my rancher connections and yours on the business side, we can reap bigger benefits than either of us can alone. We'll do an even split on the commission and fees. While I'm soothing ruffled political feathers, you'll be making the streets safe for those Eastern bankers and mining executives."

"Smells good," Wyatt said.

"I figured you'd like my plan." Johnny pulled me closer; as he looked down at me with a crinkly smile, triumph flickered in his eyes.

"I was talking about Miss Josephine's strudel."

"Feel free to take some home for Mattie," Johnny said. That's about when I lost interest in their business talk—it was news to me that Wyatt was taken. It surprised me how much it stung, even when I was sitting there wrapped in a Johnny Behan blanket. Without noticing my sudden stiffness, Johnny prodded, "What about my idea, Wyatt?"

"I need time to figure out how *that* smells." Wyatt stood up.

"According to my sources in the legislature, we have some time before the government sorts out the new county," Johnny said. "Just don't chew on the offer too long." He pushed me off his lap like a cat as he stood up. "Josie, please get Mr. Earp's hat."

I crossed the room and stretched up to reach the still-damp Stetson. When I delivered it, Wyatt looked down and thanked me for the hat and coffee with punctilious manners, no eye contact. I worried that I'd exaggerated our intimacy in the kitchen. I could have sworn he felt the same electricity I had when our hands touched. And who was this Mattie that Johnny mentioned?

Maybe there was an Earp sister starching Wyatt's shirts, stuck away somewhere on the outskirts of town.

Wyatt nodded good-bye to Johnny, who poured another whiskey and showed no sign of showing him out. I accompanied Wyatt to the door and then followed him out onto the porch to get some fresh air and catch his eye one last time. The afternoon was dark and foul-tempered, but Wyatt walked straight out from under the roof, catching the rain with his broad shoulders.

I watched Wyatt enter the road—a trim, tall, determined figure. I smiled to think of that hard man disappearing into the murk, preferring ice cream to whiskey. When I couldn't see him any longer, I looked across Safford Street toward the Dragoon Mountains. Lightning cracked like a mule-driver's whip, and I thought I could distinguish Cochise's Stronghold, where the woods rose up to meet the mountain's granite domes and steep cliffs. A decade earlier, Johnny had explained, Chief Cochise had retreated to those crags with his braves, ferocious and double-crossed. The government executed Cochise's brother, two nephews, and his father-in-law in attempts to pry the Apache leader loose from the sheer rock.

With my arms crossed over my chest, I watched the fireworks, loving the unpredictable ferocity of the brilliant blue lightning bolts cracking the horizon. I heard Johnny call from within and looked down to discover that my feet were wet from the rainwater on the porch. Dusk threatened, and I'd have to run to collect Albert from school. But first, I needed my boots and raincoat—and to rescue the strudel from the oven before it burnt.

CHAPTER 7
JANUARY 1881

When I next saw Wyatt—in late January—he didn't see me. He stood on Allen Street in front of Vogan's Saloon and Bowling Alley. He cradled a rifle in the crook of his arm, holding off a lynch mob hungry to hang the teenage gambler Johnny-Behind-the-Deuce. I blundered into the riot while testing Albert on his spelling, looking more governess than deathly beauty. I'd become accustomed to domestic life on the fringe of action, but I was restless and ready to stir up trouble of my own. Anything that happened in Tombstone I pretty much read about in the newspapers or heard about from Johnny.

While I tended Albert, Johnny fought crime and collected taxes, wheeling and dealing as deputy sheriff. When he wasn't wearing his badge, he was tending bar at the Grand or playing poker. Since women considered "wife material" weren't received in bars, I saw my man only on his night off or between shifts. I've never been short of imagination, and because Johnny was so social, I couldn't help but suspect that Miss Timberline or some such experienced femme fatale spent more time with him than I did.

Johnny had yet to set our wedding date, and I was anxious to leave that Safford Street cottage where I was as underfoot as a braided rug. But I was just stubborn enough—I won't say upstanding, because that would be giving me too much credit—not to shack up with Johnny even though we'd pretty much done everything that Rebecca deemed kosher before marriage on the Joneses' living-room sofa. That might have been another reason I'd worn out my welcome.

Among the greatest pleasures of those early months was getting to know Albert, who in no way resembled his father. The boy's pale, transparent skin laced with delicate blue veins would have been beautiful on a girl. Large and wide-set, his pale-gray eyes stared out above an overly generous mouth set beneath a solid column of nose. It was a face he would grow into in time, but in a beef jerky–tough town where the fathers' rough-and-tumble ways filtered down to the sons, he was at a loss for how to compose it. His face betrayed him with a series of flushes and twitches that he tried to conceal beneath his longish blue-black hair. He was profoundly unhappy. I tried to ease his pain as much as I could.

I warmed to Albert immediately, but not as a mother. He already had one of those. The first Mrs. Behan had remarried that fall and released Albert to Johnny while she started a new family in Tucson. Most weekdays I walked Albert to school. He returned to the Joneses' house for lunch by himself, and then I'd accompany him back in the afternoon, enjoying the opportunity to stretch my legs. That's how we wound up on Fifth Street that day, arms linked like he was my little gentleman. I walked on his left since he'd lost most of the hearing in his right ear from scarlet fever. This disability, and the misunderstandings it generated, was another source of embarrassment for him.

The two-syllable words on Albert's vocabulary list bored him, so I was peppering the boy with my hardest words: *epidermis* and *loquacious* and *subterranean*. True, if he'd misspelled them, I may not have known the difference. I was not much of a speller, unlike my Hen, but I could use almost any word in a sentence. Given our preoccupation, we weren't paying much attention as we stepped down Fifth Street toward the Oriental Saloon. Assuming Albert was slowing his pace to delay his return to class, I didn't notice how empty the street was for that time of day. No loungers catcalled from the boardwalk, no fancy girls paraded the boards, and no cow ponies rushed past.

Albert spotted the mob first. He nudged me and pointed. A wall of men, maybe five hundred miners and ranchers, marched toward us on Allen Street. They carried guns and rifles and were calling for the prisoner's head. Albert rushed toward the action. I caught his collar at the same moment I felt a tug at my sleeve.

"Albert's mum," the gentile giantess Delia hissed. I hadn't seen her since the day I arrived, but I immediately recognized her. The reedy redhead wore watermarked yellow silk and carried a parasol. She stood close, her musky perfume nearly gagging me. "They're after Johnny-Behind-the-Deuce," Delia whispered, although she didn't have to, since the roar of the mob drowned out everything else.

As I looked up into Delia's dilated eyes, she explained what had happened. Itinerant gambler Johnny-Behind-the-Deuce had cleaned out local mining engineer Henry Schneider during an all-night poker game in nearby Charleston. Afterward, Schneider was standing outside grousing and discussing the weather with friends. Johnny agreed it was cold. The popular engineer told the professional gambler to mind his own business. Johnny refused. Cheating might have been mentioned. Schneider pulled a knife. Behind-the-Deuce raised him a pistol. Schneider died, and the crowd from Charleston craved revenge, following the fugitive nine miles to Tombstone.

"What has that got to do with me?" I clutched Albert's hand. "I have to get the boy to school."

"School is suspended this afternoon, Albert's mum," Delia said gently, as if I might be in shock, if not outright stupid.

"Then I have to find Johnny and tell him."

"Johnny knows. That's the business of deputy sheriffs."

Delia guided me toward a lemon-painted, two-story frame house. My grip on Albert's hand remained tight despite his attempts to squirm in the opposite direction. As we neared the building, Delia addressed me in a measured, calm voice. "If you want to help Johnny, spare the boy and yourself. Slip upstairs with me and pray a stray bullet doesn't call us home."

I gazed at the gaudy house with its lavender door. "What would Johnny say?"

"I hope he'll say you're alive." Delia led me over the threshold. I pulled Albert along, his eyes lingering on Allen Street and the scrum of gesticulating men.

Once inside, we shuffled past a parlor concealed by pocket doors. Melancholy cello music escaped from within. As Albert and I followed Delia upstairs, my chest tightened. I realized that I'd betrayed Johnny's trust by shepherding his son into what could only be a brothel. Ascending these steps reminded me of our fight on the Grand Hotel stairway, and I felt ashamed. I was once again out of my depth, following a woman I hardly knew in order to escape a mob on the street, with a brokenhearted boy in my care. I heard my mother's disapproving voice: *this was exactly where your footsteps led when you left home on Shabbat.* And yet, now that I was here, what choice did I have? Outside was a lynch mob, inside—this!

On the landing we turned sharply into a freshly painted room—pearly pink—with fresh yellow roses arranged in crystal vases on every available mahogany surface. An embroidered satin quilt smothered a large canopy bed, which I made an effort to avoid, pushing Albert wide of its path. The room faced Allen Street. Tall, shuttered French doors opened onto a balcony where a young blonde, hardly more than a child, lay on her belly. She peered between the wooden gingerbread slats that decorated the terrace, then swiveled her head to report: "The Earps took Johnny-Behind-the-Deuce into Vogan's Bowling Alley, Miss Delia."

I watched Delia's reaction to the news: stone-faced, she took a nip from a medicine bottle on her bedside table. She paused, considered, and took a longer swig. She dabbed the brown liquid from her mouth with an embroidered handkerchief. While Delia hesitated, Albert dropped my hand. He slithered out to join her maid, April, who was only twelve or thirteen, as she avidly watched the action below with a pillow tucked under her thin arms.

I crawled out after Albert, only half believing it was for his protection. I'd been stuffed away in the Safford Street house for too long, and this was the result. I was tired of being a mouse in a closet while Tombstone's thrills raged around me. Damn Mama's caution, her intrusions into my thoughts. Since I was dead to her, I'd live for me.

Once flattened on the balcony with my head raised on a bolster, I threw my left arm over Albert's shoulder to protect him from gunfire. He shrugged me off, knowing as well as I did the futility of the gesture should bullets fly. Sensible citizens would have closed both the doors and the wooden shutters and hidden behind a solid mahogany wardrobe.

From the balcony, we had an unobstructed view of Wyatt. He guarded the street in front of Vogan's Saloon and Bowling Alley, a narrow brick building that could safeguard the accused behind impenetrable walls. The deputy US Marshal appeared larger than any other man on the scene, though I knew that was physically impossible. With his jaw set, he focused on the oncoming mob's miners and cowboys united to lynch Johnny-Behind-the-Deuce for gunning down Schneider.

Wyatt must have come in a hurry, because he was hatless. A shotgun rested in the crook of his arm, lock open, but it was as threatening as if his forefinger stroked the trigger. I couldn't keep my eyes off him. I wasn't alone; Albert stared, too. When outnumbered, Wyatt's fearlessness compelled men and women alike—and incensed his enemies.

Wyatt's older brother Jim emerged from Vogan's, where he tended bar right-handed. His useless left arm dangled from his mangled left shoulder, a parting gift from the Confederates. Wyatt had wanted to enlist in the Union army alongside his older brothers, but his parents vetoed the plan; he was too young. Jim leaned in close and whispered to Wyatt, who nodded without looking away from the mob, and then advanced toward the boardwalk's edge.

To the west, the street was empty. Shutters banged. A dog yelped. To the east, five hundred frontiersmen pushed forward on foot, led by John Ringo. Gentlemanly and tall, the cowboy gripped his saddle rope, slinging a noose. I never forgot him after that day, though I relied on April to fill in the blanks on who was who in that sea of angry and aggrieved faces. Black armbands marked Mr. Schneider's mourning buddies. They had followed Ringo from the killing in Charleston to Tombstone. The millionaire mine owner Dick Gird, one of Tombstone's three original founders, fumed beside Ringo. The New York native had gathered his local employees, graveyard-shift miners milling around before they hoisted shovel and ax, rallying for one of their own. On the fringes stood curious citizens drawn to the noise. Some people couldn't resist joining a throng once it started to form.

"Where is he?" the mob cried.

"At Vogan's!" a bystander yelled from the street below our perch. The mob wheeled, filling Allen Street from curb to curb.

"Go in and drag him out," cried someone in the back, echoed by others: "Drag him out!" "Go in!" "Drag him out!"

April gasped, but I couldn't tell if it was excitement or terror. I reached for Albert. This time he grabbed my hand back. We didn't know the man hidden behind the bricks across the street, but we feared for his life. And I trembled for Wyatt, standing so solitary. "Boys," he said in a deep, calm voice, "don't you make any fool play here; that little tinhorn isn't worth it."

Wyatt's calm had no impact. From the back came hollers of, "Earp can't stop you." "Go in!" "Drag him out!" The pressure from the rear urged the front lines toward Vogan's. And then the stamping started. The commotion was outside but felt like it pounded inside my chest. I panicked and looked back toward the room where Delia clung to the creamy velvet curtains. She seemed to swoon as the stamping became rhythmic and ferocious.

"The Apache War Dance," April said, her voice quivering as if from past experience. From behind, Delia said, "No more," and retreated deeper into her bedroom.

Shouts and shrill whistles followed. A whiskered old man in a stovepipe hat started the cry: *"Yi-yi-yi-yi! Y-a-a-a-hoo!"* As he tapped his mouth in the Apache yell, the crowd joined in. The stamping increased. A stifled sob escaped April's lips, as if she were hiding in a cabinet and didn't want anyone to hear, but horror overcame her sense of self-preservation. When I reached over Albert to pat her shoulder, she flinched.

Across the street, Wyatt swung his shotgun so it faced the crowd, snapping the lock shut and touching the trigger. But that was one gun against an armed crowd: the men carried rifles and pistols, glinting in the wintry sun. In the back, the men aimed their firearms at the sky and began blasting, aggravated by the pressure of those in the front retreating in the face of Wyatt's double-barrel. We buried our heads in our hands, but no bullets hit nearby, so we looked up again.

The whiskered old coot whooped again: *"Yi-yi-yi-yi! Y-a-a-a-hoo!"* The crowd returned his cry, magnifying it. April whimpered again, the strain intolerable, and this time Albert reached out to comfort her.

Down below, a bearded cowboy in a beaded buckskin jacket said, "Rush him." A second cowboy called out from behind the first: "He'll quit! If he don't, blast him! String up the tinhorn and finish the job!"

Wyatt covered the crowd with his shotgun, swinging it back and forth at chest level. "Don't fool yourselves," he said to his challengers in the front row, using that same unnaturally calm voice. His jaw was tight. He looked from one face to the next, making it personal. "This man's my prisoner. You know I'm not bluffing."

They were at a standoff. The stamping continued, and guns in the rear popped like Fourth of July fireworks. April whimpered, covering her head with her hands. I urged her to go inside and see to Delia. The girl wriggled backward, leaving Albert and me alone. We watched Wyatt scanning the crowd, tight-eyed and tense. I had never witnessed such bravery—not that it was the kind of courage required on the sedate streets of my San Francisco. Even among this throng, who'd confronted Apaches, bears, and enemies in war—whether Rebel or Union or Mexican—Wyatt's valor registered. He had a steel spine.

A growing feeling emerged, unbidden, from the swirling emotions of excitement and fear the spectacle inspired. Right there I became infatuated with Wyatt in the way I might fall for the handsome actor in emerald tights playing Romeo, or the tenor in *Aida*—all from the distant balcony. And so I watched this lone gunman stand strong against the crowd. I recognized greatness in Wyatt. I perceived the trust he placed in his conscience. His inner strength was as much a weapon as his shotgun. He'd put his life on the line to uphold the law, even if it meant sacrificing himself to protect a lesser man.

I feared for Wyatt's safety. I wanted to be beside him in my infatuated state. I wanted his protection and his respect; I yearned to protect him in whatever way I could. I looked down, wishing for him to see me there on the balcony—more than a face in the crowd—believing in him. Naturally, he did not see me. His gaze focused on the mine owner, Dick Gird. The middle-aged man pointed his rifle at the dirt. He employed most of the miners surrounding him, and drank with them, too; he beat them at cards when they weren't beating him. He was well liked. He and Wyatt were friends, for that matter—when they weren't squared off on opposite sides of a shotgun. And when there weren't folks in the back forcing the issue, crying: "Cut Earp down! Turn loose on him! You'll get him!"

"Stop where you are, Dick," Wyatt said. "Sure, you can get me. I'll take eight or ten of you along. There's eighteen buckshot in this gun, and the wads are slit. One step more and it's Boot Hill for some of you."

The men in the rear pitched forward, pushing Gird and his mining associates within twenty feet of Wyatt. The deputy US Marshal stared the mine owner down and said in a voice so conversational they could have been sitting across a poker felt with fair-to-middling cards, "Nice mob you've got, Dick. You're first. Three or four will go down with you, Bob here and Jack. Your friends may get me, but there'll be my brothers. It'll cost good men to lynch that tinhorn, and number one will be Dick Gird."

There was a long pause. Those in the rear still pushed forward, but Gird and his friends faded back. The stamping stopped. The war cries fizzled. Only the dogs barked down the lane. A rooster crowed. And then Gird turned his back on Wyatt and threaded through the crowd. Gird's friends followed behind him, taking the local miners with them. The Charleston miners followed in their black armbands.

After the front line crumbled, the Tombstone thrill seekers retreated to the far sidewalk with the old-timer in his stovepipe hat. That left about fifty furious cowboys. The men had ridden down from Charleston agitating for a fight—gentlemanly John Ringo, ranchers Ike Clanton and his brother, Finn, with roots in Tennessee, and an assortment of armed men in bright bibbed shirts and silver-buttoned jackets. They were mostly Texans and transplanted Southerners, Democrats, and Confederate sympathizers who resented the Republican law-and-order Earps and the business interests they defended. Many had come west to Arizona to escape Northern domination.

Wyatt returned his shotgun to the crook of his arm. Still facing out to the street, he said, "Jim, have Charlie Smith drive his wagon up here. I'm taking the prisoner to Tucson."

The double doors opened behind Wyatt. His brothers Morgan and Virgil flanked Johnny-Behind-the-Deuce. The slight prisoner blinked in the sunlight, looking impossibly young. He was shorter than average, with a dandy's slim mustache; strong, dark eyebrows; and black hair pushed back from his fair forehead. He seemed spent, what with shooting a man in the morning and nearly being hung in the afternoon before his twentieth birthday, but he was making an effort to hold himself together under the glare of John Ringo and his crew.

With a sense of relief, I looked down Allen Street. There was Johnny. My heart skipped a beat as it always did when I first saw him in those early months. Here was my man, the brave Arizonan who had wooed and won me, so handsome under his silver Stetson. He rolled toward Vogan's with a take-charge walk. Beside him marched Ben Sippy, who'd beaten Virgil in the race for city marshal two months prior. The pair climbed the curb in tandem with their hands on their pistols. They locked in behind Morgan and Virgil to form a wall around the prisoner.

Right then I saw Wyatt's friend, Doc Holliday,

who was standing half-hidden behind the prisoner, guarding his back. I watched how the slivery Georgian sneered as Johnny assumed a spot beside him. Doc hissed at Johnny under his breath. I picked at my lip, wondering what Holliday had said with such vitriol, which led me to ponder where Johnny had been all this time while Wyatt faced down the crowd. Johnny was deputy sheriff now. It was his turn to show Tombstone why he was the best man for the job, why he deserved the badge. But while Wyatt confronted the rabble, where had Johnny been?

A tug at my hem distracted me from concerns about Johnny-come-lately. Delia said, "If you don't want Behan to see you and the boy, you'd best withdraw."

I gazed down for one last glimpse of Wyatt and Johnny, but they were already gone, having vacated Vogan's front walk to escort the prisoner to the waiting wagon. They swept the bystanders along with them, leaving behind a street littered with shell casings. Albert and I retreated on our knees like children in a parlor game. Back in Delia's boudoir surrounded by yellow roses, she helped me up, her eyes dilated and distracted. She took my hand and led me out the thick mahogany door and down the carpeted stairs, our feet hardly making a sound. I hastened to leave the house, but as we reached the bottom step, the pocket doors slid open on well-oiled tracks.

April stood primly beside the portal to the parlor like a maid taking her mark in a play, her face red from scrubbing and wearing white gloves and a starched apron. She smiled shyly, and I noticed for the first time her exaggerated buck teeth. She said, as if she was running lines, "The madam requests your company for tea in the parlor."

"I have to get Albert home," I insisted.

"Albert," said April, "would you like cocoa and cake with me in the kitchen?"

Before I could stop the boy, Albert was heading down the narrow hall with April toward the cinnamony smell of baked goods. The pair resembled Hansel and Gretel as they receded. April reached for Albert's hand; to my surprise, he gave it willingly.

Delia stepped back. She faded against the canary-striped wallpaper in her yellow silk dress, as if she were a chameleon in an interior jungle. Alone at the threshold to the parlor, I felt myself in intimate and unknown peril.

CHAPTER 8

"*Entrez*, Josephine," came a seductive voice from beyond the pocket doors. I shuffled across the threshold, pausing in a seemingly empty room. Then I saw the diminutive madam, propped up on a rich, red Renaissance Revival sofa, a cello leaning against its arm. She was doll-size, with a pompadour of crimped purplish-brown hair. Her pale-gray eyes were hooded by dusky half-moons covered in powder (thwarting efforts to guess her age). A Japanese kimono the color of cherry blossoms draped low, revealing a stemlike neck, bare shoulders, and deep cleavage. Her near-nakedness shamed me. I felt tainted just by sharing the same room, breathing the same rose-scented air. Gazing down, I noticed the woman's slim calves beneath rolled silk stockings; the robe's train had been swung carefully forward so it swirled at her feet, where white cranes flew among silver peonies. The birds' red-dot eyes shocked like tiny bloodstains.

For all this, her mustache was the tiny woman's most unsettling and obscene feature. The auburn bit of fuzz, pomaded and twisted left and right under her pointed nose, didn't make her appear manlier—oddly, the unusual facial hair heightened her femininity. She introduced herself as Eleanor Dumont, but I'd already heard of her. She was Madame Mustache, Tombstone's infamous French bawd.

Miss Dumont smiled, her pointed teeth tinted green from the liquor she drank. She motioned me to a moss-velvet chair. Dispensing with small talk, the madam asked, "Having a little look around our establishment? There's another big bedroom in back if you're interested."

"I have a place to stay, thank you," I said, horrified at the thought. "I'm with Mr. and Mrs. Jones until I wed Johnny Behan. Do you know Johnny?"

"We all know Johnny." She raised her glass, sipped, licked the green from her lips with her pointy tongue. "Do you know *our* Mr. Behan?"

"What a silly question. I wouldn't be foolish enough to travel all the way from San Francisco without knowing my fiancé."

"I retract my question, Miss Marcus." A sugar cube–size emerald flashed from her ringed fingers as she shifted her kimono to reveal even more skin and reached out to ensure that her cello was at hand. "But he is a man."

"That's for sure." I straightened my spine and preened, displaying my engagement ring with its comparatively small diamond.

"But what kind of man is he?" A memory appeared to slide across her hooded eyes, perhaps a recollection of men she'd known, or men she wished she hadn't. Perhaps it was a memory of Johnny. The madam blinked. She sipped. She licked. She said, "I think, Josephine, you do not entirely understand your predicament."

"What predicament?"

"You are in a precarious position." She retrieved an ivory-inlaid box, withdrawing a black-papered cigarette with a gold filter; she extended the box toward me, presumably aware that I would reject

107

the offer and her generosity would cost nothing.

"It's not the least bit precarious, as if it is any of your business," I protested, my voice rising. "We're engaged. Johnny and I will soon be married. He is the deputy sheriff, you know."

"Pardon me if I don't salute. My experience with men has left me skeptical. And, trust me, my little bunny, my experience has been substantial. So let me ask: Are you married today? Certainly there's a justice of the peace to be found, and you have that itsy-bitsy ring on your finger that you repeatedly attempt to flash in my direction, if only it had power to shine. So, Miss Marcus, why not today? We can decorate the parlor for you right now. We can assemble roses for your bouquet. Cook makes a wicked angel food cake so light it flies into your mouth on wings of sugar. Poof! Heavenly! If that seems a bit of a rush on a day that has already had so much excitement— compliments of that rascal Johnny-Behind-the-Deuce—and you don't want the blessed event upstaged by murder and mayhem, why not tomorrow? Or a week from Tuesday. What's the delay? Will Johnny love you more in a week?" she asked, leaning forward and staring directly into my eyes. "Will you love him more?"

I flinched as this freakish foreigner pressed my most vulnerable spot. I craved a witty retort but couldn't manufacture an answer. An awkward silence ensued. I felt like we were playing cards and I'd lazily discarded the knave of clubs my opponent desired. I knew this woman was an adversary, not the ally she presented herself to be. I loved Johnny. I did. But doubts plagued me despite my belief that I'd kept my misgivings hidden. If I were so madly in love, and Johnny was the only man for me, how had these sudden flushes of infatuation for Wyatt emerged when I watched him confront the lynch mob? I could deny that the feelings were mutual, but not their intensity, and not on my side. Actions are true, and desires are fickle, but more than once my thoughts, unguarded, had wandered back to our cozy time in Kitty's kitchen on that rainy November afternoon. We had an ease even in silence that I lacked with Johnny. Wyatt radiated a sense of security, and although he was a few years younger than Johnny, he seemed older, more grounded, more patient. But anything between Wyatt and me was a fantasy on my part. I knew that. Somewhere down Fremont Street, he had a wife who ironed his white shirts and brushed his black coats with such devotion that even the desert dust hesitated to soil them.

And I had Johnny.

Wyatt wasn't responsible for my insomnia. Late at night, alone on a cot on Safford Street, I worried. I overheard Kitty and Harry bicker and whisper conspiratorially in the next room, Kitty sobbing and sighing. While the couple did not epitomize love eternal, it irked me that Johnny and I had not yet wed and moved in together as man and wife. I'd done my part. I'd cut my bonds with my family and traveled to Tombstone. But he dragged his feet despite the engagement ring that he insisted demonstrated his honorable intentions.

I attempted to deny the precariousness of my situation, but the green-fanged lady sitting opposite saw through me. Facing the madam, I tried to rally. I romanticized my plight, imagining it to mirror that of the character of Josephine in *Pinafore*. She loved one man, yet her father promised her to another. I followed my heart and disobeyed my mother's wishes. Yet my guilt was only compounded by the possibility that my situation in Tombstone might result in abandonment rather than a loving and secure union.

Looking into Dumont's chilly eyes, I summoned my strength. I was no quitter. I had no reason to suspect Johnny. I recalled him astride his stallion beside the stage when I arrived in Tombstone, carrying a bouquet of yellow roses (even that raised muted alarm now, awash in those flowers as this awful place was). And then his hands encircled my waist as he swung me into his arms and the crush of his embrace. I loved the surprising little sweet kisses he gave me, like a boy in the schoolyard, when I least expected them.

I shut my eyes and imagined Johnny's arms around me, then opened them and looked straight at the madam. "I love him now," I said, "and I will love him more." Even as I said it, my thoughts betrayed me. I beheld an image of Wyatt standing tall in front of the mob, defending that boyish captive—sitting close in Kitty's kitchen with a charisma that drew me toward him despite Johnny's imminent arrival. But I sublimated those visions and continued, "Johnny loves me now, and every day he tells me he loves me more. I have this ring on my finger, and he says I have a silver rope around his heart."

"Oh, that is pretty talk." Miss Dumont paused to sip and savor while letting her words hang in the scented air. "Ask Johnny: What's the difference between a silver rope and a silver noose? And if you pull too hard on your silver rope and ask him to marry you tomorrow, what will happen? What will he say? Where is his last wife, and how could she have let this most amazing catch escape? Oh, little bunny, all this talk of true loves, of rings and silver ropes, is way too fancy for a poor, petite French girl like me, raised on goat milk and rancid cheese."

Miss Dumont looked flirtatiously at me in the moss-green chair from her lurid sofa, her eyes now alight and mirthful. She wiggle-waggled her shoulders, and her breasts shimmied from side to side, breaking against each other like waves. She feasted on my discomfort. "You're a pretty little thing," the Frenchwoman said, apparently changing the subject. "The creamy skin, dark curls, dark eyes, those endless lashes. That is all good, if you lean toward the naturalism of a prize mare—and I know some men that do."

The madam reached forward for another sip. "The brows could use a mow, the cheeks, rouge—and you must spend more time on the hair. You are no longer a schoolgirl memorizing your multiplication tables; if you do not know nine times nine by now, you never will."

"Eighty-one," I said. I had recently tested Albert on that one.

"Oh, goodie, goodie," Miss Dumont snapped. "But you can't eat numbers from the air. You're not nearly as calculating as a frontier boomtown requires. One always needs an alternate plan, a back door, a saddled pony waiting in the alley for a quick escape, perhaps a friend to hold it, perhaps not."

The madam continued: "A ripe beauty needs to be a step ahead of all those men with their smoking six-shooters before she is not so ripe. It's true, you have natural advantages. I can hardly see your shoulders or your arms in that nun's habit you insist on wearing, much less your legs to see how you're put together. But you have a full bosom and the benefit of youth without the weight of disappointment, and fresh flesh not yet fallen or dimpled or scarred by childbirth or the pox. A pretty little thing, it's true, like a German porcelain doll still on the shelf, not yet played with or chipped. The men aren't lying when they tell me that Josephine Marcus is the prettiest girl to see Tombstone since Ed Schieffelin found silver at the Lucky Cuss. Find silver, and pretty girls will follow; find gold, and you can't keep them out of your pockets."

April tiptoed in and settled a fresh liqueur glass in the sticky circle left by the previous one. She discarded her employer's ashes in a tray and retreated, eyes downcast so that I could not catch her gaze and ask after Albert. By the Ansonia mantel clock, it was past four. Should Johnny come straight home from sending the prisoner off to Tucson, he might well wonder what crack had swallowed us up.

The heavy, sweet scent of Miss Dumont's tobacco, so different from what men smoked, made me lightheaded. Smoke formed swirling clouds around the madam's pompadour. "Miss Josephine, I am surprised that the men haven't revealed your greatest asset, probably because they're not an objective judge of female flesh like I am. Your gift is not your lips or your eyes or your cheeks, but your vivacity, the way your spirit lights up your skin right through the pores, lifts you up so you're almost not walking on the same boardwalk as we poor mortals. Your optimism sends your hips floating as you trod the street, expecting the best, protected from the worst. You have dancing hips, little bunny, and there is nothing practiced or put-on about your gait; it is who you are for now. Keep that, and your health, and you'll have more than a few years on you."

I was at a loss for words, unsettled as much as pleased by Madame Mustache's flattery and the notion that men discussed me in town. The woman lit another cigarette. Where was Madame Mustache going with this puffery? She continued with a grand arm motion, as if to a crowd of avid listeners. "All right," she said, "you've convinced me, Lady Josephine. I am overcome with remorse for bringing wrinkles to your brow, wrinkles that will immediately fade, unlike my hard-won creases."

Madame Mustache reclined against her pillows and puffed thoughtfully for a moment, leaving the mantel clock to tick the time. "I surrender to your optimism. You know the world better than I, I'm sure. I see you and your faithful, love-besotted Johnny together in a little cottage, picket fence, villains in jail, a bun in the oven, an orange cat on the hearth with mice in her tummy, and a sudden bonanza in the silver mine. Your husband purchases you an even bigger ring and bangles and baubles and a three-story brick house with an even taller fence. But please, just hear a foolish, frightened old *Française* out. What if something happens?"

Miss Dumont dropped a long ash, then raised her

eyes to the ceiling in thought. "Suppose Johnny rides off on a posse and catches a stray bullet or a rattler's naughty fang, or his breast stops the shrewdly placed arrow shot from a distant cliff by one of those rude Apaches?" As she spoke, she'd reached over to her cello and now twanged the strings to mimic the bow's lethal sound. "What then, little bunny? What will happen then?"

"That's not going to happen," I said, my voice tight in my throat and unfamiliar. "Why should you think the worst?"

"Expect the best, prepare for the worst: isn't that the English expression? Always so practical and dull, like my mother's second husband! I could never love a man who smells like cabbage. But you distract me. God forbid, something happens to your man. Big tears. There is an outpouring of sympathy; the church league brings you casseroles for a week. Oh, maybe not. You're Jewish, no? All right, Miss Kitty and her friends supply the succor. The fireman's league helps out as well with blankets and coffee. Other men step up and offer their protection, but they smell wrong and you are heartbroken. *Très désolée.* The only man in the world for you has been taken away. You are true to the one, the only, the Johnny. You are desolate, inconsolable, and in two weeks' time, broke, down to your last petticoat."

Beginning to sweat, I said, "I think I'll have one of those green drinks."

"That's a girl," Miss Dumont replied, ringing a little bell. April entered, carrying the second drink, which she placed at my knees on the marble-top table, and vanished. "You, Josephine, must learn to live in the moment and plan for the future. Where was I? Oh, yes, you were desolate, crushed, and I wondered: What shall we do, we who care so much for your welfare? Will we put you on the next stage home to your joyous parents, happy to receive their favorite daughter like a Union soldier back from Chickamauga? But isn't that really just running back to Mummy and Daddy? I can't imagine that would be your first thought, otherwise you wouldn't have traveled all this way over thistles and thorns." Miss Dumont took a long drag on her cigarette. "And then there's the question: Will they have you? You have to admit, you are no longer the little girl in pigtails who skipped off into the wild. Will they look at you the same, now that you've run off with a man? Will they introduce you to potential suitors, their unmarried daughter, as only slightly used goods available at a discount? Think about it, Josephine. Can you return to your little bed by the dark stairs, taking up your old ragged dollies and teddy bears after you've seen the moonrise over Tombstone?"

"You don't know my parents," I stammered, although she did seem to have a pretty good fix on my mother. "They would welcome me with open arms."

"Open arms and worried looks, I expect. But still, that would make you a very lucky girl. Of course, there are other alternatives. You could resume your glorious singing career. Find a *Pinafore* troupe and go backstage and see if they'll have you. Have you been practicing your sailor's hornpipe? If that doesn't work, perhaps a magician will come to town and you can be his lovely assistant onstage, pick a card, any card, get cut in two in his Chinese box, show a bit of knee and a length of arm as you dismount to keep the gentlemen returning for a second show. I see in your eyes that won't do; perhaps you want something more respectable. Can you sew? No. Even if that were an option, you would need to make three shirts a day, a twelve-hour task, and that would only earn you one dollar a week, maybe two dollars if you do really fine work. That would barely keep you in flour and butter."

Here in this moment, I was more anxious than when I entered the lavender doors with a lynch mob at my back. Madame Mustache leaned forward, her powdered breasts visible from collarbone to nipple. She continued: "Or, my little bunny, should lightning strike, you could take the large room upstairs, beside Delia, and help me entertain. Nothing would make me happier: *très contente.*"

"Albert!" I cried out, upsetting the green liquor on the Persian carpet as I rose. No sound came from the back of the house.

"There would be fine gentlemen lining up down Fifth Street," the madam went on, "freshly bathed and pockets larded with bills, checking their golden pocket watches as they waited to call on the lovely, lively Miss Josephine Marcus, formerly of San Francisco, star of the stage and famous heartbreaker, the silver queen of Tombstone."

"Albert!" I shrilled.

"If that doesn't quite suit, take Delia's room."

Albert appeared beside me, cake crumbs on his vest and surprised by my alarm. Miss Dumont took up her cello again. Opening her kimono, she placed the instrument between her thighs and gave Albert his first look at lady parts.

Albert froze in place. I grabbed his wrist and dragged him through the pocket doors toward the entrance where Delia leaned against the front door. She ate a green apple, her wrist loose on her arm, her elbow an infinite weight as she raised the fruit to her pale mouth. She hardly blinked in response to my panic and haste.

"I suggest you leave by the back door," drawled Delia. She revealed no recognition of Albert or me, though she'd invited us in earlier like a web shot out by that patient spider, Madame Mustache.

CHAPTER 9

"If I were you, Mr. Behan, which happily I am not," I said, curling my arm around Albert's shoulders and pointing at Johnny's chest, "you might rejoice to see us walking down Safford Street with four arms, four legs, and two heads. How are we, you might wonder with concern, if you were husband-and-father material. Are we hungry? Tired? What happened to us?"

"Don't point your finger at me, Josephine. I know you weren't at the schoolhouse. We both know it was shut tight after lunch."

"If you knew that, I wish you'd bothered to warn us at lunchtime before we rolled into the middle of a mob," I said, climbing on my high horse and adjusting my tiara. After tea with Madame Mustache, I dismissed his reprimand. "We discovered a necktie party is an academic holiday. Did you know that?"

"Don't get smart with me, Josephine. Where have you been all this time?"

"All this time? We've been gone no time at all, and you can see we're safe and sound. I understand with that irate Charleston crowd, your nerves are on edge. But, please, don't take it out on us."

"Here I am, rushing home to ensure you and

Albert are safe when I should be accompanying the prisoner to Tucson. You have no idea the danger I was in trying to keep that mob from hanging that foolish kid."

"I may have some inkling. While you've been striding the streets with your pistols and badge for company, Albert and I have been playing catch with stray bullets while that throng serenaded us with the Apache war cry. I'm a bit frazzled myself. You might, God forbid, thank me for preserving Albert for another day of multiplication tables."

Johnny's face darkened. He jerked his head toward the Joneses' cottage. "Albert, go inside."

The boy clutched my waist with both arms. He was clingier now than he had been on the bullet-strafed balcony. In turn, I felt braver speaking in his defense. He inspired the mama lion in me that I didn't know existed. We swore we wouldn't tell Johnny we'd seen Wyatt hold off the mob single-handedly, or found sanctuary with Madame Mustache. I was miserable keeping secrets. Suddenly, there were so many.

I blinked away the ash drifting from garbage burnt in nearby fire pits where yapping dogs fought for scraps. Standing at the crossroads of nowhere and nobody, I missed my gentle father who never raised a hand. Johnny was different. I feared releasing Albert, as much for my own protection as the boy's.

Johnny stepped closer. "Now, git, son, or you'll cut me a switch."

I detached the frightened boy as if unbuckling a stiff leather belt. When Albert dawdled, I gently pushed his rounded shoulders toward his father. Johnny took a swipe at Albert's head, cuffing his son and causing the boy to stumble. Albert slunk through the whitewashed gate that lacked a picket fence to give it meaning. When he slammed the front door, the facade shuddered.

Kitty peeked out from behind calico curtains. I raised my eyebrows in her direction, not one to mind an audience as long as I didn't have to carry a tune. If Kitty wanted drama, the sailor from *H.M.S. Pinafore* would deliver more than an Irish hornpipe. I was tired of her, too, and weary of being bottled up in some fake sense of Christian propriety only a few streets from Vogan's Bowling Alley and Madame Mustache's lair.

"You may be my fiancé, John Harris Behan, but you are not *yet* my husband." I extended my left hand with its secondhand engagement ring. The diamond solitaire had comforted me among strangers from San Francisco to Tombstone, and I had feared it would attract robbers, so extravagant did I consider the gem then. But that was before I viewed Miss Dumont's topazes and emeralds. Her diamonds sparkled with real fire, not an occasional twinkle if held up to the light. I don't know how much of Madame Mustache's voice spoke through me, but she had clearly stoked my gall: "Trust me, Mr. Behan, I won't be yelled at in the streets of Tombstone as if I were a rabid dog."

"Don't use that tone with me, Josephine." Johnny put his hands on his hips near his holsters, only to inch his right hand higher to apply pressure to his stomach. "I will not have it—not here, not ever. Do you know who you're fooling with?"

"Is this a trick question? Why don't you enlighten me, Deputy Sheriff," I said, harsher rather than softer. I stood taller as if I were willowy Delia rather than shrubby me. "Or do you plan on shooting first and asking questions later?"

"I scared off seven hundred men to preserve the life of Johnny-Behind-the-Deuce today," Johnny began, with a hectoring voice, "and ensured the poor fool got justice instead of a long neck."

"Did you accomplish that all by yourself, a posse of one?" I retorted. "I heard that Wyatt had a little something to do with it!"

"Who told you that?" Johnny reached for that stitch in his side again. Recognizing it for the pain it was, I knew I'd pushed too far. I mentioned Wyatt. I promised Albert we wouldn't reveal what we'd witnessed from the bordello balcony. It dawned on me that all mention of things Earp irked Johnny. I was intended to live in a world that orbited my man and him alone.

"Who told me what?" I played for time as everything but the truth of the afternoon vanished under Johnny's interrogation. He advanced. He shoved his forehead close to mine, his brows squeezed together, eyes glaring. I retreated. He pursued, making his proximity a physical affront. For the first time since my arrival, I was not only afraid, but frightened of Johnny. If I revealed what I'd witnessed, there would be hell to pay. I opted for the plausible: "That dressmaker Addie Bourland told me."

"What does that busybody know?" Johnny sneered, still standing uncomfortably close. "Was Addie there with a shotgun? Not likely! She was hiding under her skirts, if I know women! I'm the deputy sheriff. I handle the law, not Wyatt, and I can handle one ill-tempered girl."

"Do you want me to cut a switch, too?" I'd seen Wyatt in action. He was the law if anybody was. "If so, can I borrow your pocketknife? They discourage women from carrying weapons around here, so we have no choice but to hide under our skirts."

Johnny smirked. "Can I can trust you with my knife?"

"Can I trust you with my heart?" I had that nasty habit of taking a specific skirmish and exploding it into a larger battle. "If you have a problem with keeping a body waiting, then do tell: When do you plan to marry me, Mr. Behan?

Because until that date, I'll do as I please. I'll walk where I want, when I want, and with whom I want."

"Not if I have anything to say about it!" Johnny grabbed my wrist. I tried to twist away but failed as he marched me toward the cottage. Even on that sparsely populated street, a crowd had begun to form. Tombstoners enjoyed their entertainment however they got it. A domestic dispute was a free, standing-room-only drama. It hardly compared to a lynching, but it passed the time at the end of a long day in the mines.

When Johnny and I reached the porch, I wriggled from his grasp. "If we're getting married, set the date. Are you free tomorrow?"

Johnny's face fell. To my surprise, the fight drained out of him. He retreated from me and wiped his brow. Injured, he looked like I'd hit *him* with a switch.

"I apologize, Josie. I didn't want to tell you, but my finances aren't where I thought they'd be when I trucked you down here. Some investments haven't panned out. I'm confident they will, darling. I love you till death do us part, but I just can't afford a wedding yet."

I choked on the smoky air, ashamed. I'd never seen Johnny so crestfallen. His shoulders sagged. Clearly, his belly ached. I approached him tenderly, as if Johnny were Albert, not his father. I placed my hand on his cheek, rubbing against the stubble. "If only I'd known, Johnny! Why didn't you confide in me?"

Confronted with Johnny's wounded pride, I acquiesced, unaware that I was being played with the twin fiddles of his remorse and anger. "If only I'd known, I wouldn't have pushed you. Let me help. I'll write my father for a loan. We can get all the money we need from him." I made it sound like Papa was a banker, not a baker.

"No," Johnny said with moist eyes. "I won't permit that, Josie. I'm a grown man. Asking your father for money would be an admission of defeat, that I couldn't shelter his little girl."

Johnny continued to protest, but I convinced him there was no shame in requesting help. My family would support us in this time of need, I assured him. We would repay them in the future, with money and grandchildren. I became a woman possessed, intent on proving Miss Dumont wrong, painting myself into a domestic situation for which I was unprepared. Grandchildren? Where had I cooked that up?

Even as I cajoled and reassured Johnny, now cheek to cheek in affection, no longer angry, my thoughts returned to my bitter departure from San Francisco. The ripping sound as my mother tore her collar. The sheet draped over the mirror. Ma's horrific recounting of her Atlantic crossing, the cat-gruel soup that poisoned my unknown aunts.

To give myself hope, I conjured up Papa's final

embrace. I focused on his letter with two twenties secretly stuffed in my hand, as I assured Johnny that families stood together. Charitable actions during times of need proved our love, not yellow roses or engagement rings.

The next day, I wired Papa. I anxiously awaited his response, Madame Mustache's ominous warnings playing in my head as I walked Albert to school. On my return, I stopped at the post office, joining the long line out the shanty door—the miners expecting letters from home, the entrepreneurs awaiting cash infusions. Within the week, Papa sent the princely sum of $300. I don't know how he gathered so much money. I felt like an emotional prospector who'd struck precious ore, which may have been why I failed to register the concern in his letter's conclusion: "We pray that we will soon hear of wedding bells there, but if there is a glitch, you are always welcome in *your* home."

I signed the money over to Johnny that day, along with the cash from pawning my engagement ring. Bit by bit, wall by wall, Johnny began to build a three-room frame house on his lot at Seventh and Safford near the Joneses' cottage. Never attentive to finances, I neglected to worry that while the house was in my name, the deed for the land underneath was in his.

CHAPTER 10
JANUARY 28, 1881

"I have no problem with your Judaism, Josephine, but refusing to enter a Christian house of worship is unacceptable," Johnny said when I wouldn't attend the church service for Mrs. John Clum. Mollie, the *Epitaph* editor's sweet wife, had died a week after delivering a baby girl. Most of proper Tombstone would be there to pay respects. "I do not expect you to convert," Johnny said, as if that were generosity personified, "but I rely on you to accompany me."

"I have no problem with you being a Christian, John, but I will never cross a church threshold, not even on our wedding day—or Albert's, for that matter."

We stewed on that for a while. Johnny did not want to attend alone, but I refused to kneel beneath a crucifix or hear "Jesus" in the same breath as "Our Lord and Savior." I never had. I never would.

Our dispute meant we joined the funeral cortege en route to Boot Hill. Silent and at odds, surrounded by hundreds of mourners, we held hands to maintain appearances. At the cemetery, the baby Bessie bawled, her mother in a pine box, the grave a shallow slash in hard earth.

A priest in a shabby suit read from the New Testament. Johnny stood beside me. Together, we made a flimsy family of two without a legal bond. I felt exposed. I yearned for relatives nearby to buffer the pain on that lonesome hilltop. This was my first burial. The infant's squalling escalated the event into an operatic spectacle. Women cried inconsolably as if they were the chorus and the baby the prima donna. The sound sliced through me like the bitter wind. Bessie's *geschrei*, her scream, reminded me that I had a living mother, and I was dead to her. Was that separation as final as this? It felt that way on that day when I would have given anything to be surrounded by kin (except return to San Francisco).

The wretched fate of baby Bessie and her brother, Woody, crushed me. Despite my disagreement with Johnny, I now reached for his comfort. He relented, putting his arm around me and squeezing me closer. He handed me his handkerchief. When Johnny introduced me to Mr. and Mrs. Clum on my arrival, I had warmed to them immediately. I'd hoped that after Mollie delivered, we would get better acquainted—and that eventually Mr. Clum and I might produce the amateur theatrical of *H.M.S. Pinafore* we'd discussed upon meeting.

I recalled first spying two-year-old Woody, half-hidden in his mother's skirt, the shyest boy I'd ever seen. I tried to blame the stinging in my eyes on the wind. I failed. He'd been such a beautiful mama's boy, with girlish curls that had never been cut. Now the tragic little lamb, curls shorn, stood beside the stoic grandmother whom he'd just met that winter. Amanda Ware, unlike her daughter, did not let Woody cling to her skirts, detaching him again and again with a bothered expression. She carried the baby but lacked the emotional reserves to comfort the irritable infant. The Cincinnati widow had traveled eighteen hundred miles from Ohio to help her daughter through the birth. According to Kitty, Mrs. Ware had begged Mollie to lay-in with her back East. Mrs. Ware might have expected the unexpected in Tombstone, but even she was unprepared for mourning her only daughter in a barren cemetery, with its wooden markers askew—no marble crosses, no granite obelisks, no stone angels. Here, there were as many old whiskey bottles as jars of dead flowers on the surrounding graves.

As for the widower, the vitality had been sucked out of Mr. Clum. A typically robust and energetic figure, the New York native who'd played football for Rutgers until he ran out of tuition money was often the first to volunteer for civic duty and the last to leave. His time as an Indian agent on the San Carlos Reservation earned him the Apache nickname "Boss with the High Forehead." Now, that balding head sagged toward his chest. Behind him, Wyatt—Clum's close friend and political ally (and ever a hero on the pages of the *Epitaph*)—stood sentry. The pair shared a law-and-order sensibility regarding the protection of business interests, with the hope that they would both rise along with the town's economy.

I hadn't seen Wyatt since the attempted lynching, but I contemplated him often, a greater disloyalty than shunning church. Then the priest mumbled his prayers and raised a hymn familiar to everyone but me. Afterward, the grave diggers lowered the casket into the ground with a thud. The baby hollered. Mrs. Ware's stone exterior crumbled. I'd never seen anything like it in public: the sobs of the red-faced granny as she rocked the wrinkly infant at the edge of her daughter's grave, the rhythmic scraping of a shovel scratching up dirt and tossing it on the cheap casket. Woody stepped forward and began throwing earth into the grave, bigger and bigger clods, at first with one hand, then two. He wouldn't stop. That was when Clum's knees buckled; Wyatt caught his friend before he hit the ground. Wyatt whispered something in the widower's ear that seemed to steady Clum as much as the big, pale hands supporting him.

I snuffled into Johnny's handkerchief. He gently patted my back with one hand and twisted his mustache absentmindedly with the other. Looking up, I saw him staring keenly at Wyatt and John, as if assessing their bond and what it meant for his plans. But that was speculation, and I was overcome with uncertainty: Would Johnny's death affect me as Mollie's had cracked Clum? Would Johnny and I ever get that far—become parents and comfort each other through personal tragedy? Would we rest side by side in a cemetery that was neither Christian nor Jewish, just a repository of bones at the end of their usefulness on Earth? I couldn't envision ending up here, far from my family, amid the whiskey-bottle offerings and the rough wooden memorials, next to this man named Johnny, a man I still wasn't sure I really knew— or trusted.

Sometimes, when I noticed Johnny in my peripheral vision, it was as if he were a stranger wearing a familiar tie. Who was this divorced father of another woman's child, so much older and more experienced than I was, with a temper that flared as easily as mine? It bothered me that he expected loyalty and wifely behavior, yet wouldn't commit to a wedding date. In my uncertainty, I thought of my mother, solid and stable, her hair tightly coiled around her head in the same way every day. Who had she been at my age, and what risks had she taken? I'd never given much thought to her first husband, the red-haired man whose face shaped Rebecca's. Mama never mentioned him, and Rebecca had only the briefest of memories of a trip to Coney Island. How different would my mother's life have been had he survived to father more children? Who would my mother have become then?

I keenly felt the pain I'd caused her—and continued to produce from afar. She had declared me dead, but no doubt she still mourned the loss. I did. A loud clacking yanked me from my morbid thoughts. The grave diggers shifted from shoveling dirt to stacking stones atop the coffin. Rocks on the graves restrained predators from desecrating the corpses. Thereafter, at the sound of boulders breaking at the mine, came an echo of clattering rock upon that gentle mother's grave.

Through Wyatt, I discovered that some men grow in stature when times are hard, refusing to shy away from the rocky soil of heartbreak. It's their land and they plow it. Wyatt didn't flinch at sadness, which is a different kind of courage from shooting a rifle at an outlaw when the odds are stacked against you.

Watching Wyatt and Clum, and hearing the baby howl, I, too, began to cry, albeit quietly. I'd never known anyone who'd died. That changed drastically that bloody year.

I glanced away from the grave toward Wyatt's brothers, Virgil and Morgan. They stood together on the periphery of the mourners. They appeared like slightly inferior carvings of Wyatt—Virgil heavier in the face, Morgan more mischievous and carefree. The pair shifted their feet to stamp out the chill, and looked down toward the raw earth to block the cold wind of such powerful emotion. This wasn't their first funeral, and there was an impatience to their posture to escape the mound. They escorted two shabby women that I'd never noticed before in town. The scrawny, sharp-eyed prairie hen in front of Virgil could have been mistaken for a girl if it weren't for the wrinkles on her sour face under her old-fashioned bonnet. She wore Sunday black with shiny patches at the elbows and an awkward, new lace collar ringing her neck. She placed a rough, protective hand through the arm of her big-boned female companion. The taller woman kept her pigeon eyes trained on Wyatt. She was a sad-sack floozy in black-and-beige plaid taffeta with five rows of ruffles at the hem. It was as if she'd insisted on wearing her finest dress, even if it was better suited for a saloon than a funeral.

"Who are those women?" I whispered to Johnny as he rocked back and forth on his heels.

"The little cuss is Virgil's missus, Allie."

"Is the taller one Morgan's wife?" It shocked me that a handsome young charmer would settle for that unpleasant party.

"No, that's Wyatt's woman, Mattie."

"Wyatt's 'woman'? They're not married?" I tried to sound blasé, but a lump formed in my throat. While I'd heard her name mentioned before, I'd never seen her.

"Maybe, maybe not."

"What do you mean?"

"I don't see a ring. I doubt there's a license. Wyatt did name a claim after her. Now, hush, Josie, people are watching!"

Those same staring townsfolk could say the same about me now—no ring, no license, just airs. I studied Mattie. Her fine shape pushed out the taffeta plaid dress of a bygone year in well-proportioned curves, but above her pressed collar, Mattie's blunt face was pasty, as if roughly formed from homemade soap. Her deep-set eyes and frown contrasted with the well-kept dark curls that attempted to soften her features. It was an unhappy face rather than an ugly one. Perhaps if she had been animated, she might have achieved the pretty side of plain. Mattie didn't seem to fit with the meticulous man I was coming to know. He carried himself like a bachelor when he was with me. He behaved as if *I* was the one with obligations he was intent on respecting—not him.

When the preacher shut his book with a dismayed amen, echoed by those on the hill, Virgil's Allie turned away from the grave and caught me staring at her friend. Her fierceness set me back like a slap. Her glare communicated an incomprehensible rage, as if Allie already knew me for an enemy. It wasn't impossible: in some ways it was a very small town, and gossip traveled its own paths. I looked away, my eyes darting toward Wyatt, his black frock coat in perfect concert with the day's event. Wyatt did not look up and catch my eye. We had no more contact that day than we had the day of the lynching, and yet he hovered in my thoughts.

Johnny squeezed my arm, and I returned my attention to him. With his confident hand on the small of my back, Johnny guided me toward Mr. Clum. Wyatt melted into the crowd as we approached the inconsolable widower to offer condolences. We promised baked goods for which he had no appetite, saying words that had no meaning.

As Johnny and I headed back toward town with plans to see the progress of our house, two miners walked behind us. "Well," said one to the other, "it's not San Francisco or Cincinnati."

"Or even Prescott," said his companion. "We really are at the end of the world."

The first miner, waxing philosophical, said: "We're surrounded by crazy optimists, Arthur, all hoping that the next strike, or the next round of cards, or the next horse, will win them forever ease. Mollie's death reminds me how quickly dreams are snuffed out, and how little justice exists in Tombstone."

"Women can die in childbirth anywhere, Max. Mollie just happened to die here and not Cincinnati."

"I sure as hell don't want to be buried in this

dump among the gunshot cowboys and whiskey bottles, Artie."

"All this talk makes me thirsty, Max."

"You just want to have something to blame your tears on."

"Maybe I do," said Arthur. "Maybe you do, too."

Johnny, who was eavesdropping, said, "I could use a drink, too, Josephine."

"Maybe I could, too." Something wet hit the back of my neck as we traveled back to town. "Let's walk faster. It may start raining."

I touched my nape, surprised that the liquid I found there was thick and slippery. I brought my fingers to my nose. They smelled foul. I looked over my shoulder to see that Allie had her lips pursed. I was still busy denying the clear truth of the matter—what could these women possibly have against me?—when Mattie mouthed a single word: "Hussy."

CHAPTER 11
FEBRUARY 1881

February found me cranky. Kitty hinted I might be pregnant, skeptical that I was still chaste after all those months. I wasn't (with child) and I was (a virgin). We were spending too much time together in that little saltbox. I'd begun to pace, and she'd begun to pick. I hadn't yet cast aspersions on her tufty flamingo red hair or that third roll of fat forming beneath her chin, but I was on the verge. Even in San Francisco, I had experienced more freedom, walking the streets with Nathan and Hennie, attending performances with Rebecca. Yet here, where cowboys roamed the streets spitting and cursing and shooting for sport, Kitty, now hardly the carefree coquette she'd been in San Francisco, expected me to behave like a hausfrau, too, baking biscuits to accompany her dreadful boiled beef.

Each day I awoke from my cot in the living room to the sight of Harry Jones, clad in red long johns, headed out to the privy, feeling I couldn't ditch the Joneses' house soon enough. I wanted to move into the home built with my father's money and tuck Johnny in beside me. I wanted my life, my real life, to begin. How did it happen that I was again trapped in a domestic situation in which I had no control, and no father to protect me from Kitty's relentless criticism?

But the winds disrupted my plans. The gusts were so fierce that building stopped: frame a house one day, discover a pile of lumber the next. I looked out the window and thought I saw a flying sheep. It might have been a tumbleweed. If I left the porch, filth clung to my skirt and *schmutz* to my skin. One afternoon a hen hit me in the side of the face. I wasn't sure who was madder, me or my sister bird. Navigating the street, zephyrs slapped me sideways, making me nearly as cussed and cranky as cowboy Curly Bill Brocius.

Inside, the cottage beams creaked. Windows banged. I felt as if a great gust could have lifted the house off its foundation and flung it into the next yard like a plate pitched in anger. As for me, I could have thrown plenty of dishware, and a few teacups, too. I was restless—for marriage, for adventure, for my own place out from under Kitty's critical gaze.

On this particular February afternoon, after a lunch of Tombstone a-town-so-tough beef stew, Kitty sat propped on pillows reading the *Nugget*. I flopped on the mohair divan opposite with the *Epitaph*, having sent Johnny back to work. Now that the governor had created Cochise County with Tombstone as its seat, Johnny had begun slurping his share of the spoils. On February 10, Fremont appointed Johnny sheriff. He was now busier than ever, setting up a new office and hiring staff.

Johnny promised to bring home the bacon. I said I'd prefer lamb. The difference was lost on him.

Across from me sat Kitty, clucking whenever she read something of interest. "Well, I don't say," she said, sipping oolong tea she bartered from the Can Can's Quong Lee.

"You did say, Kitty. Spit it out and get it over with."

"The judge freed Curly Bill Brocius!"

"Impossible."

"Marshal White must be rolling in his grave." Kitty reserved her greatest sympathy for those already interred. "That fool judge acquitted Curly Bill of murder. White's dying words were that the shooting was an accident, but, in my opinion, a mishap is tripping on the boardwalk and ripping my hem. It's not blasting a pistol into a man's stomach, however unintentional. If Curly Bill hadn't been drunkenly shooting up the town, White would still be alive." She shook her head. "Cowboys get away with murder around here. These outlaws and rustlers lack respect for decent society, and it's only getting worse. They're downright un-American."

Kitty read on, then snorted. "Wait until you hear how that scoundrel celebrated his release—"

"I'm guessing it wasn't singing 'My Country, 'tis of Thee.'"

I recalled bumping into the bearlike bruiser Brocius with his haystack of wiry black hair the day I arrived. In general, I didn't yet have a strong dislike for cowboys. The town was as divided in its opinion as the major newspapers: the Republican *Epitaph* criticized the lawless cowboy element and had ample ammunition to do so, while the Democratic *Nugget* was increasingly their apologist in slant, and continued to report news like Brocius's misbehavior, because shootings sold papers.

The cowboys' mayhem largely occurred outside the saloons or on the range. In town, these rough-riding men, when I saw them, seemed intent on a good time and had money to spend. They were lively and extroverted, colorful in dress and speech, and unlike anyone I'd seen in San Francisco. Since I was usually on Johnny's arm when we encountered them, their outlandish presence didn't threaten me. I was a tourist, then, and they were part of the sights, like rowdy sailors in the port of San Francisco. Their roughness—they didn't bow to anybody or abide by standard social conventions—was part of their appeal.

Johnny influenced my opinion by praising the ranchers and *cattlemen* (the less incendiary term for *cowboys*). He appreciated their potential to expand his tax-collecting plans to the far reaches of Cochise County, where he couldn't safely travel. To him, these men meant money and votes, which were as valuable as any banker's, as Johnny would need to seek reelection. Since the cowboys skewed Democratic and Southern, he considered them allies. But my man was to belatedly discover that, whether approached in friendship or enmity, the loosely associated cowboys were human dynamite.

"Are you listening?" Kitty asked, and then

continued to read aloud: "On Saturday night, Curly Bill and Pete Spence snuck into a Mexican fiesta in Charleston."

"Isn't that Marietta's husband?"

"Marietta who?"

"That sweet little Mexican woman who traveled with us on the stage from Tucson. I'm sure she said she was marrying Pete Spence."

"Oh, the smelly one with that awful mole? Well, she knew how to pick 'em. According to the paper, Spence and Brocius pulled their pistols and halted the band. Then Curly Bill said, 'Strip, every one of you. Now strike up a tune.'"

"And did they remove their clothes?"

"What choice did they have? They were as naked as pigs in a sty."

"That's disgusting." The shocking prank inspired nervous, inappropriate laughter in me.

"That's an understatement. You wouldn't find it funny if it was you and Johnny at the dance," she said, snapping the paper. "I bet he still hasn't seen you in the altogether."

"You know he has not! Not until after the wedding."

"Don't wait too long."

"What do you mean by that?" I asked, swinging my feet off the divan and planting them on the floor. I hated Kitty poking her nose in my business just because we shared a roof.

"I mean nothing at all, Josephine."

"Like *what* nothing?"

"Settle down. I said and meant even less." She raised her eyebrows at me with a look that contradicted her words. Raise her eyebrows at *me*—really. Maybe if it wasn't February, with those irritating high winds that put me in a foul mood, I could have ignored the gesture. But she made my stomach turn like food poisoning. I looked at the teacup she set down on the table and imagined the lovely sound it would make smashing against the wall.

"This shack is too small for this discussion." Kitty was not one who liked the taste of her own tongue when bitten. "I'm going to mind my own business for a change, and leave it to Curly Bill to strip people naked."

I simmered in silence for a while, reading about Mr.—now Mayor—Clum and his plans for Tombstone's future. Kitty couldn't let it go: "Just so you know, one married woman to another not yet wed, I wouldn't wait until June to become a bride."

"What makes you say that?" I folded my newspaper once, then again in a way I knew bothered Kitty. Who knew there was a wrong way to fold a newspaper? Kitty.

"For men and loose women, Tombstone is an all-night town. A lot happens while we're tucked under the eiderdown. Of course, Harry gives me no cause for worry. He's as true to me as he is to his fork and knife."

"Mr. Jones may be true, and he may like his food, but he doesn't seem to enjoy your company any more than I do." I regretted the words the minute they flew from my lips. I still needed a roof over my head—not the canvas of Johnny's tent and half of a bedroll. "Now, out with it. What about Johnny? Who are these women?"

"I declined to mention them the first time, so let me politely decline again," Kitty sniffed. "But someday you can ask your white knight what destroyed his marriage and listen to the answer he serves you with a rich sauce."

"Don't provoke me, Kitty. I'm in no mood. That whipping wind has got me crawling in my skin. Tell me. What broke up Johnny's marriage?"

"Oh, honey, that's not for me to say." I could tell she was desperate to gossip.

"Say it anyway."

"I have said enough, even if their divorce made the Tucson papers and is a matter of public record. Remember, you remain here by my generosity, not because of any perceived charm you may have to Mr. Behan. I've lived a good sight longer than you. If I can read the inexperience on your face like a newspaper headline in the *Nugget*, imagine what that shrewd Johnny can see there. He might be blinded by your pretty airs for now, but he will soon discover what a lazy, nasty piece of work you are."

My last nerve scraped, I hopped off the couch.

I had perfected my chokehold on my brother Nathan, and now Kitty's fat throat was calling out to me. Horse hoofs pounded outside, interrupting my rage, their rhythm punctuated by pistol blasts and their riders' hoarse, triumphant yelps.

"Curly Bill!" Kitty cried with the exaggerated fear of a child interrupted by a sudden noise during ghost stories. As I approached the window, Kitty warned me away; she was not so angry as to wish me gunshot. She yanked me beside her on the floor, and we took refuge beneath the dinner table. I grasped Kitty's hand, wrapped her in my free arm, and rocked her. Our differences disappeared with the gunfire of unknown origin. I was afraid, true, and exhilarated. Something was happening, and it wasn't just in newsprint. Meanwhile, I realized lonely Kitty, despite her barbs and innuendoes, required my company more than I hers.

After lunch the following day, once I'd dropped Albert at school, I stopped by Johnny's office as I frequently did since he'd set up shop in a little room behind the tobacconist. I interrupted him entertaining a group of fellow Democrats celebrating his recent appointment by Governor Fremont. After they left, showering me with compliments, Johnny sat me down beside him at a partner's desk too big for the room. I was studying building plans and thumbing through the

Montgomery Ward's catalog when Wyatt entered an hour later, a pair of Colts strapped to his hips.

"Miss Josephine," Wyatt said, removing his hat. He turned to Johnny—as much as any big man could in that tiny office—and said, "Now that you're sheriff, it's time for us to settle up. I held up my end of the bargain. I dropped out of the race and didn't oppose you. When do I start my job as undersheriff?"

"Good of you to come," said Johnny.

"Nothing good about it. I'm busy over at the Oriental, so let's hammer out the details. I'm ready to start today. Curly Bill's back in town."

"Drink?"

"Don't indulge."

"I'm not sure I trust a man who doesn't drink."

"You'll have to get over that."

"Mind if I have one?"

"I'm undersheriff, not judge."

"Well, my good man, the deed is done." Johnny retrieved a bottle from his top drawer and poured three fingers of whiskey. "We can say *hasta la vista*, Pima County, and *buenos dias* to seven thousand square acres of new Cochise County. It's a gold mine in silver country. But, Wyatt, can you give me some time to get myself sorted? What with the tax collecting and the law enforcement and the lack of infrastructure, I have to crawl out from under this pile of paperwork first."

Wyatt just stood there looking at Johnny and

letting some quiet hang between them. I wasn't sure what game Johnny was playing; I'd seen him promise Wyatt the job. The lawman was just there to collect a debt, and it made me uncomfortable to see him dangle. I was sensitive to such dangling, given that Johnny had promised to follow my engagement ring with a wedding band, and here I was sitting beside him without either ring on my finger.

"Right," Johnny said, cracking the silence. "I suppose I'll get back to work. I'll be in touch, Wyatt, don't you worry about that."

"I'm not worried," Wyatt said. But I was.

Johnny turned to me. "Now, Josie girl, isn't it about time you pick up Albert?"

"Sure thing, Johnny." I shuffled the house plans and placed them on an empty corner of his desk in hopes that he might review them later.

"Aren't you forgetting something?" Johnny asked.

"I don't think so," I said, reaching for my bonnet. "I'm leaving the plans for you."

"Those aren't the plans I had in mind." Smiling with a side of wicked, Johnny drew me into his arms—pulling back the bonnet I'd so carefully secured—and kissed me long and hard, as if the Sahara and a band of raging nomads had separated us. I tasted whiskey and cigars—which are not nearly as flavorful secondhand on a whisker. I flushed with embarrassment as Wyatt stood nearby, breathing up most of the air in that small room behind the tobacconist's.

The my-regiment-leaves-at-dawn theatricality of the kiss bothered me—was Johnny showing off to Wyatt while dangling us both?—but I always warmed to Johnny's kisses back then, and I was willing to meet him halfway and ignore my gut if this alliance would move us closer to our house and a wedding date. So I kissed Johnny back for all it was worth, giving as good as I got.

Wyatt turned before exiting. "When I come on board, we'll need a bigger office."

With Wyatt gone, Johnny pulled away and put the desk between us. I straightened my bodice and sorted my bonnet, then stepped outside to find Wyatt lingering in the doorway of the adjacent cigar shop with his hands in his pockets, exchanging stories with Dave Cohn, the tobacconist.

When I'd shut Johnny's office door, Wyatt turned to me. "I thought you could use an escort through town."

"Thank you, Wyatt." I wiped the remaining liquor from my lips with my handkerchief. I felt pleased for the company after all those long days cooped up with Kitty. I wanted mischief, but I didn't want to court catcalls from the Allen Street loafers while I walked to the schoolyard flushed from recent kisses.

"Do you know Mr. Cohn?" Wyatt gestured at the

tobacconist, busy with his inventory atop a ladder.

"We have a nodding acquaintance."

"Dave, I want to introduce you to Miss Josephine Marcus."

Mr. Cohn bobbled the cigar boxes he was inventorying as he scrambled down from his ladder. He squeezed out from around the counter in his overstuffed shop, clearly flustered. With a constellation of moles on his flushed cheeks and a sparse blond beard, he was a few years older than I was but obviously more industrious. He wore a yarmulke at a rakish angle that matched his jagged but jaunty smile. "Finally, an introduction," he said with a thick German accent. "A pleasure! I've heard so much about you."

"All good, I hope."

"Not bad!" Dave needled back, revealing a mouth as crowded with crooked teeth as cigars filled his shop. "I'm always happy to meet another member of the tribe."

"What tribe would that be, Mr. Cohn?"

"It's not the Apaches, Miss Marcus!"

"Cheyenne?" I felt as if I was suddenly the straight woman in a comedy routine. What next? An illusionist sawing me in two?

"The *mishpocheh*. There aren't many of us Jews here, but we've got a minyan of ten men. The Jacobs brothers own the Pima County Bank with Frenchy Lazard. There's Judge Wallace. And Abraham Hyman Emanuel is a super over at the

148

mill. The Calishers run the dry goods store just across Allen, and if you want a French hat, tell Mrs. Gotthelf that Dave sent you."

"That's very generous, but I don't have anyplace to wear a *chapeau*."

"We'll have to change that. Mark your calendar, Miss Marcus. Rosh Hashanah begins on September 23, and I promise you a service you won't forget."

"Thank you for the generous invite. I'm not planning that far in advance. I'll rejoice if I make it to June. In the meantime, it was a pleasure meeting you, Mr. Cohn."

"Call me Dave." He grinned with that mouth full of yellowed teeth, eager to please. I smiled back with more reserve. He wasn't my type, and I was already taken, besides. "I'd give you a cigar, but you don't look like a smoker. Take a Swiss chocolate, my treat."

Dave dropped a square, wrapped chocolate in my gloved hand. A maid in a red dirndl winked at me from the paper wrapper. I marveled at how far that tiny European had traveled without breaking. What stories could she tell? I wondered. Wyatt extended his left arm, through which I laced my right glove. I justified my familiarity by telling myself it was good to get better acquainted with Johnny's future associate. It's amazing how much a girl can lie to herself, but there it was, me feeling every movement of his ropey muscle. Wyatt was truly a gentleman—even if he wore Colt six-shooters with the casual pride with which other men (like bankers and businessmen) wore pocket watches or lodge stickpins.

"Wind's up," he said. A twelve-mule wagon thundered past. We crossed Allen Street, me trying to keep pace with his long strides as we dodged men on horseback, their noses and mouths hidden by bandanas to strain the soot.

Anchored to Wyatt's arm, the wind didn't irritate me. Feeling secure, I raised my chin and studied the scene around me; I didn't worry what strangers saw when they looked at me. My adventurous side, tucked away in Kitty's cottage like socks in a drawer, unfolded. I lacked the urge to lean in to Wyatt as I did with Johnny, to curry favor and flutter eyelashes, to be cute or clever. The unprecedented sense of freedom—from myself, most of all—made me feel giddy and bold.

"Good people," Wyatt said as we climbed the boardwalk across Allen Street.

"Excuse me?" I asked.

"Dave Cohn. Good people. He's a bachelor, you know."

"Is he?" I was beginning to see where this topic was headed.

"He'd like to marry."

"I suppose there aren't many eligible women in a mining camp."

"Short supply, big demand."

"I hadn't noticed."

"Your mind is elsewhere." Wyatt guided me to avoid flying tobacco spit. "Dave's predicament is that he's seeking someone who shares his faith."

I stopped and squinted up at him. "Mr. Earp, are you matchmaking?"

"Not at all, Miss Josephine, I'm just stating fact. Good folks."

Not wanting to seem conceited, I neglected to explain that if I'd wanted to marry a nice Jewish shopkeeper, I had my share waiting in line back in San Francisco. And there were handsomer, richer men in my sister's congregation attracted to my looks, if not my station in life. I knew too well my value as a beauty without a dowry. Mama had made it very clear that my impulsive actions had cost her a rise in social standing and living standards. Bless Mama for lighting the Shabbat candles every Friday night, but keeping house was no more my destiny than it should have been hers. She should have been a Torah scholar, with an entire *shtetl* tending her needs while she dove into the Talmud, but that was hardly possible back in Europe, much less America.

Wyatt smiled down at me, perhaps recognizing that I wasn't budging on this topic, and changed the subject. "Are you going to eat that chocolate?" he asked.

"I don't want to muss my gloves, but I'm happy

to share." I handed it over and Wyatt stripped the wrapper and cracked the morsel in two. I clasped my hands behind my back, closed my eyes, and opened my mouth, receiving the luscious treat. When I opened my eyes, Wyatt was smiling down at me, amused. He quickly looked away. He tossed his half in the air and attempted to catch it in his mouth. It bounced off his broad mustache and tumbled to the dirt.

"Well, that was a waste of a perfectly good chocolate," I said.

"It was worth a try. I wagered my aim was better than that."

We strolled on toward the schoolyard. I kept my mouth shut to preserve the luxurious aftertaste of Swiss chocolate from the Arizona grit. Wyatt seemed content to pick our route while I blindly followed his lead, watching the town unfold before me.

"Do you have any sisters for Dave Cohn?" he asked.

"Oh, I have sisters all right. A pair: Rebecca has a husband, and Henrietta is too young to marry. But if I lured Hennie to Arizona, it would break my mother's heart. It was enough of a *shonda* and sorrow that I ran away unchaperoned."

"Did you leave home because you were unhappy?"

"Not desperately, but I wasn't the dutiful daughter Mama demanded. My folks are good people—and I still moved away." I would have left a placeholder back on Perry Street to marry whatever man she considered suitable if possible. But I yearned for a connection that always seemed out of reach, across the wrought iron fence and down the block. "I hate all the heartache I've caused. But, the first time adventure came calling, I answered. I don't suppose you want to hear how a nice Jewish girl who couldn't carry a tune got it into her head to join Pauline Markham's Pinafore on Wheels and hit the road?"

"I suppose I do."

"Didn't you ever run away from home, Wyatt?"

"Home had a habit of running away from me, Josephine." His mood darkened as he chewed his mustache. "But tell me about you."

"Some people might think that's my favorite subject, but they'd be wrong." I took a deep breath. It would have been easy to blame the whole *mishegoss* on my best friend, Dora Hirsch, the daughter of my music teacher. Or I could curse *H.M.S. Pinafore*. My sister Rebecca and I saw it three times. I identified with the heroine, "the lass that loved a sailor" and shared my name, Josephine. You couldn't turn a corner in San Francisco in 1879 without seeing a kid in a sailor suit or hearing a bank clerk whistling "Sir Joseph Porter's Song."

One afternoon, Dora told me the famed Broadway actress Pauline Markham's Pinafore on

Wheels was casting for the road company bound for San Bernardino, Prescott, and Tombstone. I immediately caught Dora's hysteria, although I knew very well I couldn't carry a tune. Dora, a talented singer, explained that running away was our only option, since our mothers wouldn't approve. As in most things Dora, I immediately agreed.

We left on October 19, 1879. I prepared for my day at school, my hands dappled red with nerves. I could hardly button my dress. When I went to stand for inspection in front of Mama, instead of pecking her on the cheek, I threw myself around her with a great big hug and a kiss. She peeled me off and felt my forehead with the back of her hand, but a fever didn't explain my strange burst of affection. She sent me outside with a cluck and a shake of the head, missing the tears that were beginning to form.

I embarked on my first great adventure armed with a pile of schoolbooks tied with a leather strap. I didn't pack a toothbrush or a change of underwear. I didn't even have a stamp to send a letter back home if disaster struck.

Crossing Perry Street, I approached Dora's apartment, pining to return home and confess. But I persevered, more terrified of Mama than what might happen to a pair of penniless flirts on the road. Dora answered her front door before I knocked, slipping out with a satchel tucked under her raincoat. She grabbed my hand, and we ran down the slippery wooden steps toward the docks in a rush to start our glamorous new lives.

At the time, I was ignorant of the tour's impetus: the recent Chicago arrest of Miss Markham's husband for embezzlement had stranded her on the West Coast. Compelled by financial necessity, Pauline launched her own company: she needed to raise money if she was ever to see Broadway again before her face fell and she aged out of prime roles. The scandal, and the weeping it inspired, had added a second little pouch beneath her right eye that collected powder like alms for the poor.

The company embarked on the SS *Drake*, a drab steamer lacking the romance of the titular schooner, the HMS *Pinafore*. Dora and I spent the journey practicing, since our first performance was scheduled for Los Angeles.

My debut as the cabin boy, not quite the heroine with whom I identified, failed disastrously. Some performers get butterflies in their stomachs—I got buffaloes. I felt hideous in my sailor-suit costume, my hair tucked tightly under a cap, my chest wrapped to camouflage my curves. Once the curtain parted, I managed to strut onstage with my fellow sailors, rolling my hips from side to side as rehearsed. And then I turned and registered the audience. All those strangers peering at me. I froze. While my fellows sang,

"We're sober men and true and attentive to our duty," it was obvious I was no man, sober or true. I could not control my face: one minute it was ecstatic; the next, I struggled to subdue tears of fear and shame. Being onstage had appeared easier from the audience.

Later, when the time arrived for me to perform my solo—the sailor's hornpipe—my feet felt nailed to the boards. The sailor chorus repeated my cue—once, twice, three times. When the audience became restless, Dora crept up behind me and pinched my behind so hard that I stumbled forward, clutching my rear end. The audience howled. The actor playing Dick Deadeye grabbed me roughly on one side. The one playing Ralph Rackstraw lifted the other. I danced between them, my feet treading the air as the men performed the familiar steps on either side of me. It was an inauspicious beginning for my brilliant stage career.

During the next performance in San Bernardino, I faced my failure. Sweating in my costume, hands shaking, terrified of my cue, I realized I was no Sarah Bernhardt. While I was deeply disappointed in myself, I recognized that the offstage adventure thrilled me. Bouts of homesickness appeared like waves of nausea, but returning to the normalcy of Perry Street didn't appeal to me.

I stuck it out all the way to Arizona and even survived a terrifying brush with renegade Apaches.

But this is where I fudged the story with Wyatt. Discussing the braves led directly to meeting Johnny. I skipped that part: after all, *I* was telling Wyatt the story, not the *Nugget*.

CHAPTER 12
MARCH 1881

In mid-March, Johnny and I shacked up together in the house my father funded on Sixth Street and Safford, a fishwife's yell from the Joneses. Albert curled up in the loft, which seemed sturdy enough to hold him. He didn't eat much. Though we'd yet to stand together before a judge, I began to use the name Josephine Behan when I visited the post office. I told myself I was now a daring Tombstone resident when I was actually a typical greenhorn: gullible and giving it away for free. Madame Mustache could have told me that— and essentially had—but I might as well have jammed my fingers in my ears and sung *"lalalala"* for all the attention I paid to advice that didn't suit me. I was adventurous enough to get into trouble, but not enough to exploit my situation. Every time I got fed up with Johnny and threatened to leave, he called my bluff and reeled me back with charm and yellow roses.

It took more than smiles and flowers to believe

that what we hastily built on Tombstone's northern fringe was truly a home. The February winds had limited construction, and spring arrived with its itch, so we didn't wait until it was finished. It was going to be as grand as Kitty's—or at least have more than a roof and a few walls. I envisioned a white-painted home with gingerbread trim on the gables, a three-piece Eastlake parlor suite, and vases filled with flowers from the garden.

I never got it.

The only finished room, top to bottom, with walls and a window and a door with a brass knob, was the bedroom. A big brass bed dominated the plank floor. A side chair, a chest, a hat stand, and a rag rug showed a woman's touch—but not mine. Lacking curtains, the room had an unobstructed view of the Dragoons and Cochise's Stronghold, where the woods rose up to meet the mountain's granite domes and steep cliffs. Everything else was slapdash, with a hammer here and a saw there. Oilskin stretched over the window frames in place of glass.

I gave myself credit for keeping my knickers up for five long months, though I didn't exactly begin as Joan of Arc. Ever since Johnny had guided me upstairs at the Grand Hotel that first night, I'd been fighting a losing battle. While I'd held firm that night, keeping my thighs together and corset tight and turning us around when we met the seductive soiled dove Miss Timberline, I was flirting with surrender. Desire unleashed my operatic streak; I was running toward passion, playing with fire, poking the sleeping lion. I wanted to run free—damn the costs—which seemed to be the prevailing attitude in Tombstone.

From the very start—farther back than the night Johnny taught me how to kiss behind the barn— I wanted to yield my girlhood and become a woman. I was tired of playing with dolls, and I had no desire to be a porcelain princess on a shelf myself. But I resisted, heeding the voices of Mama and Rebecca and that spinster scold, Common Sense, who restrained my inner compass.

Johnny pursued and pursued and pursued, and every fiber in me wanted to relent. I didn't want to surrender but to join him as an equal, to uncover what lay beyond the kiss and the caress. I despised ignorance and craved knowledge of what happened when all the clothes came off in a private room with the rest of the world locked out. Every day, as the frame rose for our house, as the hammers banged and the saws sang, that eventuality neared. And every day I felt more inflamed, more impatient, more agitated. In a town where marriage was optional and men lived like bachelors, their wives in distant cities, the old ideas of love and marriage seemed more flexible.

In the new order, love was the commitment, not the law—or at least that was the line Johnny was selling. To share a roof was to be man and wife, he insisted. *Take my name. You have my heart.* While I wouldn't have believed Johnny in my damp, dark chamber on Perry Street with Mama down the hall, I wanted urgently, with every passing day, to embrace our union in windswept, starlit Arizona, where I was unfettered and adrift.

I awoke on the morning of March 15 to a surprise snowfall—and Harry Jones thudding by in his long johns while scratching his bait and tackle. I received Kitty's shrill rebuke to get my lazybones out of bed. I'd had enough. They had, too. I figured they wanted to be left alone so they could fight it out in peace: he was never good enough, and nothing ever satisfied her.

But the Joneses' marital discord disappeared from my thoughts when I stepped on the porch. The dizzy snow fell softly, chaotically, stirring me. I felt energized, embracing the morning, wanting to unwrap myself beneath the flakes and inhale the cool vanilla deliciousness. The air seemed alive with promise. It rarely snowed in San Francisco. This was new and magical, as if the real world only existed in places of extreme weather—cold and heat, thunder and wind, flash flood and drought. I descended in bare feet and raised my face to the sky. The powder dropped on my cheeks and eyelashes. The fresh white slapped a coat of paint on the house, giving it a fairy-tale glow. A northern cardinal—a flash of vibrant persimmon, a male—paused on the roof, then teased me with its flight, disappearing into the dancing whiteness.

Johnny had promised to come by for me that evening and show me how the house was progressing. He planned to take the night off, explaining, "The bedroom is finished." Those words filled me with anxiety and anticipation: what would it be like to share a room, not with a sister, but a man? What could that intimacy be like, and would I at last experience the bliss I expected sex to be? I fretted like a silly hen that I wouldn't live up to all the expectation in Johnny's eyes. That led me to wallow in my inexperience while I did the baking and scrubbed the linens, which prompted deeper worries about where that disappointment might lead. Would it change the way he saw me? Would I rise or fall in his esteem?

The day seemed interminable as I flipped and flopped between hope and fear. At dusk Johnny arrived, flashing his easy smile and familiarity; I was both relieved and uneasy. He hurried me down the street past the empty lots of houses to come, and the rubble of camps disbanded, his muscled arm wrapped securely around my waist.

At the threshold of our cottage, Johnny gathered me up and carried me into the house. Our bodies together made the statement. I knew we couldn't wait any longer. Or maybe I didn't know, because it isn't a thing of the mind, but accepted, unfolded, relaxed, surrendered, finally, to the natural flow of man and woman possessed. Between kisses and calling me his bride, he said something like, "Who needs floors when we have love?" or "Who needs a stove when we'll be cooking in the bedroom?" Aloft in his arms, I was so infatuated that I failed to notice that the snow had begun to waft inside through cracks in the walls and roof, puddling on the unfinished floors.

Johnny walked the plank bridge between the entrance and the bedroom, crossing the parlor, which had been roughed out but not yet filled in. He kicked open the chamber door and tossed me on the bed. Taking a match from his vest pocket, he lit candles, risking all we'd built. Moonlight entered the window, turning the snow crystals at the corners into small chandeliers to rival those at the Grand Hotel.

Johnny removed his hat, jacket, and vest. He turned to me and said, unknowingly echoing Kitty, "Get up, lazybones." I laughed and obeyed. I felt a tingling in my fingers—and between my legs—that life was about to change between us in a way that had nothing to do with legal papers. If we were going to cross a border together, I was ready. I rose beside the bed and awkwardly began to unbutton the back of my blouse.

"You never have to do that by yourself again," Johnny said, loosening the fastenings, kissing me slowly, then adding the tip of his tongue. My knees loosened. He pushed the blouse off my shoulders. The room was so cold I could see my breath mixing with his; I didn't feel a chill, but a slow flush.

With a quick hand, Johnny unhooked my skirt, which pooled at my feet. That left that garment that had always been between us: my corset, my bodyguard. He untied the top with gentle hands. I wondered how he could advance so unbearably slow. I attempted to help, but he pushed away my hands. He held my gaze until he bent down to loosen the remainder with his teeth. I held his head while running my fingers through his hair, rubbing the tips of his ears. He'd taught me so many little pleasures—but now the feast.

My corset dropped. Johnny inched down my chemise, exposing my breasts to the moonlight. I had never been naked in front of a man. Doubt overwhelmed me. I feared I would disappoint him. He might laugh and turn away in rejection and loathing. I struggled against the instinct to cover myself. And then I watched the reaction in his candlelit eyes, which awakened with new interest. They flamed with an unfamiliar—but not unwelcome—light, and what seemed to be a deeper appreciation of what I brought to this party.

Not only did I not disappoint, I exceeded expectations. Viewing that fire in Johnny's eyes unleashed a *chutzpah* in me previously unknown. I felt comfortable in my flesh as I had never before, even when bathing alone. I rubbed my belly as it curved toward my hips. I pushed back my shoulders so that my breasts rose with each new breath. I raised my chin to flatter my cheekbones. I had known stage fright. Now I encountered its opposite: a bold physical freedom that surprised me as much as it delighted Johnny. I wasn't ashamed. I would *not* be ashamed. In fact, I was unleashed.

I reached up to pull out my hairpins, releasing the curls slowly as Johnny watched. He undressed, as if reluctant to tear his eyes from mine and break the spell. My hair sprang wild and loose around me as I cupped my breasts and approached the edge of the bed where he sat. He clasped my thighs tightly between his, brushed my nipples lightly with his palms, and in a sudden motion, took my right nipple into his mouth, sucking hard, then soft, then hard. My head fell back. He reached around my bottom and settled me onto his lap, my legs split. He caressed and resettled and caressed, until he eased me onto his manhood. A painful, awkward moment passed as he tried to break through my seal. He held my waist while trying to gentle me through the rough passage, but forbidding my retreat. At last the barrier broke. I tumbled as he pushed deeper inside me. We stopped there, and I felt what it was like to have bare skin against bare skin, and my arms around those broad shoulders I loved so well.

It was a closeness I'd never before experienced.

"My love," he said, brushing away my curls so that he could regain eye contact. He rocked me from below, slowly and rhythmically, and I took quickly to the dance. My knees gripped the bed and my hands his shoulders as he guided my hips, rocking me back and forth, faster and harder, slower and gentler, until I broke free from his control and found my own rhythm. He lay flat on the bed, feet on the floor as I rode him out, pressing hard against his pelvis with my own until I felt a cataclysmic release. Afterward, I collapsed on his chest, drenched in sweat. Tears ran down my cheeks onto Johnny's chest as I curled into him, our bodies illuminated by the hot, yellow candlelight and the cool, blue moonlight.

After I caught my breath, Johnny grabbed my hips, flipping me onto my back. As I lay there, hands outstretched on the pillows in surrender, he entered and stroked, fast and slow, his eyes closed in concentration, until he had nothing left to give. I felt his liquid warmth deep inside as he relaxed above me. The urgent pounding of horse hoofs outside ended our short-lived moment of complete union. Someone hammered the front door; a horseman's face appeared at the bedroom window. He banged on the glass. I covered myself with a quilt.

"Get your skinny ass out of bed, Behan!" yelled the horseman with a scar from ear to chin. "Bandits held up the Sandy Bob stage bound for Benson. Philpot's been shot, and a passenger's down. We got to round up a posse, man, not a pussy."

Johnny hopped up and hurried into his clothes, skipping into one boot while holding his other and hat as he headed for the door. With one hand on the knob, he spun around, shot me his most charming smile, and said, "I would have liked an encore, sweet pea, but duty calls. Don't wait up."

CHAPTER 13
MARCH/APRIL 1881

I awoke on March 16, swoony and saddle-sore in a house with neither kitchen nor privy—and no John Harris Behan. He was leading Wyatt and Virgil and Morgan and pretty much every leathery local on horseback to capture masked bandits who'd attempted to rob the Benson stage. Outside of nearby Contention, the trio shot driver Eli "Budd" Philpot while miner Peter Roerig caught a stray bullet. The thieves failed to seize the $26,000 in silver bullion on board, thanks to shotgun messenger Bob Paul. The former sheriff of Pima County, moonlighting for Wells Fargo, blasted the assailants while crying, "I'll stop for no one." And he didn't: the spooked horses bolted. A mile later, Paul regained control of the team, saving the silver and the remaining passengers.

This wanton violence scared bankers all the way to San Francisco. I knew my parents would read about the attempted robbery and fear for my life. As for me, my thoughts remained between my legs, as if I were the first woman who'd ever had sex, which meant I was worried for Johnny. Afraid to be alone with the fugitives at large, I returned to Kitty's house. She snorted when she saw me coming, but softened to give me a hug and a pinch. We were that way with each other, chafing then bonding. Life could be hard, and men could make it harder. If you didn't have some kind of sister to share your crazy stories with, who would believe you?

While I huddled with Kitty, watching the world go by in newsprint—she read the *Nugget* (recently purchased by Democrat Harry Woods), and I preferred Clum's *Epitaph*—Johnny chased the bandits, risking bullets and a broken neck in rough country. I missed him more now than ever. In his absence, I felt as if my skin had been peeled away, like he'd taken part of me and ridden off. I went to bed hungry for him like a starving orphan. I awoke craving him like water in the desert.

Lovesickness—I had it bad. Kitty tried to convince me that it was good. At least I felt something. Even my pain made her jealous. She claimed she could do with less of her husband, not more, but the lawyer wasn't the rugged type to join the posse. As the days passed, riders thundered in and out of town, carrying bits of news. Gradually, Jim Crane, Harry Head, and Bill Leonard emerged as the villains. Luther King had been the fourth man, holding the robbers' mounts. Some even hinted that Wyatt's friend Doc Holliday was an accessory before the fact and implicated the Earps. I didn't believe the rumors.

The weather warmed up. One beautiful day of blue skies and breezes followed the next. While Johnny roamed the countryside on horseback, I was stuck in town with the other posse widows. I spent my days ensuring that Albert attended school, and completing our house. Not with my bare hands, though. I couldn't hit a nail on the head with a hammer. No one in my family had ever used anything more than a rolling pin. But I was determined. With money and a honeyed voice, I asked Dave Cohn if he could find me a carpenter. He brought me two. Working steadily for cash to pay their overdue rent, the unlucky miners laid the floors with simple local pine and raised the walls. Dave found a worker to dig the privy, and a glazier to fit the windows.

One afternoon in late March, I was feeling pretty proud of my frontier skills, hemstitching gingham curtains to keep the perverts out of my business. Less impressed, Kitty was criticizing my messy stitching when she gasped at an article in the *Nugget*. "Did you know this?" she asked.

"Know what?" I pulled a stitch too tight.

"Johnny just named *Nugget* editor Harry Woods his undersheriff?"

"That can't be true. Johnny all but promised the job to Wyatt. I was there."

"Well, he promised it to Wyatt, but according to Woods's newspaper, Johnny appointed Harry. What does a newsman know about upholding the law?"

The news made me feel clammy. I paused with the needle above the fabric, the only weapon I knew how to use, and that just barely. If Johnny would betray Wyatt, who was packing heat and had brothers at his back, how could I trust his promises to me?

With an unintentional prick of my finger, I marked the moment the tide shifted between Johnny and Wyatt. A person could do a lot of things to Wyatt—the scuttlebutt was that his pal Doc had sorely tested their friendship, constantly getting drunk and courting chaos—but disloyalty was another matter. Lying to his face was intolerable, and Wyatt had just learned before I did that Johnny was capable of saying anything to get his way.

Time passed. The Benson stage robbers evaded capture in the mountainous and vast territory that bordered Mexico. The posse remained on the range. I rarely saw Johnny. Finally, he captured accomplice Luther King and jailed him in

Tombstone. Allegedly, King held the robbers' horses during the crime and, since he could identify the villains, became the prime witness. Meanwhile, Johnny and I made the most of our brief time together. He hardly noticed my home improvements from our bed. Between rounds, when Johnny wasn't snoring, he grumbled about the conflicts among the posse members, cursing "those damn Earps" for not recognizing who was boss: him! These rising tensions—exacerbated by hunger, thirst, and mistrust—escalated on the night of March 28, when King escaped.

Kitty and I learned of it, and more, when Harry came home at lunchtime the following day, dumping his newspapers on the breakfront and sitting down to Kitty's tiresome beef stew in silence. He looked like he'd aged five years overnight.

"What happened?" Kitty asked. He just shook his big balding head and chewed his meat like an old mule over his feed sack. Kitty coaxed and prodded, trying to get Harry to talk.

"Kitty, leave off," he said.

"Tell me, you old fool, or I'll take your plate away from you."

"I've had enough of your disrespect, Kitty, especially in front of *her*." He shot me a look, his face flushed with anger. "It's nothing I can say with Behan's girl sitting here at our table."

"I can leave," I said.

"Sit still, Josephine," Kitty said, "and don't break anything. This is not about you. Harry, tell me what happened, and tell me now. Whatever it is, we will work it out."

"I've been hoodwinked," he said, pushing away his plate with a rare lack of appetite. He reached for his pipe. "I had the wool pulled right over my eyes. I can't even bear to let you read the newspapers."

"What do they say?" Kitty asked.

"It's too mortifying." He shook his heavy chin with a sigh, tapping out his pipe and pausing in a way that would normally send Kitty into paroxysms. She waited him out. "Luther King escaped from custody last night."

"How does that involve you? You're not a lawman."

"I was in the sheriff's office drafting a bill of sale for King, who wanted to sell his horse to Johnny's corral partner John Dunbar. That gabby new Undersheriff Woods was jawing about something or other he'd written in the *Nugget*, and how the Democrats were being robbed worse than the Benson stage. He'd been advised to chain up the prisoner on warnings that King might bolt, abetted by the cowboys swarming into town. While I was finishing the paperwork, King strolled right out the back and disappeared on a horse that was tied behind the office."

"How is that your fault, Harry?"

"It's a bad thing, Kitty, and I am deeply shamed. I was there with Behan's cronies, profiting off the prisoner when he should have been under lock and key. These thieves killed two good men, and King was the link to their discovery. Now I appear tainted, as if I colluded with the escape, as if I freed the rascal myself. How will I be able to show my face in town?"

"You're exaggerating. It cannot be as bad as you say."

"Am I ever one for exaggeration? Read the newspaper and weep." For once, Kitty let her husband have the last word. He was right. King's escape was a black eye for Woods, and by extension, Johnny. At best, they were negligent; at worst, complicit. The breakout soured Harry's partnership with Johnny. The lawyer tried to put distance between his reputation and that of the sheriff, and to expand his clientele to the growing law-and-order set rallying around Mayor Clum and his Republican *Epitaph*.

Kitty now began to visit me across the street on the excuse that we were setting up house and needed her assistance. She had a point: I could raise Cain quicker than curtains. As for my opinion of Johnny, ours was not a business arrangement. I was incapable of such distance, as Harry demonstrated. Every day that Johnny pursued Leonard, Head, and Crane on the range was another day my body longed for his. In

Johnny's absence, my love grew exponentially, so that at last his homecoming in April was explosive. Any reservations I had about the man's integrity hardly concerned me in my rush to return to the sheets beneath the crooked homemade gingham curtains.

Once Johnny returned to our new home—having postponed finding Leonard, Head, and Crane to resume collecting taxes—I wanted to see him as much as possible to make up for lost time. He spent long hours in his office and frequent nights at the Grand Hotel bar, where proper women were discouraged. I begged Johnny to teach me how to ride so we could be together on the range. I loved horses (although I'd never had so much as a pony ride at a fair).

My affection for animals was unique to me: Mama had no patience for pets. She could not comprehend the attention people wasted on their dogs and cats. It was as if there was only so much tenderness in the world, and it should go to family and the congregation. If there was an extra scrap at the end of the week, it should be shared with widows and orphans, not animals.

Like so many young girls, though, I became horse-crazy. I would beg to see the beasts in Golden Gate Park. Mama would occasionally take Hennie and me there for Sunday strolls. I loved sitting on a bench by the bridle path to watch the equestriennes. They balanced high in their sidesaddles, with their backs straight and swan necks elongated—princesses in a pageant that didn't include a Jewish baker's daughter. The horsewomen wore tall silk hats with ethereal chiffon veils. They inclined their heads ever so slightly in acknowledgment when a dashing male acquaintance (or possibly a stranger) trotted by in the opposite direction, tipping his hat to prolong the encounter, and perhaps enticing a reciprocal glance from under the veil.

For me, horseback riding exemplified the height of San Francisco sophistication. I aspired to make my way into this larger circle that ignored me on my dingy public bench, my hair in pigtails tied with plaid ribbon. It's not that I wanted to pass myself off as someone different. I wanted to be recognized for the bold beauty that I was becoming. I felt confident that I could compete, given half a chance. If I had a stylish riding habit and a horse to match, I, too, could rise in society. I don't think Hennie shared this ambition to break free and move up the caste. But I'd already begun to see the light in men's eyes when they appraised me. I knew that at least in that way I was different from my sisters and mother.

No one guessed my aspirations; my mother dismissed them as airs. I would sit beside Hennie, my legs dangling beneath my short skirt, attempting a perfect posture I would never achieve, haughtiness inappropriate for my status.

Mama would unfold newspaper-wrapped sand-wiches or an orange that dripped as we slurped the slices, licking our cuffs like peasants. Our mother had little patience for my raptures, dismissing the riders in her heavy accent: "These women ride and ride and never go anywhere."

I intended to ride and ride and get somewhere in Arizona. Johnny agreed to teach me. Headed for Dexter Livery Stable, where Johnny owned a half interest, we walked arm in arm (mine shaking in anticipation). Johnny raised his hat to passersby, calling most by name and asking after their kin or business or livestock. Albert lagged in our wake, hidden behind his fringe. He owned a sleek black gelding that Johnny had bought him in Prescott to smooth the parting from his mother. Albert had named him Geronimo, after the rogue Apache chief still at large, and spent his free time currying the horse and mucking out stalls at Dexter's for ice-cream money.

When we arrived at the corral, Johnny called out, "Hey, Dunbar," to his partner, a rangy blond with a florid ginger mustache that parted like velvet opera curtains. "Get the swiftest horse for Josephine! She claims to be a fine San Francisco horsewoman, and she's here to prove it."

"I said no such thing, Johnny. I've never even been on a horse."

"Modesty doesn't suit you, Josephine."

John O. Dunbar led a battered bay named Sally

Sue out to the paddock. Johnny's partner had recently added the title of treasurer to stable owner, a political appointment courtesy of his older brother Thomas, the territorial legislator who introduced the bill to establish Cochise County. And it was thanks in large part to Thomas that Johnny—not Wyatt—had become the new county's first sheriff.

But I wasn't considering politics that day, just the sheer mass of this homely old bay. Sally Sue was tall and brick solid; a network of veins stretched across one side of her long face from a previous and brutal owner. She gave me a baleful stare, as if I were a bucket she could kick just out of spite.

"Do you have anything smaller?" I asked.

"We're not trying on boots," Johnny said. "She'll do fine."

"She's gentle as a tarantula," John Dunbar chimed in. "Not afraid of anything . . ."

". . . but mice," Johnny said.

". . . and snakes," said Dunbar.

". . . and scorpions," said Johnny, slapping the horse on the rump. Sally Sue twitched her rear and backed away. Mr. Dunbar grabbed hold of her bridle and yanked her into submission. Then she stamped twice. I squealed.

My call-and-response with Sally Sue drew the attention of the idlers collected nearby. They gathered around to watch the fun. Among them was Newman H. "Old Man" Clanton, who'd just left his horse to be watered. The last time I'd seen him was atop the stairs at the Grand Hotel, buttoning his vest while the overly familiar Miss Timberline passed Johnny and me in a cloud of attar of roses. I'd wanted to run then. Now I wanted to disappear.

Old Man Clanton chewed on a cigar, an imposing grandfather from Tennessee. His spikey brows overhung deep-set eyes that had no patience for fools who weren't related by blood. According to Johnny, Clanton had enlisted in the Confederate Home Guard out of Texas and then deserted without ever losing his antagonism to Northern intervention. Eventually, he established the Clanton Ranch nearby on the San Pedro River, where it became an unofficial hub for local cowboys.

Clanton's eldest son, Isaac (called Ike) sidled up beside his father, laughing at the joke he'd just finished sharing with the Mexican stable boy. Ike was nearly respectable in a dark three-piece suit, a spit curl adorning his tanned forehead. With a jovial "Howdy, lads," and an outstretched flask, he approached the handsome McLaury Brothers, Frank and Tom. The inseparable pale-eyed siblings, one clean-shaven and the other with a dandy's goatee, stood together like a shiny pair of pistols. Beside them, Peter Spence wore a large, droopy sombrero and a shirt red enough to startle a bull.

I tried to ignore the corral rowdies, but my stage fright rose in reaction to the unwanted attention. I wanted to learn how to ride, not star in my own rodeo. My palms began to sweat, which would hamper holding the reins. I looked to Albert for moral support, but he'd slipped out of the crowd into the stable and his beloved Geronimo's companionship. I tried to remain steady, approaching the musty-smelling bay as if I wasn't in the least intimidated. The mare turned her head toward me and snorted, sending me flying backward into Johnny's arms.

The men's derisive laughter hardened my resolve. I would neither pout nor cry nor chastise these cowherds and ranchers for their bad manners; that would only worsen the situation. Getting a rise out of me was clearly part of the game. I harnessed my reserves of willpower, raising my head like those San Franciscan pony princesses and attempting some semblance of a haughty look. I tossed back my curls and gathered my skirt in one gloved hand. "Boost me up, Johnny."

Ike Clanton stepped forward. "*I'll* give her a boost."

Johnny displaced Ike, laced his hands under my boot, and hoisted me onto the two-pommel sidesaddle. I perched uneasily, clasping one horn without the security of a stirrup until Johnny raised it, and raised it again when it finally reached the sole of my left boot. At his instruction, I balanced on my left foot and lifted my right leg over one pommel so that it rested in the valley between two curved leather horns. The position was awkward, but the saddle supported my right thigh and lent stability without my having to hike my skirt up and reveal my knickers.

I folded forward to pat Sally Sue, wanting to convey that we girls were in this mess together. She jerked backward and passed gas, sending a shudder through my chicken heart and a gale of laughter through our audience. The mare snorted again. I did a jump-and-squeal. The growing crowd roared again. One sour, unamused face I would later have cause to loathe floated among the merrymakers. Dunbar's wife, a weather-beaten brunette with her hair in two Indian maiden braids, had joined the onlookers. She regarded me with a cynical look on her pinched face, as though plotting her future duplicity.

I became more angry than terrified. I would not be shamed for wanting to gain a skill many of the folks in the corral had acquired before they learned to read; I could read in two languages and swear in three. I kicked Sally Sue with my left heel, timidly at first, then harder, as much to escape the stable monkeys as to ride. Albert appeared up ahead, exiting the stables on Geronimo. To my great relief, he and his beautiful beast sidled up to us, taking my reins. He said,

"Miss Josie, tighten your belly and squeeze with your thighs. I'll do the rest. Only please, no more squealing. Horses never attack; they react. Miss Sue already fears that you're a predator. If you scream like a mountain cat, she's likely to want to toss you off before you set your claws into her back."

"Thanks, Albert." I tried, but failed, to match my voice to his gentle tone. My hands shook on the saddle horn as Sally Sue walked along Allen Street and then followed Geronimo up Fourth toward Fremont. Johnny caught up on his gray stallion as we passed the post office and its long line of gawkers.

"I'll take over from here," Johnny told his son. Albert returned my reins and faded into the side street, trotting off with a wave of his right hand.

I wiped my palms on my thighs and repositioned my hands on the reins, firmly but not tightly. We soon were at the outskirts of town, the shacks and shanties of Tombstone's crust. Without an audience, a weight lifted. I resettled my bottom on the saddle, increased the pressure in my thighs, and felt Sally Sue submit to the inevitable and settle into an unhurried gait, following Johnny's stallion. On the plateau, desert flowers had begun to bloom. The sky above was denim blue, the cottony cumulus clouds heavenly and brushed with pink shadows, the air clean of Tombstone's burnt garbage smoke. I felt the freedom of distancing myself from the boomtown with its mobs of men. Only five minutes had passed since we'd crossed Safford Street, but looking cautiously back over my shoulder, Tombstone already seemed small and inconsequential, a town made of matchsticks and canvas cuttings.

Johnny rode beside me, as easy in his skin as his stallion in its curried coat, smiling slowly over at me with that twinkle. "You can do it, baby girl. Just hold on and that sweet nag won't let you down. A big horse like Sally Sue makes for a smoother ride. I won't let you fall. Don't forget: she's more afraid of you than you are of her."

"That's small comfort," I said. And then I stopped talking altogether, reluctant to let my vibrato betray my nerves. My self-control returned slowly, along with an increased security on my mount—not enough to be chatty, but enough to nod at Johnny and hold on. As we cut through the chaparral on the well-worn horse path to the Dragoon Mountains, Johnny taught me how to turn left, then right, and how to pull back to a stop. He showed me how to get the mare going again with a firm kick, and how to refrain from sending mixed messages of stop and go, left and right. We repeated the actions, Johnny circling me atop his stallion, until I began to feel comfortable.

Relative to the fancy San Francisco equestriennes in their tight, tailored jackets and tall, polished boots, I had a long way to go. But at least I'd made the leap. I'd climbed on horseback. And I kept saying to myself, *I'm riding, I'm riding,* even if I was afraid that I would fall and be crushed. But between those waves of fear, I began to experience exhilaration. I forced myself to embrace the present thrill. I was on a horse. Even if she wasn't the most beautiful, she was moving.

Above us, the sky stretched blue, and for as far as I could see there were no people other than Johnny and me. I could follow Johnny out of a walk and into a trot. I began to feel the breathless excitement of forward motion, of flight into the unknown.

As we approached the mountains, I fell behind. I watched Johnny's hat shrink in the distance as his trot exceeded mine. Then he stopped abruptly. I assumed he was letting me catch up, but when I looked ahead to the foothills, I saw what might have been the figure of a man, a flash of white that could have been a sleeve. I trotted toward Johnny and began to see the outline of a stocky, dark-skinned native in the foothills, a red bandana on his long black hair, a rifle strapped across his chest. He was too far away for me to see his eyes or distinguish his features. Then I saw another figure, and another—rifles, bandanas, a feathered headdress, long black hair, the flash of white shirts against dull leather vests.

My fear of Sally Sue was small in comparison to the terror that these rifled men inspired. I gripped the reins too hard. The mare resisted. She shook her head from side to side, which hardly bothered me in my frightened state. I forgot to breathe and became lightheaded, but realized that now I must master this horse because my safety depended on my resisting the reactions of fear, even if what I wanted to do was scream.

Johnny wheeled around and raced toward me, his hat flying behind on the leather thong encircling his neck. "I'm going to teach you to gallop, Josie," he called as he neared me, and then as he passed, "You are going to learn on the fly."

I hardly had to kick my mount with my left foot for her to turn in Johnny's wake and follow. Sally Sue knew how to gallop. We followed Johnny, flying at a pace that left me gasping and holding on with my small hands, my thighs, my hopes. And here was the odd thing: there was something glorious about it, an adrenaline high—nothing else in the world existed except rider and horse and speed. Johnny looked back to ensure I was following. He looked past me; I couldn't tell what he saw. But I could read his lips, mouthing *Faster, faster*. We accelerated. At this speed, I couldn't manage to look back, but in my mind's eye, I envisioned dark-skinned riders on painted ponies, and I dug my left heel deeper. All ridiculous thoughts of Sunday San Francisco horsewomen escaped my head, replaced by my desire to survive, to hold on to Johnny again on our brass bed beneath the gingham curtains.

From this distance, Tombstone was a dirt clod dwarfed by the open spaces surrounding it. Gradually, the town grew until its tent cities and stucco shacks and gaudy facades resembled a child's village made from matchbooks and thimbles and playing-card packets. It seemed like the domain of a spoiled child who might just as easily step on it as over it when his attention waned.

Once Johnny and I reached safety on Safford Street, he stopped, and I pulled up beside him, breathless and frazzled. "We're safe," he said, holding on to his saddle horn and reaching over to give me a kiss, which I returned with pleasure, and without tears. We paused for a moment at the outskirts of town. I savored the aftermath of another scrape we'd survived together, another crisis that brought us closer and widened our circle of trust. And then we walked on past the post office.

When Sally Sue saw the stables, she broke into a canter, but I held firmly, my back straight and my eyes forward, refusing to give the cowboys at Dexter's the satisfaction of hearing me squeal again. General applause greeted Johnny and me when we entered the corral. To my confusion, I saw money changing hands. Albert later explained that bets had been placed on whether I would even get up on the horse. Others took odds on whether I'd stay on the mare beyond the town limits, where I would fall off, whether I'd cry, or if I'd return on the back of Johnny's stallion with Sally Sue in tow. I discovered that Old Man Clanton, counting his cash, had bet the long shot: my returning in one piece still on horseback, dry-eyed. He won the day, an excellent judge of horse flesh and human character.

If only I'd put money down on myself returning in one piece. But I got my reward: satisfaction. I felt like a tougher, braver woman than the squealer who'd climbed on the mare's back earlier that day. I was a Westerner; and the next day I had the saddle sores to prove it.

Months later, Wyatt told me those men in the foothills weren't Apaches, but costumed cowboys pulling a prank. I was never quite sure if Johnny was complicit or not—and by then it no longer mattered.

CHAPTER 14
MAY 1881

As I settled into our new home, I surprised myself by preferring the open sky of the outdoors to the low-ceilinged shelter within. Most evenings, once Johnny returned to Allen Street, I left the dinner dishes on the sideboard and Albert with his sums, then stepped into our backyard, which was really just a square chip of scrub marked off with rope. I sat alone on an old canvas camp chair, with a tumbler of whiskey to soften the night.

Peering out, free from small talk and local politics, I watched the light change incrementally, bringing the distant Dragoons into relief. The mountains seemed almost close enough to touch in the sharper light before softening into the distance—in shades of violet, ultramarine, and smoky quartz. I shared the ever-changing view with a legion of small animals and birds that appeared once I achieved a state of quiet watchfulness. The hawks with their majestic wingspans circled above; and sadly, I heard the death cry of a rabbit plucked by its feathered predator or abducted by a coyote. I was not so soft, then, that I mourned the bunny for long. One animal feeds on another. Only the cleverest survive.

Fox eyes flashed. An owl hooted. I gazed at the stars, gradually making out the Big Dipper, the planets Venus and Mars, fat Orion's belt. I awaited a wishing star, only to realize that this was my wish: this serenity—without Kitty's chatter or Mama's judgments or the pressures of an arranged marriage—was what I desired.

The rapture I experienced beneath the naked sky inspired my religious philosophy, one as passionate as my mother's Judaism, but disconnected from its rituals and words. I never questioned my mother's faith: she believed in right and wrong. I respected her commitment to education and betterment, her concern for the needy, and her disdain for the materialistic. My mother's God was just and passionate. Her belief in his power to guide her toward goodness and protect her loved ones may have been tested by her voyage to America and my disobedience, but her faith did not bend or break.

I never rejected Judaism, but I did not share my mother's orthodoxy. I had yet to light the Shabbat candles in my new home. I could roast a chicken on Friday night, I could make soup from my mother's recipe—but I did not yearn to indoctrinate Johnny or Albert. There were no Sabbath services in Tombstone—and I doubt I would have attended them if there were—and I didn't go to Sunday church with Johnny and Albert, either.

Mama never missed synagogue on Friday nights and Saturday mornings, joining in prayer with a larger community. The rituals and holidays, the blessing of the candles on Fridays, and the nightly prayer, *"Lieber Gott,"* while kneeling at her bedside, were a constant reminder of her devotion and gave her life meaning. These acts were archways to a higher communion. We both shared that trust in God, only I found my faith in the desert stars and lighting campfires instead of Shabbat candles.

I spent more time with Albert in our new home—not quite a mother, but more than a governess. We often rode together. One May afternoon, I met him near the schoolhouse; he was furious. After careful prodding, I chiseled out the source of his discontent: Three older boys had teased him for chewing on his pencils. I argued that there was nothing wrong with chewing on a pencil as long as he didn't swallow it point first, but he said the trio told him it was disgusting and would cause lead poisoning.

It steamed me that boys could be so cruel over so little: What was so awful about a child chewing pencils anyway? A nervous tick: Albert was bored, plain and simple. I encouraged him to ignore his schoolmates, bolstered by the knowledge that he was cleverer and handsomer, but that didn't help him survive the long, lonely school days. Albert was more sensitive than I had been at school—I was usually the one teasing and troublemaking. But through his eyes I understood how much their taunts stung and rankled. He thought of them over and over, which only led to more pencil chewing. He lashed out in response to their needling, which only satisfied the other boys. They egged him on until Miss McFarland— overburdened with nearly a hundred students— noticed and sent Albert to face the corner for being disruptive.

Albert hurt badly. He missed his mother (although he mentioned her less and less) and off days at school stirred up more sadness in the boy. Out of pity—and an excuse to satisfy my sweet tooth—I steered Albert to Lottie Hinkley's Ice Cream Parlor on Allen Street. We raced each other upstairs to the second floor of the tall, narrow adobe. Our moods lifted with every step.

The sound of the tinkling bell as we crossed the threshold instantly revived us. Across the otherwise empty ice-cream parlor we spied Wyatt. He spooned vanilla ice cream from a tulip glass, his back against a mirrored wall. My heart skipped a beat and dropped toward my knees. I felt doubly guilty because I was standing beside Albert. Had he looked up from his shoes in that moment, my expression—reflected across the parlor mirrors—would have betrayed my feelings. Or could he sense my feelings by proximity?

Wyatt motioned for us to join him. I took Albert's hand, which he immediately yanked away, and approached the lawman. "What brings you here?" I asked. Albert and I stood side by side like schoolchildren in the principal's office.

"Ice cream," Wyatt said.

"No law against that."

"I'd have to arrest myself if there was."

"Wyatt, have you met Johnny's son, Albert Behan?"

"A pleasure, Mr. Behan."

"I'm just plain Albert, Mr. Earp," said Albert. "My father's Mr. Behan."

"I suppose you're right, Albert. I hope you don't take offense if we don't shake hands; mine are sticky. Have a seat."

Albert scraped back a chair and settled down. Before I could give Wyatt the opportunity to rescind his invitation, Lottie shuffled her wide hips over and took our order: chocolate for Albert, and cherries jubilee for me. As we waited, Wyatt scooped another bite of vanilla and let a pause rest between us. He had pale, long fingers with square-trimmed nails buffed shinier than my own. They were well-cared-for gambler hands because, according to Johnny, Wyatt dealt faro, a popular and easy-to-master game of chance, at the Oriental Saloon and Gambling Hall. It was among Tombstone's most luxurious spots. I'd never gotten any closer than peering through the windows; Johnny told me the Oriental wasn't a suitable place for proper women.

Lottie Hinkley's was a safe destination, so it was funny that Albert and I now shared a table with Wyatt Earp, the man who owned the Oriental's gambling concession. I wondered what a person could tell about a man by watching him eat ice cream. Wyatt was slow and deliberate, not wasting a motion, not rushing toward the end. He was as smooth as vanilla, but he wasn't soft: even here he was packing pistols.

"Are those Colts?" Albert asked.

"Sure are," Wyatt said. "You shoot?"

"Squirrels, mostly. Nothing fancy."

"I've sent a few squirrels to heaven and slaughtered some tin cans. I don't believe in fancy shooting myself. I learned most of what I know at the feet of better men in Kansas City, summer of '71, sitting on a bench in front of Marshal Tom Speers's office. In the quiet between buffalo shooting seasons, men like James B. Hickok—"

"Wild Bill?" Albert leaned forward on his elbows.

"The very same." Wyatt nodded his head in confirmation. "Hickok, Jack Gallagher, the scout, and Cheyenne Jack were all there. In the lazy afternoons, they held an informal school for shooting before they made for the gambling houses and variety shows. Wild Bill could do fancy, but when he faced down a man, there was nothing tricky about his gun handling."

"Could Wild Bill shoot two pistols at once?"

"He could, when he was showing off. He could fan his guns, shoot from the hip, and fire two pistols at once. Grandstanding was what it was. When Hickok got serious, confronting an enemy, he shunned tomfoolery." He scooped his dessert, licking the drips off his mustache while pausing to consider the past. I could read it in his eyes, the way he shuffled through the stories, figuring which were suitable for a young boy.

Lottie, with her cotton-candy hair, returned with

our ice cream. She asked Wyatt if he wanted seconds, but he ordered a coffee—black, with five sugars—and continued: "There wasn't a man in Kansas City who knew more about hunting buffalo than Gallagher, but when you wanted shooting advice, you turned to Bill. He had a reputation for being the deadliest living pistol shot. And he was courageous, too, wouldn't back down or slink away from a fight, whatever the odds. I didn't say much those afternoons. I listened and learned lessons I still use today. I wasn't much more than twenty myself that summer, not much older than Miss Josephine."

"But a little wiser, I hope," I said.

"I wouldn't bet the payroll on that," Wyatt said. He looked me straight in the eyes until I glanced away. Lottie watched us closely from behind the counter.

I looked down at my ice cream and pecked at a dainty spoonful, though I wanted a bigger bite. It was delicious, with a wicked hint of rum. Part of me was as excited as Albert to be sitting with Wyatt, buffalo hunter and Dodge City deputy. We'd witnessed this man tame a lynch mob to rescue Johnny-Behind-the-Deuce. I felt starstruck and deeply curious: What was Wyatt like when he wasn't shooting or fighting or dealing faro at the Oriental? I also wondered whether I needed to be wary of Wyatt, sitting in Lottie Hinkley's as if he was just waiting for us to arrive.

What I observed was that even while Wyatt ate vanilla ice cream with a little silver-plated spoon in a room with pink-striped wallpaper, he had gravity. It was as if all the rivers flowed in his direction. He could take his time because the world was coming to him and not vice versa. The man had a square-faced solidity, a powerful stillness that forced others to react to him: even me, sitting with my Medusa curls and my fiancé's son, trying not to flirt since I couldn't possibly impress him with my bravery. I can't deny wanting to make a positive impression on him.

"Please, tell me more about Wild Bill," Albert said between bites. A chocolate mustache formed at the corners of his mouth; I left it there, knowing it would be more embarrassing to Albert if I pointed it out or reached over with my napkin.

"They were a pretty woolly crew back in Kansas City. When they weren't discussing buffalo, they were debating guns. Who shot who? Who met an untimely death and where? After a night drinking whiskey, they passed those hot afternoons target shooting, competing to prove the best aim."

"Did you try to win?" Albert asked.

"Sometimes, but I didn't always succeed. I grew up shooting guns. I had a keen eye and a quick hand. When I was in my teens, I crossed from Missouri to California with my folks, shooting game for the convoy. I earned respect with my rifle. My skills served me well, but a cool head served me better. By the time I turned up in Kansas City, I was a decent hand with a rifle, shotgun, and pistol, but I still had plenty to learn."

Wyatt sipped his coffee. He took a long look my way. It embarrassed me that I was so disheveled and off balance, so casual in Albert's company, but it didn't seem to deter Wyatt. The intimacy of afternoon ice cream on a safe patch extended to all three of us. However, Wyatt's gaze attached to me for long enough that Albert became impatient for more stories. The lawman swiveled toward the boy and continued his gun talk. "Sure, Gallagher and Hickok taught me about marksmanship, but also which weapons performed best, and how to wear a gun to get the quickest action in a fight. Speed and accuracy was their goal. They hadn't lived as long as they had by being flashy. There's a split second between life and death, and those gents knew how to make the most of it."

"How, Mr. Earp?" Albert asked, his spoon abandoned in his ice cream, his gray eyes sharp and focused. I appreciated the way Wyatt drew Albert out, and silently thanked him. Albert was no longer worried about chewing pencils.

"Hours of practice, sure, Albert, but the wisest lesson I ever learned was that the gunman who takes his time survives. A gunfighter has to be mentally calculating, and muscularly swift. The

Kansas City gang taught me that if I hoped to see twenty-five, tricky shooting was poisonous. It would get me killed in a flash of gunpowder."

"Who knew there was so much to consider?" I asked. "I thought it was point, squint, and shoot."

"Don't be so girly, Josie," Albert said.

"Get a bit older, son, and you won't be saying that!" Wyatt told Albert with an open grin that set his eyes dancing.

I flushed, studied the dregs of my cherries jubilee—I never ate ice cream slowly—and tried to ignore Wyatt's comment. After a beat, I slowly peeked out from under my lashes, only to get caught in Wyatt's unapologetic stare. He smiled right at me. I may not have known how to pull a trigger, but I could flirt. I'd started at three on young David Belasco from down the street, and I'd been honing my skills ever since. I recognized that there was nothing unintentional about this man with the black Stetson. Unlike Belasco, who never succumbed to my baby charms, Wyatt was toying with me right there in front of Albert and Lottie.

"I may be as girly as they get," I said, to get the conversation back on track, "but if I behave as if I know everything there is to know, I'll never learn anything new!"

"If you want to learn something new, Miss Josephine, I'll take you out shooting."

"After my riding lesson with Johnny, I'm not ready for guns."

"You weren't *so* awful, Josephine," Albert said.

"Thanks for the compliment, little Mr. B., but the world isn't ready for me to pack a pistol."

"There's a right way and a wrong way—and it's important to learn the difference, Miss Josephine," Wyatt said. "The first lesson: learn what's comfortable for you and stick tight. When I'm packing, I wear two guns in open holsters, like this, one on each hip. I shift 'em down low because my arms are long. That's how it feels right for me. I got one set to go, and one in reserve. That second gun shows I'm serious."

"I don't need to see two guns to know you're serious, Wyatt."

"What about you, Miss Josephine?" His eyes studied mine. I made an effort to hold his gaze. "What are you serious about?"

The question gave me pause. I'd finished my ice cream, so I couldn't use eating as an evasive maneuver. I wasn't serious by nature, but I was passionate enough for two. Right then, I should have immediately thought "Johnny" in theater marquee–size letters. I didn't.

Wyatt pulled my heart in a different direction, one that conflicted with my current domestic status. Was I suddenly feeling something deeper than I had before? Or was I being feckless and foolish?

Though Johnny and I shared a roof—and there wasn't a wifely act I didn't perform—he didn't seem any more serious about marriage now that he had a regular income as sheriff than he had before. Maybe if I showed an interest in Wyatt, Johnny would become jealous and get busy making us legal. But I knew that wasn't why I was flirting, if that's what we were doing. It had nothing to do with Johnny and everything to do with Wyatt. Given the flush I felt, he had me reconsidering things I thought I knew for certain and solid.

Albert pierced the awkward pause with a new question: "Ever kill a man, Mr. Earp?"

"Nope, but I've scared a few." His eyes slid off me. "I prefer talking a man out of gunfire or clocking him on the side of the head to snuffing out a life—but that's me. And the choice has bit me in the chaps more than once."

"Are you really as dead a shot as they say you are?" Albert asked.

"Don't believe everything you hear, young Albert," Wyatt said, wiping his hands on a napkin, tapping his holsters, and preparing to leave. "I learned my lesson in Kansas City: be fast, be accurate, and be alive."

Wyatt rose and waltzed around the table, easing out my chair behind me. "Put all three on my tab, Lottie," he said as he escorted us out the door, down the stairs, and onto the wooden sidewalk.

Wyatt paused, a piece of warped board creaking under his boot, as if weighing what to say next.

"Thanks for the ice cream," Albert said.

"Thanks for the company," Wyatt said. "Eating ice cream can be a lonely business."

"Albert and I are always happy to keep you company." I blushed and added: "And put you out of your misery."

Wyatt tipped his Stetson and backed away, turning and rambling across the wide road between the horse-and-wagon traffic. He passed Marietta Spence and her old mother carrying brooms and buckets, and gave his hat another tip before leaping onto the opposite sidewalk and disappearing into the Oriental.

Albert and I walked in the opposite direction. Once out of earshot, I said, "That man actually knew Wild Bill Hickok. What do you think about that, Albert?"

"What I think is that the man's sweet on you."

"He is not! What a thing for you to say, given your father and all. It was the ice cream that made him so sweet. I'm an almost-married woman."

"Almost."

"You are wrong." I blushed, hoping with every fiber that Albert was right. True, that emotion was disloyal, but I couldn't smother the genuine smile Albert's words inspired despite my impassioned denial: "Wyatt didn't have a word to say to me; all we talked about was guns."

"Shoot, Josie!" He rolled his eyes.

"Is that a joke? Shoot? It's a miracle!"

He punched my arm before taking my hand and smiling up at me with a string of even, white teeth. He'd be a lady-killer someday, no pistols required.

CHAPTER 15
MAY 20, 1881

It was one thing to observe the notorious Curly Bill Brocius stomping down Allen Street, cursing and laughing, spitting tobacco, surrounded by his cronies in bright bibbed shirts. But it was another to invite him over to play poker like Johnny did.

I would have called Curly Bill a colorful character of the Western frontier if I was a tourist ignorant that he'd killed Marshal White the previous October. He wasn't just wild, he was feral. Even if the judge acquitted Brocius after two months in jail, the outlaw was dangerous. Maybe that shooting was accidental. Maybe it wasn't. But he wasn't just a harmless public nuisance: he celebrated his freedom by shooting at the toes of a preacher, making the clergyman dance in front of his congregation to the bullets' beat. Bill had a prankster's sense of humor, but it wasn't particularly funny if you were the butt of his joke. I discovered that he had neither manners nor morals—he had no respect, but a surfeit of self-regard. There were bears in the wild that were more civilized. I learned that the hard way under my own roof.

Johnny invited William Brocius, Johnny Ringo, and their ilk over for Friday-night cards, which seemed harmless enough. Since I was the woman of the house, Johnny insisted I stay and play hostess, bake oatmeal cookies a la Harris House, serve a roast—that kind of thing. Curiosity won out over caution. I was eager to throw a party in my own house for the first time in my life. That wasn't something we did on Perry Street. I had no reason to argue since I trusted Johnny's protection and infallibility. He was the sheriff, after all.

During pillow talk, Johnny shared his plans for a business alliance with the cowboys. They tended to be Democrats and Southerners like himself, and they were rule benders rather than makers. Johnny's strategy put him at odds with Wyatt. The Earps disliked Brocius, even if Wyatt and his brothers inevitably drank and gambled with the cowboys in town. When balancing the two prongs of the sheriff's office—law enforcement and tax collection—it was the latter that prevailed for Johnny. He loved money, and that's where the biggest profits lay. Wyatt, on the other hand, would always balance the books on the side of the law.

That night, Johnny and I looked happily around

our new living room, the deviled eggs I'd prepared on the sideboard. But the room that had appeared spacious suddenly seemed overrun when our guests arrived. Brocius, who was in his midthirties, was oversized in everything he did; he entered following three bangs on the front door at 10:00 p.m., flung his coat on a chair, and slung his guns on the wooden hooks. Suddenly, it was as if his bear-size personality sucked the air out of the room.

Like Curly Bill, most of the Cochise County cowboys were damaged goods. I did not approve of them in general but had never been close enough to be justifiably fearful. That night, I still felt that Johnny knew what he was doing and that he was in control, despite rumors that Bill had murdered at least one man in Texas before he encountered Marshal White. Johnny Ringo, who was part of Bill's loose circle, had been fourteen when he saw his father take a misstep off the wagon while heading west and shoot his own head off with a shotgun. Their wounds—and those they inflicted—bonded these men together. They were not easygoing men yearning to be yoked to responsibility and respectability. They were rustlers and thieves beyond the pale. Drink became a sort of religion that washed away their sins, as likely to bring chaos as communion. For some reason—whether arrogance or a faith that individuals with common interests would pursue them like gentlemen—Johnny apparently believed he could play with fire and not get burnt.

"Let me plant a kiss on the hostess," said Curly Bill. Without gaining permission, he grabbed my shoulders in meaty paws and attempted to land his rubbery lips on mine. I managed to twist away at the last second. He only got a portion of my cheek—but it was a very big slice, which he sucked like a peach. His smell repelled me: the foul breath of unbrushed teeth, tobacco, and a rangy ripeness covered in whiskey.

To my surprise, Johnny laughed at this "mischief." When I glared, he pointed to Bill's Stetson banded with silver conchos and said, "Take the man's hat." I bit my tongue out of deference to Johnny, playing hostess to his host. Still, it surprised me that my man was suddenly free of jealousy just when I could have used his green-fueled outrage. I should've known better. Johnny and Curly Bill had already forged an unusual business partnership. Along with his deputy, Billy Breakenridge, Johnny had the inspiration to recruit Curly Bill to collect taxes from the ranchers and rustlers on the range for a percentage of the take. Bill the Bully turned out to be a highly efficient tax collector. Few Cochise County citizens—on either side of the law—had the power to defy him. Since Johnny received 10 percent of all taxes collected, this was a good deal for him. The alliance also appealed to Brocius's dark sense of humor. He was a stick-up man for the government, ambushing rustlers. The irony appealed to Curly Bill.

The poker game was, in part, a celebration of this lucrative confederacy. Bill straddled a chair at the dining-room table where Johnny had draped a large square of green felt. The cowboy rearranged his black, snail-like curls on his freckled brow—his vanity exceeded that of Napoleon's Josephine—and popped his cuffs to show he had nothing up his sleeves but wrists. To his left, two sealed twenty-card decks waited beside the seat Johnny set aside for himself. At each place stood a bottle of whiskey—apparently the good stuff, not the home-brewed brown liquor made with snake venom, which often passed for scotch.

The other guests began filing in, their boots pounding on the thin pine floors: Ike Clanton and his brother Phineas, Frank and Tom McLaury, and Deputy Billy Breakenridge. The McLaurys had better manners than the rest at the beginning of the night, but as the cards were dealt and the whiskey cracked, the group got rowdy, egged on by Curly Bill, who seemed to grow larger as the night wore on and the room shrank. Albert remained in the loft, but I can't imagine he got much sleep.

Johnny presided as the gracious, impeccably dressed Southern host, his pocket watch dangling from a heavy gold chain. He ensured that each guest got what he wanted, keeping the card game moving and the conversation lively. He let the poker players tell their tales. When there was a lull, he contributed an anecdote that was often at his own expense. When conflicts arose, whether it was a debate about cards or who among them was the better shot, Johnny interceded to smooth out tempers. Billy Breakenridge insisted that Curly Bill was the room's finest marksman, able to shoot a jackrabbit midhop, and a quarter out of a piker's fingers. Curly Bill called up to Albert to help him demonstrate. But before Curly Bill could rise, Johnny Ringo stood up; he was a quiet, bookish man until he was liquored up. He claimed to be the deadlier shot.

"True, Ringo, if your opponent is unarmed," said Ike Clanton, laughing like a wheezy hyena. He shared a large adobe with his brothers on the ranch their widowed father built on the San Pedro River. Timing had been everything. The Clantons settled to raise and rustle cattle right before the Schieffelin Brothers and Dick Gird discovered silver nearby in 1879, named the town Tombstone, and launched the boom that primed the local beef industry. Ike pushed back his chair, which clattered behind him, and said, "Let's pull."

"Why don't we go outside and test it, you belligerent braggart," said Ringo, straightening his belt and squaring his hips, "I'll even give you a head start—or did you forget your guns in your Pappy's pocket?"

"Ante up," Johnny said. "Are we here to play poker or measure our manhood with yardsticks?" I blushed at the comment, realizing that while Johnny may not have been the fastest draw in the West, or the bravest lawman, or the first on the scene, he could talk a snake out of its fangs.

Johnny played cards as I watched, ignorant of the rules but trying to learn on the fly. My man got flushes and three of a kind and even won a hand with two pairs. The cowboys were folding around him, tossing cards and cursing the devil for dealing bad hands. Johnny glowed as he reached forward to scoop gold coins and dusty dollar bills. He separated them into neat piles, each win calling for another shot of whiskey. I began to speculate that this wasn't an ordinary poker game among friends. They could have played on Allen Street anytime. This night of cards, in the privacy of our home, was intentionally rigged with the mutual consent of all involved. Johnny later hinted as much (without drawing a map) when belatedly trying to justify the party. *Lie down with dogs, get up with fleas,* was all I could think. The game enabled Brocius and the cowboys to deliver kickbacks to the sheriff for the beneficial tax-collecting scheme. As a side bonus, their losses functioned as bribes for ignoring rustling and roughhousing beyond the town limits.

There was no sign of the game ending at 4:00 a.m. Their drunken slurs became impossible to follow, the clashes more frequent, the threats more violent. Phineas Clanton sat on the sofa, his mucky boots on the armrest, his greasy head thrown back. Snorting snores escaped his lips. His brother Ike pelted Phin with biscuits from the sideboard, and then a chicken leg. When Ike raised an empty whiskey bottle from the green felt and stood up to aim, Johnny stopped him. "We're not in a saloon, Ike. Sit yourself down and play cards."

"Who are you to tell me what to do?" Ike slurred.

"I'm not going to pull out my sheriff's badge," Johnny said, dealing out another hand. "Let's just say you're in my house, my rules. No throwing bottles after midnight."

"That seems fair enough, sir," Tom McLaury agreed.

"No bottle tossing after midnight," concurred Tom's brother, Frank, as he examined his fresh hand, his features revealing nothing. He could have had aces or eights and no one at the table would have known.

"I'm a rule maker, not an order taker," said Ike. "And I'm certainly not going to take any horse crap from a half-cocked, half-breed, badge-wearing son of an Irish Catholic bastard like you, Behan. You are no Southerner in my book."

Brocius fanned his cards, then looked up and waded in: "You have a book, Ike? That comes as a mighty shock. How about this: your granddaddy and Behan's both owned slaves, so I'd say that makes you both princes of the Confederacy. Now, are we going to play cards here or lady-talk?"

My drowsy eyes popped open. Did Curly Bill just say that Johnny's beloved Grandpa Harris owned slaves? That was a story that the voluble Johnny had skipped. Maybe it was just late and I misunderstood. I didn't know what disgusted me more, the past or the present. A headache began to thicken above my right eye. So these were the men Johnny was cultivating. He dumped Wyatt for these scoundrels. I glanced at Deputy Breakenridge, who was cleaning his fingernails with a serrated knife, just watching the show, and taking it all in, not interfering. So, this was the law in Tombstone.

I felt nausea coming on as the headache deepened. I abandoned hope that the men would leave before they asked me to cook them break-fast. I touched Johnny's shoulder, and he didn't look up, so I slipped wordlessly out of the smoky room into our own.

I rubbed my stinging eyes and removed the false smile I'd plastered on my face until the last hour. I undressed, unfastened my boots, and released my corset stays with a sigh of relief. I never felt entirely free all strapped, my breath shortened and my waist cinched. While the atmosphere among the men in the other room grew increasingly oppressive, my wardrobe reminded me in a visceral way of my limitations in mixed company, trussed like a chicken and expected to behave like a hen.

I stood in my chemise, allowing my body to readjust to its rightful position. My stomach expanded and my breasts fell from my throat; I rubbed the life back into them. This was me, unfettered. I inhaled deeply, gulping like a drowning woman to clear my head, and stretched my arms to the ceiling and then to the floor, sensing each vertebra as I rose back up. I removed my hairpins slowly, shaking the locks loose, left and right, down and back. I rubbed my scalp to relax away my thoughts and concerns: that Johnny had allied himself with these ruffians and invited them, like demons, across our threshold and into our life.

The inky sky had begun to brighten infinitesimally into the cadmium blue of early morning, which gave me enough soft light to slip under the covers without lighting a candle. With my head on my feather pillow, I curled up with the belief that Johnny would wrap himself around me sooner than later; overcome by exhaustion, I fell asleep instantly despite the hootenanny in the adjacent room.

Not much time elapsed before I awoke to the sound of the door opening. Suspenders snapped. Heavy boots thumped on the floor. The sound of the poker party flooded in through the open door. I first thought it was Johnny coming to kiss me good night. But he smelled wrong. Suddenly the room was ripe with sweat and unwashed feet and peculiar cigar smoke. I hoped I might be dreaming until the mattress sank and the bed frame squawked in a way that was unlike Johnny. I experienced a fear and foreboding that was more nightmarish than any dream I've ever had, a terror that crawled up my spine and raised the hair on the back of my neck.

I did not allow myself to wait for what would happen next, but leapt from the bed toward the window and grabbed my shawl. I hoped my fear was all in my imagination and that I would be alone in the room. But there in the early morning light lay Curly Bill. He was naked atop the coverlet: his muscular biceps flexed, his hands rested behind his head, his armpits and the meeting of his mighty thighs furry pelts.

I screamed for Johnny, then waited to hear his response or his boots rushing across the living room to my aid. It was oddly quiet in the next room, except for some stifled giggling. My voice rose with panic as I called again. To my horror, there was no response, except what might have been the sound of a scuffle. When the loft stairs creaked, an unfamiliar voice hissed: "You, back to bed," apparently to Albert.

Untouched by my horror—entertained, even—

Curly Bill leered at me from Johnny's side of the bed, flexing a beefy bicep for my benefit. "I won you fair and square in the last hand," he said.

"That's impossible." My voice squeezed tight with fear. Once I found my breath, I pointed to the door and yelled, "Get out of my bedroom!"

"I'm not going anywhere. I had aces over jacks. Johnny had two pair."

"Johnny would have to possess me to gamble me away, you devil, and he doesn't." It was unpleasant enough having the man under my roof; sharing a bed with him was inconceivable. I would not submit. Or, at least, I would not surrender quietly. I imagined those couples that Curly Bill had forced to dance naked and flushed with horror: it had seemed altogether different when read in newsprint. I had no leverage over this man except Johnny, and he wasn't running to my rescue.

"You're as good as hitched, Mrs. Behan, living together under the same roof." He twisted a snail-like curl on his damp forehead. He patted my side of the bed with his meaty hand. "Come back to bed, darling."

"Get out of here!" The door was on his side of the mattress. I felt guilt and shame. Had I somehow invited him into my bedroom by going to sleep while the men were still in the house? Had I sent a signal of which I wasn't aware? Had my smiles in service of Johnny's politicking signaled an invitation that I didn't intend? Or worse: Had shacking up with Johnny before marriage signified a willingness to ignore all legal convention? It did me no good to surrender to my doubts. However I felt, I knew I had to remain strong, aggressive even, so I said: "You reek."

"You smell nice, too, Miss Josephine. And you're even prettier when you're angry."

"You have not seen angry yet. I am not a horse to be bartered."

"But I will ride you."

"You will not."

"You know that you want it." I knew I did not, but had I asked for it by leaving the protection of my home for Tombstone? I was momentarily struck dumb. "Don't be coy with me, Josie girl. You know you're a fine piece of horseflesh: all that flouncing about and eyelash flutter and wiggle. Why give it away free to that little man Behan, when you can have a real man with something worthwhile in his pants and gold in his pockets?"

Curly Bill lunged across the bed and seized my wrist. I screamed as if I was on the verge of being scalped. While the grinning brute held fast to me while kneeling atop the mattress, I thrashed and yelled with a new edge of desperation, calling Albert, too, and again for Johnny—this time, as if the call for law enforcement might have more impact than the ties of love, I called "Sheriff." I heard no movement from the other room. It was silent, an audience engrossed in the heroine's tragic predicament—Aida in an opera, not Josephine in an operetta.

Appearing disgusted with me and the racket I was raising, the beast released his hold on me and got to his feet. "I'm going. It was just a joke. You're no fun at all. You should have played along." A red bruise circled my wrist.

But Curly Bill showed no signs of moving. He stood at the foot of the bed, undressed and aroused, his smile having taken a nasty, sneering turn. He looked me in the eye. "Remember this," he said, lowering his voice, "I know where you live."

Only then did the outlaw climb back into his clothes and boots, making a slow show of it. At the door, Curly Bill paused to leer at me again before exiting.

"I told you my Josie wouldn't buy it," I heard Johnny say.

"It's my turn now." I recognized Ike by his slurry voice and hyena laugh. "You've been flaunting that fancy dancer from San Francisco for months, Sheriff Slicker-than-shit. I'll teach her how to ride. You got your cash. Now give us a little fun."

"Shut it, Ike," said a voice that I didn't recognize. "You're so drunk you couldn't even tickle her with that limp rope."

"Not like your old man and Timberline," said another with a similar twang. "Your pa's a goat with that old bitch." As I heard chairs scrape outside and something crash, I flung a jug at the wall to register my anger heard. I was shocked, ashamed, and humiliated—but I wasn't going to let one more man through that door as I sat down with my back against the wood, nursing hot tears.

CHAPTER 16
MAY THROUGH JULY 1881

Johnny and I never recovered from our night with Curly Bill. That didn't exactly make us unique— just ask the dancing preacher over in Charleston if his congregation ever showed him the same respect following their Sunday prayer meeting with Mr. Brocius. As I said, the rustler's antics were always more amusing when they happened to someone else, preferably in another town. And, while Johnny was a natural-born storyteller, he'd failed to mention the darker side of his family history. When I pried further, he shut me down. Even his smooth tongue couldn't turn that awful night around. Maybe that was Johnny's tragic flaw: he loved company but lacked loyalty. I guess it was a little late to discuss *that* with the first Mrs. Behan.

The next week, Curly Bill's peculiar sense of humor got him into more trouble. On the way to the mining village of Galeyville in the mountains about a hundred miles east, he shot Jim Wallace's horse out from under his outlaw buddy. Wallace had to walk the rest of the way into town. Like me, the weary cowboy failed to appreciate the joke. But unlike me, he had a gun and was fully clothed. The Arizona newspapers reported that on May 25, after a round of drinks at the saloon on the banks of Turkey Creek, the drunken pair quarreled, insults slung and apologies withheld. Wallace apparently had had enough bullying, and while Brocius threatened to fire, Wallace took the initiative, shooting his companion first. The bullet entered the left side of Bill's neck and exited his right cheek. His jawbone shattered.

When I heard news of the "tax collector's" grave injury, I rejoiced. While rumors that the cowboy was on his deathbed were exaggerated, I knew the wounded brute wouldn't be coming to collect his debt at my house anytime soon. That in itself was a tremendous relief. But in the aftermath of his poker-night antics, the damage to my affections for Johnny had already been done. I just didn't know how to extricate myself. The prospect of leaving Johnny after investing all of my father's money in the house we shared worried me to no end.

Meanwhile, Johnny and I pretended that nothing had changed. We attended the Redpath League's Grand Ball at the brand-new Schieffelin Hall on the corner of Fremont and Fourth to benefit the Irish (Johnny was on the committee and wore a green ribbon on his chest). We dined out a little more often, even returning to the Grand, but not sipping unlimited Champagne. Though the romance had faded, any change in Johnny's demeanor was undetectable out in public. We finally had a roof under which to make love, but the act seemed tainted after Brocius laid his curls on Johnny's pillow.

The injured outlaw became the proverbial elephant in our bedroom. I could understand why he'd bullied Johnny into that joke. Curly Bill was the kind of belligerent prankster who would have shot a man who didn't laugh. Johnny, feeling physically threatened, didn't want to be that man. But I couldn't forgive him for abandoning me. Even if Brocius wasn't rising from his sickbed anytime soon, I doubted Johnny could or would protect me from the other cowboys with whom he increasingly associated.

My trust in Johnny, already frayed, became too thin to support our better selves. At home, talking became as good as arguing. Johnny's expectations—that I would have food on the table whether he showed up for dinner or not, that I would spread my legs or roll over on demand in this pose or that pose whenever he entered the door—ended our short honeymoon even before we wed.

Our love was burning out into ashes just as a devastating fire threatened Tombstone. A cigar spark ignited a whiskey cask at Allen Street's Arcade Saloon. That scorching afternoon topped one hundred degrees, and the flames spread swiftly. The fire feasted on the flimsy wood-frame buildings, destroying a swath from Fifth to Seventh Streets and Fremont to Toughnut. The volunteer fire department lacked the necessary equipment, trucks, and hoses that Mayor Clum was just then buying on a trip east. The next day, I read in the *Epitaph* that the blaze consumed sixty-six businesses and cost $175,000 in damages, but fortunately, no lives lost. The newspaper survived, too.

While the town pulled together, Johnny and I struggled to survive the blaze. It's an odd thing how a man who doesn't want to be saddled with a particular woman anymore keeps upping the ante until she walks away from him as if it were her choice. In that, Johnny was typical. He didn't exactly want to dump me, but now that money was coming in and he wore the sheriff's badge, I didn't add value to any of his schemes. He didn't want to marry me, although he didn't have the guts to admit it. Instead, he gave me a demonstration of the fact, as if one were needed.

I don't recommend ending an engagement by discovering your oily partner clamped onto another man's wife. That's what I recall about July 11, which became an anniversary of sorts—a day I would come to observe with a sense of relief for having dodged a bullet. I'd taken Albert to Tucson for a visit to the ear doctor. When we returned home earlier than anticipated, dripping with sweat and thirsty and out of sorts, I expected the house to be empty and Johnny at work. I heard something in the bedroom that sounded like a cornered raccoon. I went to see what the racket was about and staggered when I glimpsed Mrs. Dunbar's chicken legs stretched over Johnny's broad shoulders. With his muscular buttocks bared, Johnny kneeled and grunted on our brass bed (which came with a lifetime guarantee).

Disgust and horror surrendered to anger and rose up my spine like lava. I felt more exposed than the naked pair: he was the only man who'd seen my bare breasts, shyly at first, then brazenly, comfortably, and joyously. My nipples were his nipples, twisted and toyed with by sure fingers, but now I knew the awful truth. He had seen me, squeezed me, taken my virginity, and moved on. I wasn't his one and only; I was his one of many.

Despite Johnny's candied words, I was nothing special to him. I was not a unique beauty of rare quality, but merely another conquest. The injustice stung, but a more hideous realization followed. From the first moment I'd arrived in Tombstone, my status must have been apparent to everybody except me. Even Kitty must have known that first Friday in San Francisco, awaiting my comeuppance, the surrender of youth and beauty to a charming womanizer.

How could Johnny betray me after I'd traveled so far and sacrificed so much? After I told him every secret in my heart, every fear, small and large, every dream and nightmare? I would only realize much later that his rutting had little to do with me, and everything to do with his own nature. But that broiling afternoon I felt intensely small and unworthy and abandoned, like a disgusting wad of tobacco chewed up and spit out. I didn't know whether to yell at Johnny or berate myself for being the fool my mother always believed me to be.

But I wasn't alone in that stifling bedroom. As shame and anger fought inside me, Albert's strangled exclamation awoke me to responsibility. I covered the boy's eyes from the barnyard spectacle. This wasn't only happening to me: it was a setback for this beautiful, sensitive child struggling to overcome his parents' acrimonious public divorce following his sister's tragic death. Albert was striving to view his father in a better light than the one his mother shined on her ex-husband—and this primal moment only confirmed her low opinion.

Our once-happy home ended that day. Over Johnny's sweaty back, I nodded to the wide-eyed Mrs. Dunbar, the wife of Johnny's business partner at Dexter Livery Stable. I saw every rib on her scrawny body. But I didn't blame her—it was Johnny who couldn't recognize a good woman ready to follow him to hell and back. Or at least Tombstone in the summer, which was close enough.

Johnny had his rear to us, athletically occupied, grunting and oblivious to our presence. I wanted to scream that he would never find a better woman than I, or one who loved him more, but my voice failed me. And good seemed less important than having gymnastic tendencies, in which case I had to defer to the flexible Mrs. Dunbar. I turned on my heel and exited the house without stopping for so much as an extra pair of drawers, still holding Albert's clammy hand.

We rushed together down Safford Street and away from the house we shared together. Hot and sweaty and fatigued, we both cried. Albert slowed down as we put more distance behind us and the new cottage. Then the boy stopped. I didn't know where I was going, except away. I looked into his eyes, realizing he already knew that he couldn't run any farther than the corner of Dust and Ash. I wrapped my arms around him, but it was too hot, too humid, too soon. He pushed me away, shrinking from my touch. Any comfort I could give him was only temporary. I was not his mother and I never would be. And I could only guess that he had fewer illusions about his father than I. "I must go back," he said, and left me there, sweating through every pore, crying to bust my tear ducts, alone and feeling every inch of my isolation and abandonment.

CHAPTER 17
AUGUST 1881

Upon reflection, escaping my partnership with Johnny was a *brocheh*, a blessing. I did call myself Josephine Behan for a bit. I wanted to believe in us, Mr. and Mrs. John Harris Behan of Tombstone, an entity that never existed, much to my shame. Afterward, Albert told me that if I would wait for him to grow up, he would make amends. How that sweet boy came from such a father I'll never know.

For the next three weeks, I alternated between weeping and railing, no fit company for even the softest shoulder. I'd put all my eggs in one leaky basket. After four days, Kitty and Harry suggested the door. I found a room at a boardinghouse that was one step above a jail cell but within my meager budget. I could hardly stand myself for being so gullible.

When I wasn't beating myself up, I was aching for Johnny's touch, missing the way we spooned each morning. He'd walk his lips up the back of my neck and behind my ear to that sensitive, ticklish spot. I awoke wanting Johnny (and having him, his hand reaching down between my thighs while I was distracted by his lips).

I swore I'd never sleep with Johnny again, even when he came sniffing around to deliver "rent" money on my house where he and Albert continued to live. He turned up everywhere I went, begging forgiveness without offering me any more security than before my view of Mrs. Dunbar's skinny ribs. But that didn't mean my body agreed with me. My desires didn't end until Wyatt stopped that backward-looking nonsense with a period and an exclamation mark.

One morning I awoke in my dim room, looked in the warped shaving mirror, and realized my eyes could not get any puffier without doing permanent damage. I didn't have the energy to brush my hair or lace my corset. I could tell by the way my breasts fell that I was losing weight. I had to find a reason to pull myself together before I disappeared entirely and was no longer the most beautiful woman in town. Call it vain, but it was go back to Johnny, go home, or cut a new deal with my future. Mining wasn't really an option: me with a pickax?

I realized I had to take responsibility for myself.

If my rough encounter with Curly Bill had taught me anything, it was that I required protection. My damsel-in-distress act was now wearing thin. There was only so long I could be tied to the railroad tracks with the engine roaring my way. If I fainted now, who would catch me? I feared it would be someone less cultured than Johnny and more dangerous. At night, cowboys circled beneath my window as if I was a table scrap. I feared what might happen to me, without kin or clan at the edge of the world.

Bedazzled by my own beauty from the time I began to develop at twelve, I had no real skills beyond my value to men. I discovered that being free to choose my own man was not quite the liberation I'd anticipated, and began to wonder if I would have to sell my own flesh in order to eat flesh again. That was when I recalled Madame Mustache's offer that I had so swiftly rebuffed. She'd been my Cassandra, suggesting the day might arrive when I could no longer rely on Johnny. She'd alluded to his death by rattler or errant gunshot, but I realized she'd anticipated that our match would falter. This was not magical foresight. She must have been aware of Johnny's infidelity long before I did. She'd probably profited from it under her own roof, taking her cut from Delia.

I sat on the edge of my cot with its graying sheets and knew that as bad as things were, I was too stubborn to quit. I regarded my trunk and my carpetbag and imagined them in the San Francisco foyer. I felt physically sick, like I couldn't pour myself back into that woman I was, that I'd rather live a dismal day here than a proper day under my mother's roof.

To a point, I was grateful that she'd made it so difficult to return home. Even Madame Mustache must have known I was exaggerating when I explained that Ma would welcome me back to San Francisco with open arms.

Despite such limited options, I rejected marrying a bachelor from the Tombstone Hebrew Association. Dave Cohn, Tombstone's earnest tobacconist with his constellation of moles, sparse blond beard, and shop-worn yarmulke, had certainly smiled at me. A young miner with the fringe from his *tallis* visible beneath his coat pinched my cheek while I was at the hardware store and promised me a silver menorah when he struck it rich. I may not have been a virgin, but I was of the faith, so an exception could easily have been made that would have returned me to the road of respectability. But I was no more inclined to keep a kosher house in Tombstone than in San Francisco, and I hadn't risked outlaws and Apaches to spend my days stacking shelves and serving customers for pennies an hour placed in the housekeeping jar.

I'd visited the fair and I couldn't backtrack.

Some might cluck that Johnny had spoiled me for proper society, but despite my comeuppance, I felt like I was just beginning to get the hang of living. What would it be like to never experience the pleasures of the bedroom, only the duties of a wife, like my sister Rebecca?

Determined to make my own way, I craved more star-filled nights and passionate kisses. I just didn't know how to make that leap, or if it was even possible. When I ran out of money to pay my room and board and the owner made the lewd suggestion I knew he'd make, I faced a difficult choice. I could beg from Johnny, seek out Wyatt (who'd been strangely silent in the aftermath of my disgrace), or accept the madam's protection and her offer: the room beside Delia's.

I'd been trying for so long to conceal that crack in my character, denying its truth, that I almost didn't believe it happened. But it did.

I had never turned a trick, but if that was what it took to stay in Tombstone and not be stuck in false propriety in a flimsy saltbox, so be it. Before I could think any more about it, I returned to Madame Mustache's yellow house that very morning. Somewhat surprisingly, though she was happy enough to receive me and show me to my room—she was, above all, a businesswoman, and I would surely be good for business—the madam didn't gloat. On the contrary, she treated me with what almost amounted to kindness.

Still, Medea had nothing on my rage that sweltering Tuesday night in early August when I reported to work for the first time. Now I possessed the key that the madam had given me. Pausing, I heard the giant, teeth-gnashing sound of boulders being broken at the mill. When I opened the lavender door—advertising the house's business with the subtlety of a striped barber's pole—I was desperately ashamed. I feared what I would find there and the stranger I would become.

It was midnight. It had been so hot that people, like lizards, crawled out from under their rocks only in the night's relative cool. Most of the proper women—the wives of mining executives, doctors, and lawyers—had left for San Diego or Los Angeles or anywhere but this desert at Mexico's backside. I'd spent most of that day wrapped in a wet sheet, but now, here I was in a borrowed apricot silk dress carrying a bag with indoor slippers, rouge flushing my cheeks, and my eyebrows plucked into surprised arches.

April (the maid who'd been so frightened of the Apache war cry) greeted me in the foyer. Wearing a starched white pinafore (and a smirk), the girl took my things as I entered. She removed my street boots and offered me new slippers with white-gloved hands.

Neither Madame Mustache nor Delia appeared to receive me, though I could smell heavy perfume.

Perhaps someone had just glided the parlor door shut. Seeing the prominent hall mirror, I couldn't bear to glimpse my reflection. It was as if, sitting *shivah* for my own *neshama*, or spirit, I'd cast a sheet over the mirror as I'd seen my brother, Nathan, do upon my departure. I mourned the relatively innocent girl who'd first entered Madame Mustache's establishment.

April led me up the stairs. I kept my eyes on the ruler-straight part at the back of her drab blonde hair, pulled tightly into two schoolgirl braids wrapped with pale ribbon. The bow at her back was tied in a knot that she couldn't possibly have made herself. April, too, was acting her part in this pantomime—the anonymous servant with no past, ascending one stair at a time, unhurried and blank.

As I climbed the narrow steps, I remembered with sickening clarity my first night in Tombstone when Johnny had led me up the staircase at the Grand Hotel. I recalled the melancholy Miss Timberline with her jet-black hair and heavy silver jewelry, mined without a pickax. Above her, Old Man Clanton smugly secured his vest over his thick waist, his wiry beard bushy enough to hide a canary.

Anxiety surged through me. What would I find on the other side of the door at the top of the stairs? I could hardly breathe, thinking about it, as much from tension as from the fact that I'd tightened my corset to fit into the borrowed apricot silk tailored for some tiny acquaintance of the madam (who knows whom?).

April arrived at the landing. She stood by the door waiting for me to advance, her white gloves encircling the mahogany knob. I couldn't read her inscrutable face. I recalled Mama's mythology lesson about Cerberus, the three-headed dog that guards Hades, keeping the living from entering and the dead from escaping. The hot air suffocated me. April awaited my nod and then slowly opened the heavy door, crafted to buffer noise, providing the ultimate privacy for those within.

April closed the door behind me. I entered a bedroom decorated in lime green and peach. Apricot-colored roses filled crystal vases, perfuming the air. Heavy, horizontally striped curtains covered windows overlooking an alley—not that there was any light this late at night. The chamber was smaller than Delia's and more cramped, especially because Wyatt Earp was stretched out on the milk-colored coverlet like a toy soldier in a doll's house. He'd made himself comfortable and had propped his boots on the footboard, rested his hat on the lampshade, and hung his coat on the adjacent high-back chair.

Setting aside the *Tombstone Epitaph*, Wyatt smiled and said, "Surprise," in a low, steady voice.

"That's an understatement," I said.

So, he was to be my first client. Wyatt Earp. I'd fallen this far. This straight-arrow lawman whom I'd idolized, respected, and romanticized from day one was first in line to purchase me. All those months that I'd thought we shared a connection I'd been fooling myself. I felt sickened and saddened and shocked at my own stupidity. Beauty had its price. Just leave the cash on the nightstand.

My hands began to flutter like agitated birds in a too-small cage, and I didn't know where to hide them. I didn't need rouge to color my cheeks. I had shame for that. "Everything is a surprise to me now, Mr. Earp. Frankly, I would welcome fewer surprises."

"Pull up a chair."

"Do you want me to shed my clothes first?" I asked, trying to take some control of a soul-crushing situation that led in only one direction: my submission. The wayward daughter always realizes her mother's wisdom too late. I felt Mama's presence at my back, which was damn inconvenient. If I was going to be abased, I might as well pile on the guilt, too. I added the tears I caused Mama to my shame, although I was beyond tears. I imagined Madame Mustache somewhere in the house twirling her whiskers like a villain in a cheap melodrama. True, she'd offered me the opportunity, but I alone had taken it. If I wanted to kick anybody, it was me.

"Hold your horses," Wyatt said, raising both his hands as if I'd pointed a pistol at him. "That's not why I'm here."

"Then why are you here?" The sense of rejection I suddenly felt surprised me. "If you plan to tell me I'm on the wrong path and ship me back to San Francisco, forget it."

"I'm not about to tell you how to behave, Miss Josephine. You seem capable of walking right off a cliff by yourself." Wyatt smiled without showing his teeth. The expression lit up his eyes. I struggled to return his gaze, crippled by self-contempt. I wanted to believe. I wanted to feel safe in his company, as I had at the ice-cream parlor and the tobacconist's. However, we were upstairs at Madame Mustache's, behind a closed door with April likely listening through the keyhole.

Wyatt wasn't a man for grinning just to set folks at ease, but it occurred to me that he also seemed awfully comfortable in this whorehouse. There. I'd admitted it: whorehouse, brothel, cathouse. Not quite a crib where a single woman might service dozens of cash-strapped miners a night, but in that spectrum. I'd crossed the threshold and become another person, a soiled dove, or so I thought.

If I was now another person, who did that make Wyatt? No longer a friend, but a customer? After opening myself up to Johnny and being gambled away to Curly Bill, I felt raw and exposed. Even kindness and concern inspired suspicions. My beauty seemed more a currency than a quality. I doubted everyone, even the trustworthy. Most of all, I doubted myself. My instincts stunk.

I was in no mood to be teased about my predicament. It vexed me that Wyatt had found me in this pastel boudoir. With every breath, my breasts pushed nearly to my throat thanks to this ridiculous corset. It was shame enough without seeing myself through Wyatt's steady gaze.

I felt the pressure of tears forming behind my eyes when Wyatt said, "I am not going to let you sell yourself into flesh slavery, either. You are a smart girl, but you don't know where you're heading. I do. You are not going to become one of Madame Mustache's whiskers on my watch."

"Who gave you that power?" Still suspicious, I rose from the chair.

"Settle down." He acted as if he were calming a high-strung mare.

"I detest it when people say 'settle down.' When does that work? It aggravates me more. It makes me want to settle up and tell them off." If my agitation continued, I was never going to make money in this profession, which may have been Wyatt's point. Subservient I wasn't (and never would be). Tell me to go right and I'll go left.

"I'm not going to let this happen to you. It's a long and winding road that only leads down. I expect nothing in return. But let's pause for a minute and consider ourselves as two ordinary people—"

"—in a bedroom at Madame Mustache's."

"Let's consider ourselves two people talking to each other, two people who might, just might, have a future together that doesn't involve a woman with a lip tickler taking a percentage."

"All right," I conceded, and settled back in the chair, sitting on my hands so they wouldn't betray me. "I'm listening."

"It's about time." He smiled again. Two smiles from Wyatt in one day: it may have been a record. I began, just slightly, to unwind in Wyatt's company. At the very least, he beat Old Man Clanton or whatever gentleman with silver and an itch that might have awaited me in that room. Still, I wasn't going to make it easy on Wyatt, lying there on the bed wrapped in his infernal confidence with his polished boots and his bright white, newly pressed shirt and his long gambler's fingers tucked into his belt. I didn't know who was the cat and who was the canary right then.

"I have a few things I want to get off my chest," he said. I scooched up in the chair just a little. "I've been married once by a justice of the peace. It was in Lamar, Missouri. Her name was Willa Sutherland. I was just twenty-two, a few years older than you are now, and had made my first stake in a railroad-grading contract—twenty-five hundred dollars. I was feeling pretty manly and old with my pocket bulging. I went to visit my grandparents in Monmouth and catch up with my folks who'd returned from California. I thought I was ready to settle down, and Willa was the one to catch me. She was only sixteen; her brothers weren't convinced that I was good enough for their sister, but both my parents and hers thought we made a good match."

I had no idea where this story led, but I kept silent for a change. There was something easily companionable about the moment; it echoed our time in Kitty's kitchen months before, when I was baking and he was drinking coffee. Still, I never lost track of the tawdry surroundings and the big bed and its purpose.

"Willa was a good girl with a big laugh; I laughed a lot more then." Just the mention of other women irked me, after Johnny's indiscretion. I struggled to quiet my jealousy and attend Wyatt's words. "She was used to being around boys, surrounded by brothers like she was. She looked up to me, but not too much. She was always in motion, singing. We'd hardly moved in together after our wedding before she began to eat me out of house and home. She was pregnant. She cooked corn bread day and night—couldn't get enough of it, loved the crunchy bits. And she could shoot. Could aim with her left eye and knock a squirrel off a tree at fifty yards. I liked Willa a little wild, and I wasn't one to button her up like her mother and brothers and tell her to act like a lady. Besides, you can't be more like a lady than having a baby."

"Why aren't you still married?"

"It all went south. She got the typhus and went into labor early. The baby was stillborn. We just carved out one stone for the pair. Her brothers blamed me."

"Why?"

"Who knows? I didn't give her typhus, but I got their baby sister pregnant. We were all just so damn torn up about it, so full of love and sadness and anger. We had one big brawl; I guess I figured I deserved getting my ass whipped. But it didn't change how things were or how I felt. I didn't want to be in Lamar anymore, and Lamar didn't want me. I just saddled up and went a little crazy and quiet and rash, shot buffalo because ou can't think of anything else while your rifle's lined up with the herd. I had my life plowed out before me in neat rows with Willa, but it wasn't meant to be."

"I'm so sorry." I fumbled for words, then reached out and took his hand. He laced his rough fingers with mine. It felt right.

"Not as sorry as I am."

"I had no idea."

"No one does except Doc and my brothers."

"But why are you telling me all this?"

"Isn't it clear, Josie?" He patted the side of the bed. I confess it wasn't quite as clear as he thought it was, but I rose and kicked off my slippers. He slid over. "What does your family call you?"

"Sadie, short for Sarah, my middle name." I was confused and curious about what this had to do with sharing a blanket.

"All right then, Sadie." He patted the bed again. "I warmed up a spot for you."

I crawled atop the coverlet wondering whether I should lead with my lips. Wyatt clued me in, patting his shoulder. I rested my head on his rocky bones, trying to find a comfortable spot. I did not know yet where this was leading. I felt off balance even though we were lying down. Other than giving me a squeeze to pull me closer, he didn't touch me with his hands. It was unclear what we were doing there, but I sensed Wyatt had more to say and that it was difficult for him. He was searching for the right words. And for once I got wise, shut my mouth, and let someone else set the pace.

Staring up at the ceiling, Wyatt inhaled deeply and said, "I guess I'd better explain Mattie, too, as long as I'm carrying on like a woman. That's harder to justify. We don't have papers between us, but she's been with me since Kansas. Mattie tried to coax me out of my misery in Dodge City. She was just there, sitting beside me in the saloon when I gambled, getting me coffee, giving me silence. She didn't seem to expect anything. And that's just what I gave her. For a time, that was enough. She wanted shelter, she wanted company, and she wanted out of the game. She wanted family, too, and she got real sisterly with Allie, Virgil's wife. When it was time for me to leave, I didn't have to ask and Mattie didn't have to answer. She came, too. She packed her bag and climbed up beside me on the wagon. No ceremony, no ring."

I understood the "no ceremony" part. But I didn't interrupt, I just listened, feeling Wyatt's heart beating, hardly noticing where he began and I ended, even with all those yards of apricot silk skirt creasing between us.

"Mattie climbed into my life like a stranger climbing into a wagon. We were two people sharing a seat looking forward, facing the same dangers: Indians, outlaws, thirst. There was nothing I could do to shake her devotion, then the guilt that I couldn't live up to it."

Wyatt stopped, and I realized that I had not only entered an unfamiliar room for the first time, but into an unexpected level of intimacy with this man. He had a true and troubled heart that he was opening up to me. And his confidence drew me closer to him emotionally, even as our physical positions remained unchanged and unclouded by passion. That night sowed the seeds of a loyalty that would last decades.

"I didn't love Mattie, but I thought that was all right because after Willa I couldn't love again. It wasn't as if I'd rolled over one morning and discovered I'd fallen out of love with Mattie like a child falls out of bed. I never loved her. I never claimed otherwise. I knew the real thing.I just didn't think I could love again. But I was wrong."

"Why is that?"

"Because, Sadie, I love you."

Wyatt took my chin in his right hand and raised my face so that we were looking eye to eye—something we were never able to do while standing because he was so tall and I so short. His feelings were real and as solid as his biceps. For the first time since I'd stepped off the stage last October, I felt truly safe and truly aware of the dangers I'd brought on myself, entering unknown territory without the protection of kin. That was when I began to cry, not even knowing that the tears poured down my cheeks until Wyatt wiped them away with his handkerchief. I let myself go and admitted the extent of my terror. I'd been shouldering such a pile of fears and hurts: Johnny's betrayal and Bill's sexual taunt. Here was a man who saw me at my lowest point and opened his arms to me. He let me sob. He didn't shame me. My emotion was true and so was his. I offered a safe place for him to speak his heart, and in exchange, he would protect mine.

"If this is going to work, I have one rule," he said.

"What's that, lawman?"

"You have to be faithful to me."

"Does that go both ways?"

"It wouldn't be fair otherwise."

"Let's just have one rule then: I'll be true to you, and you'll be true to me."

"I can live and love with that."

When Wyatt finished talking, he kissed me tenderly on the lips in a way that made me want to climb on top of him, hitch up my skirt, and break the tension. I wouldn't have been that younger, foolish me if I hadn't bobbled the moment and asked, "Should I strip now?"

"No, Sadie. You'll know when I'm ready. I'll take my boots off first."

CHAPTER 18

Wyatt carried my bags upstairs at the San Jose Boardinghouse: the secondhand trunk and worn-bald carpetbag, a string of bright hat boxes, and a carton of odds and ends—theater tickets and playbills, framed photographs, a rock that meant something to me at the time. The rent I charged Johnny for the house we built on his Safford Street lot—and Wyatt collected for me—pretty much covered it. I didn't have the heart to throw

Albert out on the street, but I wasn't ever going to enter that bedroom again.

The San Jose, unlike Madame Mustache's bawdy house, was legitimate. It housed mining engineers and lawyers and politicians, some sticking their toes in the water to see what all the boomtown fuss was about. Others stayed for months, their suits improving with their fortunes—a lucky strike, a lucky hand, a clever stratagem in real estate or dry goods. House rules banned Wyatt from remaining upstairs: men were forbidden in a lady's room at the San Jose Boardinghouse. The walls were thin enough that it wasn't a rule that required policing. I could already hear the rapid gunshots of my neighbor's sneeze; perhaps he had a dust allergy, so very unfortunate in Tombstone.

"We'll work this out, Sadie." When Wyatt saw my face as he replaced his hat in preparation to leave, he said, "I'm only asking you to be a little patient. I love you and only you. *Forever.*"

I understood that he was as good as his word. But I could not get myself to feel the elation that I expected right then. I was in love, damn it. I had tasted the cheap stuff and now I knew the real thing. I loved Wyatt. His every action demonstrated that he shared my affection. Apparently sensing my uneasiness, he pulled a card from his vest pocket and handed it to me, suggesting I call in at the Fly's Photography Gallery and introduce myself to Mollie if I needed company. Then he was gone, without even a kiss (out of respect for the house rules).

Once the door shut behind Wyatt, I felt abandoned in this little box. I crumpled the card without looking at it. I couldn't see my way forward. I rose and examined the corner room, which took hardly a minute, it was so plain and small, like a cell, really. And there I was, my hair damp, my eyes drooping, staring back at myself from the plain oval mirror above the stoneware water jug and basin. I wasn't sure how I felt about this girl. No, this woman: because that's what I was after my time with John H. Behan. I had to take responsibility for the consequences of my actions.

Sitting on the foot of the bed, I picked at a crack in my nail with my thumb. To stop myself from ruining my manicure, I placed my hands on either side of my thighs. Beneath my fingertips, the mattress was of recent vintage, like everything in Tombstone. It was as new as a fresh scab.

Outside the south-facing window overlooking City Market, the deluge continued, cleaning the gutters and washing away the ash, creating ragged rivulets on Fremont Street below. I felt the desperate pang of isolation rumble like hunger in my belly, the kind I could try and fail to stuff with a sweet bun or a sandwich. For most of my life I'd shared a room with Hennie, then slept on a cot in the Joneses' front room and divided my first double bed with Johnny. Now we had "split the blanket," as the locals said, parted ways. I was learning that Wyatt's domestic arrangements were complicated, and I was another complication.

I considered Mattie, sitting in a room somewhere within a mile from here, with that disappointed face of soap she wore. I was aware that Wyatt's devotion to me came with a price—Mattie's heart, and her security—even if he deserved joy, too. I'd created another enemy in Tombstone without much effort. Wherever you turned, people were taking sides. By embracing Wyatt, I rejected Johnny, who still sniffed around begging forgiveness. He wanted me back. The feeling was not mutual. I discovered that in such a small, polarized society, taking sides meant you were actively rejecting others, animating opposition. Tombstone was evolving into a town where there was no neutral ground.

To shoo away the new-room blues, I willed myself up off the bed and onto my feet. I had no patience for being stuck. Only later would Wyatt teach me that sometimes sitting still and gathering strength is the best action to take. But this was way before I learned that lesson. I unfastened my trunk and filled the hardwood chest with its dovetailed drawers, rolling my stockings the way Mama had taught me, hiding the most intimate undergarments at the back. Then I changed my mind, placing the satin and the lace up front. Draping a red paisley scarf across the bureau top, I laid out my powder and rouge, my silver hairbrush and comb and hand mirror, my tortoise-shell hairpins. I placed the tin-framed photo of Albert and smiled at his company. It wasn't the wedding photo of Johnny and me by C. S. Fly for which I'd hoped, but he wasn't the man for me, I assured myself. And I'd come out of the situation with a son, or at least a younger brother.

Somehow I'd become a woman with a past in ten short months, although that seemed like a lifetime to me right then. I unclasped my carpetbag and removed Papa's folded letter. I approached it slowly, unfolding the rough stationery, reading my father's handwriting, labored and sincere. "My Dearest Sadie." Just those words pulled me up. I was Sadie in his eyes and Wyatt's, my true self, the big-hearted girl I could be, given half a chance, the one capable of taking and giving back. I read through the letter, which I rarely did because it opened such a well of emotion. Saving it retained its power to move:

. . . You must live in the future. You have my blessing for what it is worth. May you find love, and keep love, and have children of your own, but know that there is always and forever love in my heart for you and shelter under my roof . . .

I was living my present, charting my future at the San Jose. If I surrendered to loneliness, I had my father's love and faith to lift me up. And while I'd stumbled hard over Johnny, I had also discovered real love and would keep it. Someday I would have children of my own. And even if this roof was strange and the rain pounded atop it, I lived in the shelter of my father's love and carried his confidence in me even when mine flagged. I was my father's favorite no matter where I was, whether on Perry Street or Fremont.

Holding on to this unbreakable bond as if it were a locket, I glanced at the writing desk overlooking Fifth Street and considered composing a letter to Papa, but only managed to lay out my stationery on the leather blotter. Where would I begin? I had to inform him of my new address, but that would entail explaining the why of it beyond the what, and the sacrifice of his investment. I lacked the strength to describe my current situation with a plucky tone. The words would dissolve into stronger emotions and raw confidences when the ink merged with the paper. Letters with tearstains and ink smears would disturb Papa for days. That wasn't fair to him. I would wait until I could compose with more self-control, when I was more settled. If that was the case, I could elevate my mood by stretching my legs.

Thrusting my melancholy aside, I unfolded Wyatt's card and read in black lettering:

FLY'S PHOTOGRAPHY GALLERY
312 FREMONT STREET
C. S. FLY PROPRIETOR

Trusting in Wyatt, I grabbed my cloak and umbrella and tightened my bootlaces. I descended the stairs. After nodding politely to the gentlemen assembled in the parlor who were discussing the price of silver ore, I entered Fremont Street. No longer on the fringe of Tombstone, I found myself in the humid thick of downtown.

I hurried west toward the recently erected Schieffelin Hall, built by Albert Schieffelin, brother to Tombstone's founder, Ed. In the pelting rain, I distinguished what may have been an actor disappear down the alley toward the stage door. Perhaps he was rushing to a rehearsal of Tom Taylor's melodrama *The Ticket-of-Leave Man*. Was it intentional that the opera house's premiere production was about a rube nearly brought to ruin in the wicked city? The producer clearly was trying to match his art to his audience. I would have been more thrilled by a musical: a production of *H.M.S. Pinafore*, *The Pirates of Penzance*, or *Evangeline, The Belle of Arcadia*.

Ducking out from under the arcades, I cut across Fourth Street. I passed the offices of the *Nugget* to my left and the *Epitaph* across the road to my right, the rival newspapers positioned to face off, even down to the street on which they stood.

Pausing to ensure I wouldn't be knocked over by a horse and rider, I plotted a shortcut down the alley leading to the O.K. Corral from Fremont, which put me squarely before the modest storefront labeled FLY'S PHOTOGRAPHY GALLERY (C. S. FLY, PROP.) on its shabby, two-story facade. Four slender pillars supported the eaves. I ascended the porch, free from the rain and shaking my wet ringlets. I might have turned around and left—I was a mess. However, the rain resumed, achieving the intensity of a monsoon, and meeting strangers seemed the lesser of two evils.

An immediate answer greeted my hesitant knock. The wooden door creaked open. A bell tinkled. I found myself staring eye to eye at a woman with thick black hair pulled into a bun. She had a broad, flat nose and a rounded chin that rose up to meet it, like a crescent moon, and curious eyes that took me in even before she reached out a hand to grab my arm, ending all hesitancy that might have remained.

"Please tell me you are Josephine," she said as she reeled me into the studio, which smelled of chemicals and mint.

"How do you know my name?"

"Who else would you be but Wyatt's woman? If someone has a reputation for being the greatest beauty in Tombstone, I have an obligation as a photographer to see her, even if she has not seen me. Call it professional curiosity."

"I'm flattered." And flummoxed, too, although I didn't say so aloud.

Mollie had the ability to read even the densest and most complicated facial expressions like simple prose. Seeing my confusion, she laughed, and said, "I am Mollie Fly, proprietress. Buck—that's C. S.—is off in a tent somewhere shooting Apaches with his camera and tempting scorpions with his skinny ankles." She paused to laugh at her own image. "The building says 'Fly's Photography Gallery,' but I'm as much an owner as that gadfly Camillus Sydney. We're both camera-crazy, even if polite society hasn't accepted female photographers. It's easier to give the man credit where it's not due. Here, what kind of hostess am I? Let me take your wet things." She carelessly tossed them on a cast-iron hook without stopping when they puddled on the floor.

Mollie looked to be about Wyatt's age, give or take a year, although her features weren't as worn by sun and sorrow. Short, bristly brows sheltered sharp, deep-set eyes. The oddity of her visage was how long the canvas of her face was, and how her petite features clustered together in the middle, between a broad forehead and heavy jawline. She was a plain woman if beauty was judged from the outside, but she was far more beautiful than I was if judged the other way around. She would have protested she wasn't photogenic, but that was likely because she preferred composing the image from behind the camera rather than posing in front of it. And she preferred shadows to sun in general, security to exposure outside the walls of her beloved studio.

"How about I pour you some mint tea and we get acquainted." She rolled down the sleeves of her white blouse and tucked in the shirttails more neatly around her waist. She walked with purpose, passing the imposing mahogany-and-brass box camera labeled Scovill Manufacturing Company, NY. The contraption dominated the room atop a tripod, its open black bellows forming an impressive proboscis. She led me to a pair of green-velvet parlor chairs—one large, one little—arranged side by side like a married couple. Mollie motioned me to the smaller one while taking a tall wooden stool herself. She winked and said, "I usually need the stool so I can see eye to eye with my customers, but that's not necessary here. It's nice to see that you're human-size, with all these six-footers galumphing around. You are a darling, and I bet you're photogenic."

"I'm not," I said, though the fact was I'd never had my picture taken. Johnny and I had intended to visit Fly's as a couple for an engagement photo. It was just more writing on the wall that we'd never made the short walk to 312 Fremont Street.

"No false modesty here, Josephine. I am sure the light loves you as much as Wyatt. Why not embrace our virtues as long as we admit our vices, too? Some folks consider me too forthright, but Buck likes me this way, says it keeps him honest. We ditched propriety in Napa when we wed two years ago. We both love photography. We wanted to create pictures together, along with all the other treats of marriage and adventure. My first husband dismissed my passion for cameras over cooking, and that's why I have a second one."

Mollie poured tea from a big brown pot into an earthenware mug. That explained the minty scent. The taste made my tongue tingle and warmed me from the inside out. While I drank, my hostess continued her story without giving me the time to realize I was no longer lonely. She said, "We crated our equipment and decided Tombstone was booming, and that's where we were bound. We began our studio in a tent. You'd be surprised how many lonely men will pay thirty-five cents for a picture to send back to their families. I had sticky fingers with Buck's carousing money, and we built the studio and the twelve-room boardinghouse." Mollie paused to refresh my tea. "Now I run them both in Buck's absence, and typically, in his presence, too. He's not much for the studio portraits. They bore him to death. But these pictures butter our bread. And I like the job. I've met nearly everyone in town, from sinner to saint. While Buck prefers natural light, I am content to shoot my photographs within these four walls, looking for the innate glow within my subjects. Now that I see you, I want you to pose for me. Josephine, you have a glow. Capturing it would please me to no end."

A rap at an internal door interrupted the offer before I had time to respond. "Come in," said Mollie.

The man was nearly six feet tall and reedy, almost painfully thin, with hair parted on the side and smoothed with scented pomade that was a mix of blond and gray so as to look ashen. His square face with a well-kept English mustache would have been handsome if it weren't for the weariness he carried and his fair skin's ghostly pallor. He wore a double-breasted, dark suit with sleeves that belled out slightly, revealing white cuffs with gold-crested cuff links. In his right hand, he carried a solid chestnut cane with a brass tip. The peculiar knob at the top resembled a monkey's knee, which he used to clear the way to the larger parlor chair, sitting down with the grace of a dancer, folding one long, spindly leg over the other like a grasshopper.

The stranger used the cane tip to knock at the side of the Brown Betty kettle and asked, his voice soft for a man so tall, "Mollie, should you be drinking this swill so early in the day?" He raised his blond, almost transparent eyebrows at me as if we were doing something wicked, which confused me.

"Knock it off, Doc," Mollie said. "Put that cane

away before you hurt yourself. This is Josephine Sarah Marcus. Josephine, may I present John Henry Holliday, my boarder, dentist, and adopted baby brother."

"I have only accepted in anticipation of the windfall inheritance from the family Fly," Doc said with a straight face. He appraised me. He took my hand; his was surprisingly cool. He brought my fingertips to his lips for a dry and polite kiss while he stared into my eyes. I looked back into his, a blue-gray like some predatory bird, and tried to hold his gaze. Even in his weakened state—he suffered from tuberculosis and had come west for relief if not a cure—he had enormous charisma. He smiled at me with a fine set of teeth, an advertisement for his award-winning dentistry.

"Where are you from, Miss Marcus?" he asked, laying his cane to the side and retrieving a clean handkerchief from his jacket pocket.

"San Francisco," I answered. And there was an awkward pause while he waited for me to reveal more.

"Were you born there?"

"No, I was born in New York, but I don't remember it."

"So your parents were from New York?" Doc's smile had disappeared.

"No," I said, made uneasy by his quizzing, and feeling every bit the dunce. "They were from nearby villages in Eastern Europe, but they met in New York."

"What about their parents? Where were they from?"

"My grandparents?" I shrugged. "I never knew them."

"On either side?" He appeared incredulous, although I may have been projecting my unease on this gentile stranger. Shame engulfed me. I could not name my own kin. My mortification grew because I believed that this was some sort of test that I was failing. We were Jews that had leapt off the European continent like rats from a sinking ship, fleeing something that my mother had never repeated to me, something awful enough to justify her tragic passage across the Atlantic. I had the power to lie, to say that we were German Jews from Nob Hill, but it was too late, since I had confessed my parents met in New York.

"Oh, Josephine, Doc's just getting all Southern on you," Mollie said. "He will keep asking about your ancestors to see if you are in some way related. This is as Georgian as red dirt and grits. It's what they do when they meet someone new. Probably so they don't sleep with their own cousins."

"So politely put, Mollie," Doc said, putting his index finger between his stiff collar and his neck. "I'm feeling a bit parched."

"I'll get the decanter, since you seem to lack the power of your own legs," Mollie said. "Since I doubt Josephine has kin in Valdosta or Griffin, Doc, you can desist this line of questioning for now." Mollie hopped off her stool, leaving the two of us alone.

Doc wasted no time. The moment Mollie turned her back, the dentist leaned over toward my chair, his minty breath all that I could inhale, grabbed my wrist in the vice of his long fingers, and focused those intense eyes on mine. He said in a low and threatening voice: "If you mess with Wyatt, Miss Josephine, you will answer to me. As a dentist, I have the power to rearrange those pearly teeth in your mouth."

The threat registered. His sudden rage frightened me, his vehemence entirely unexpected.

When Mollie returned with the hooch in a cut-glass carafe in one hand and two tumblers in the other, Doc dropped my wrist and captured my hand, cradling it with gentleness as surprising as his anger. "If you are loyal to Wyatt as you should be, I am your friend for life and will defend your safety to the death." He smiled generously, his eyes now jolly and light, then turned his pale face toward Mollie, taking the brown liquor.

"She'll make a pretty picture, don't you think, Mollie dearest?" Doc downed the whiskey.

"You should be a magician the way you make

that booze disappear in one swallow, sir," Mollie said.

"Ah." Doc sighed appreciatively. "The day begins ladies, the day begins."

CHAPTER 19
SEPTEMBER 1881

In the weeks to follow, I became *Ivanhoe*'s Rebecca and *H.M.S. Pinafore*'s Josephine. To portray Shakespeare's Lady Macbeth, Mollie draped me in tartan blankets borrowed and begged from across the camp. During those long, hot September days, I became the photographer's muse and playmate. While the Mexican Marietta Spence and her gnarled mother cleaned the boardinghouse's dozen rooms, Mollie retreated to the studio, and our collaboration started as a way to kill time. During those hours, Camillus had packed a mule with camera equipment and departed for the wild. Wyatt was busy, as tensions between the cowboys and the town's businessmen simmered, and Fly's Photography Gallery was often empty for long stretches between customers who popped in unexpectedly at odd hours. Mollie awarded me a fancy title—artist's model—and fed me and filled me in on all the news that wasn't printed in the *Epitaph* or the *Nugget*. Since countless individuals flowed in and out of the gallery and lodgings, 312 Fremont Street became a clearinghouse for information and gossip.

Mollie's company and the creative stimulation suited me. Despite my stage fright, I relished the attention—and I didn't have to sing a note. Mostly, it was the pair of us, Mollie behind the big box camera fiddling with the plates and lenses, or staging me, adjusting my costume, angling my chin up, my hands down. I began our sessions as stiff and self-conscious as Abraham Lincoln with a migraine. These first photos showed no great aptitude on my part. I recoiled from my homeliness. Such a beauty, as my mother said. My right profile was hideous: my nose too large, my lips stingy, and my close-set eyes dark, expressionless caverns.

"No more profiles," Mollie insisted, no more cardboard poses. We were on a tandem search to create a naturalness that so few of her patrons allowed her to achieve in their thirty-five-cent portraits. "Let there be flaws," Mollie cried, as she worked the bellows and switched from portrait to landscape in the 8 x 10 camera, placing me upright leaning on a pedestal or reclined on a chaise. "Let there be misfires and blemishes, but let's also capture your glow when you're animated, your sensuality in repose."

I didn't know I had sensuality in repose, but it sounded positive, so long as I didn't view myself through my mother's eyes. I discovered that this voluptuousness that Mollie sought to extract from me was not a quality for which I had to strive. In fact, it was the opposite. Pouting my lips, gazing intently, thrusting my bosom: all false and stilted. I had to ease into it, to float and forget. When I became untethered from the ordinary (forgetting that just beyond the wooden door there existed a world of horses and men and conflict), the poses and their imprint on the albumen paper began to emerge with an enchanted realism. The images resembled me, but, through Mollie's gaze, I emerged in purer focus, as a stranger might encounter me in a moment of intimacy. I found that drinking sherry helped.

Mollie rarely invited Doc to attend our sessions. She joked that she couldn't afford his whiskey budget (or his way of alienating paying customers). Still, the classically educated gambler shaped Fly's portrait photography. While studying dentistry in Philadelphia a decade earlier, Holliday had regularly visited the Pennsylvania Academy of Fine Arts when staring down teeth became too much. There he encountered the work of the American realist painter Thomas Eakins. The Academy alum had recently returned to his native Philadelphia from Paris and Spain. Eakins exhibited his first major oil painting drawn from life, *Max Schmitt in a Single Scull*, in 1871. His bold portrait of the athlete on the river (the first ever of the popular sport, according to Doc, who liked to lecture us on the subject) raised conflicting responses among the staid local critics, but not Holliday, who idolized Eakins.

Never one to mince words, particularly on subjects about which he had encyclopedic knowledge, Holliday hectored Mollie and Camillus to create portraits that revealed the human figure realistically. He appealed for photos that were fluid, not brittle, that used the relatively new technology to embrace contemporary life rather than embalm it. Doc argued that even the most ordinary local event was extraordinary compared to the otherwise dull Philadelphia and his native middle Georgia. By extension, he argued that I, as the belle of Tombstone (his words, not mine) would make an ideal subject for these studies. That is, if I could only sit still and silent long enough to listen. He explained, as if there were decades between us and not just a little more than one, that there was an exalted history in art of portraiture of the female form, clothed and not.

Holliday still corresponded with friends in Philadelphia, who wrote that Eakins had begun experimenting with the camera to capture the human form, first as a teaching tool for anatomical studies, and ultimately as art in its own right. Eakins was as likely to use men as women as subjects, Doc said, and women even numbered among his students at the Academy of Fine Arts where he was now a teacher. Doc saw the artistic potential in Mollie's portraiture, never judging her the lesser artist for being female, which endeared him to her. Mollie, the pragmatist, was keener to try "French postcards" than I was in those early days, aware that there was an international market for such images that could address our income problems and possibly underwrite a new level of independence, or at least pay for camera supplies.

However, Mollie had no intention of pushing me in an uncomfortable direction. It was in the cocoon of Mollie's studio where I discovered the serenity of which Doc also spoke, the poker player's composure. I learned to quiet my thoughts so that I could increase my awareness of the world around me, which is something both Doc and Wyatt had learned as hunters and marksmen from an early age. I also gained a new community of friends that accepted me for who I was as I evolved into what I would be. Tombstone was a fluid society, so young that there was no inherited wealth or privilege, no glue to bind individuals to one station or another. People rose as quickly as they fell, and there was an exciting friction to this dynamic, which created fireworks as exhilarating as they were dangerous.

I had believed my big leap was leaving San Francisco's *shtetl* by the sea. That was only the beginning. Mollie encouraged me to discover my own identity, to explore the nooks and crannies that existed in every individual and therefore were simultaneously unique and universal. Although Mollie was plain, she was shrewd and self-confident, completely free of jealousy. She wanted to capture my image in albumen prints as she saw me in motion, or at rest when no one was watching, the way that my personality animated my features and lit them from within, or the moods that overcame me in silence. Mollie envisioned a partnership: she was the gaze, and I was the subject. She would look up and out boldly at the world through her lens, but bow her head if the scrutiny was reversed. We were opposites in that way and complementary.

Mollie focused her Scovill camera on me between paid portraits of mining engineers and shop owners who projected the seriousness of successful businessmen that could easily be confused with constipation. Doc first noticed that I might appear more natural if I lacked a corset that sucked my breath and constricted my waist. He wasn't being impertinent, at least in that—simply contributing to the process as a knowledgeable critic who had an idea in his head of what he thought the effect of these portraits should be. Mollie, who had the ability to take direction from any quarter without offense, found inspiration in a photo of the famed French Jewish actress Sarah Bernhardt. One afternoon,

Mollie ushered me behind a screen, unlaced my stays with a nurse's nimble fingers, and draped a theatrical red-velvet curtain around my bare shoulders. I reentered the main studio like Queen Victoria in royal drapes.

That afternoon, when I leaned on one elbow on a pedestal with my hand cradling my left cheek, I felt how free my body was beneath the heavy fabric. I inhaled deeply and exhaled and let my features rest, not summoning a false smile, but letting thoughts run through my head like water, about Mollie—my new mother-sister—and Wyatt, Doc, and even Johnny. I sensed that I existed only in the moment, a gilded urn in a still life, a camellia, a poker player with three queens hoping to draw a full house.

In the resulting images, Mollie revealed beauty in the strength of my cheekbones, the thick, expressive brows, silky skin on the shiny albumen surface, and the suggestive curve of shoulder. She also captured mystery and moods, rapture, worry, regret, pensiveness, mischievousness, and a self-possession I did not know I had. The photos, seen together, were both solid and shifting. It was the same woman, but within me there were so many different shades and shadows.

Mollie often talked as she worked, stopping only to carefully adjust the lens, the shutter. It would be quiet, and I would be lost in thought, or hungry for an egg, and she would ask some unexpected question like, "Who are you more like: your mother or your father?"

Instantly, my face would shift, and she would capture a picture as I began to speak. "I am my father's daughter," I said.

"But do you resemble him?"

"Do I look like him? Yes, around the chin. I have his nose, his eyes. Although I have my mother's thick dark hair, and he has hardly any."

"But are you more like him than her?"

"I am not nearly so gentle or accepting," I said, and I smiled to consider him—not a portrait grin, but one of mutual unconditional love recalled, his great gift to me. I looked up at the rough, unpainted ceiling, considering what mix I was of father and mother, even of grandparents I'd never known, and never would know, dead aunts and cousins untethered and alive in distant cities. "I would like to tell you that I resemble my father, to say that I am as kind as he is, as hardworking, as free from pretense. But he is mild, and I am not. He is also loyal, which I believe I am. And intimate. It's easy between us, not like Mama and me."

"What can you say?" Mollie asked, and she raised her chin with her index finger so that I would do likewise, and lowered her eyes momentarily to signal to me.

I followed her direction while thinking of my parents, trying to see them clearly but without forcing the insights, to glimpse the truth in the periphery. "I don't know if she is an angry woman or was made angry by experience. Mama stands in judgment always. Nothing is ever good enough, which does not diminish the hardships she's survived." I crossed my hands on the bare, slightly sticky skin of my chest, looking right while turning my face left. My mouth pinched as I continued the thought: "Mama carries around her sorrows and indignities in a burlap sack. To be near her is to try to keep on the still waters of the surface. It is a risk to peek below, to disturb the *dybbuks* clinging to her ribs."

"How has her fear shaped you?" Mollie asked, skillfully changing the glass plates.

"I am not that person," I said. "I want the shallows and the depths, the hunger and the satisfaction that comes from feeding it. She is afraid, and she spreads fear. I want to be fearless and spread life."

CHAPTER 20
SEPTEMBER/OCTOBER 1881

Rosh Hashanah came and went in mid-September. While the more observant traveled to Tucson where there was a rabbi, I ignored the communal rituals and turned, as I often did when I wanted to feel a sense of family, to baking. Because I couldn't use the San Jose's kitchen, I went to see the Flys, passing a sooty group of ragged, ill-humored miners on the street. I made Papa's raisin-studded challah recipe in Mollie's oven. Her Camillus had just returned from Apache territory with a mustache full of dust and a bad case of sunburn. He was treating it with whiskey taken internally.

Mollie and I dipped the fresh-baked bread in honey to commemorate the Jewish New Year. We embraced our newfound friendship and collaboration as among the year's sweetest surprises. Lacking horseradish, we shared a cigar and drank brandy shots to rinse away the smoke's bitterness.

Not all the bitterness I'd tasted would be rinsed away. Johnny's betrayal still hounded me as the liquor burnt my throat.

Johnny's mistreatment had diminished me. I feared that I was a laughingstock in Tombstone. And yet, rationally, I knew that when I broke with Johnny, I'd dodged a bullet. President James A. Garfield, in the more civilized district of the country, had not. The object of assassin Charles Guiteau, the president had taken two shots—in the arm and back—on July 2 at the Capitol's train station. While the president had survived the Battles of Chickamauga and Shiloh, rising to be a major general in the Union army, his peace-time wounds festered and proved fatal. Garfield lingered through the summer but died on September 19.

In reaction, our town not only mourned the Republican's untimely passing while in office, but revisited Abraham Lincoln's assassination, only sixteen years before. That critical event was burnt into the memory of most of my neighbors. No one had forgotten where they were when they got the news, and the deep emotions it aroused. Lincoln's death was my first memory: Papa returning early from the bakery, unexpectedly opening the door, and the unearthly sound of keening outside entering with him. Mama disappeared upstairs, returning dressed in black. We joined the flood in the streets to mourn together as a city and a nation. Men and women wept openly and, although my mother did not, I cried, too, only half knowing why. I felt a genuine sense of loss, that something obscene had transpired, and America had been divided into a before and after marked by Lincoln's assassination.

Then as now, citizens wore black to mark the event. Riders draped crepe—a stiff, crimpled silk—from their saddles. The dressmaker Addie Bourland sold out of her darkest silks by noon. While national events often seemed muffled (a distant sound and fury) compared to the chaotic news of Cochise County reported in the *Epitaph* and the *Nugget*, Garfield's shooting disturbed the boomtown locals. What were free elections if one crazy individual could veto the rule of democracy? And while local lawlessness thrived—drunken gamblers shooting one another over a card game, stage robbers shooting Wells Fargo agents—assassination remained taboo, the province of cowards and savages. If the president could be cut down in a busy train station, no one with a public profile was safe in the heavily armed, deeply polarized aftermath of our least civil war. Women wailed out of sadness and fear: Who would protect them if their husbands and fathers died? How many widows lifted their skirts nightly at the town's bordellos, or bent over endlessly at the dark cribs on the edge of town where miners lined up after their work shifts?

As the town continued to grieve, Yom Kippur arrived on October 3. I fasted, having refused food and water since sundown the night before. I felt penitent for the grief that I'd caused my family, although I had yet to mend the broken bonds with my mother. I was at a loss for how I would accomplish that from afar. I knew that a thousand miles away, she was in synagogue, wearing white, attending the rabbi's drone, the cantor's sweet voice, in perfect harmony with her God, if not with me. Hennie would be at her side, sharing the shame that I wasn't seated with them, dead to my mother with the entire congregation as witness. And yet I was not going to *schul* to make my peace with God, to atone for the rupture between us that I'd caused of my own free and errant will.

In the afternoon heat, hungry and testy and starved for company, I exited my airless room at the San Jose. Lightheaded and lonely, I sought out Dave the tobacconist, who might share my Yom Kippur sorrows. Even on that holiest of days, he kept his shop open. He offered me a lemon drop. I rejected it, referring to my fast. As he saw my knees give way, he found me a short wooden stool. Dipping his handkerchief in water, he wiped my brow and said, "*Gut yuntiff,*" or "Happy holiday," in Yiddish, and "a pair does not a minyan make."

I put my head in my hands and waited for the ceiling to return to the roof and the floor to make itself solid below my feet. Dave held the cool handkerchief to my neck. Behind me, the door to Johnny's office opened. The damp handkerchief moved on my nape and was no longer still, but stroking gently. I put my trembling hand to the back of my neck, and it was grasped by a familiar hand. My stomach lurched, and I could not distinguish the inspiration: hunger, queasiness, or lust.

With an effort I raised my heavy head. It had begun to throb. (Unlike Mama, I'd never had a talent for fasting. This was not the first time someone had to catch me with a chair.) I hardly lifted my eyes when they were caught in Johnny's intense and welcoming gaze. They seemed to say that he knew I'd return—that I couldn't stay away. He knelt at my side, sitting on his heels, his hand moving down my back. I felt the wet stripe form.

Johnny flashed his shiny teeth, perhaps mistaking my pale face for penitence, my liquid eyes for lovesickness. That was just about when the nausea that had been subsiding rose again. I heaved but had nothing but mucus in my empty stomach, and such bile that went along with it, but the mess was enough to soil the knees of his trousers.

"Jesus, Josie, what kind of greeting is that?" he asked, standing up so that he towered above me.

"None at all," I said.

"Isn't it time you stop fooling around and come back home?"

"I can't come home, because you're still living there. I think you owe me rent," I said, miserable and angry at putting myself in Johnny's path. Only then did I question my own motives, visiting Dave's shop knowing that Johnny's office lay just beyond. My actions were suspect. He still stirred me, after all that had happened. My heart rose to my throat when I saw him after time spent apart, and scrambled my words. Just seeing those familiar laugh lines at the corner of his eyes made me melt, even if that attraction paled to what I felt for Wyatt. I knew who Johnny Behan was as a man. Standing beside his only son, I'd seen him clearly with Mrs. Dunbar on the bed we'd bought together, and here I was again. I would not blame God on Yom Kippur for making me face my mischief. I'd walked over in the heat of the day, a damsel one fainting spell away from broken promises. If I hadn't already been nauseous, this realization would have made me sick to my stomach.

"Dave," I said to the tobacconist, "I'll take that lemon drop now."

"Take two," he said.

I rode beside Wyatt for the first time bound for a night of camping in the Dragoon Mountains. I had rarely felt such peace before that moment, and it was a feeling that I would return to again and again with Wyatt. It was October 7, and he'd promised me a full moon and clear skies, beans and beef jerky. It was not the Grand Hotel, and I rejoiced in that. We would not travel far— Apaches had hopped the San Carlos Reservation, and they were at large—but we were safe within a few hours' ride of Tombstone.

Wyatt set an easy gait. My horse followed suit. My anticipation of our night alone under the stars, lying rough, focused and clarified my senses: we scared a doe from her hiding place, sent jackrabbits scurrying for cover, and watched hawks swirl in liberated arcs above us riding the air drafts. The sky was a melting watercolor of lavenders and violets and a streak of peony pink that I would have called my favorite color except that it could not be captured; it changed from moment to moment, defining itself against the darker sky, and then disappearing as we neared camp.

I shed my impulse to control the situation, to question our destination, to wonder about my looks and if they would suit. I trusted in Wyatt and the quiet that wrapped us together rather than separating us. I trusted my hold on my mare and her easy trot, my heels digging into the stirrups. My fears dissipated. I drew my strength from her rather than trying to dominate the animal. If I absorbed her ease, then she would be easy with me. As it was with the horse, so the man.

The quiet company of the ride out was something I learned to love—the sharing of the view, Wyatt's intimate knowledge of the wilderness and his reading of its signposts that meant nothing to me. But that day in October was different. It was twilight, and the full moon had begun to rise over the Durango Mountains. The air was fresh in the way it is in early autumn, welcome after a hot summer and slaking a thirst for coolness that had built up over months. I felt my love and anticipation building deep inside of me and ignored my impulse to verbalize it, to deflate it, leaving it coiled and ready.

When we arrived in the foothills, we didn't climb far, finding a ready-made curve against a rock wall. A fire-licked circle of stones already marked the protected spot facing north, away from Tombstone, toward the entirety of the Americas. Wyatt dismounted while his horse was still in motion, taking the leather reins over its head and tying them to a bush.

Meanwhile, I dug my ankles into the mare. She stopped in time for Wyatt to turn to me, taking the reins and throwing them over the horse's head. She stood at attention as he reached up, his large hands encircling my waist. He hoisted me off the horse, but when we looked eye to eye, he stopped. With his arms wrapped tightly around me and my feet still weightless above the packed earth, he leaned in for a kiss, his chapped lips rough but their touch gentle. His contact communicated what we were beginning that night even before our horses were watered and fed. That part of me that was coiled inside met his kiss as an equal in love and passion, but I held back the full weight of my desire. This was only the beginning, the raising of the curtain, the taste of what was to come. When he set me down on the rough, packed earth, I floated upward, wanting more but trying to wrap myself around the patience he was teaching me.

Wyatt unstrapped a camp chair from his saddle-bag, unfolded it a few feet from the fire ring, and motioned to me to sit down, holding my hand to steady me. He retrieved a pile of kindling hidden beneath the bush and set it alight at my feet. Before he continued the business of making camp, he poured me a thimbleful of brandy that he carried but did not indulge in himself. He left the flask at my side. While I appreciated the light changing and the rising sound of crickets and toads, soprano and bass, he laid out the buffalo-skin rug, the bedrolls and blankets, together in the elbow of the rock. I knew we would end up there, and I walked a tightrope of desire and restraint, knowing that on any spectrum I was closer to the former than the latter.

When Wyatt finished his preparations, he walked the perimeter. Then he cooked beans, which we consumed with the clatter of tin spoons on similar bowls. We ate, and it was simply eating, sustenance. With him at my feet, we watched the moonrise, holding hands until I got familiar with every callous and scar. The sky darkened around us, and the light's alteration first brought the bushes closer and then made them disappear into the shadows. All that existed was the tight circle around us with the campfire at its center, and then above us the large pale moon at its fullest in the cloudless sky. It was one of those all-seeing moons that looked down upon us, blessing our unity, and saw, too, all who were not hidden under roofs, or buried underground, Apaches and cowboys alike, sparrows and snakes. It did not see Mama, but it saw me.

I could feel myself unfold in the cool, bright light, letting go of all the lies of my existence, the promises to false men, the restraints of daughter-hood, and the expectations of becoming a wife. In my thoughts, I called out to a God who saw everything from on high but refused narrow judgments, a world parsed in Ten Command-ments and subdivided in countless customary restrictions between men and women, both the foolish Adams and Eves and the wise.

Sitting beside Wyatt, I felt my legs fall loosely from my hips and my sex rise up, releasing as if ready to accept all of the outdoors—the moon and stars, the flesh and bone. I began to grope my hair for the pins to release the curls from their bondage, and Wyatt kneeled beside me and finished the job until my hair was as wild as a mane and fell darkly down my back to where it now arched.

Wyatt took my right hand in his and eased me up off the stool. He was so big and powerful this close that what I'd begun now frightened me: those broad shoulders, the muscular arms, the narrow hips above forceful legs. And yet I let that go, too—my natural fear, my worries, my second guessing, for I felt my pelvis press against his thigh, and his fullness against my bosom. His knowing hands turned me around and herded me, as ablaze as the moon above, toward the buffalo rug and the layers of bedding he'd spread there.

He holstered his Colt .45 revolvers and set the pair by the head where folded Indian blankets served as pillows.

Wyatt removed his boots. We smiled at each other. And then, slowly, we unbuttoned, unlaced, unwrapped, wriggled out of, and set aside the clothes that were between us. All the cotton and the wool, the silk and the leather, the ruffles and the rough, fell into one pile. Standing on the soft bedclothes, I approached him with my hands behind my head, following my nipples as they approached the warmth of his skin, feeling the heat before we even touched.

Leaving his hands at his sides, Wyatt waited until I brushed against him. I heard his deep intake of breath. He reached around me, the roughness of his palms pleasurably scratching my sides, grazing my hips, and cupping my bottom. He bent his knees, raising me up, my arms ringing his neck, as he pierced me. There was such a groan between us that the unsettled horses chittered nervously at their stand.

CHAPTER 21
OCTOBER 1881

Apaches raided outlying areas, frightening prospectors on remote claims. Curly Bill recovered enough from his May injuries to pilfer cattle. The tensions between the Earps and the Clantons and the rest of the cowboys simmered. But on those nights when Wyatt booked a room at the Cosmopolitan Hotel, our trysts began late in the coolness of the night and lasted until deep into the morning, when Morgan would bang on the door to raise Wyatt for another day at the Oriental, and give me a wink. It was as if he'd known from the moment he handed me off the stage that this is where I'd arrive, as if he knew the future. But, if he'd really had foresight, he would have insisted Wyatt pack up and get out of Tombstone while the getting was good, and followed him down the road.

During that time, I might have known that Wyatt returned home in the mornings to get clean clothes (and dirty looks) from Mattie. But we didn't dwell on that. The situation was temporary. All situations were temporary. At lunchtime, Virgil's wife, Allie, cooked for all the brothers and their womenfolk. They sat down together in a little house on Fremont Street only a few blocks west of Fly's Photography Gallery. Allie could, and would, beg to differ, but I knew where Wyatt stood with Mattie, which was his business, not that of Virgil's wife. I understood what Wyatt and I did together was making love, the hard stuff, not cheap beer.

After those long nights, I'd stroll to the San Jose nearby in a happy haze and rest. Then I'd typically amble over to socialize with Mollie and hear the daily news and gossip, and knock heads with Doc if he was in town. The week leading up to the gunfight, he'd been in Tucson playing faro at the Augustin Feast and Fair when Morgan tapped him on the shoulder and requested Holliday's company back in Tombstone. I learned this from Doc's girlfriend, Mary Katherine Horony. She sat in the green-velvet lady chair at Fly's Photography Gallery a little after noon on October 26 wearing a fringed, multicolored kimono over her camisole and petticoat. Still, little was left to the imagination: she was a big-boned, high-breasted woman, a little past thirty, with a large oval face as flat as a platter, with a domed forehead. Although her nickname was "Big Nose Kate," her nose was not large but long, the bridge beginning high on her forehead and ending in a small curved beak at the tip.

Kate was nosy, radiating the kind of curiosity that could get you killed if you hung around the wrong places with secretive people. Born in Pest, Hungary, a doctor's daughter, she'd been orphaned in Iowa, and then stowed away on a riverboat to Saint Louis. Kate despised rural life. Her strong features had nothing on her temperament. After a legendary bender and brawl the previous July, Kate had—either coerced by Johnny Behan or fueled by drunken rage—signed an affidavit drawn up by the sheriff that declared Holliday a coconspirator in the failed Benson stagecoach robbery that killed Budd Philpot. Kate recanted when she sobered up the next day, but the damage was done. Johnny arrested Holliday.

When Johnny liberated Doc for lack of corroboration, Holliday gave Kate money and sent her packing back to Globe, Arizona. She didn't want to return to the boardinghouse she ran there, practicing the bedroom arts far from Doc's gaze. And yet Kate was the only woman in Doc's life, as he often told me, for good or ill. She alone could soothe his consumptive coughing fits and get him breathing right again, but it had been four months since Kate had hung her corset at Fly's.

Kate and I bonded over our shared dislike of Johnny, whom she didn't find sexually attractive. She sat drinking coffee in that fuzzy hungover way that gripped a town where many folks retired drunk as the sun rose. Kate was thumbing through Mollie's photographs appreciatively, returning again and again to one of me draped in red curtains with just a little more shoulder visible than the other pictures, and a faraway look in my eyes—as if I could see the future, and it was a pleasure.

"Too much clothes," Kate said, shaking her head. "I appreciate the composition, but I've seen nuns wearing less."

"Where was that?" asked Mollie. "In Buda or Pest?"

"Don't tease," Kate said. "I'm trying to talk sense. There's money in these pictures. Haven't you ever heard of French postcards? I know you have, Mollie. You're too shrewd by half. Send them to New York or, better yet, London or Paris, and you will make money without any man drooling on your flesh, unless you prefer their slobber."

"I prefer spit," I said, trying to sound more jaded than I was to impress Kate.

"Since when, baby girl?" Mollie stared at me until I looked away.

"At least she's no longer a virgin," Kate said. It shocked me to hear my business discussed so openly, and only made me aware that it had always been a topic of conversation in rooms I didn't occupy. "I bet cash money that first night at the Grand Hotel. I lost big."

"Can we remove the focus from between my legs?" I sat across the studio on the chaise, wrapped in a freshly laundered Mexican shawl the color of old blood, and a peasant skirt borrowed from Marietta Spence. Mollie intended to create a portrait of me as a senorita.

"You put the conversation there," said Kate.

"Let Josephine focus, Kate, or I'll toss you out of here," Mollie said, but with a cushion to her tone that made it clear she never would. Mollie had borrowed massive silver earrings for the shoot, and the heavy jewelry tugged my earlobes. I had to keep my neck straight and the crown of my head upright to maintain balance. Behind me, Marietta Spence sat sideways on a chair, scraping a comb across my scalp to create a straight center part. The house cleaner's fingertips smelled of corn as she pulled my oil-slicked hair into a tight braid at the base of my neck. She was gentler than Mama when plaiting my hair, and Marietta's attentions relaxed me.

"Josephine, I do not know how you didn't see through Smiley," Kate said, using one of her many nicknames for Johnny. "I've hosted Be-Handy in Globe often enough. He's quite the little athlete. He considers himself a Southern gentleman, but I don't think what he does with a walking stick is quite what his beloved grandmother had in mind."

"Spare the child," said Mollie. "I don't see the point."

Kate was never one to apply the brakes: "And all those yellow roses? When you arrived on the stagecoach, a beauty queen expecting her bouquet—well, he took them from Delia's room at Madame Mustache's when she was done with them. If Delia never saw another rose, it wouldn't be too soon. And that goes for all the flowers of the field: she can get hives just looking at a daisy. She had a soft spot for Johnny, too. Delia just doesn't rely on him for rent money."

While I no longer loved Johnny, Kate's comments still stabbed like a dental probe into an abscess. Did knowing more about Johnny make him easier to hate, or did it just make me more mortified for being such a foolish tenderfoot? Bile rose and burnt my throat. Kate laughed generously and deeply, and said, "We have all been fools for love, Josephine. I don't mean to pillory you, but to invite you to join our sorry sisterhood. None of us is safe. Doc is my second dentist. And, Lord love the man, I'm the only woman for him. Mollie exchanged her first husband for Camillus. How we pick ourselves up and grab the reins defines us, and I consider myself pretty well defined. You've dumped that scum-sucking, two-timing creep, but still, I would remind you that he has his finer qualities. He's a charming storyteller who could talk Abraham Lincoln out of his beard, and persuade him to purchase slaves. Even I, who betrayed Doc at Behan's hands, cannot blame Smiley for seizing the opportunity I gave him. I was drunk. He was canny. He's neither Curly Bill nor Johnny Ringo, but a small, dapper man driven by self-interest and that lizard in his pants."

"How is that supposed to make Josephine feel better, Kate?" Mollie approached her camera, preparing to begin the shoot.

"I didn't realize that was my job, Mollie. I'll try to improve next time." Kate rested her Moroccan slippers on the coffee table. "But Josephine does take a pretty photograph. These haven't quite captured her beauty yet, though. Still, too much clothes."

Marietta smoothed the hair on either side of my part and came around to wrap the *rebozo*, or shawl, correctly across my chest, giving the free end a twist over my right shoulder. I placed my hands in my lap, the left cupping the right. As directed, I looked straight into the lens, balancing the earrings and clearing my thoughts. I pushed aside Johnny and men and false roses, considering only the mesa, the open spaces, the tight white sky, and the woven shawl made by the *abuelita*, the dear grandmother, I never had. I breathed deeply, relaxing my lips, my chin, and my brow. I focused my gaze on the camera as if it were a friend I considered an equal, looking beyond the lens into the trust I felt for Mollie.

The door flew open and I flinched. A Winchester rifle appeared, followed by Ike Clanton. His skin had a sickly, sweaty glow. He was hatless and disheveled, his trousers wrinkled, his coat collar askew, as if he'd been up all night. He reeked of perspiration and alcohol. Waving his rifle, he asked, "Where is that sonofabitch?"

"I'm looking at him," Kate said.

"Don't play with me, woman."

"I wouldn't if you paid me, Ike. Which sonofabitch is that?" Kate asked, tossing the pictures to the table without rising from her plush chair.

"Doc," he said, yelling over the din of horses clopping outside on their way to the O.K. Corral. He continued to yell once they'd passed. "That damned sonofabitch has got to fight."

"I haven't seen that damn sonofabitch," said Kate. "But when I do, I'll tell the cocksucker you're looking for him."

"You do that." Ike retreated the way he'd come, banging his rifle into the side of the studio door that opened on the empty lot with a view of the rear of the O.K. Corral. Once he disappeared into the clamor of hooves bound for the stable, Kate said, "Ever since that Mexican posse ambushed Old Man Clanton last month in Guadalupe Canyon, Ike has been out of control. He's a headless chicken. The Mexicans butchered Papa like the tough old steer he was for sneaking Mexican cattle across the border." Kate stood up quickly, pausing to hold her head after an attack of vertigo. "Better tell Doc that he's going to have company later."

Kate disappeared behind the door that connected to the boardinghouse to wake up Doc. Twenty long minutes later, Doc entered the studio, dressed in a tailored black suit over a fresh peach-colored shirt. His ash blond hair was slicked back, his mustache combed, his cheeks pink from shaving. Mollie offered him coffee. Doc requested brandy. She filled a tumbler, which he inhaled, his nickel-plated pistol visible in his waistband. He pulled on his gray greatcoat and was headed for the studio door when Kate returned from the oppo-site direction wearing a snug blue dress. "My apologies, Kate, I will be unable to take you to breakfast. You'll have to eat alone," he said as he opened the external exit, inviting a great yawn of cold air.

Mollie rushed to shut the door to keep out the dirt and then turned to face the room. Kate raised Doc's glass, motioning to Mollie for a refill. "I hate waking Doc up," she said. "I'd rather stick my head in a lion's mouth. The breath would likely be sweeter." She downed the brandy. "When I told him he had a rifle-carrying visitor, Doc said, 'If God will let me live to get my clothes on, he shall see me.' He is not one to be rushed. And if you ever seek a male model, look no further than my man, although he won't have time for it today. It's going to be a hell of an afternoon, and your Earps are going to feel Ike's wrath, too."

"Can I have a drop of medicinal brandy, too?" I asked.

"What ails you?" asked Kate. "You're not going to grab a pistol, too, are you?"

"I fear for Wyatt."

"I have more reason for concern than you do. Doc's already dying: the question is whether that death will be fast or slow. Wyatt has an almost supernatural power to emerge from danger alive. I'm worried for everyone around them, including us. Sisters, we are the sty in the eye of the storm. Morgan didn't drag Doc back to Tombstone because he was lovesick. From what I can gather, Ike was liquored up and thirsting for a fight, the way men do—standing on each other's pickles and beating their breasts. He said this. He said that. There isn't enough rope to hang all these men. They are fighting to be the top of the dung heap. No one will win."

"And some poor mother will lose," said Marietta in her heavily accented English, to my surprise. I'd forgotten she was still in the room.

CHAPTER 22

The worry became deafening as Camillus "Buck" Fly entered the studio from the street. Ike's barrage of threats that had been carried through the town like the sound of tom-toms had forced the hand of Virgil, who, with three years of active Civil War experience, was at that time both city marshal and deputy US Marshal, and often deputized Morgan and Wyatt. Now all the parties were up and out of bed, some shaved, some not. It was illegal for civilians to wander the streets armed, and Ike had flaunted the law with his Winchester. Fly reported that first Virgil had disarmed and buffaloed Ike, who held his own bleeding head and told the marshal, "If I had seen you a second sooner, I'd have killed you" before being hauled before a judge by the three brothers.

Buck talked to Mollie and me as he cleaned and loaded his own rifle, shaking ammunition from a box and inserting bullets into his empty bandolier. That was nearly as frightening as anything he said. A county clerk at the courthouse had told Buck that Wyatt had finally blown his cool and told Ike off, saying something along the order of, "You cattle-thieving sonofabitch, you've threatened my life enough, and you've got to fight."

Ike volleyed, unfazed by his bloody skull. "Fight is my racket, and all I want is four feet of ground."

Buck, getting the drift of the rising tensions, had hurriedly concluded his errands. While he was heading home, he heard a rumor that Wyatt had left the courthouse, encountered Tom McLaury on the street, and pistol-whipped the brother during an escalating argument. With this new information, Buck detoured at Spangenberg's gunsmith shop to top off his ammunition. There he saw Ike and Tom, both with bandaged heads, weapons shopping. On the way out, he encountered their brothers, Billy and Frank.

Back at the studio, Buck readied his rifle and then prepared his portable camera equipment. Mollie helped him pack the lenses while I drank brandy. She forbade me to leave the studio to walk the streets alone in search of Wyatt, or news of him. She explained if we just remained where we were, most news and gossip would arrive in the safety of those four walls. We received the odd assortment of men and women who stopped by to share information or to learn the latest from Buck. Around about 2:30 p.m. it got oddly quiet. Mollie noted the pause in horse traffic in the alley that led to the O.K. Corral. A mining engineer who had an appointment for a portrait failed to arrive.

Buck stepped out on the porch with his rifle to assess the situation (he was a better shot with his camera), then swiftly retreated behind the door. "I can't explain it, Mollie, but I count five men congregating in the vacant lot. Ike and Billy Clanton, the McLaury Brothers, and Billy Claiborne—and two horses besides. Those boys look jumpy, which I don't like to observe in a man with a gun. When Billy Clanton saw me, he put his hand to his pistol. I'm mystified why they'd pick this godforsaken spit of dirt."

"Doc," Kate said, as she returned through the boardinghouse door, "I think they're lying in wait for Doc."

"Josephine," Mollie said in a high, tense voice, "maybe I should have dispatched you to the San Jose."

"It's too late now." I tried to keep my panic at bay. Wyatt was out there somewhere on hostile streets, nearby but unreachable. I knew he was less vulnerable without me. Still, I wanted to run to him immediately. Armed men, some whom I'd welcomed into my own house, loitered just outside with malicious intent. They were wicked and unrestrained, as I experienced on poker night with Curly Bill. And I had heard them speak ill of Wyatt and all he stood for: the rule of law, a fair fight over an assassin's bullet.

My hands shook as I raised the brandy to my lips. The wind whistled through the cracks in the siding. No horses trotted down the adjacent alley. An uneasy quiet settled among us in the large rectangular room. Buck rechecked his camera equipment. Few things clarified love's potency more than the threat of imminent, violent loss. I wished I'd never encountered Johnny, but then I never would have met Wyatt. How could a thing so bad lead to one so good?

Despite the chill, my palms began to sweat. My

eyes teared up. I couldn't stop myself. The fact that I could not protect the man I loved unhinged me. I had seen him risk his life to preserve Johnny-Behind-the-Deuce, and now, only his brothers and Doc stood with him against a cowboy mob. My tears became wild, uncontrollable, followed by gulps and sniffles. I remembered Delia the day of the near-lynching, sucking at the laudanum bottle, shrinking into the wallpaper, disappearing in plain sight.

I could not recover my composure. I tried to talk myself down, to explain that my outburst did Wyatt no good, nor did it help us, stranded as we were in the studio surrounded by long-simmering hostility soaked in alcohol and vengeance. As my weeping bubbled over and my sobs grew louder, Kate crossed the studio from the entrance, moving fast. Squaring off before me, she looked down and backhanded me across the face with the force of a strong follow-through. It stung. No, it hurt and stunned and shamed. This was not the first time Kate hit somebody. She'd been taught, and had practiced, that maneuver.

My cheek blazed like sunburn. Kate's angry, pale-moon visage eclipsed mine as she got right up close to me and said, "There may be a riot outside, but don't you start one in here. I can't hear what's happening in the yard with your blubbering. You're not a widow yet. Stop, or I'll shoot you myself before you ever become a bride."

Kate's act was uncomfortably intimate—she hadn't just whacked a stranger; she'd hit *me*. My mother had slapped my face, but with the intention, if she was that aware, of exorcising her anger and shaming me—not causing physical pain. Kate acted out of necessity. We were only as safe as our weakest link and, at that moment, that was me. When I looked around the room—at Buck and Mollie—I saw exasperation and impatience on their faces, not sympathy.

A seething anger at Kate burnt through my veins, which prompted adrenaline and chased away the tears and sorrow and despair. Now all I felt was antagonism, but less for Kate than for the outlaws outside acting as judge, jury, and executioner of the man I loved and the brothers who resembled him in a way that made them all larger and more powerful. They were a pack—Kate's man, Doc, included for his devotion to Wyatt and deadly aim—and they were in mortal danger.

Kate cracked open the door, stepping out onto the narrow porch and allowing us all to eavesdrop on the angry discussion between the McLaurys and the Clantons in the vacant lot. "I'll kill Virgil on sight," said one, and "I'll kill the whole lot of them Earps," said another. The wind carried a yell from Fremont Street: "Here they come!"

Kate ducked back inside and closed the gallery door.

"What did you see?" asked Buck.

"Looked like Frank McLaury and Billy Clanton cocked their pistols. Maybe Tom McLaury stepped behind his horse and reached for his rifle."

"You sons of bitches," called a deep male voice that could have been Wyatt's, "you've been looking for a fight and you can have it."

"Throw up your hands," a voice that could have been Virgil's shouted to the cowboys.

I heard two shots so close together they were nearly one. It was so concussive it felt like my eardrums were being smacked. The explosion echoed off the nearby buildings. A horse screamed and a rider said, "Whoa."

A pause of an instant followed, and then gunshots exploded simultaneously, impossible to count, with the added percussion of a shotgun blast. I retreated to the farthest corner from the action where I typically posed, ducking behind the props and the chaise. Someone flung open the gallery's street door and shoved Billy Claiborne inside at a run. Claiborne had gunpowder on his pants leg, but I could see no blood. Johnny tumbled in behind him, flushed and florid, hardly the dapper man I knew.

Johnny saw me across the room. He ran over and snatched a rough kiss, turning me around physically and emotionally. I shoved him away. "Sheriff Behan, go out there with those guns on your hips and stop this slaughter."

"I can no more stop the snow," he said as shots burst outside, "than these bullets flying."

"Coward."

"You'd prefer corpse?"

"Yes," I said, indignant and on fire in my ridiculous senorita costume, the heavy silver earrings straining my lobes. "Once again, you plan to arrive at the curtain call to take credit while other men risk their lives."

"Talk to me when you've faced gunfire, Josie. I need a drink." Johnny showed me his back, fleeing to the sideboard with the decanters beside the interior passage to the boardinghouse. "Mind if I pour my own, Mollie?"

Johnny sucked down the first shot of whiskey and had poured his second when the interior door banged open, admitting Ike—unarmed, his bandaged head bleeding, his eyes wild. (I made the connection that this wasn't the first time that Fly's, Doc's home in town, had been used as an escape route or hideout.)

Ike pried the glass from Johnny's fingers. He gulped the dregs and tossed it to the wood floor, where it shattered. Then he recklessly threaded his way through the studio, nearly upsetting the one standing camera. He left the battle he'd started at his back. Grabbing the brass doorknob, he took the customer exit opposite, letting in a lick of cold from the vacant lot and a sulfurous smell.

On the far side of the room from where I stood,

Mollie and Buck busily tried to protect the precious photographic equipment from flying glass. A round of bullets smashed outside beyond the row of shuttered windows on the studio's west side and ricocheted against the walls. The sound slammed my inner ears, but I didn't flinch, although I felt the rounds deep in my belly.

The bullets stopped. The quiet held. Each one of us in the room registered if we'd been shot, or any of our companions. The battle lasted no more than thirty seconds, although terror had stretched time. The photographer, now carrying his rifle, exited the gallery door that opened onto the vacant lot. I foolishly followed him, running to Wyatt.

In the narrow lot between Fly's and Harwood's House (a shack, really) hung acrid smoke, the iron tang of blood, and the odor of horse crap dumped by a frightened animal in flight. I had never seen such carnage. That bloody mess Billy Clanton sank down on his haunches against Harwood's. He was trying to reload his pistol with his left hand, hampered by his bullet-shattered right wrist. Buck walked straight over through the heavy haze of white gun smoke to Ike's younger brother. He took Billy's empty Colt Frontier revolver. Billy, clean-shaven and not yet twenty, keened in pain from his wounds. It would come out that he'd also been shot near his nipple and navel, so that a pierced lung made breathing labored. The sound of injured men groaning came from Fremont

Street. A whistle pierced the cries from the steam hoisting works.

Wyatt stood in the middle of the lot, alone, the last man standing with his guns loose at his sides. This was the stranger I'd seen from a distance that day so many months ago when he stood off a lynch mob, solid and steely in danger. Morgan was down, and Virgil clutched his own bloody calf. Doc was absent. I watched Wyatt in profile as he looked through the haze assessing the damage, focused and steady. A bullet hole pierced his long coat, but I witnessed no matching bloodstain. I ran toward him. When he turned and saw me, I read confusion in his eyes, and the ferocity behind it. He didn't recognize me immediately. I was still in costume, a senorita in Marietta's peasant dress, my curls slicked back. But he was only bewildered momentarily, as I ran to him and his sadness. "You're alive!" I said, embracing him shamelessly in public.

"I am." He was stiff to my touch in the scorched air. He didn't holster his guns. And yet he bent down to give me one kiss, heavy and sure, to communicate our connection when words failed and the sky had fallen. This was truth and reality, live flesh. This was love worth living for. Billy Clanton and the McLaury Brothers were scraps of beef, dead or nearly there. Doc could be heard cussing on Fremont Street. Nearby, Billy's unceasing groans sent shivers through me. A second whistle filled the streets with armed men, joining the curious who appeared on the street from their houses and businesses. The local vigilance committee made their first appearance too late to alter the outcome.

"I have to get Morg and Virg home."

"How can I help you?"

"Go back to the San Jose right now. Sit tight. I'll send word."

I jumped. Johnny had crept up behind me. "I want to see you, Wyatt."

Wyatt pressed me behind him. "You deceived us, Sheriff. You said they were unarmed. I won't be arrested, but I am here to answer what I have done. I am not going to leave town."

CHAPTER 23
OCTOBER 27, 1881

A soft rap came at my bedroom door, followed by the porter's urgent statement: "Miss Marcus, a visitor downstairs." I bolted upright. A knock this late boded ill—the portent of sudden death and imminent disaster. Good news can wait until morning. Dread followed me up from the pit of my dreams, where I wandered strange, empty rooms hewn of rough, warped boards, one chamber in a line with the next. Not a single exit presented itself. I'd begun to search for windows, and slashed my hand on broken glass. Awake, gripping my right hand, I lay fully dressed on my bed at the San Jose. Marietta's Mexican costume rested on a side chair, the ghost of another woman.

I snatched my heavy cloak and stuffed my stockinged feet into my boots, leaving the laces for later. In my haste, I nearly tumbled down the stairs carrying my candlestick. That would have been memorable: I would have become the careless girl who set Tombstone aflame.

Downstairs, in the parlor, a tall man with close-set eyes awaited me, his hat in his right hand and held over his heart. I sensed his reluctance to be there. He carried worry along with the war wound that had shattered his left shoulder, leaving the attached arm dangling below, his fingers twisted and withered.

We'd never met. Shyness overcame me. I tried to smooth my hair out of a nervous reflexive vanity and nearly set the curls afire with my candle. He removed the light with his able hand to set it on the mantel. It was 3:00 a.m., according to the clock.

The stranger didn't introduce himself, but I knew he was James, Wyatt's older brother, the outlier, the bartender. I'd seen him across the road from Madame Mustache's balcony during the lynching, stepping out from Vogan's Bowling Alley to whisper in Wyatt's ear. In the sparse candlelight, he looked much older to me now, the creases in his forty-year-old face deepened in shadow. A half twitch in his right eye came and went, which would have made him useless at the poker table.

"How are Virgil and Morgan?" I asked.

"You'll learn soon enough, Miss Marcus," James said. He sounded like Wyatt, his voice deep and rich, but cracked by fear. He lacked the wherewithal to shield me from it, the way Wyatt would have. "Accompany me to Fly's. The town is too hot for Wyatt."

"Is he all right?" I asked, suddenly uncertain if more disaster had befallen him since we'd parted in the bloody yard beside Fly's.

"He is what he is," James said cryptically. And then there was an awkward pause during which I clumsily laced my boots. "Since I'm here, I have my own message for you, Miss Marcus. Wyatt was a lonely man until you arrived in Tombstone. You changed that. We brothers appreciate that you gave him something to live for. What makes Wyatt happy matters to us boys. We'll protect you to the death."

"I hope it doesn't go that far, James." I smiled at him but got none in return. "I am deeply touched." I'd been accepted into the Earp clan by the power of Wyatt's love. Here was another sign that his affection was true. Despite the fear in the room, I floated up inside myself, raised by Wyatt's affection and by my own powerful reciprocal feelings. Death circled us with jagged claws and bloody teeth, with savagery, and forged the untried steel of our love into something stronger. I had to see Wyatt. "Let's go."

James led me out of the San Jose, keeping silent as he guided me skulking through the darkness of Fremont Street. We dodged the few windows that still had light at this late—or early—hour. We made slow progress, as James paused to check that each new shadow didn't conceal an armed enemy, and glanced up at every second story for potential snipers. His fear became contagious, particularly in light of the fact that this tall man had enlisted, and ridden into battle, with the Union army. I wanted to fly in the opposite direction, back to the safety of the San Jose. But I would have to pursue that alone, and I couldn't bear that, either, so I clenched the rough fabric at his elbow as he picked our way through the darkness, seeing hazards I never would have recognized.

James stopped twice to attend to sounds in front of us, or check for tails behind us. At last, we arrived at the familiar back alley that fed into the O.K. Corral. Hearing distant gunfire and rough laughter, we flattened ourselves against the cash-store wall, and he placed his right arm protectively across me. I could hardly breathe. I didn't want to fail Wyatt, but the thought of going farther brought the image of Billy Clanton, bloody and dying, to my mind. One minute he was standing, belligerent in the backyard, the next broken, bleeding, bellowing. How easily that could happen to me without even a pistol to protect myself.

James and I had paused in an inky pool beneath the eaves to listen. When he seemed satisfied, we ran across the alley, him pulling me faster than I had ever run. At the familiar door to the gallery, James knocked twice, then once, then opened the door slowly and pushed me ahead of him.

I could smell cigar smoke mixed with the photographic chemicals as we entered. And then I spotted Wyatt at the opposite side of the room, perched on the green-velvet man chair, smoking a cigar visible only by the light of its ember. His eyes appeared as he inhaled, disappeared into smoke when he exhaled. The door to the boardinghouse shut, possibly behind Doc.

Rushing across the room, I felt ahead of me like a blind woman for tables and chairs that had shifted since I'd first arrived the previous morning. "Come," Wyatt said. "Sit on my lap."

I stumbled toward his voice until I felt his strong gambler's fingers, his muscular arms, his hard knees. I crawled into the cave he created, holding my heart to his, my face hidden in his neck. It was a reunion both physical and emotional. He was sanctuary to me, and all the dangers around us disappeared. I believe for him, that connection gave him a reason to rally, to stay and fight and scheme, to raise his head one more day in the war against the sons of bitches, the cattle thieves. Because we knew, sitting together in the dark, guarded by James and Doc and who knows who else, that the gunfight that afternoon had not been an ending but a beginning. There were casualties on our side and fatalities on theirs. But that was recognition of an external danger, and this was intimacy in the moment, sitting crossways over Wyatt's long legs, his arms pulling me closer and tighter, smelling the bitter cigar smoke. I threw my right arm around his neck. We were a unit. We were love.

Wyatt offered his cigar. "Want a puff?"

I took a drag and coughed it out. When I'd stopped hacking, he kissed me long and hard. The cigar taste wasn't so foreign because it clung to my tongue, too. I had never known a kiss so powerful and communicative, which wrapped up caring and compassion, fear and ferocity. He would do anything to save me, his kiss said, and I responded that if he did not survive, my life was not worth saving. Our kiss was as secure as a fortress, as flammable as gunpowder. Nothing has ever meant more to me than that connection.

Wyatt pulled back, first gently caressing the curls that had escaped in my rush to meet him, then lacing his fingers deeply into my hair.

"Sadie, we never wanted a war. James can tell you that."

"I know," I said. "You did not start this fight."

"Now, Morgan took a bullet that entered one shoulder and exited his other. Virgil took a hit to the calf."

"Will they be OK?" Terrified, I knew the agony they must be suffering and the fickleness of frontier doctors. If the country's best medics could not save President Garfield from his gunshot wounds, how would these two survive?

Wyatt shared their pain: These were his brothers, his arms and legs. They carried his memories and hopes. Together, they formed a pack. "Virgil is better off than Morgan. Recovery will take time. I pledged to protect my brothers, and then this happened. We did not stir the pot, and yet it is stirred by these Southern, cattle-thieving sons of bitches. I feel a weight of guilt that I was unscathed, and a responsibility to set things right. This town has become twisted, and I don't know how to put it straight."

"It will become clearer in the morning," I said, a salve with only placebo properties.

"We came here to buy land and mines and businesses, to sink roots and prosper together. Keeping the peace is something we have a knack for, but marshaling wasn't our original plan: to be guns for hire, a shooting gallery of cowboys popping up like targets at the fair. We wanted to maintain the peace for ourselves, but that seems unlikely now."

"Why do you say that?" I asked. "You're heroes."

"Today, maybe, but tomorrow? Together, we're the Earp brothers, but the Clantons and the McLaurys are brothers, too. Every time a cowboy dies, a harsher enemy rises among his kin. I'm not worried about our actions, but our opposition." He paused to puff on his cigar. I felt the weight of his free hand on my knee. There was no filter between us, no scrim.

"Before we entered the yard," he continued, "your Johnny ran up, warning us there would be trouble. When Virgil told him he was going down to disarm them, we both heard Behan say, 'I have disarmed them all.'"

"The *liar!*" The familiar seething anger of betrayal drew new blood, a thumb twisted in an old wound.

"After that, Virgil put away his rifle and grabbed Doc's walking stick in his right hand, and we turned the corner into the yard at a walk. But those boys were armed."

Johnny had betrayed me in the bedroom. Now he had betrayed Wyatt, Doc, and the brothers on the streets, a battlefield with no boundaries.

"Tonight, Johnny called at Virgil's house uninvited. That two-timing sheriff sat right there by my brothers' sickbeds and claimed, 'I was there *for the purpose of* arresting and disarming them.' That's quite a different tune. We walked into danger, and Behan muddied the waters. We may be considered heroes for a moment, Sadie, but I'm uncertain for how long. We acted in self-defense in a fair fight, but—"

"But what? Doesn't that end the matter?"

"Johnny intends to arrest me. He said as much—you heard him—if not today, then soon."

"But you did nothing against the law."

"Tell me this, Sadie. What's the most direct route for Behan to dispose of a rival?"

Horror gripped me. "Get him killed?"

"Or get him arrested. Wrong or right, if I get sent to jail, please, Sadie, don't visit me."

"It won't happen, Wyatt. I won't let them take you."

"I cherish the sentiment, but I don't see you having any sway in this department. Stay clear of the jail. I couldn't bear up if you saw me behind bars. I will send messages to you here, through Buck and Mollie."

"Don't get ahead of yourself, Wyatt." But I knew he wasn't one to exaggerate. I feared we would be separated so soon after we came together. If Johnny jailed him, he jailed me, too. I could not bear to be ripped from this man who meant everything to me, and have him living on display in shame like some caged beast with John Harris Behan as his zookeeper.

"Let's face the reality of the situation together,

Sadie, the bitter and the sweet. We have to stop and look the future in the eye. I have to know: Are you with me all the way?"

"What does it look like? I could not be any closer if I was your eyelash."

"That's true now, but I need to know you understand the ramifications of remaining true. This morning, Tombstone may have our backs. We have the *Epitaph* in our corner, even if we can't trust Behan. But I don't know where we'll stand by sundown. There are real risks: jail, assassination, loss, exile. I'm staring down a hard road. I need you to contemplate that before you commit. If you leave this room allied to me, which means to my brothers and Doc, too, then our burdens become your burdens."

"Isn't that how it's supposed to be?"

"It is and it isn't. My life is in danger. Doc's a wild card. Virgil and Morgan are bedridden. They should recover, but there are no guarantees. I'm going to have to shift them to the Cosmopolitan Hotel for safety, and that will include Allie and Mattie, too. So that's going to mean no room at the inn for you and me. It's going to get really ugly, really fast, around here now."

"What do you want from me?"

"I am here to make a vow," he said, and then he paused, his voice catching, "or cut you loose."

"I'm not leaving." My throat tightened. Tears swelled my eyeballs. "What's the vow?"

"I have one rule for us, and only one."

"What's that?" I asked, and nervously joked, "Don't shoot each other?"

"You wouldn't stand a chance." He gently lifted me up off his lap and settled my feet on the floor, then slid off the chair and down to his knees. Taking my hand, he said, "I vow to be loyal and faithful to you alone from this day forward. Do you agree?"

I kneeled with him, the darkness above us a *chuppah*, a canopy. There were no witnesses. We didn't need anyone else. In a strong, clear voice, infused with affection, I said, "I vow to be loyal and faithful to you alone from this day forward."

We remained kneeling in the dark for a long time, knowing that this was our choice, to be together, my little hands in his callused ones, my large spirit dancing around his heavy weather. Slowly, the room lightened with the dawn, and the tumble of camera equipment, the photos of strangers that covered the walls in witness, became visible. When we dropped each other's hands, we could not guarantee our future together, but now there was an *"us,"* a *"we."* I was an Earp. This was real, as real as the shooting at the yard and the puddles of fraternal blood that darkened the raw earth. And it was sanctified—not by a rabbi or a priest—but the true feelings in our hearts, and the sacred vow we'd exchanged.

Wyatt protected me to be my true adventurous

self. I held his heart in my hands, blowing light and life where there had been ashes and the tiniest of embers. Our kiss was a quiet breath held together. A soft knock at the internal door interrupted us. Doc whispered, "Wyatt, we have to go."

CHAPTER 24

Wyatt nailed it: our lasting devotion—and his fleeting hero status. Tombstone awoke on the morning of October 27 with a horror hangover. The folks living in the town named for a grave marker—with a newspaper named the *Epitaph*—had boasted about having their men for breakfast. But it had rarely happened. Now we had three corpses for supper, which inspired mass indigestion.

The initial response had been pro-Wyatt. The *Epitaph* ran the headline "THREE MEN HURLED INTO ETERNITY . . ."

Editor and Mayor Clum wrote:

> The feeling among the best class of our citizens is that the Marshal was entirely justified in his efforts to disarm these men, and that being fired upon they had to defend themselves, which they did most bravely.

Since the *Epitaph* was syndicated, Clum's favorable opinion echoed across the country—and would likely have been read out loud by Mama to Papa. Even the *San Francisco Exchange* hailed my Earps:

> Marshal Earp and his assistants deserve well of their fellow citizens, and we hope the Tombstoners appreciate the fact. The cowboy class are the most despicable beings on the face of the earth. They are a terror to decent people and a disgrace to even frontier civilization.

But local opinion in the saloons and stables, the tobacconists and sewing circles, was woefully split. Nothing made that clearer than two days later when Ritter and Ream, City Undertakers, displayed the bodies of Tom McLaury, Frank McLaury, and Ike's little brother, Billy, in their picture window following their date with the coroner. Above the three corpses hung the sign MURDERED ON THE STREETS OF TOMBSTONE. As I hurried by on an errand to the shops, avoiding the crowds, it became abundantly clear that a difference of opinion existed within the town limits about who were the heroes of the gunfight, and who were the victims. My concerns for Wyatt grew along with the gawkers outside Ritter and Ream.

When I dropped by Fly's and told Buck what

I'd seen, he set aside his whiskey, grabbed his camera equipment, and headed for Fifth Street in a visible adrenaline rush. Buck had moved to Arizona to be the first photographer on the scene at just such events. He planted his tripod center front of the plate-glass window, shooing away the growing crowds with an air of self-importance and entering what Mollie called his "fugue state."

According to Mollie, Buck left his camera outside and entered the funeral parlor, where the undertakers had propped the cowboys up in their three identical silver-trimmed ebony caskets adorned with leaf motifs. The victims wore formal suits and ties. Their bloody wounds had been tidied. Ignoring the throng outside, Buck began setting the scene with an officiousness that took the undertakers aback. Ignoring their protests, he removed his coat, rolled up his sleeves, and composed his death photograph. He tucked a collar here, smoothed a cowlick there, and crossed pale hands over chests with an eye toward visual harmony. He ordered the undertakers to raise the wooden boxes higher so that the faces became more visible, without the bodies sliding in an ungainly posture from their final resting places.

The clean-shaven Billy looked impossibly young, a spring leaf fallen prematurely from a great oak. The McLaury brothers might have been twins, with their identical black mustaches and goatees, their dark brows over sunken, sightless eyes. The trio could have been biblical martyrs in their serene seriousness.

Buck, with Mollie assisting, exposed plate after photographic plate to create a photo that would become nearly as legendary as the gunfight itself. In death, the corpses rose again, and Tombstone flooded with aggrieved cowboys and ranchers from the outlying territory. The influx climaxed with the largest funeral procession ever seen in Tombstone. A brass band led the cortege from the funeral parlor to the cemetery at Boot Hill. Clanton reposed in one hearse. The McLaurys followed in another. Three hundred pedestrians, a four-horse stagecoach, twenty-two buggies and carriages, and a string of men on horseback filled the funeral procession, while onlookers occupied the sidewalks. The event's scale, the outpourings of sympathy and grief, the tears and outrage, shocked me and surprised the local law-and-order crowd. Even the cowboy-friendly *Nugget* seemed taken aback, running this headline: "AN IMPOSING FUNERAL," followed by the text:

> While it was not entirely expected, the funeral of Billy Clanton and Thomas and Frank McLowry yesterday was the largest ever witnessed in Tombstone.

The crowd gawked and mourned the dead, but I feared for the living. In the funeral's aftermath, curses filled the street. Well-heeled horsemen itching for a fight converged on Allen Street. That night, an endless wake flowed from one saloon, one long bar to the next. Quiet reigned at the Cosmopolitan, the Earps' territory.

From what I gleaned from Mollie and the newspapers, the town feared cowboy retribution, which in turn made businessmen jittery. The entrepreneurs and miners needed peace to draw cash investments from Eastern bankers, and all that money flowed down into small concerns like the studio and the boardinghouse. The merchants and miners only supported my Earps to the extent that they kept the peace, and did not necessarily have the backbone to support them once violence broke out.

True to form, Ike Clanton took the opportunity to behave despicably. He had drunkenly threatened Doc and the Earps from one bar stool to the next all over town on the eve of the fight and deep into that morning. Wyatt had let him leave the yard because Ike alone was unarmed, which was when I saw him flee through Fly's with crazy eyes. Yet, within days, Ike filed murder charges against the Earps and Doc, and Sheriff Johnny had the nerve to carry them out now that public opinion was swaying his way. He'd played his political cards like a true gambler. On November 1, Johnny arrested Wyatt and Doc. Those Earp brothers who were bedridden remained free under the watchful eye of Virgil's wife, Allie.

November was bitter and difficult. The tide of town sentiment turned against Wyatt and his brothers following the funeral. The fear of cowboy reprisal was palpable, and it was only going to worsen with Johnny fanning the flames against my man.

Wyatt and Doc hired high-profile lawyer Thomas Fitch for their defense. After Justice of the Peace Wells Spicer set bail at $10,000 each, they raised the money from their supporters and their own pockets. Even after their release, I rarely saw Wyatt, although I read about him daily. He sent me a single "I love you, Sadie" scrawled on a scrap torn from a legal document. I tucked it into the envelope with the letter from Papa. I had to have the strength—his strength—to cling to what that represented. Meanwhile, Judge Spicer convened a preliminary hearing to determine if the facts warranted a murder charge and a formal trial. Although I wanted to attend, I laid low. My presence would have made the courtroom hotter for Wyatt, particularly since Johnny was the key witness for the prosecution.

Johnny first testified on November 2. When I read the newspaper account, my jaw dropped. I had seen Johnny in Fly's. He had fled when he should have disarmed the cowboys and protected the town. Instead, he let others do his dirty work, waited for the smoke to clear, and double-crossed them. Johnny was a coward. He was a liar. I knew this! He had reneged on his vow to make Wyatt undersheriff. On the stand, he asserted that Billy Clanton and the McLaurys were unarmed victims shot with their hands in the air. I knew that was false. I witnessed Buck removing Billy's pistol from his bloody hand.

But there was Johnny, in the power of print, alleging that he'd met the Earps on Fremont Street and attempted to dissuade them from entering the yard, to no avail. Despite his best efforts, they'd murdered three harmless innocents. What slayed me was that Johnny smooth-talked the court into believing his version of events. His testimony, backed by his authority as sheriff (the high-paying position that he'd weaseled from Wyatt), sabotaged Doc and the Earps in the courtroom. Dropping the newspaper, I became furious, then nauseated. I knew Johnny was in bed with the Clantons, the McLaurys, Curly Bill, and Johnny Ringo, and knew all too well how persuasive he could be. If he could convince the court in the same way he had snookered me, Wyatt would hang.

Under cross-examination, the defense failed to shake Johnny, shifting the tide of public opinion away from the Earps and Holliday. The prosecution scored a victory when Judge Spicer revoked bail on the strength of their case. Johnny jailed Wyatt and Doc.

Johnny, a lesser man, had shamed Wyatt in public and now held the key, not only to his cell but to his future. I empathized with Wyatt, knowing the disgrace of his incarceration, a lawman treated as a murderous criminal with Doc railing at his side. Wyatt had infinite patience, and yet it stabbed to be stuck behind bars, robbed of his agency, reduced to a caged gorilla. And why— for protecting the town against armed outlaws while defending his brothers and Doc against threatening, murderous thugs?

This was justice turned on its head, and all Wyatt wanted to do was right it. Adding salt to the wound, it was fork-tongued Johnny who triumphed in Wyatt's catastrophe. The moment I heard that Wyatt had been taken prisoner, I wanted to run from the San Jose to the jail, hatless, uncombed. I needed to reach through the bars and touch his hand—to comfort him, I told myself, but it was my own desperation to feel his skin's warmth, the muscle beneath, the solidity and certainty that was Wyatt.

That urge was shabby of me: to desire his protection and comfort when it was he who needed salvation. I forced myself to accept the bitter truth: I was incapable of consoling him in jail. He did not want me to see him reduced to criminal status, unwashed, defeated, surrounded by lesser men in more powerful positions. My arrival would embarrass him in front of the throng, my inevitable tears forcing him to raise a brave face—and show his hand. I struggled to maintain my promise: to leave him be in jail and wait to celebrate his inevitable freedom. But that freedom felt anything but certain, given Johnny's testimony. I rose and rushed to the door multiple times, ready to fly to him, ready to break my oath. I made it as far as the landing only to return to the edge of my lonely bed and look out the window, waiting, picking at the coverlet, anxious and crawling out of my own skin. Panic was my only company.

Heightened nervousness ran like a current through town. Johnny, apparently fearing that the Earps' allies would spring the prisoners—I would have done so if I could—charged the inept editor turned Undersheriff Woods with assembling a heavy guard. But lynching was as likely as a jailbreak. Despite Woods's guards, the citizens' vigilance committee encircled the jail to ensure the prisoners would remain safe from external threats. There were many sore-headed men anxious for payback now that Wyatt and Doc were unarmed and vulnerable. I could hear the angry calls for the noose from my window. Even when I went downstairs for supper, the talk among the gentlemen residents of the San Jose was of a possible necktie party, and how this was bad for business, although the discussion ended when I entered the room. I had seen this bloodlust bubble up for Johnny-Behind-the-Deuce, and only Wyatt had saved him from the mob. That November day, "murderers" was a common cry. If I heard it, Wyatt did, too. Again, I lamented for his state of mind. I knew my own was shattered.

The following day, Johnny brought Wyatt and Doc to court in shackles. Billy Claiborne took the stand to hammer another nail into the defense's coffin. Clearly, Claiborne and Behan had synchronized their stories. The cowboy testified that he had been in the yard for sixteen to eighteen shots before he entered Fly's. He claimed both Clantons raised their hands up before Virgil, and that Tom McLaury was opening his coat to prove he was unarmed when the shooting started. This contradicted what I'd seen: the panicked Claiborne running through the studio after only two rounds. Yet he testified that Doc shot first, Morgan second, and, together, the Earp side fired the first six bullets. Coupled with Johnny's testimony, this was damning evidence.

The defense experienced their darkest hour. *Hanging* was the word that seeped out from the courtroom into the streets.

CHAPTER 25
NOVEMBER 1881

The night that Billy Claiborne testified, there was partying in the streets and the sound of pistol fire. Every time I heard a shot, I didn't know if it was a liberating or lynching party at the jail. I had to do something.

I couldn't visit Wyatt. I considered visiting Morgan and Virgil, but instantly knew that a rancorous encounter with Allie and Mattie would be inevitable. Wyatt would not want me to stir up that hornet's nest of resentment. But I could no longer sit on my hands as darkness fell and the night lengthened and cold chased the revelers into the saloons and brothels. The only way to escape my panic was to take action, and the only leverage I had to spring Wyatt was with Johnny.

My thoughts spun: Could I move Johnny's conscience to save Wyatt from the noose without placing myself in a dangerous and vulnerable position? I had no clarity, only fear and loss and a need to make things right, as Wyatt would if I were at risk. Only my skills were not in my steely nerves or sharpshooting.

All I could think, in my plain bedroom over-looking Fremont Street, was that I had to act. The walls were closing in on me. I looked at myself in the mirror and saw the familiar features: the heavy lashes, the eyebrows—one higher than the other—the full lips, and the dilated eyes of fear. Thanks, in part, to Mollie's labors in the photography studio, I saw a woman, not a girl, and I saw my power over men. I looked away when I thought of how that power had emboldened me and then let me down when I found Johnny twisted around Mrs. Dunbar. Wyatt had rescued me with his love and unleashed a depth of feeling in me that I'd never known, but he could not erase the shame embroidered in dark thread on my heart. I felt it tug as I put on my armor, strapped on my holsters, my weapons of beauty: I painstakingly created a series of small braids and twisted them around my heavy curls in an ornate hairstyle. I rouged my cheeks. I plucked my brows. I struggled by myself with my corset to constrict my waist even tighter than the norm. I doused myself in cologne. I tried on one dress in front of the mirror, fussed at a stain. I exchanged it for another, the red taffeta, the one Johnny favored, the one that was cut lower at the bust than the rest.

Once dressed and powdered, I resisted catching my own eyes in the looking glass. I would see the woman who loved Wyatt judging back at me. I could not afford to face her disapproval. I could not sit and do nothing. I could not pine patiently, knowing that Wyatt was passing the time on a hard bunk with Doc bellyaching, surrounded by gloating jailers, and gawkers stopping by to see the mighty fallen. Even though I knew that Wyatt had the patience to see the preliminary hearing through and wait for the right time to act, sit tight, or fold—and would disapprove of my impulsive actions—act I did.

Concealed beneath a silk paisley shawl, I descended the San Jose stairs. As I passed the parlor, I again overheard guests discussing hanging and the price of silver, and the sound of newspapers being flapped and folded. Wordlessly, I snuck out into the brisk night air bound for Sixth and Safford Street. On the way, I jumped at every shadow, shuddered at a mongrel's growl. I hewed to the darkness approaching the town's outskirts, shivering from cold, fearing my safety as I passed the empty lots on Safford Street, the lonely canvas tents, the campfires whipping up sparks.

Damn the court: I would see Johnny to plead my case.

On our familiar corner, I paused in the blackness to observe the sweet house with the lacy fretwork on the eaves that I had called mine. I had loved the hopes of that house, planned every corner and cornice, felt an affection for every window for which I'd fought against the constraints of the budget. I had envisioned planting climbing pink roses and baking birthday cakes for the children who would inevitably arrive, buying the best oven possible in the Montgomery Ward "Wish Book." Now, from across the street, even the cottage betrayed me, with its welcoming lights and a lantern hung from the porch, as if I'd never left. I could see the gingham curtains I had stitched and bled over. I would rather share a thousand campsites with Wyatt than spend one more night under that roof with Johnny, yet here I was, and I could already feel Johnny's pull, remember the first time we'd made love, and how that freed a wild self in me that I never wanted to contain.

Contain. Jail. Wyatt.

My fury rose as if it were yesterday when Albert and I caught Johnny with that floozy. How could someone uphold the law and betray his beloved and shame his own son? Johnny had robbed me of my home and heart—and arrested other men for lesser burglaries. Even as I blamed him, I had only myself to chide for returning to his door in my current reduced state: standing in the shadows in red taffeta and rouge, a beggar with only beauty in my basket. While my jaw stiffened with my resolve, my feet dragged up the narrow path whose construction I had overseen myself. I climbed the porch on tiptoe, raised my fist to rap on the front door. This had been my door. I had chosen its height and girth. I had always opened it freely—and I remembered how it slammed when I left for good, still holding Albert's hand in mine, stunned by the carnality and betrayal that had confronted us.

Rage and jealous fury fueled my urgent knock. Johnny had stolen my heart, dragged me to Tombstone, and ditched me. I wouldn't let him steal Wyatt. I was not the wide-eyed girl I had been when Johnny first grinned at me with those shiny teeth and I mistook him for the tenor to my soprano in a fantasy operetta of love.

The door opened and there they were: the shiny teeth in Johnny's welcoming, even cocky, smile. His eyes were merry upon realizing it was me at his door. I swallowed, overwhelmed by how swiftly my rage dissipated. Seeing him again revived all those old feelings: how handsome he was, how warm his eyes that looked straight into mine without shame, his hair barbered, his mustache combed. I've always liked a man with a small waist and broad shoulders, and that was Johnny. He reached to embrace me, front to front. I retreated from the precipice in time, fronting him a cheek to buss. Slipping past, I entered the parlor, our parlor, with the suite I had so carefully picked from the catalog. I noticed a cigar burn on the red Renaissance Revival gentleman's chair. A dark stain of unknown origin crawled across the settee. I'd had such pretentions, such baseless hopes for Mr. and the second Mrs. Behan. Seeing the nearly new furniture already marred, I said, "I like what you've done with the place."

"It could use a woman's touch," Johnny said. "What brings you to the old neighborhood so late at night?"

I had not considered even my first move, the pawn of my attack, through all the long time I had braided my hair and changed my clothes and plucked my brows. Was there not a strategic bone in my small body, besides my small body?

"Am I unwelcome in the house I built and paid for?"

"Money is so important with you and your kind."

"And what kind is that?" A religious slur. Now I would see how low Johnny could stoop, as if I needed more proof.

"Womankind," he said, raising his thick eyebrows and observing my response. "You claimed your father was rich."

"And *you* said you'd marry me."

"You left me, Josephine, not the other way around," he said, as if my departure had been a rainy-day whim rather than a desperate exit on seeing him mounted upon another woman. Just thinking about that afternoon brought the image to my eyes. I recoiled.

"I suppose you could say that I am not good at sharing." I could hardly bear hearing myself, so weak, so defensive, while standing on my back foot.

"As you explained to me," Johnny said wryly,

"this is still your house in deed. Regardless of your opinion of my behavior under our roof, you know that the bedroom door is always open."

"It is much too crowded for my taste." I must have been probing for remorse on his part, for a way to gain his sympathy and then try to parlay that into mercy for Wyatt. I thought Johnny owed me, but I sensed the feeling was not mutual.

"I like a full house over a pair," Johnny said. "I'm not alone in that. What you call a crowd, I call a party. You cannot deny that we're a good match, although we love better than we fight. I admit: I did the horizontal dance with someone else. You caught me. Guilty as charged. Now you have bedded down with Wyatt. We're even. I won't hold that against you. You can only lose your virginity once. You gave that to me, thank you very much."

I sputtered. Johnny's words reduced what we had to less than nothing, and I feared they were truer than the last illusions I carried. His cavalier attitude shocked me. I had been in love with him. I had believed we would marry and remain together. And yet he had never shown me this side of him, his morals nowhere near as tailored as his suit. I said, "You betrayed me, Johnny, all while pretending it was true love."

"OK, maybe I strayed. Maybe I strayed more than once. But I only *love* you. I only *adore* you. I brought you here. You were mine first. We butt heads, but we also make love. We fight, but we also make up."

"How dare you! We are not getting back together, Johnny," I said with a tremor in my voice. "We are as through as Billy Clanton."

"We'll never be through, Josie. I know you. I know how you like your nipples rubbed." I blanched. He did—and how many men had he told? "I know how you scream and sigh for more. Your nightmare is awakening in your mother's house without my arms around you. You can't return to San Francisco, an unmarried lady with a wife's worth of experience. We can only go forward. Now you truly know me," he said, opening his palms in front of me. He smiled his most winning, cunning, ingratiating smile. "The gloves are off."

It suddenly hit me that I'd made no headway. I'd wandered off the track and landed in the territory of the wolves and coyotes. My purpose had never been reconciliation, but protecting Wyatt. "Are we having an argument, Johnny? That was never my intent. Tell me, instead, that you are incapable of letting Wyatt hang, knowing the truth as we do."

"Wyatt hangs, we get back together. Why should I separate the two? You have an inflated notion of Earp. You think your deal with Madame Mustache escaped me? I might have played a little fiddle there, expecting you to return to me, but Wyatt beat me to the punch. He scooped you up. Wyatt is not the hero you think; he is an opportunist of the first order."

"You, sir, are the opportunist," I said, "putting Wyatt's life at stake for your gains." Shaking, I gripped bunches of my skirt in my fists, tempted to shred the fabric. I longed to slap his smug face.

"Josie, I can feel you trembling across the room. Even your anger is an invitation. You can't stay away from me forever. Wyatt is in jail for a single night. Where do you run? To my arms, that's where you come. What do you *want* from me, then, Josie, in your red dress and your rouge?"

His question, calling me on my bluff, humiliated me. I was no seductress. This woman he saw before him disgusted me. He'd seen through me from the moment I banged on the door, and had set out to exploit my desperation. Even when I wore a corset, he'd seen me naked and loose-limbed, wild-haired, flushed. I'd tried to seduce him to free Wyatt; he'd known that he held the winning hand. Perhaps he expected me to return to him for protection. That was not going to happen, not by the chin hairs of Curly Bill. There was no going back. Still, one last time, I tried to appeal to Johnny's conscience, to the honorable man with whom I believed I'd fallen in love.

"I insist you tell the truth on the stand," I said, straining to keep from shouting, as I'd seen my mother do so often at home.

"Or what will you do, little lady? I am telling a

truth—my truth," he said, relaxing now that I'd begun to play my hand and lose my temper. "It's very compelling, and I don't need a pistol in my hand to enforce it. Would you join me in a cognac? You look like a little peaked. Can I pour you a digestif?"

"No, thank you. I read your testimony, Johnny, and caught you out in your self-serving lies. You promised to appoint Wyatt as undersheriff if he dropped out of the sheriff's race. I was there. You welched on that deal when it no longer suited your schemes. You made an enemy where once stood an ally."

"Not much of an ally steals your girl," Johnny said.

"Wyatt had nothing to do with your losing me. You did that all by yourself," I said. "The day of the gunfight, I saw you and Billy Claiborne skip into Fly's after two shots. Again, I was there."

"Who will believe that story? And to whom will a woman of your reputation tell it?"

"And who ruined my reputation?" I said, finally releasing the shout that I'd contained until now.

"I did not abduct you, Josie. We are a long way from San Francisco." He sipped his drink and thumbed his vest pockets in search of who knew what. As we talked, he inched between me and the entrance, preventing my exit and herding me toward the bedroom. "My love has not abated.

Come, feel me. My ardor for you remains. Tell me: What do you want from me?"

"The truth, Johnny, I want the facts," I said, retreating. "Wyatt is no murderer. Four men's lives are at stake in Judge Spicer's courtroom, three of them brothers."

"And three men are dead and buried, three friends of mine, and all of them brothers. Calm yourself. All this yelling will get you nowhere. What next: tears? This is a negotiation. What would you be willing to yield? Judge Spicer is currently overseeing the preliminary proceeding. Considering the prosecution's dominance, and my role as witness, a murder trial will ensue. I will be called to testify again. I cannot afford to risk my reputation, but perhaps I can be less emphatic. Perhaps I can drop a few salient points of evidence. Maybe only a few bullets discharged before we entered Fly's. Out of court, I can no longer offer you marriage—fidelity is not my forte—though I will honor you in my way, first in my heart."

"What guarantees would I have?" I asked, worn out and outmatched, and deeply saddened that I'd opened my heart to this man. Still, I could see the charm, still, the intelligence, but where was his sense of right and wrong?

"Tell me your alternatives. How else can you save Wyatt? I am your sole leverage." He was now clearly blocking my path to the front door.

"Let's seal the deal. You will not regret it, Josie. Our times together will be as sweet as ever. Remember when we first met and we would head out behind the barn for kissing lessons? I am hungry for more. We have had good times, Josie, you cannot deny that. We have tasted Champagne and, now, the tax money is flowing. There will be a future for us. Albert misses your company. It would be a matter of moments to bring you back under our roof. Who would blame you?"

"I would," I said. "Wyatt would."

I saw myself through Wyatt's eyes—posing in red, eyelashes inked, and offering myself up to his rival. Repulsed, I rallied. This was a deal with the devil, and I would not make it. To cheat on Wyatt would annihilate our love. I had vowed fidelity. I realized, perhaps too late, that even if I embraced Johnny to rescue Wyatt, our love would be compromised. As Wyatt knew, there was right and there was wrong. This was all wrong.

The front door flew open, and Ike Clanton entered without pausing to knock, like a breath of foul air. "What's *she* doing here?"

"She's jumping to the winning side," Johnny said with a smirk.

"She's too rich for my taste," Ike said. "Besides, I don't trust her. She's Wyatt's damn spy. Soon that sonofabitch will hang with Doc. My only regret is that I didn't shoot them myself when I had the chance."

"You had the chance but ran like the coward you are," I shrilled. Ike grabbed his head like my voice cut him.

"Josie, leave off now," Johnny said. "You're upsetting our guest. Ike, tomorrow you will testify to the aggression of Wyatt Earp and Doc Holliday that cost you your brother. We will dispatch that lot like the garbage they are, and we will do so legally," said Johnny. "How are you feeling?"

"I'm getting one of my headaches," said Ike.

"Did you run out of your cocaine drops? I can get Claiborne to stop by the pharmacy tomorrow. Have a drink for now and see if that dulls the pain." As Johnny walked toward the decanters, I saw my opportunity to escape. As I rushed out the door, the last thing I heard was Johnny saying, "Tomorrow, Ike, you will have your day in court."

And Ike did, many days. On November 9 and 10, his statement for the prosecution dovetailed Johnny's. Ike appeared the grieving brother marshaling his facts. He denied ever threatening the Earps or Doc. He claimed he had no stomach for a fight and tried to drag Wyatt bodily out of the line of fire into Fly's. Then, on the third day, a recess had to be called; Ike's neuralgia had flared up again. A day later, when he returned to the stand to face the defense, he was manic and arrogant, possibly due to the effects of cocaine drops commonly used to treat neuralgia of the head. Inconsistencies, lies, and tall tales riddled his testimony. The prosecution witness became the defense's star, and the team pursuing Wyatt and Doc never recovered their advantage.

The hearings persisted until the end of November, with a short break for Thanksgiving. When both sides rested, Judge Spicer exonerated Wyatt and Doc. He set them free, but they were never safe in Tombstone again.

CHAPTER 26
DECEMBER 1881

While behind bars, Wyatt had ample time to wonder about the nature of right and wrong, law and order—and whether he would live or die in Tombstone.

After Judge Spicer liberated Wyatt, he was not free as he had been before the gunfight. The anticipation that enemies could target him on the street at any moment restricted his movements. Typically, he and his brothers traveled in pairs (which cramped our romantic life). The Earps were always heeled, a pistol on each hip and a rifle stashed somewhere in town with easy access. Doc returned to Fly's, but the Earp family, Mattie included, exchanged their unprotected casitas on Fremont for the Cosmopolitan Hotel. I avoided what had become "our place." Although

I wasn't happy about it, I refused to add to Wyatt's worries.

December was the long pause between beats. While Wyatt assured me that life would settle down again, his eyes said otherwise. He was unconvinced. I tried to be strong for him, to provide a haven within my arms and not burden him with my fears. I understood Wyatt's love life was the least of his concerns. I struggled to believe that we had a future together where every night would be ours alone, whether in fancy hotels or under the stars; it didn't matter which. That month Wyatt and I developed trust like a muscle and exercised it. It wasn't always easy, but we were gentle with each other, and patient, forging a bond in adversity that transcended the bedroom and grew into a deep sense of mutual support and companionship that neither of us ever found elsewhere.

Wyatt was as steady as ever, but the town remained jittery and divided, jumping at every gunshot, fearing a fusillade. The long hearing had exonerated the Earp faction but failed to assuage the hunger for revenge among the cowboys. The conflict struck an old nerve, according to Wyatt, whose older brothers had fought for the Union. To the rural cattlemen on the range—many of whom had fought with the Confederates or lost kin in the War Between the States—the Earps represented the Yankees coming all over again to pass judgment and steal their lands. This was just what they had traveled west to escape. The Clantons and such had lost one war. They would not surrender easily. They craved blood for blood.

Having lived through rough times in Dodge City and Wichita, Wyatt knew that the surviving Clanton and McLaury brothers would not rest until they had avenged their kin. Kill one brother and you might as well kill the lot—but Wyatt was not that kind of man, not yet. He still had all his brothers. The law disappointed him. His arrest and time before the judge had disgusted him. But he still believed, like the true Lincoln Republican he was, in justice.

That changed shortly after Christmas, a holiday I tried unsuccessfully to ignore.

In the early-morning hours of December 29, the porter rapped at my door at the San Jose. I awoke with immediate foreboding: there was no good knock at 5:00 a.m. Who had died now? It had to be Wyatt. I wrapped myself in a robe and pushed my feet into slippers, banging my head on the door in my haste. I rushed downstairs, expecting James or Morgan. I could hear the cook in the kitchen battling the stove to get the biscuits started, and the clink of milk bottles on the porch as they were delivered. I turned into the parlor expecting the worst, feeling an egg rise on my forehead where I'd bashed it.

Wyatt dominated the room with his hat in one

hand, his vest unbuttoned, and his coat dusty. His nails were filthy. Blood soaked his cuffs. His raw, red eyes signaled that he'd been up all night. Deep pockets of gray skin sagged below. The first look I saw was one of despair, fatigue. There was no light of love or affection. Yet I had never been so happy to see another person, all six feet of Wyatt, long arms dangling, high-waisted, and all man. I ran to embrace him, but he held me back.

"You don't want to get blood on you."

"Is it yours?" I said, searching his arms with my eyes and dreading his answer. Panicked and desperate, I had feared Wyatt's wounding from that day of the attempted lynching of Johnny-Behind-the-Deuce in front of Vogan's. He could not evade his enemies' bullets forever.

"No. It's Virgil's."

A momentary wave of relief crashed against a new horror: "No! Not Virgil!"

Wyatt collapsed onto the settee, his hands between his knees, his head bowed. I threw myself beside him, arching my arm around his slumped shoulders, and kissed his neck, salty with sweat, his chin stubble. He shook his head like a tired old nag responding to a fly but did not rebuke me.

"There's no justice. There's no law. There's just blood and piss."

"What happened?"

"Assassins shot him in cold blood."

"Is he alive? Tell me he survived."

"He's alive. He's conscious. But it's touch-and-go. The shooters blasted his shoulder with heavy-gauge buckshot. They wounded his thigh but missed his spine. I didn't quit his side to come here until I was sure he was going to make it through the night. He may lose his arm. I left him and Allie battling the doctor not to cut it off. She said she'd sooner slice off my arm. The sound of Allie cursing me for every rotten thing that ever happened to Virgil drove me out of the room just to give my brother a moment of peace. That woman has the personality of a porcupine."

"How did it happen?"

"Virgil left me at the Oriental for the Cosmopolitan a half hour before midnight, and the villains ambushed him. He says two or three snipers fired double-barreled shotguns from behind the adobe walls at the Huachuca Water Company. Damn cowards shooting to kill in cold blood. It was Ike and that cowboy vermin, maybe Curly Bill or Johnny Ringo, Frank Stillwell or Joe Hill. They've been threatening to kill us for months, and the hope of a hanging must have whetted their appetite. I heard the shots and was heading for the door when Virgil fell back through the doors of the Oriental and into my arms. Over his squalls, I heard cries in the street of 'There they go' and 'Head them off,' but I wasn't giving chase. I'll have time to figure out who pulled the triggers, but first I had to see to Virg. We sent for the doctor and carried him to the Cosmopolitan where we could guard him."

"So he's safe now?"

"As safe as any of us—that is, not safe at all."

We sat through a long silence, as I studied the bowed head of the man who always sat upright, with his eyes facing forward. This Wyatt whom I loved was now shattered and grief stricken, neither hero nor villain, just a man who'd witnessed more carnage than he could stomach. Yet, he forever felt an obligation to shoulder the load, to make things right, even if they were unrightable, unfightable wrongs.

"Tell me what's in that hard head of yours, Wyatt." I placed a hand on his nape, the other on his knee, my touch softening my words. He remained still, silent. "You can bottle it up. I understand. I won't force you to talk, or to listen, but I'll speak until you cry 'enough'!"

"Go on, Sadie, I'm listening."

"Maintain a tough front with your brothers. I understand. You aren't the oldest, but you are the fiercest among strong men. You are their leader, their anchor. That's clear to everyone. But you don't always have to be tough with me. You rushed to protect me, and warn me, as soon as you could get free. I hope you also came for another reason, whether you accept it or not: you came to unburden yourself. Wyatt, you cannot carry this weight on your shoulders all day, all the time, behind bars and on the street, heeled or not. You are not a pack animal. There was no joy for you in the deaths of the McLaury boys and Billy Clanton, no satisfaction."

"Lord have mercy, no," he whispered.

"I know this. Your brothers do, too. The guilt will kill you. It will sap your strength. You cannot preserve people that do not want to be shielded. Wyatt, you cannot even protect people from themselves. The fiends tried to assassinate Virgil, unarmed, unwarned. They're animals."

"Cow-thieving bastards."

"Virgil may die. He may not. He may be crippled. But *you* did not shoot him. He called you to Arizona for the opportunities he saw. He wore the deputy US Marshal badge as well as the name of Earp."

"He *wears* the badge and *bears* our name. He is not yet dead."

"He will not die, Wyatt. Look at me. *Really* look at me." Wyatt gazed up, balefully, without raising a wall of strength, without smiling to make me smile. I took in those sad, tired eyes and stared back, radiating love and light. "This is who I am for you. Talk to me, tell me your troubles. I may flinch at a gunshot, but I will not flinch at anything you tell me. Good, bad, or indifferent. I will hear you out. I know down deep you are a good man. You can parse right from wrong. But,

331

please, do not feel obligated to be an angel in my eyes. You are a caretaker and a lawmaker, but you are no good for nobody a broken-down heap."

I held my breath then, wondering if I had gone too far, pushing a man already down too hard, when all he wanted was a bit of soft shoulder and a place to rest. Then he spoke: "You don't know what it's like to see Virgil broken again after all that time in bed with his leg. There was so much blood, and his arm just hanging like a bent branch. No way I could lie and say it was a stitch away from being fixed. Virgil survived the war without seeing a bullet, only to be wounded leaving a saloon. I never wore a uniform. Now I'm shooting men on the street. And, look, this blood on my sleeves is all his, not mine."

"You can't blame yourself for being lucky, baby."

"But I do, Sadie. Every day while I'm walking and my brothers carry the bullet scars that ache when the weather turns. Now, tonight, Virgil took buckshot in cold blood—not a fair fight by any reckoning. I have hunted buffalo to forget my sorrows over Willa, one falling after the other, without remorse. Now cowboys hunt my brothers and me as if we were beasts. There is more than enough silver in these mountains, and gold in these saloons, to satisfy. It's just the gamble: some win, some lose. Apaches aren't our foes; they fight for their territory just like we would. Rattle a

332

hive and hornets sting. The braves do not enter our saloons, get drunk, and shoot up the town, dropping an enemy in the dark from behind a blind. This is white men gone wild. This is evil. And when the cowboys control the local sheriff, that smooth-talking ass-licker Behan, it is a dangerous world. Damn that fool Ike, he dropped his hat running from the scene tonight—with *his name* in it. His whining and threatening whipped up that damn gunfight that got his brother killed—that got my brother killed tonight, or close to. Now, I've killed men, too. How am I different from Ike in the eyes of the law, and how can I prove myself a better man?"

"Are you a drunk, Wyatt? Are you a fool? No."

"No, Sadie, I'm not."

"You are a true man, but now may not be the time to act. Standing against the cowboy crew is a big and, perhaps, impossible job. Consider your kin: Virgil's life is hanging by a thread. You are that thread. Stand beside Virgil now and tell him what he means to you while you still can; he needs you. He *will* be avenged. But what good does that do him now?"

"It has been so long since I could rest, since I could just lie back in a field and watch the clouds pass overhead. It has been duty and responsibility, burying the dead. I have the strength to stand off a lynch mob, Sadie. I do. I can pull my gun in a vacant lot and shoot faster than the man whose gun is pointing at my heart. But there is a toll on me. A man doesn't see the light go out in another man's eyes during a senseless squabble without knowing that death comes to us all, to his brothers and mine. And," his voiced cracked, "I cannot bear to leave you, or lose you."

"Hush," I said, deeply moved. He had so often been strong for me, and here I was protecting him without a pistol. "I am not going anywhere, and neither are you. I cannot pull you on my lap, but come, rest your head."

I took Wyatt's hat and tossed it on the empty chair, lowering his head gently onto my thighs. I combed my fingers through his hair, finding the tangles and running them through. I smoothed his thick eyebrows, lightly, gently. I circled the depressions above his ears with my fingertips, and felt his shoulders relax. I rubbed his temples. His legs extended. His right arm fell over my knees, his hand opened, callused palm up.

While I wanted to beg Wyatt to leave Tombstone with me immediately, I knew that was impossible. I stroked his head, letting the love I felt for him flow through my hands. My needs were nothing in comparison to his: I was all for Wyatt.

We shared the settee for a long time, until the clattering in the dining room increased. The maid set the table. The cook barked that the toast had burnt. A gentleman in pressed pinstripes and a pocket handkerchief blundered into the parlor and then retreated as if he were on fire.

I did not stay my hand until Wyatt stirred beneath it. "I have to go back, Sadie."

"I know," I said, in the peace between gunshots. "I'm here. I love you."

"I love you, too. I just want to be free to love you all the time, always."

CHAPTER 27
JANUARY 1882

Wyatt and I lay in a knot of sheets, entangled, loose-limbed like big cats. My cheek rested on his chest. I like a man with chest hair. I attended his heartbeat, calm now and rhythmic while my own quickened, ascending again as my free hand flattened on his navel, feeling the warmth, the rise and fall of him. He lay with his arms splayed out, legs heavy, naked feet oddly vulnerable with their gnarled toes, the smallest ones curved under, half-hidden.

We'd become acquainted with each other's bodies, the quirks and quiet spots. Our knowledge was just the beginning of a long journey we would take to please each other. This peace at dawn was something that we'd taught ourselves: spend the night together as if there was no day, no tomorrow, no eddies of enmity swirling around the town. No Johnny Behan. No Mattie. As if we were absolutely alone, no armed guard in the alley, another in the lot, where three men died and reputations soured. A third posted on Fremont Street, one knee bent and boot propped on the facade of Fly's Boardinghouse, leaning casually with a hat tipped over his forehead, but every nerve awake.

That frigid, fragile month, we hoarded our time together. I sensed this night would be our last. At first light, Wyatt was leading a posse with a warrant for the arrest of the remaining Clanton brothers. He would ride as a deputy US Marshal, having requested and received Virgil's appointment following his shooting. The badge was no use to his older brother. Bedridden, Virgil fought daily for his life, at the very least his arm, up in the Cosmopolitan Hotel with Allie as nurse and jailer. Across Allen Street, the cowboys had assembled in the Grand Hotel, shooting distance from the Cosmopolitan, capable of firing at any moment. If Virgil could be attacked on Allen Street, it was open season on the Earps in town and in the vast surrounding wilderness.

A dusty light had begun to seep beneath the shutters on January 23. I glanced at the bedside table, observing an oval portrait of two plump young boys in a silver frame. The smaller, cherubic child in christening white was Doc. His cousin Robert, the slightly older, darker-haired boy, sulked beside him, shooting baby daggers at the photographer. Behind that was a dark picture of Doc and his mother. He was slightly older than in the other photograph, scowling over Alice Holliday's lap as the bonneted woman looked up and away from her ghostly son with his tiny clutched fist. I had asked Wyatt where Mrs. Holliday was now. He said, "In the ground." She had passed her consumption on to her sensitive son, born with a cleft palate and lip, before she died. He had loved her very much. His father remarried three months later.

Doc had ridden to Contention to gamble and lent us his room at Fly's. It was a small cabinet of oddities: a dental cast of teeth, a skull, piles of letters in brown ink—some unsent, others captured in grosgrain ribbons of red, mauve, and black. There were books in towers in the corners of the room, the stoutest at the bottom, Latin and Greek, philosophy and art. Pages from some had been pulled and tacked to the walls, marked with his calligraphic penmanship: notes to remember, truths to retell.

Wyatt shifted under me and said, "The light."

"Shut your eyes, then," I said. But he wouldn't. I felt his muscles tense beneath me as he retook his arms and legs from us. The mattress complained as he planted his feet on the floor. He reached to the foot post to grab his long johns. I was a harsh taskmaster and would not let him love me separated by cotton despite the chill.

I kneeled on the bed behind Wyatt, encircling his chest, finding the sweet spot at the bend of his neck with my mouth and kissing him there until he softened. I felt his shoulders release beneath my breasts, and I waited for him to fall back. But he didn't. He leaned forward, putting on his drawers, reaching for his shirt, his socks, his pants, his suspenders, his vest, his coat, until the man who rose beside the bed was the stranger Wyatt, the cardboard cutout, still handsome but without the warmth I knew so intimately. He pinned on the badge. He strapped on his holsters.

"Let's not make a fuss," he said. "I'll be back when I'm back."

"You're the one who fusses," I said. Still kneeling on the bed, I stretched my back muscles with my hands splayed on my hips, shaking my loose hair until it tickled the top of my buttocks.

"Don't send me away like this," Wyatt said, looking down.

"Then go, now, because if I kiss you the way I want to, it will be broad daylight before you leave this room."

Wyatt leaned over and pecked my forehead. I raised my lips and our mouths met, closed and soft, a good-bye kiss. He smelled of me. He would carry that on the trail with him. Wyatt turned, grasped the doorknob without looking back, and disappeared. I heard a stranger's deep voice in the hallway say, "Wyatt."

"Let's ride," Wyatt said. Their boots echoed in the hallway. The boardinghouse door opened and shut. I could hear the sound of water splashing and Marietta scolding someone in Spanish. The day began for working folk.

It was getting lighter as I lay crumpled in the middle of the bed, surrounded by books and photographs and sepia-toned secrets. I didn't want to be alone. The clopping sound of horses became more frequent on Fremont Street. The traffic increased on the alley to the O.K. Corral. Somewhere deep in the house, I heard Mollie calling cheerily, "Marietta, *venga*." I smelled coffee. The day began. Wyatt was already in the saddle. He could have been a mile away or ten or two hundred. If he wasn't in bed with me, I felt I would weep for loneliness. But I stopped myself: falling into a farewell funk, I would not rise until dark when the sadness would be there to meet me, an unwanted guest that refused to leave.

I slid off the bed. Reluctant to shed the night's languor, I decided to seek Mollie's company, comfort, and coffee in the studio. Buck was off on one of his photographic adventures, and we would have the place to ourselves to play. It was still too early for customers. I reached behind the door for Kate's kimono. I gave a little hop to release the heavy silk damask from the hook. It was peach-colored, stitched with peonies and cherry blossoms and golden phoenix birds in flight. The lining was cream silk satin. The robe swam around me, so I wrapped it and tied it closed with a cerise sash I found on the floor. Pushing my cold toes into Kate's red embroidered mules, I snooped absentmindedly at the papers tacked to the walls until I saw a photograph of Doc reclining in Fly's studio, naked except for a handkerchief across his lap. He looked at the book he held open in one hand, his other propping up his head to reveal ropy biceps, a pointy elbow, and visible demarcated ribs.

It was a rare oddity, a photograph of a naked man, and I found that while I wanted to look away, disturbed, instead I moved closer and stared, intrigued. I was flushed and ashamed, but knew that if Doc had wanted to keep this secret from me, it would not have been there on the wall of his private room. In the photo, his skin resembled marble. He was more muscled than I imagined, since his suits often hung off his shoulders, too large as he slowly disappeared from his life on earth, consumed one cough at a time. He had long since abandoned keeping up the appearances that his good Georgia breeding had once demanded.

Rather than hiding my discovery, I took the photograph and pinned it upside down so that Doc would know I saw it.

I opened the bedroom door, leaving my day clothes scattered around the room and shuffling down the hallway to the studio in Kate's big slippers. It was then, when I saw Mollie waiting at the table with coffee poured and Mexican pastries piled on a silver tray, that the tears began to press against my eyes.

"Don't." Mollie leapt from the lady chair.

"What have I done? Should I not be wearing Kate's things?"

"No," she said. "Kate's kimono suits you. I don't want you to cry. I'm no meteorologist, but I can see the flood coming. Look at my finger. This is the dike. We are going to plug up those tears and let the melancholy emerge in every other way, like sweat from your skin. Just whatever you do, Josephine Marcus, don't weep. It will ruin our pictures. Hold it all in and release the sorrow through your body."

"I just want to cry on your shoulder."

"I empathize, yet I have a scheme that might distract you. Trust me?"

"Always—we survived gunfire together."

"The bullet holes in the walls prove how close we came to our—what do they call them? Dirt baths? What an awful term, yet it is so descriptive."

Mollie removed her apron and folded it, flaglike, in triangles. Inspiration flared in the small woman's eyes. "Goodie," she said, as much to herself as me. "I'm so glad you're here today—and Buck's not. He's off in search of the next big death or disaster—even if it's his own. Men need to risk their necks. I have no desire. We have life overflowing right in this room that Buck cannot be bothered to capture. Come, Josie, sit down and have a coffee and a sweet roll."

After making me comfortable in the lady chair that she'd warmed, Mollie bustled to the studio's center and her camera tripod. She placed the back of her Scovill in the landscape position, the prepared glass plates already stacked on the long worktable. She glanced at me over her shoulder and wagged a finger. "No kisses and coddling this morning. Suck those salty tears in and have another pastry. Concentrate on the sugary sweetness. Marietta doesn't have a light touch with it, and she makes the best coffee. You'll have time to milk that sadness soon enough."

I obeyed. I shut my eyelids, the crying urge pressing behind, a single drop or two still clinging to my lashes. Savoring the sweet bun comforted me. And then there was the awakening fire of cinnamon. I opened my lids, reached for another roll, and doused my dark coffee in thick cream until it was the color of a dun pony.

The camera viewed a new setup. Heavy tasseled drapes formed a backdrop behind a narrow stage. A long, low upholstered chaise with bun feet stretched across the platform, arousing my curiosity. I recognized the furniture from the picture of Doc.

Mollie rose. "Josie, leave your coffee for now.

You'll have time for more between setups. Would you do me the favor of lying on the chaise with your back to me?"

While it seemed odd to pose for a photograph facing away from the camera, I acquiesced. I felt so much like my new self and unlike my old self, draped in silk with nothing underneath but my own limbs and bumps. I longed for Wyatt between my legs and in my heart, but concentrated instead on the aftertaste of sugar and cinnamon, the coffee's homey aroma, and steady Mollie's instructions. I climbed the platform, which was covered in a Persian carpet. Scuffing off the red mules with their feathery pompoms, I reclined on the chaise, arranging the pools of fabric around me, propping my head up with my left hand as I studied the swags of the curtains, a view of next to nothing.

"I want you to be comfortable in everything we do today," said Mollie. "Do you feel comfort-able?"

"I'm twisted up in this kimono," I said, tugging at the silk here and sliding it there, and looking over my shoulder at Mollie.

"Don't look at me—yet," Mollie said. "I'll tell you when. For now, I don't know who you are. You are a beauty in a kimono. You could be Japanese, your hair is so dark, your skin so pale. Imagine that. You are Japanese. You are a foreigner. You are lying in a garden surrounded by peonies and cherry blossoms. A phoenix wanders nearby. Consider how the silk feels against your skin, the chill against your naked toes, and the sugar on your tongue."

"How will you get that in a picture, with my big behind facing you?"

"That's my concern, Josephine," Mollie said with studied patience. "Just follow my voice. Listen to me. Relax your shoulders, let your head fall into the crook of your elbow, feel the silk. Try to notice wherever the silk touches your skin as if it were a man's hand, Wyatt's hand."

I felt my body relax. My shoulders dropped. I released my neck, stretched the fingers, and then let my free hand fall heavily where my legs intersected. I bent my knees and curved my feet around each other. I heard Mollie behind me, exposing film, changing glass plates, moving the camera closer, changing lenses. As she did this, I relaxed more deeply—not dozing, not forgetting my pain, but suspended in the camera's eye.

"Now, shrug off the silk," Mollie said. "Start with your shoulders. Don't worry where the robe falls. We want random folds. Kick back the material with your top leg. There. Now you've shed your second skin to reveal a new, lush layer of silk."

The air chilled me. Excitement stirred. My nipples hardened. Goosebumps formed, raising the hair on my forearms. I had been on the verge of arousal when Wyatt left. Now it returned, and I felt my thighs tighten and my pelvis rise. True, I had in my mind the photographic image of Doc, reclined, so much himself before the lens, but also the reality of Wyatt, his long legs over mine until I didn't know where he began and I ended. I held myself between two beats, relaxed in my body and aloft in Mollie's gaze. I again heard the glass plates slide into the camera, the shutter close, and then the sound of Mollie's deliberate footsteps as she approached.

"I've warmed up my hands," Mollie said. "Now I'm going to compose you. I will start at the top and work down. Tell me if you ever feel uncomfortable. Just say, 'Stop.'"

Mollie began with my hair, pulling out the strands so that they cascaded down my back, looping it in the messy braids so carefully plaited the night before. Her gentle touch relaxed me. Her soft, warm hands moved to my shoulders, straightening their alignment. She pushed my top hip toward the drapes, tucked my left knee under my thigh with two hands, tucking my left foot back so that the sole faced the camera. Her final touch was to elongate my right leg, curling my left toes around my right ankle.

I let Mollie shape me as if I were bread dough, as if I were that little flour banker with the egg-yolk hair I showed to Wyatt so long ago in Kitty's house while baking strudel. Mollie rolled me this way and that. She started gently and, when I didn't complain, became firmer, more matter of fact. I heard her footsteps retreat to assess her composition, and then felt the return of her warm hands, her soft coffee breath. I was not the actress at the center of the stage, not Pauline Markham, who could seduce the stoniest heart in the audience. Instead, I became the image of beauty at the center of my friend's photograph in this game we played together while everyone else was out of the studio. This was performance, even if it was not movement.

"Now, Josephine, slowly raise yourself on the pillow and twist your face toward me. That's not going to work. Try this: throw your left hand over the back of the chaise without arching your back. That's it. Hold on gently. That's good. Now bend your right elbow. Goodie. Use your right hand to position your face toward me, resting your cheek on the palm. Your hair is perfect just as it is. Leave it."

Mollie stepped away again, and I tried to hold the position. I breathed deeply, not considering my nakedness but the puzzle piece my body had become. She said, "There's one problem. Can you take that left breast that's getting crushed and push it out just a smidgen? No radical movements, mind. This is a small shift. Try arching your back to release it. Now relax your back again. Your hips are still facing backward, your head forward. Perfect.

"Now," continued Mollie, "although you might want to shed tears from the torturous twist, I want you to consider your feelings as you entered the studio this morning. Resist tears and let it flow through your gaze, your lips, or the reach of your neck. Feel it in places that you think the camera won't see, and it will be visible elsewhere. Bring Wyatt back with your eyes, not your words."

The pressure behind my eyes returned with full force. I projected the emotions as if my pupils were pistols. In my head I could hear my voice, and it said, *One more time, come back to bed. Let the Clantons run until high noon. This may be the last time, our last time.* Liquid welled beneath my eyes. *Wyatt, please, stay, but if you must go, know that this is what you are leaving behind—and let that knowledge bring you back to me.*

"Beautiful," Mollie said. "If I were Wyatt, I'd turn my horse around right now. Can we risk one more shot? I have an idea."

"What's that?"

"Untwist yourself and I'll tell you," Mollie said. "I have a prop."

Slipping the silk kimono around me, I slid off the chaise. Mollie left the room. She returned with a gray box tied in a black ribbon. After carefully opening the box, she rounded her shoulders and seemed to pause, as if trying to decide whether to reveal its contents. Then Mollie removed a long black-net widow's veil.

I shuddered. "What's that?"

"I bought it from Addie when Buck stayed away longer than intended on the trail of Apaches. Have you ever bought an umbrella to keep it from raining? That's why I purchased this veil: hope and fear."

I fingered the fine mesh. "If it's some kind of superstitious protection, I'll buy in."

"No need for your pennies. Maybe we should wait for another day. It's getting time for customers to come knocking. I don't want to risk it."

"Just tell me what you want. If we hear footsteps on the porch, I'll run behind the curtain."

Mollie retreated behind the tripod, switching the camera back to the portrait setting. "Drop the robe and kick it aside. I don't want it in the shot."

I covered my head and draped the veil over my shoulders and breasts. Below my navel, I clasped my hands.

"Raise your chin, Josie. Show me a pout."

I gazed at Mollie's lens with a controlled intensity. In my mind, I conjured Wyatt and felt desire rise in me, driven by the memory of his passion that had washed over me again and again the night before. I felt, for a moment, triumphant. I sensed the power of my body and how it vibrated with life. It was an ecstatic moment.

But it was only a moment, a moment draped in black: it was possible that I would become Wyatt's widow before I became his bride.

CHAPTER 28
FEBRUARY 1882

Dark days followed, accompanied by heavy snows. At Fly's, I monitored daily dispatches. The surviving Clantons eluded Wyatt. His posse, including Morgan and Doc, scoured Charleston and the county's farthest corners armed with shotguns, Winchester rifles, and pistols. No Ike.

A week later, I heard that the Clanton brothers surrendered to a second posse, claiming they feared for their necks in Earp custody. As if Wyatt was capable of such lawless brutality while wearing a badge! Those brutes returned to Tombstone, facing charges for Virgil's shooting. In early February, Ike had his day in Judge Stilwell's court. The prosecution's evidence—his hat at the scene—was circumstantial. Seven alibi witnesses testified he was in Charleston at the time of the shooting.

Ike was acquitted. I was enraged. It got worse.

Exonerated and emboldened, Ike filed a new murder indictment—this time in Contention, not Tombstone—against the Earps and Doc for October's gunfight. We were going to be dragged under threat of the noose again. Johnny, ful-filling the arrest warrant, first sought Wyatt at the

Cosmopolitan Hotel. He took Morgan into custody there, leaving behind the wounded Virgil.

Sheriff Behan, armed and empowered, now walked door to door in all the familiar places—the Oriental, Vogan's, the Alhambra Saloon, the tobacconist, even the ice-cream parlor—to flush out his rival in love and law. While Mollie and Buck discreetly walked to the post office, gleaning the gossip on the streets, Wyatt and I huddled at Fly's Gallery. We had a sliver of time together before Johnny's inevitable arrival to arrest Doc—and him.

Wyatt, pacing the boards, ignored his coffee, although Marietta brewed the best in town. Having downed mine while I waited for his arrival, I felt wide-awake and deeply anxious. I dreaded separation, whether it was jail or Wyatt scouring the territory for violent offenders at the head of a posse begging for a sniper's bullet.

I wanted to stake my future on this beautiful man from Illinois. The feeling was mutual. Together, we had carved out time amid the chaos of clan warfare and complicated domestic arrangements. During those intimate moments, I was as closely connected to another human being as I'd ever been and, I felt, ever would be. I did not want to abandon that. And then, along came Johnny, who couldn't value what he had, but put a price on what he lacked. His jealousy, coupled with his sheriff's badge, terrified me. I sensed my time with Wyatt was about to end. My sadness drove a great anger: I wanted to shoot Johnny myself. I knew Wyatt wouldn't do it. He was no killer.

That critical morning, I took comfort that Wyatt wanted to spend his last free moments with me. I tried to moderate my emotions to support him, rather than increasing the tension. Perched on the edge of the chaise, I waited for Wyatt to make his point. He'd talked to his lawyer. Ike's filing wasn't double jeopardy because the first go-round in Judge Spicer's court had been a hearing, not a trial.

Observing Wyatt's frustration, my anxiety rose. He had explained that in a dangerous situation, one's own panic served the enemy. The adversary, whether Apache or cowboy, was waiting in the dark or behind a tree, counting on this weakness. If I could learn to control my hysteria, I became an ally, not a burden. It was the difference between fearlessness and bravery. I focused on Wyatt. He would not break. Neither would I.

Wyatt turned to me, his face somber. "Johnny is the law in Tombstone. We've both been fooled before, Sadie. We won't be fooled again."

"Amen."

"If I'd been named sheriff, believe me, the cowboys would never have risen like this. But that's over and done with. Mad dog Clanton won't let go. He's set his teeth in me."

"He's a slobbering bulldog, Wyatt. They'll set you free. You said it yourself: they have no new evidence. This will blow over."

"Sad to say, Sadie, this will not blow over. It will blow up. Ike has Johnny to do his dirty work. Nothing makes Behan happier than cuffing me and jeopardizing you."

Wyatt was right. Danger didn't just knock. It pounded. Now wasn't the moment to persuade him otherwise. While I wanted to soothe him and prompt the comfort of his reassurance, I followed his lead. I stuck to the facts: "What is our plan?"

"I'm considering and sifting our options. Today, I have no choice." Wyatt raised his forearms in mock surrender. "Johnny will find me soon enough. I'm prepared if it only means jail and justice. What disturbs me is that I'm a lawman by nature and now lack faith in the system. I've done my month in court, my weeks in jail. It's cost me dearly in cash and credibility. I won't be caged again. I've called in all my markers and mortgaged my house to raise attorney fees. Virgil will never regain the use of his arm. His Allie blames me as if I had loaded the shotguns. She thinks I'm impervious to her opinion, but I'm not, given that she slings it at me day after day."

"You are brothers together. When has Allie's carping ever affected you?"

"I'm worn down, Sadie. My hopes for making a

respectable life here surrounded by my kin, with real estate and businesses and bank accounts, died in jail. Between us, I'm concerned. We ride over to Contention and we could get shot at any point along the way. These cowboys are brazen. We sit in jail there, we're begging for the rope even if Ike's suit is unfounded. Behind bars we're sitting ducks, as vulnerable as Johnny-Behind-the-Deuce."

"What can I do?" I could not bear the thought, after so much death, of adding Wyatt's corpse to the pile. How would his strong face appear when no longer capable of expression, those lips robbed of kissing, those thick muscles slack? For a horrifying instant, I saw the image as it would appear in a C. S. Fly photograph, and then I chased it away as best I could. How do you describe premourning: the fear borne by women left behind when dispatching husbands and sons to prison or battle, that impossible agitation edged in hope that you will see them again, safe and unbroken? It was like weighing odds at the faro table, gambling on life and fearing death. I reined in my tears even though I wanted to hide Wyatt in the cupboard with the cameras. We could wait until nightfall and flee together. But, no, he wouldn't have submitted. Instead, I steadied myself for the reason he'd called me to him. I sensed he was about to lay down the law.

Wyatt reached out his hand. I shuddered,

knowing how close I was to tears as I took it. I kissed the inside of his palm, the callus at the base of his ring finger. Horses wheeled in the alley. "I am no outlaw. Sadie, this is not your fight."

"It's not yours anymore, either. You did not want to fight Ike. You spared his life. And now, here you are, dumped into the cowboy muck again. You will be exonerated. You will have your chance to see justice served."

"That might be true, Sadie. It might not. But that's irrelevant. If I am ever to get out alive, I need a reason to continue: our future together."

I longed to kiss those lips to seal that deal, so reassured was I at his dependence, but we had so little time. The risk of separation might extend beyond weeks and months. It was unbearable, but I said, "Do what you believe is right, Wyatt. And tell me what to do."

"Leave here now. Get out tonight. I'll settle your debts. I booked you passage on the Benson stage and the San Francisco train under the name Joanna Brown. Forget good-byes. Send letters to your friends once you're safe. Pack your trunks and leave them in your room for James to ship directly. Take only a carpetbag, as if you were just doing an overnight errand. Leave your parents' address for me here. I will come and get you when this is over."

I gulped, clutching Wyatt's hand. "When will it be over?"

"I'm no fortune-teller. When I'm free and clear, I'll kiss you in San Francisco."

Boots scrambled on the gallery porch. The door banged inward, introducing wind-borne dirt and horse-crap stink, shaming the cheery jingle of the customer bell. Johnny swaggered in and muscled between us. "Wyatt Berry Stapp Earp, I arrest you for the murders of William Clanton, Frank McLaury, and Thomas McLaury."

I felt inclined to spit, and jeer: *"Hypocrite. Whoremonger. Coward."* I wanted to run to Wyatt and wrap myself around him so they couldn't capture him. Instead, I respected that Wyatt wanted to take the high road as he was dragged down the low one. Without so much as a parting kiss, he disappeared in the stamping of boots and the clamping of irons. Doc's curses came from the other room, and Kate cussed like no man I'd ever heard, in filthy English and undecipherable Hungarian, and then Doc, too, was gone.

Alone in the studio, I stood immobilized. I wanted to crumble. But that wasn't Wyatt's woman. I sat down at Mollie's rolltop desk, pulled a sheet of stationery from one of the cubbies, and sat staring at the blank page embossed with the words FLY'S PHOTOGRAPHY GALLERY. Looking up at the slots in the desk, I saw, half-hidden amid the piles of photographs, the most recent intimate images of me. I took two and placed them side by side on the desk by the blotter. I was no longer the girl in too-tight braids tied in tartan ribbon.

I had my inspiration. I wrote simply:

Dearest Wyatt,
Come back to me.

The words mattered less than the photograph. It was my image in the widow's veil. In it my chin raised to emphasize my cheekbones, and my eyes gazed out from the heavy paper with a knowing expectancy. My curves beneath the veil pleased me: I saw myself as Wyatt saw me, creamy-skinned and inviting. Mollie had captured in film what Buck had yet to do: she'd caught life on camera, not death's stillness. This was a photo of a woman in love and lust demanding her man remain safe, if only to return to her bed. I slid the photo in the envelope addressed to Mr. Wyatt Earp from Miss Josephine Sarah Marcus above my parents' San Francisco address, then cleared away everything else on the blotter and placed the envelope at its center where Mollie would be sure to see it.

I placed the second photograph in an envelope, put on my coat and gloves, wrapped myself in a shawl, and left through the boardinghouse. From Doc's room, I heard crockery hit the wall and shatter. I kept walking until I arrived at the Fremont Street door. On the porch, the wind whipped up the dirt, and I paused to cover my head with the shawl, concealing my face. Without stopping at Addie Bourland's directly across the street to cancel a dress order and bid good-bye, I hastened toward the San Jose, my mind now full of the details that amass when one is leaving a town where one has lived for over a year.

Crossing diagonally at Fourth Street, a small woman blocked my way amid the horse traffic. "You don't remember me, do you?" Allie Earp asked.

I could hardly see Virgil's wife with the wind whisking the dirt into my eyes and my head full of bees. I couldn't proceed without knocking her down, so I looked at the tiny, sour-faced woman beneath her old-fashioned bonnet. I remembered her from Mrs. Clum's funeral, although we had never been properly introduced, as many hours as I'd spent in Virgil's company with Wyatt.

"You're—" I began.

"Allie," she said. "Allie Earp. Mrs. Virgil Earp."

I applied a pleasant smile. "A pleasure; I'm in a bit of a rush."

"I'm sure you are. But before you swan off, I have a few things to get off my chest. I hardly register in your opinion, but I remember you from the first day you stepped off that stage."

"You have a good memory," I said. "But I don't think we should discuss this in the middle of the street. Getting trampled would please neither Wyatt nor Virgil."

Allie didn't move. She railed on. "Who are you to speak for Wyatt? Mattie is his wife, though it gives her no pleasure, and he never made it legal."

I felt a headache coming on after hearing her refer to Mattie as Wyatt's wife. "Now is not the time."

"Isn't that too bad, Miss High-and-Mighty. I have something to say, and I'm going to say it. Stay away from my kin. You've brought bullets and Behan down on our heads from the day you arrived."

"I hate Johnny Behan. He just took Wyatt from me."

"I hated you from the moment you climbed off that stagecoach. Virgil told me about you: the Jewess Johnny Behan shipped down from San Francisco. I was heading to the post office when I caught you smiling at Morgan. Then you did that double take we all do the first time we see a brother Earp. There was that cuss Wyatt, although I despise speaking ill of kin, in his black hat and coat, as neat as a pointy pin, thanks to Mattie's hard work."

"I don't remember seeing you."

"Why would you? You wouldn't have the time of day for me. But I saw you smile at Wyatt, you man-eater. I wouldn't let you near my Virgil. You and your airs, as if Johnny was a prince—and we all know how true that was. Behan shamed you, and then you had to get back at him with Wyatt.

Wasn't there anyone of your own kind you could cleave to and leave us alone?"

"I don't have to listen to this." I felt the urge to shove her and find Wyatt. The tears that I had withheld were knocking at the door of my lids crying, *Let us out!* But Wyatt had told me about Allie and her meddling ways. I remembered his words the first time he showed his hand: he had never loved Mattie. He never would. All that mattered was that we would be together.

A horseman in the street denounced us. Allie shook her fist at him and stood her ground. "Yes, Missy, you do have to listen now that you've gotten all twisted up in our business. I married Virgil, but I got five Earps. It was no bargain, five for the price of one. We're fine when it's just the two of us, but that hasn't happened since you brought the sky down on us in Tombstone."

Rage rose up in me. "I am not to blame."

"Beauties like you never are, gathering the silver that working men mined. When you stepped off that stagecoach, I felt a shiver run through me. I had a premonition. I turned around, went home, and cut the cards in the middle of our bed to see the future. Out they came: all black, all spades. I'd never seen the like. There were five of them: a spade flush, ace high."

"Isn't that a lucky hand?"

"If you think a pile of death is lucky. That spade flush was the five brothers, all devilish handsome and doomed to die together. The cards don't lie."

"They're just made of paper, you superstitious witch. Wyatt's flesh and bone, and he's all mine."

By midnight that night, Tombstone was at my back—but Allie's words haunted me all the way back to San Francisco.

CHAPTER 29

I found Mama alone in the concrete backyard behind Perry Street, a spot tighter and narrower than the vacant lot beside Fly's. Settling my carpetbag on the back steps, I watched the white linen ballooning in the breeze and knew I'd abandoned the land of zephyrs and dust, where clean sheets hung out to dry were likely to come down dirtier than they began. I'd returned home with less baggage and more heartache. I desperately missed both Wyatt and who I was with him.

I watched Mama. Clarifying my emotions, I reckoned that I feared rejection and exposure. I considered hiding my pain so that Mama would not immediately see my vulnerability—and feast on it. She sucked two clothespins in her mouth, which added to her face's determination. She had aged, the worry lines deepening above the prominent nose, canyons cutting at the corners of her lips. She held the clothesline and the linen in her left hand, and clipped with her right.

Despite the chilly weather, Mama lacked a sweater. Sweat stained her armpits. She worked against time, raising her eyes to the sky. Above, the clouds hovered and indicated no reprieve. Would the sheets dry before the rain came? She returned to pinning without looking forward, where she would have seen my face. She hung her head. I wondered if that had always been her posture and I hadn't recognized it before, or if shame of my opprobrious behavior had bent her. Perhaps it was also the weight of constantly being submissive in the larger society, taking the load and not talking back to anyone who had power over her.

I approached and took two clothespins from the cloth sack hanging on the line within Mama's reach. I grabbed a damp pillowcase—the easier task; she would have noted that—and hung it on an empty line. I returned again, taking clothespins, pillowcases, sheets. Whether or not she would acknowledge it, we pinned linens together.

Seen objectively, perhaps from a neighbor's window, we were mother and daughter doing the wash. Except that I was in traveling clothes, my hair piled on my head and twined in tiny braids, my cheeks rouged, my eyebrows plucked. Tucked in my bag was a hidden photograph that captured the essence of me and my beauty, reclining in

Mollie's gaze—an image that would confirm every judgment Mama had mustered the day of my departure, and every day since.

There was too much linen for one small family. Mama was taking in laundry again. Resentment edged her movements. I hesitated among the sheet ghosts, my arms already weary from the unaccustomed menial task, and began the speech I'd prepared on the long train out of Benson. I spoke in an even tone, not attending an invitation that might never arrive. "I have seen enough death since last we were together to mourn loss, Mama."

My mother continued hanging without pause. I said, undeterred: "I saw young men shot for pride and misunderstanding and drunkenness, lying together in cracker boxes. I have witnessed heroes shot to bits that would give anything just to be able to raise both arms and pin laundry."

"Who told you to go?"

"It was my choice. I left alone and unprotected. You were right to be fearful." I intended to be conciliatory, to ride out the hostility and prove that I was the bigger woman for it. "I discovered that families must stick together no matter the cost, a lesson I learned from Wyatt Earp and his brothers, Morgan, Virgil, Warren, and James. In that light, it strikes me as unjust to sit *shivah* for the living."

Mama sniffed, not in sadness but disgust, clearly unimpressed.

I approached, faced her, and said, "See me? I am alive. I am your daughter. I am myself."

Mama looked back at me, sharp-eyed. "I see you. You are alive. You are my daughter, whoever that is today, and whenever that changes tomorrow."

Her response fell like a weight on me. I reminded myself that it would take time to heal. Look how long it took Virgil to regain his strength. I must retreat and lower my expectations while I awaited Wyatt. I could not expect the kind of embrace from Mama that I felt I deserved; the kind she'd always withheld.

"Your father has been in mourning since the day you left."

"Is that because he misses me," I said, losing my composure at the suggestion of his complicity in her religious charade, "or because I left him with you?"

"You talk like *that* to your mother?"

"It's just words, Mama. I'm not pointing a gun. I've heard of plenty of people who got shot for less."

"Is that why you came back?"

"I didn't come back. I'm running, Mama, I'm running."

I didn't even feel like crying. My actions didn't shame me. They shamed Mama. I'd staked out a life in the wider world. I had to walk the higher road because I had seen farther. I had to make peace with myself in this situation, not with Mama. We were, and nearly always had been, like two antagonists on a narrow stage. I had to make my exit or be consumed in our mutual rage. We fell into each other, fed on each other. Papa needed me at home to take the heat. He also needed my companionship in a hostile house where he earned the money but ceded control to Mama.

Feeling like a beggar, I asked: "Can I stay here with you and Papa?"

"Where else are you going to sleep?"

As if I were a polite stranger at an inn, I said, "Thank you." And then I continued. "Thank you for marrying that sweet, sweet man. Thank you for the sisters and brother. Thanks for the sheets, the blankets, the schlepping and schooling."

"Well, suddenly you're grateful. I never would have known."

"You've worked hard, Mama. Thanks for all the burdens you've shouldered. *But:* taking responsibility does not excuse the not-quite-loving. Your feelings need no excuse, but it would help if they were out in the open. I had an obligation to advance our fortunes in the Jewish community by marrying well. Instead, I served up shame."

"You have no idea."

"I think I do. I'm not your favorite child, or even your third favorite. I'm shallow, slutty, and vain, if you are to be believed. But I'm Papa's favorite, and that's more than enough love for me."

"You should hear how your father talks about you."

"I thought he didn't talk since I left."

"You think I don't consider walking away? You think you are the only woman that was ever young and beautiful and wanted the world? I had Rebecca when I was your age. And her blessed father, the ginger from Poland, he did not die. I was never a widow. He was a Torah scholar, a rabbi's son. He was a *goniff* who took me and left me pregnant. I was not good enough for his father. I was not of their congregation. I had no family. I found your father through the goodness of a neighbor, and he was too foolish to shun me, too much in love with my looks to see my pain. There is my romance. There is my love story. There is Rebecca, then Nathan, and you and Henrietta. There is *my* shame."

I approached Mama, arms out, for a hug, to offer comfort. She was now crying, but her pointy jaw was tight. She swiveled away from me, plucked another sheet. "I don't have time for talk. This wash won't wait."

Clothespins in her mouth, her cheeks red as if they'd been slapped, Mama moved from sheet to sheet. She stretched the crumpled bundles into wind-blown sails. Finishing one, she immediately bent for the next, her hips stiff. I raised the basket and followed behind, passing her fresh clips. This action suggested a truce. We moved together down one line and up the next. My back ached from my trip.

A raindrop landed on my cheek. Mama hissed. But there was only a drip or two.

Mama took the empty basket from me. She looked down with anger in her eyes and said, "You think you have seen death, have you? Have you seen shame? When my own daughter left my house on Shabbat for a gentile who refuses to marry her, it reflects on me. You think you have it bad? Look at me. I'm not young or beautiful. My life is a worn rug behind me and in front, wet wash."

"How can I help?"

"You can dump the dirty laundry water down the drain." Mama turned her back, mounted the stairs, and kicked aside my carpetbag. She disappeared into the house. I looked down at my stylish narrow wool traveling skirt, unbuttoned my lavishly decorated bodice, and stripped to my shirtsleeves. I approached the back of the yard to topple the heavy tub and rinse it under the pump.

My return to Perry Street was a homecoming, if not a welcome home. I had expected my mother's response to be yes, or no. You can stay here or you can leave. You are my daughter or you are a harlot. But this would be another siege. Sleeping in the back bedroom and staying in the shadows so as not to magnify the *shonda*.

I contemplated three ways to handle my unfortunate situation as I waited for Wyatt. The first was the route of my nightmares. I could regress to the claustrophobia of being my mother's unloved daughter, sitting *shivah* for my true self. The second was the way of anger, the destructive force I'd frequently witnessed in Tombstone. This was fighting with my mother even if that meant breaking the family as collateral damage.

And then there was the third way, which required my higher self. I was bigger than this backyard, this house. I would reject my position as the lightning rod for my mother's anger. She blamed me for having to take in laundry. If I'd accepted an arranged marriage, she would be better off. She had expected to trade on my beauty—how dare me for stealing the benefits of an advantageous match.

Mama raged against her situation and spat it out at me. I would not spit it back, but I would not let her tie me up in the backyard as her scapegoat. I would find comfort in Papa and my siblings, in the knowledge that Wyatt would prevail. I'd grown strong enough to defend myself, but feared lashing out when provoked and prolonging the bitter cycle of our mother-daughter drama.

Let it go, I said to myself as I picked up my

carpetbag and reentered my house. *I know love, and I can give love.* A stirring in the parlor gave me hope that we were no longer alone. Perhaps Papa had returned and I would get that hug I craved.

CHAPTER 30
MARCH 1882

A month later, I discovered my rising desire was no longer for physical congress, but the fetal position. I had surrendered to house arrest, mitigated by the company of Papa, Nathan, and Hennie. Rebecca's husband forbade her from seeing me, as part of my shunning by proper San Francisco Jewish society. I'd never wanted to attend *shul*, but now Mama forbade me from accompanying her even though I was desperate to escape Perry Street—even if it meant attending temple. At home, she groused around the house as if she were the injured party, treating me as the scullery maid she might have gotten if I had been shrewd enough to marry well.

That morning, I had awakened early to bake a honey cake out of season for Papa and start the chicken stewing. I had cooked lunch, washed up, and laid out the dishes for the Sabbath meal. Now, two hours before Shabbat began, as the light softened, I still had piles of laundry to hang that would have to be left up over the following day. I wore an old skirt that I'd left behind, and a stained blouse. I hosted a blemish on my chin, and it was about to give birth to a brood. My hair, locked down in a single braid that pulled at my temples, had frizzed in the humidity of the hot water. My cheeks flushed from work. I smelled like a miner. And that was when Johnny Behan parted the sheets.

I hate to admit that Johnny looked dapper—hat, tie, tailored town suit, cufflinks, pocket watch and silver chain—but, after Wyatt, he also looked short, and sleek as a snake-oil salesman. Affection radiated from his eyes as if I was the most treasured woman in the world, the biggest beauty in Tombstone, if not Arizona and California both. My stomach flip-flopped, but I considered it merely a bodily betrayal, like gas, rather than a sign of something true destined for greatness. I'd had my itch for the wolf dressed in sheep's clothing, the bad boy with the charming airs. I'd scratched it. I was lucky it hadn't gotten infected.

Now, we were in San Francisco. A lot had changed. I pressed my chin's flaming spot. It was still there. It might have swelled over the hot wash.

Johnny approached through the sheets, as if that was how he always wooed washerwomen. "How are you?"

"It's getting better."

"I'd hate to see worse."

I shrugged. "Not quite the Grand Hotel . . ."

Johnny handed me a double bouquet of yellow roses. "These are your favorites, right?"

"I like roses," I said flatly. They were lovely and extravagant and fragrant, even if I preferred red, or pink. I considered tossing the blooms in the wash bucket but instead dropped the bouquet on the remaining damp laundry (and thought of Delia with her room full of yellow roses, by now possibly out of Madame Mustache's and a step down in a crowded brothel).

"How's Albert?"

"He's spending a lot of time on Geronimo. He misses you nearly as much as I do, and that's saying something. Let me take you away from all this," he said, his arms rising, the affection in his eyes dialed up to undying-love intensity. Placing his handkerchief on the ground, he kneeled. "Marry me."

It was all I could do to keep from laughing, although having him on his knees was the most entertainment I'd had since I arrived in the city. "We've done this dance before, Johnny. You had me and you wouldn't wed, as much as I begged. You had Wyatt as a loyal ally, and you fought with him behind his back."

"Wyatt is over. He's played out."

"Not from what I've read in the papers, and not

in my heart. Are you taking advantage of his political weakness to visit me? Or are you on the prowl again? Is this your game—propose to as many girls as possible to see who's dumb enough to believe you? Now you say that you *really* want me, and you know I *really* want out of here."

"True, that's not quite the red dress I saw you in last time you visited me. You were a stunner that night. I was an idiot for letting you go."

"I was the idiot, not you. I won't be fooled again."

"If you don't trust me, let's go to City Hall right now."

"There are worse places than hanging sheets under house arrest. I watched a mob demand a human hanging, for one example; sharing a bed with Curly Bill is another."

"Are you going to hold a practical joke against me?"

"If it was at my expense and involved seeing Curly Bill naked, then I guess so. Tell me, Johnny, am I just one stop on the old-girlfriend circuit? Did you woo your way through Contention, Tucson, Prescott, and Los Angeles before you found me here?"

Johnny rose and shook the dust from his handkerchief. "I'll make this perfectly clear. There's only one woman for me. It's you."

"You're selling. I'm not buying. What are the

odds some lonely girl will return your smile and sacrifice her security?"

"That's crazy talk."

"How much of your pursuit today is to snatch me from Wyatt while he's fighting for his life and livelihood?"

"Maybe I could see where you'd end up: abandoned. Look in the mirror, Josephine. Have some self-respect. Put some witch hazel on that thing. Aren't you ashamed of how you've let yourself go?"

"I am not ashamed of how I look today. I regret how I looked at you."

I lied. I *was* embarrassed. I looked like hell. I did occasionally glance in a mirror, but less frequently than before. Meeting my former flame looking my worst humiliated me. I admit that vanity, and I am not alone in it. Couldn't he have sent a note first?

Wretched at being ambushed in this condition, I surrendered—I was a scrawny, unkempt washer-woman under siege, awaiting a rescue that might never occur. I wanted a night of lovemaking, and the sleep that followed in my lover's arms. I wanted a restaurant with Champagne and items in French on the menu. I'd do almost anything to get it—except take Johnny back. I could reclaim my beauty, but I knew Johnny could never regain his integrity.

As angry (and lonely) as I was, I returned to

hanging sheets, setting the roses aside. Let him see the sweat stains, damn him. "I don't regret running off to Tombstone with you, Johnny. How else would I have met Wyatt?"

"Wyatt isn't coming."

His certainty flattened me, but I held on to my mistrust. "You don't know that."

"It's too hot for him in Tombstone, but he's too stubborn to sell out and leave."

"I'm sure, as sheriff, you're doing everything you can to protect him and his family."

"I'm not battling Wyatt, here. I'm fighting for us."

"You shot that horse months ago, you hypocrite. You have blood on your hands even if you did not hold the gun and shoot that afternoon on Fremont Street. You fanned the flames and perjured yourself. Now, before my mother flies out and flogs you with her broom, shoo, and stay shooed. You are nothing to me but Albert's father. His mother was right: he deserved a better man than you."

Johnny walked over to gather his roses, and I said, "Leave them. Buy more for your next date."

Johnny disappeared behind the sheets as he'd come, and I almost wondered if I'd imagined it all—except for the yellow roses at my feet.

As I entered the kitchen with the empty basket, I registered the anger in Mama's eyes. She'd seen

Johnny from the window, and she would have no bitten tongue for dinner. "Who was that?"

"John Harris Behan."

"Was that your fancy man from Arizona with his big gold watch? What did he want?"

"It may surprise you, but he wanted me."

"He took one look and left."

"I took one look and chased him off."

"That was a long look, then. What did you discuss?"

As drained as I was, I knew I had to draw a line in the kitchen. I didn't want my anger at Johnny to upset the delicate balance I was trying to achieve with Mama. If I lost my temper and expressed my conflicted emotions to her, who knew what upsetting confessions she would make to me about her own rage and sadness. I had to protect myself, so in answer to her question, I said: "We discussed the weather. It rains and then it doesn't."

I put the roses in water in a milk bottle, and gathered with my family at the dining-room table. I noticed that the big mantel mirror was gone, so I couldn't see myself reflected as Johnny saw me. I took my place beside Papa as Mama lit the Shabbat candles, her cracked hands gracefully circling over the flame three times. I noticed that the candleholder was new and brass; the silver one was gone, probably sold.

My family had sacrificed to rescue me from Johnny. Although I'd begun to send money home before I left Arizona, it never replaced that first $300 that bought the house. Maybe Mama wanted to know if Johnny had brought money to repay me. I hadn't even considered asking. I could have told Mama that Johnny had taken so much from me that cash was the least of it. The harder truth was that I'd given so much freely and without coercion. Although I was a sucker to offer my affections to him, young girls can be asses. I discovered I had something to offer: love. It was a powerful emotion that was not exclusive to those with beauty.

After Papa blessed the bread, I served the meal, rising to clear the plates after each course, and bringing in the next. Mama met Papa's comment that the soup I'd prepared was especially tasty, with a grunt. Otherwise, no one talked; no one made eye contact. Papa retreated into himself. I stewed in my choices: rebuffing Johnny, waiting for Wyatt. I tried to model my patience after his. I had to wait this situation out, and Perry Street was as much of a safe haven as I had at my disposal. I had to convince myself that this was not a step backward but a way station. I had to avoid the electric current of my mother's rage, knowing that once unleashed it would scorch my heart and zap my strength. It was not an easy battle within me, but I tried to find oases of contentment in this small house with no privacy— and that was my time with Papa.

After washing the dishes, storing the leftovers, and scouring the countertops, I rolled down my sleeves. I would be able to rest until sundown the next day. I carried the flowers and a footstool into the parlor, past the last flickers of the Sabbath candles. Papa sat alone with his glasses and his newspaper, reading the sports scores. I placed the milk-bottle vase atop a *schmatte* on the scratched oval table in front of his secondhand gentleman's chair. I plucked a pillow from the mismatched settee and made Papa shift forward. I placed it behind the small of his back, which tended to ache from standing all day. He sighed with pleasure as he crossed his ankles on the footstool I placed at his feet.

Before I sat down beside him, I went to the sideboard and brought over two small glasses and a decanter filled with golden liquid that I'd sent a neighborhood boy to the store to buy. I poured a dram for Papa, and one for me, and plopped beside him on the worn ladies' chair.

"What's this?" he asked, holding the glass and squinting.

I raised my glass and motioned for him to clink the pair together. "*L'chaim.*"

He sipped carefully, then smiled broadly. "That's not wine."

"No, it's whiskey." I leaned in conspiratorially, like the image of Queen Esther pleading with the Persian King Ahasuerus for her people's freedom.

"Drinking it is pleasurable, not medicinal. Pretend it stinks or Mama will come down to see what we're doing and accuse you of being a *schicker*."

"We wouldn't want that." We downed the first glass and poured the second. Papa returned to his paper, and I began to undo my braid in companionable silence. It was so tight that it took me a while, combing with my fingers as I went, until I could shake it entirely free. "Ahh," I sighed, scratching my scalp. "Another?"

Papa raised his glass. I filled it. He shook his head and said, "That honey cake was delicious."

"Too much salt, according to Mama, and God forbid you make a honey cake when it's not Rosh Hashanah."

"Thank you. It was a treat."

"I knew it was your favorite. Why just have it once a year?"

"Leave it to your mother to look a gift cake in the mouth."

We laughed together and, yes, I poured another wee dram for each of us. It was Friday night, after all, and though he had to work the next morning (another *shonda*) this would help him sleep.

"Mama wasn't always so tense."

"I don't believe it."

"Have I ever told you where I lived on the Lower East Side? It was in a tenement on Hester Street. We men had the fifth floor because we could manage the stairs and the rising smells. We were eight to a room, hiking down to the docks, scrounging a day's work. You slept in your socks so that nobody would steal them. I kid you not."

"It sounds like the mining camp in Tombstone."

"I can see that. I had one distant cousin in New York. It took him three months to answer my note. I didn't blame him: the crossing was hard on everybody. In a world where putting food on the table was a challenge, sharing wasn't so easy. But once my cousin got his bearings, he told me there was an opportunity at a bakery. If I wanted it, I'd better hurry. It was near Congregation Shaare Zedek on Henry Street. The owners were from Poland, which could have meant anything, but I took my satchel and found my way to their shop."

"Had you baked before?"

"I'd eaten bread. I studied mathematics in the old country until my father yanked me out of school. I wasn't bad at putting things together, but rolling dough was a different story. Still, I could learn, and I was no good at selling, so this seemed like a reasonable opportunity. Listen, it was an opportunity, so I jumped. I took my satchel and went. The baker and his wife owned the three-story house above the bakery, which was a big deal in those days. The couple, their children, her brothers and various 'uncles' all lived there. For a modest fee withdrawn from my wages, I moved in, too."

"So, that was where you learned to bake."

"And that was where I met your mother. The baker's wife couldn't sit still for fixing everybody's life. She latched onto me, a bachelor without a wife back in the old country. I was in no rush to get married. I had a steady job and a little coin. I could have some fun on my nights off. This was America, and I could walk around without getting harassed or hunted. I was good enough looking, and I'd been raised with sisters: I liked women."

"And they liked you."

"Thank you for saying so. They liked me. I was in no rush to get married and add to my responsibilities. I began to relax, to play a little ball. I'd go see a baseball game in Corona, Queens, on my day off with the uncles. At night, we played cards and had a little schnapps. Not a big life, but a life."

"What happened next? When did Mama enter the picture?"

"Thank the baker's wife. If only she'd stuck to something she knew, like sticky buns. But no, every room in the house was filled, and there were more boarders to come. The wife volunteered at the Hebrew Benevolent and Orphan Asylum Society. She met the beautiful widow Sophie and her bright-eyed daughter Rebecca there. She lamented that they were too good to be living on charity, sharing a roof with who knows what. She insisted she could use more help around the house, since there were so many men, and all she bore were sons. Couldn't we find a place for Sophie? First, my landlady moved me in with her brothers, who were much older than me. Then she asked, 'How would it look: a bachelor and a widow under the same roof?' "

"It would look fine."

"Who cared? No one was looking at us. We were all *shleppers*. Sophie had a kid already, so she wasn't doing any blushing. I liked Rebecca. She was bright and quick to learn. And her mother doted on her, even though she had a high opinion of herself, forever reading books. She was very observant. Me, not so much. Still, I thought I could do worse. I was tired of taking care of myself, Sadie. I was lonely with no family, no sisters, aunts, and uncles. I had been part of a big family at home, where being the quiet one had been a blessing for the noisy rest of them. Can you fault me that I wanted a little comfort? I didn't have time for romance, and the baker's wife wanted a wedding for Sophie. I didn't understand the rush, but we stood under the *chuppah* right there in the living room, with the 'uncles' and the brothers and the kids and the neighbors and the rabbi from Shaare Zedek. My distant cousin was my only relative, and he had to work that day. Sophie only had Rebecca, who sat straight and sober through the entire ceremony. Eventually, I learned she'd been up all night with her mother, crying. Trust me: you never get used to it, the tears at night.

"Years later, your mother told me the baker's wife entered her attic bedroom on the eve of her wedding and said, 'Worst case: you'll always have bread.' I suppose it was a deal the landlady herself had made. I never saw her talking to the baker with any kind of love or affection. But she loved her brothers and her sons. That yenta filled the Henry Street house as if it was a boat sailing rough seas and she its captain. I can't even remember her name. We make our beds. We lie in them."

"We need a last drink to toast to that."

"*L'chaim.*" When we heard Mama's footsteps on the stairs, we hid our glasses beneath the table. I couldn't help myself. I giggled. Papa socked me in my arm. He whispered, "You should have seen the man from temple she had picked out for you. Some beauty he was, an accountant."

CHAPTER 31
AUTUMN 1882

My sister Hennie and I sat thigh by thigh on the stoop. To protect our dresses, we parked atop the front page of the *San Francisco Examiner*; the papers lacked news about Wyatt in Arizona, New Mexico, or Colorado, but had reported that Virgil was in town, consulting a specialist to reset his arm. I didn't visit, fearing Allie's wrath.

After months together, the affection thawed between Hennie and me. We reclaimed our old secrets. We were sisters, something I hadn't had in Tombstone. We were kin. Life had progressed in my absence. A gentleman had proposed. Hennie wanted to accept. Mama raised a roadblock because he was a gentile. But the enterprising industrialist seemed as serious as Hennie. At least he was not an unknown quantity hailing from the Wild West, but only the East Bay. I told Hennie that was in her favor. She couldn't do any worse than I did, no longer a virgin and unmarried and back at home. But, unlike Rebecca, I'd had sex that I'd relished, not bartered to an anemic younger son from a proper German Jewish family.

Hennie liked to hear about my adventures. That gave me a chance to relive them in the retelling. When she told me about her gentleman caller, I was unsure whether Hennie loved him, despite her protestations. Where was the passion? I didn't see it. Perhaps it was projecting my own concerns on her, but I wondered if she was as infatuated with escaping our house as I was, even if it took a marriage license to make the getaway.

Boredom overcame me under a brilliant October sky. The air was full of hope, but I wasn't feeling all that rosy. Lethargy was my enemy. I hated the routine and the pecking order. I wanted to break out and get back to my real life. I craved

Wyatt at my side so that we could devour the world together. If he wasn't coming, I had to formulate an alternate plan that didn't include Johnny, or dancing. I didn't know what that would be.

Given all the passing months, my concern for Wyatt only intensified. Only a week after Johnny visited, cowboy Frank Stilwell and his henchmen shot Morgan dead but failed to hit Wyatt, standing at Campbell and Hatch's saloon watching his favorite brother play pool. I mourned Morgan as much for our friendship as the knowledge that this passing affected Wyatt like a branding iron to his heart. After that, I knew I wouldn't see my man for a long time, following his vendetta against the murderers in the newspaper. I awoke each day in fear that the paper would report his death by gunshot or hanging, and that his reputation would be dragged further through the mud.

Despite that heavy angst, exile on Perry Street had improved. All it took was cash. My washerwoman days ended around April when I received my first wire from Mollie Fly. While I told Mama the funds were installments on a legal settlement for defamation, the photographer sent me royalties for the pictures she was hawking through agents in Paris, Berlin, London, and New York. That pleased me to no end: I could make money off my beauty without having strangers touch my flesh.

In May, a wire addressed to Mrs. Josephine Marcus Earp arrived at Western Union—and the funds from Wyatt came regularly on the first of the month from then on. These testimonies of spousal support came from Arizona and Colorado. Wyatt's money should have reassured me that he was committed. Still, I worried that Mattie was also awaiting Wyatt's return, her nails as bitten as mine. Was she living with his parents in Colton, California, with her sewing machine and her nerves, considered his wife by his kin?

Hennie and I people-watched. It was Friday afternoon and the fathers had begun to shuffle home from work. We awaited Papa's return. He was bound to have a big braided challah wrapped in wax paper, and maybe cherries for Mama. It was hard to believe that I had been reduced to this, I who heard gunshots on Allen Street, who saw Virgil and Morgan and Doc bleeding outside Fly's. Now the day's excitement was awaiting Papa's homecoming, with cherries or without. I came back to a city where people didn't have a man for breakfast. They had a bun. I suppose that, as a baker, Papa benefited.

Meanwhile, the back door slammed. We both flinched at the sound of Mama stomping into the backyard followed by the whump of her paddle as she beat the carpets. Hennie and I stayed put, but I felt guilty. Hennie probably did, too. I thought Hennie nudged my arm to get me to go help. I elbowed her back—and then I saw why she poked me.

Wyatt climbed the steep hill. He stood out: a giant, a legend, unlike anyone else who'd entered the neighborhood. He wore his Stetson, the brushed black coat with the silver watch chain, a starched white shirt, and black leather pants. His pointed boots beat the sidewalk and, yes, he had pistols strapped to his hips. He'd grown older, I observed, sadder: Morgan's loss, Virgil's crippling, the ebbing of their Tombstone prosperity, the press accusations as a murderer and vigilante. But he came for me and me alone, my quiet man with the big presence. And I saw by Hennie's awe that my Earp was the handsomest man she'd ever seen.

When I saw Wyatt, my first thought was: *I'm out of here.* And then came *I love you* and then, *I want you.* I rose, anticipating Wyatt's approach. I relished his thoroughbred stride. I feasted on the slow smile that crossed his face and dawned in his eyes when he saw me on the stoop, as if I'd attended him every day at this time since my February arrival. I stood on the third step with my arms open so that, when he stopped before me, we could almost see eye to eye. I wrapped my arms around him with a tightness that showed I'd never release him again. He boosted me up as if I weighed nothing; we were weightless together.

It was our first kiss in San Francisco: two sets

of lips wedded to each other, ravenous and patient, pure escape and absolute grounding. We traveled together through that kiss and, while passions do fade, that kiss never did. It was as if Mollie had captured it in a photograph. It stopped time. There was before that kiss, and after. I would return again and again to that moment that liberated me to be my wildest, truest, warmest self and freed me to meld with the man I loved. Oh, and he loved me back.

I took a breath. "Jesus, you feel good."

"You're not so bad yourself, stranger."

We kissed again. I wrapped my arms around his neck. His hands encircled my waist. If I'd pressed myself any closer to Wyatt, I would have been standing behind him. That was the kind of kiss that kept you from straying, that sealed the emotion: this love is true.

Wyatt was more than my darling—he was a hero on the Western stage. He sliced right from wrong, and I was *all* right in his eyes. That fortified me, making me strong enough to defy convention. When Wyatt had something to say from his heart, he turned to me. He knew I'd be loyal. Some may consider it a blind spot, but I never envisioned anything but the best in him. He returned to me with blood on his hands and a heavy heart after riding the range as a deputy US Marshal, seeking vengeance for Morgan's murder and Virgil's shooting. Along the way, joined by

Doc and his brothers, James and Warren, they killed Frank Stilwell, Francisco "Indian Charlie" Cruz, and Curly Bill. I knew those outlaws, and I knew Wyatt, and I knew Johnny perverted the law. My faith in Wyatt never wavered.

When we pulled away from our kiss, I said, "Sorry about Morg."

"Let's leave that for now. Good?"

"Good." We held hands as I turned to introduce him to a red-faced Hennie, who had never seen such a public display of affection. "Wyatt, this is my sister Henrietta."

"Pleased to meet you, Henrietta."

My sister went dumb.

"Normally, she can speak, Wyatt. She'd do anything for me but break the Shabbat—right, Hen?" My sister remained stunned, as if everything I'd told her had been a self-justifying fairy tale, and suddenly here was the prince to reclaim Cinderella.

"Let's go inside, Sadie. It's time to meet your folks and do this thing proper."

I let that fall. I supposed if he could handle Curly Bill and the Clantons, he could handle Mama. It wasn't easy for a boomtown love to survive the home front. In a world in flux, the Earp brothers rooted themselves in one another. So did the Clantons and the McLaurys. I saw my future as an Earp, but the summer had proved I was a Marcus, too. Navigating a way to remain connected to Hennie and my family was nearly as important as my desire to put miles between us. Well, that was an overstatement. Still, there was strength in those roots. I was a Jewish immigrant in a country of choice and opportunity.

When I think back, I know I didn't run away from home. I ran to Wyatt. He caught me, not because I was some lost sheep but because he needed who I was as much as I needed him. When the smoke cleared in Tombstone, he ran to me.

ACKNOWLEDGMENTS

When we were deep in the quicksand of the developmental edit, my brilliant believer of an editor, that book-loving feminist Danielle Marshall of Lake Union, e-mailed me: "Good Writers. Good Books." If only it were that easy. First, it took a Good Agent. At Victoria Sanders & Associates, there was Victoria, who saw the kernel of my idea and believed in the journey. Bernadette Baker-Baughman guided me through the process with grace and support. Victoria introduced me to editorial coach Benee Knauer, who rode with me through every page and character quirk, never blushing, ever generous. And another Good Editor: David Downing rolled up his sleeves and, during the developmental phase, asked questions I'd never considered but most readers would. The words assembled in the right order, the Lake Union team—including Tyler Stoops, Dennelle Catlett, Shasti O'Leary Soudant, and Gabriella Dumpit—herded cats to bring the novel to market. And then there were the Good People, the *menschen* who make my writing a life: Dennis Dermody, Galen Kirkland and Natalie Chapman, Hilton Caston and Robin Ruhf, Paula Bomer, Caryn James, Carla Stockton, Bari Nan Cohen, Nicole Quinn, Nina Shengold, Melissa

Leo, Patricia Clarkson, Mark Ruffalo for believing in poetry, Rajendra Roy, Anne Hubbell, Amy Hobby, B. Ruby Rich, Jeff Hill, Jane Rosenthal, Amy J. Moore, Elisa Kleven, those heroes of WAMC Joe Donahue and Sarah LaDuke, my local bookseller Suzanna Hermans at Oblong Books in Rhinebeck, Jacqueline Kellachan at The Golden Notebook in Woodstock, Lina Frank and Clare Anne Darragh, the power-houses of Frank PR, Julie Fontaine, Sibyl Goldman, Jada Marie Sacco, and Jill Goldstein. And to all the amazing stories out there of women who dared to want more than they were served up by society's stuffy waiters.

ABOUT THE AUTHOR

Thelma Adams is an established figure in the entertainment industry. For two decades, she has penned celebrity features and criticism for high-profile publications. Her portfolio of actor interviews includes Julianne Moore, George Clooney, Jessica Chastain, and Matthew McConaughey, among many others. While covering film for the *New York Post*, *Us Weekly*, and Yahoo Movies, Thelma became a regular at film festivals from Berlin to Dubai, Toronto to Tribeca. She sits on the Hamptons International Film Festival Advisory Board and twice chaired the prestigious New York Film Critics Circle. Her debut novel, *Playdate*, published by Thomas Dunne Books, won high critical acclaim. Adams is often recognized, as she has been invited to share her expertise on many broadcast outlets, including appearances on NBC's *Today*, CBS's *Early Show*, and CNN. She graduated Phi Beta Kappa with a history degree from UC Berkeley and earned an MFA from Columbia University. She lives in Hyde Park, New York, with her family.

Center Point Large Print
600 Brooks Road / PO Box 1
Thorndike, ME 04986-0001 USA

(207) 568-3717

US & Canada:
1 800 929-9108
www.centerpointlargeprint.com